Praise for Anna Jacobs

'[Anna Jacobs' books have an] impressive grasp
of human emotions'
The Sunday Times

'A powerful and absorbing saga – a fine example of
family strife and struggle set in a bygone age'
Hartlepool Mail

'Anna Jacobs' books are deservedly popular. She is
one of the best writers of Lancashire sagas around'
Historical Novels Review

'A compelling read'
Sun

'This is a rare thing, a pacy page-turner with a
ripping plot and characters you care about . . .
[Anna Jacobs is] especially big on resourceful,
admirable women. Great stuff!'
Daily Mail

'Catherine Cookson fans will cheer!'
Peterborough Evening Telegraph

ANNA JACOBS

The Trader's Sister

Book Two of the Traders Series

HODDER

First published in Great Britain in 2012 by Hodder & Stoughton

An Hachette UK company

This paperback edition published in 2022

I

A CIP catalogue record for this title is available from the British Library

Paperback ISBN 978 1 529 38874 9
eBook ISBN 978 1 529 38874 9

Typeset in Plantin Light by Palimpsest Book Production Ltd,
Falkirk, Stirlingshire

Printed and bound in Great Britain by Clays Ltd, Elcograf S.p.A.

Hodder & Stoughton policy is to use papers that are natural,
renewable and recyclable products and made from wood grown
in sustainable forests. The logging and manufacturing processes
are expected to conform to the environmental regulations
of the country of origin.

Hodder & Stoughton Ltd
Carmelite House
50 Victoria Embankment
London EC4Y 0DZ

www.hodder.co.uk

To my lovely niece Clare and her family: Damion, Amber, Darcy and Connie. You said you wanted your own book and here it is.

ACKNOWLEDGEMENTS

My thanks to Rondo Bernardo for his help with Chinese family life in Singapore.

Thank you also to Eric Hare for his invaluable help and mentoring in nautical matters.

I

Ireland: May 1868

Ismay Deagan watched her mother touch the letter that had arrived from her brother in Australia and had been sent down to their cottage from the big house. Ma was tracing the lines of the address because Bram had written the words and it was as near to touching her eldest son as she could get.

The sight of her mother's anguish upset her, so Ismay said loudly, 'Well, aren't you going to open it?'

With a sigh, her mother handed it to her. 'You read it to me.'

Ismay took the sharp kitchen knife and carefully slit the top of the gummed envelope, scanning the words quickly. It said almost the same as the last letter. Her brother was doing well, making a good living as a trader and . . . 'Oh, his wife's near her time for birthing the child. That's three months ago. She'll have had it by now.'

'And I'll never see the poor little soul,' Ma murmured. 'Will they even make a Christian of it in that heathen land?'

'Why do you keep saying that? Bram told us there's a Catholic church in Fremantle. He keeps saying he'll take us all out to live with him when he's more settled, so you *will* see his child. He's going to be rich, my clever brother is.'

But her mother shook her head. 'I don't care how rich Bram gets, I'm too old to be going to another land. It'd kill me, I know it would. And anyway, I have children and grandchildren here. I'll not be leaving them. If he gets rich, he should come home to live in Ireland and buy a bit of land for himself. That way we could all be happy.'

'He likes it there and he makes more money there. If he offers, I'm going to join him in Australia.'

Her mother straightened up and gave her an angry look. 'Will you never learn, girl? Your father told you last time and I agree with him: you'll not be allowed to go. I'm not losing any more of my children.'

'With so many, I don't see how you'll miss another one or two,' Ismay muttered, but she took care not to say it aloud. Her father had given her the belt last time for insisting she was going to Australia. He'd hurt her, too.

Da hadn't hit his children this much when they were all young, but then Bram had been around to jolly him out of it. Since her brother had left, Da always seemed to be angry. She couldn't help wondering if he was jealous of how well his son was doing in Australia.

While Da was beating her last time, he kept

saying she was a wild one, had the devil in her, and he was going to drive it out. She wasn't wild. She just wasn't . . . meek.

They'd brought the priest in afterwards and Father Patrick had gone on and on about the fifth commandment, 'Honour thy father and thy mother.' Well, her parents should be kinder to their daughters if they wanted to be honoured.

She realised her mother had said something else. 'Sorry? What were you saying?'

'Is that all Bram wrote in the letter?'

'No. He's sent some more money for you to Mr Kieran at the big house. He'll give it to us when he gets it, like last time.'

'I'd rather Bram used the money to come back himself.'

Ismay was sick of hearing her say that, sick of her mother closing her mind to the world out there, which must surely be more interesting than their muddy little village. Some said it was pretty, with the lough just down the road. The ducks were welcome to that. There were hills around them and green winding lanes, but she never got the chance to climb the hills or wander the countryside because Da wanted his daughters safe at home.

And there might be pretty stone houses in the village and a church with stained-glass windows, but their cottage had only two rooms, the thatch was rotten and the walls were crumbling and damp.

Her father came home just then from his day's work on the farm belonging to the big house. Most of the family worked for the Largans and the cottages they lived in belonged to the Largans as well. Da looked exhausted and his shoes were filthy, but he still walked the muck in, didn't he, even though her mother had just swept the floor.

Ismay didn't know why Ma fussed so much when the floor was made of beaten earth. She looked round angrily. The stables at the big house were better built than this, though, give Mr Kieran his due, since his father died and he became the owner, he'd made sure the roofs were all watertight and given everyone a new barrel to catch the rainwater for drinking.

Mr Kieran said he'd be building new cottages, too, when he could afford it.

No one called the new master Mr Largan because they still remembered the old master and his cruelties. There were whispers that he'd wasted the family money, but Mr Kieran would still have more money coming in each year than Ismay's family would see in a lifetime.

She had to sleep in the roof area and share it with her two younger sisters and two younger brothers. It was reached by a rough ladder in the corner and she sat on the lower rungs sometimes of an evening. Ah, she was too old to be sharing with the boys. She had to get undressed under the covers of the girls' bed, and sometimes the boys would egg one another on to tug the covers off, because they were at the age to be interested in women's bodies.

'Read the letter out to your da,' her mother said, so Ismay went through it all again, taking care not to make any comment that might upset him.

'He still thinks of us, our boy does.' Da sniffed away a tear. 'But he's so far away, we'll never see him again.'

'Father Patrick says it's God's will.'

If Ismay heard her mother say that once more, she'd scream, so she would. And as for the priest, he was a fat old man and lazy with it. He was always saying things were God's will. Well, his life was easier if he didn't have to try to change things, wasn't it?

She wanted to change them, oh, she did, she did! Especially her own life, which was nothing but hard work and little to show for it because Da took all her money and boozed away half of it. It wasn't fair when all she had to wear were rags.

If Bram really did give them a chance of going to Australia, she was going to take it, whatever Ma and Da said or did. She'd get Mr Kieran to help her. Surely he would?

On Monday, when Ismay went to do her weekly stint in the laundry of the big house, she was summoned to the housekeeper's room.

'What have I done wrong?' she asked the laundry maid, terrified she was going to be dismissed.

Ginny gave her a shove. 'Go and find out what she wants. It's not my place to tell you.'

Mrs Jamieson looked at her across her big desk. 'I've had good reports about your hard work in the laundry, Ismay.'

She relaxed a little. So she wasn't in trouble.

'Now that Mr Kieran and his wife are in charge here, things are starting to settle down and we need a new housemaid. I thought you might suit.' She stared at her, head on one side, assessing. 'You'd have to live in, though.'

'I'd love to live in,' Ismay said at once, feeling excitement bubble through her. She only had bits and pieces of work here and there, like most people in the village. That was one of the reasons why her parents wanted her to get married as soon as possible, so she'd be off their hands. If she got a live-in job, maybe that'd do and they'd stop nagging her.

'We'd have to provide you with the right clothes, but Mrs Largan says she'll do that because Mr Kieran prefers to employ people from the village.'

'I'm very grateful and I'll work hard.'

'Good. I'll speak to your parents, then. Come and see me tomorrow afternoon and we'll find some decent clothes for you.'

Outside the housekeeper's room, Ismay leaned against the wall and sighed happily. At least she'd have a proper bed to sleep in from now on and decent clothes to wear, even if the maids did have to wear those silly caps.

When she got home, she told her mother what had happened.

'But you're going to marry Rory Flynn. Your father said it was all arranged with the priest.'

Ismay stared at her in shock. 'I told Rory last month I didn't want to marry him, and I told Da too.'

'Your father says you have to marry him. And why wouldn't you? He's a fine catch, Rory is. He's been waiting for you to grow up. He's always wanted you. And he's got a good place as cowman on the home farm. You'll never go hungry if you marry him.'

No, but she'd die of boredom. He hardly had a word to spare, whatever happened, and he had big, thick-fingered hands. She wouldn't want those touching her. He'd pretended to bump into her last week after church and grabbed hold of her. She'd thought she'd be sick. 'Well, I'm not going to marry him. I don't like Rory.'

'What's not to like? He's a fine, sturdy young man.'

Ismay wriggled uncomfortably. 'I'm not talking about that sort of liking. It's . . . I don't like him touching me.'

'Oh, that! You'll soon get used to it. It's quickly over and done with. The men need it.'

'How can I get used to it when him touching me makes me shudder?'

'You'll have to. Your da's set on the marriage.'

She took a deep breath. 'I'm *not* marrying Rory Flynn.'

Ma shook her head sadly. 'Your da will find a way to make you. He always does.'

'Not this time.'

But she felt nervous about telling him, wished her brother Bram was there to help her.

When Da came home, there was much whispering in the corner, then he crooked a finger at Ismay. 'What's this I hear about you going to work at the big house?'

'Mrs Jamieson offered me a job as housemaid and I said I'd like that.'

'Well, you can just tell her you've changed your mind. You'll be getting married in a few weeks and then you'll be busy looking after your husband and having his babies.'

'I told Rory and I told you last month, I don't want to marry him.' She felt shivery at the sight of the anger on his face but nothing would make her agree.

'You'll marry him, my girl, if I've to carry you to the altar myself.'

'You can carry me to the altar, but you can't make me say the words.'

'Are you defying me?' He began to unbuckle his belt.

This time she didn't let him hit her, but ran out of the house and was off down the lane, with him chasing after her, yelling for her to come back. When the yells faded behind her, she stopped to listen but there was no sound of pursuit. She'd always been able to outrun people.

It started to rain, so she went to shelter under a tree, tears in her eyes. She wasn't going back to a beating, but where could she spend the night?

In the end she went into the church, slipping in by the side door and crouching down in a side pew when the priest came to say his final prayers. She'd stay here overnight and Da's temper would have died down a bit by the next day.

But it was a long, cold night, and although she found some old floor rags to cover herself with, she didn't sleep much.

If Da didn't stop saying she had to marry Rory, she'd run away for good and all, she would so. Better to be a beggar than wife to Rory Flynn, with a baby every year and nothing to hope for but thumps and grunts.

In Australia, Bram Deagan stared down at the bundle in his arms, his eyes full of tears of joy. His son, his first child. He looked at his wife, lying exhausted in the bed after a long labour. 'He's beautiful.'

Her smile was glorious, though her face was pale and she looked exhausted. 'He is, isn't he?'

'You've had a hard time of it, my darling.'

She shrugged. 'I'll soon be better.'

'Your wife needs her rest now,' the midwife said.

Bram planted a kiss on the baby's soft cheek and handed him back before bending to kiss Isabella.

He'd hired the best midwife he could find and, even so, she hadn't been able to ease the pain or shorten the labour. As it went on and on, he'd scandalised her by going into the birth chamber to comfort his wife. Well, he couldn't bear to listen to Isabella's moans and cries of pain without wanting to be with her.

They'd better not be having too many children, he thought as he went downstairs to his makeshift bed. At thirty-one, Isabella was old to be having a first child. There were ways to limit families and – whatever the priest said – he was going to use them.

'Arlen.' He said it aloud, the name they'd chosen for if they had a son. It meant pledge, and he saw the boy as a pledge of his love for Isabella. It was also an old family name and had been his grandfather's. He liked that, too.

He didn't want to call the child after his father. Sean Deagan could be harsh in his ways, especially with the girls. Well, Da had had a hard life and had the worry of too many children to provide for, so there was some excuse, but Bram sometimes wondered how his sister Ismay was getting on without him to stand between herself and Da.

Peacemaker, his mother had called him, and he did try to be that. Fighting and quarrelling were such a waste of time.

Within a year or two he'd have enough money to send for his parents and as many of his brothers and sisters as would come to Australia. They'd soon find jobs here, he was sure. The Deagans weren't afraid of hard work.

Sally, who was helping out in the house, smiled

at him from the kitchen, and little Louisa put down her cup, showing a milky moustache. He hadn't meant to keep the child. She should be with her mother, Isabella's cousin, but Alice always had some excuse for not taking her daughter from her first marriage to live with herself and her second husband.

Ah well, he could afford it, and he'd grown fond of her.

When Ismay risked going home the next morning, she was relieved to see her mother out working in the garden, making the most of the late vegetables. She slipped into the cottage to wash and change her clothes quickly, putting on her Sunday best, the only other clothes she had. Then she went to hide in the woods until the afternoon, keeping an eye on the activity in the big house to work out what time of day it was.

Once she was sure it was time, she made her way up to the rear door, ravenously hungry now, but relieved to have escaped her father. She was going to beg them to let her stay.

The housekeeper looked at her in surprise. 'Why have you come to see me, Ismay?'

'You asked me to, Mrs Jamieson. You said you'd find me some clothes for my new job.'

'Your father came to see me this morning to say you couldn't take the job after all, because you were getting married. Surely you knew that?'

Ismay couldn't speak for a moment, she was so

shocked, then she grew furiously angry and the words tumbled out. 'No, I didn't know it because it's not true. Da wants me to marry Rory Flynn, but I've said no again and again. I can't stand the man and I'd rather run away and beg on the streets than spend my life with him.'

'Oh. I see. But I don't think we can go against your father's wishes.'

Ismay couldn't hold back the tears, which wasn't like her, but then her hopes had never been so badly crushed before. 'If Da tries to make me marry Rory, I swear I'll run away. I will so.'

'Calm down, girl. No one can make you say the words to marry a man.'

'Da will try. He'll beat me senseless if he has to. He tried to give me the belt last night and I ran away. I had to sleep in the church and I've not had a bite to eat since I left you yesterday. Please give me a chance to be a maid here, Mrs Jamieson. I beg you.'

The housekeeper frowned. 'Look, I'll speak to the mistress and perhaps Mr Kieran too, see what they think. Go and wait in the kitchen. Ask Cook for something to eat. Tell her I said it's all right.'

Ten minutes later, her father erupted into the kitchen and stormed across it towards her. 'I thought I saw you making your way here and I was right. You're coming straight home with me, my girl.'

Ismay ran behind the big table. 'I won't. I'm not going to marry Rory Flynn.'

'You'll do as I say.' He lunged round the table,

but she was faster. Only she bumped into the kitchen lad, who was carrying a bucket of water, and spilled it all over the floor.

'Stop this!' Cook yelled. 'Get out of my kitchen, Sean Deagan.'

He didn't pay her any heed. In the confusion, he'd managed to catch hold of Ismay and now he clouted her hard across the head.

For a moment, she saw flashing lights, then she screamed and tried to wriggle out of his clutches. But though he wasn't a tall man, he was strong. He started dragging her towards the back door, with her still screaming at the top of her voice and pleading for someone to help her.

Just as they got to the door, a voice called, 'Stop that at once!'

Da didn't let go of her, but he did swing round at the sound of his master's voice.

Mr Kieran walked across the kitchen. 'Let go of her, Deagan.'

'She'll run away if I do, sir.'

'She'll stay here. Won't you, Ismay?'

His icy gaze speared her and she bobbed her head. You didn't defy the landowner, not if you wanted to stay in your cottage. This man might not be as bad as his father, but he still had power over their lives.

'Now,' Kieran went on. 'We'll go to the house-keeper's room and talk about this quietly and reasonably. Someone send for my wife, if you please.'

Cook pointed one finger and the kitchen maid slipped out of the room.

Mr Kieran turned round and led the way along the corridor to the housekeeper's room, without even looking back to make sure he was obeyed.

'You just wait till I get you home, Ismay Deagan,' Da whispered.

She didn't reply, skipping forward to stay out of reach of his clenched fist.

In the housekeeper's room, Mrs Jamieson gave up her seat behind the desk to her master and stood to one side. She pointed to a spot beside her and Ismay moved across to stand there, feeling a bit safer now.

Surely they'd not give her back to her father?

'Please stand to that side, Mr Deagan.' Kieran glanced at the girl. She was a slip of a thing and she looked terrified. She was going to have a black eye. The skin round it was already puffy and darkening. Her father must have clouted her good and hard. He didn't approve of beating women.

Mrs Largan came in and looked at her husband questioningly as the housekeeper pushed a chair forward for her.

'We have a domestic matter to settle, my dear, the one we were discussing earlier, and I'd value your advice.' He waited until she'd settled next to him. 'Mrs Jamieson, perhaps you can explain what's going on?'

'I can tell you, sir,' Deagan said.

'I'd prefer my housekeeper to explain.'

His words were calm enough, but you wouldn't want to cross him when he looked like that, Ismay thought, for all he was usually smiling and kind. Only, if he told her she was to marry Rory, she'd have to disobey him as well; she'd just have to find the courage somehow.

Once Mrs Jamieson had explained the situation, Kieran turned to Mr Deagan. 'Is this correct?'

He nodded. 'It is, sir. It's a good match and I intend to make sure she weds him.'

Kieran's wife whispered in his ear and he turned to Ismay. 'Are you with child?'

She gasped and her mouth dropped open in shock. 'No, I'm not, sir. I've never lain with a man, never.'

Kieran studied her for a few seconds. He believed her. She hadn't the face of a liar. He turned back to the father. 'If she's not with child, why is it necessary for her to marry Flynn?'

Deagan shuffled his feet. 'I want her settled, sir, living here in the village near her family. She's a wild one, Ismay is, picked up some fancy ideas at that school. I don't know why your father ever allowed it to be opened. Teaching girls to read is a waste of time when all they need to know is how to look after their families.'

Kieran frowned. He firmly believed in teaching everyone to read and most families were grateful for a little education. Even his father had admitted that he needed people working for him who could read and write. But there were plenty of men still who shared this man's views on educating women.

His wife made a sound in her throat that sounded like irritation. He knew Julia would be annoyed by Deagan's statement. She intended to make sure the girls on the estate got the same chances of an education as the boys, because it was already clear whom the priest and schoolmaster favoured. Educating girls was one of her pet projects, and he'd support her in every way he could.

The Deagan lass was staring at them pleadingly, her face white and pinched, except for where it was bruised. He'd told himself he must stay impartial in this quarrel, but he couldn't help feeling sorry for her. 'Ismay, why don't you want to marry Flynn? Your father's right, he'd make a good provider with that job.'

'I don't like him, sir. I never have. He used to pester me when we were children, but I can't bear him to touch me. Anyway, my brother Bram is going to send us the money to join him in Australia and I want to do that. There's nothing for me here but hard work and babies, beggin' your pardon.'

'Her mother doesn't want to lose any more of her children to that dam— er, cursed place,' Da said, his deep voice growling with anger.

Kieran looked at his wife as if inviting her to speak.

'I think it'd be best if Ismay stayed here at the big house for a while,' she said quietly. 'If there's no baby on the way, there's no need for any of us to act in a hurry. We can work out what to do for the best once tempers have cooled.'

Deagan looked furiously angry. 'Begging your pardon, ma'am, but she's *my* daughter and it's for me to say what happens to her. I'm not trying to kill her, just marry her to a decent fellow. What's wrong with that?'

'How old are you, Ismay?' Kieran asked.

'Twenty-two, sir.'

'Why are you not married already? Most village girls are by your age.'

Deagan answered for her again. 'Because she's full of silly ideas about love, that's why. It's all because of those books she reads. I'll tan her hide if I ever catch her with another book in her hand, and Rory says the same.' He glared at his daughter. 'You are *not* going to Australia, my girl! Do you want to break your poor mother's heart?'

Kieran wasn't having that. 'I'll thank you not to shout and make threats in my wife's presence, Deagan. And we'll let your daughter speak for herself.'

Da opened his mouth and Ismay's breath caught in her throat at the anger in his face. He snapped his mouth shut again, but the look he gave her made her shiver. He'd kill her if he ever got her alone. She couldn't go home now, whatever happened.

'Why are you not married?' Mr Kieran repeated.

'Because I don't want to live in a hovel and have a baby every year. I want more than that. If I go out to join my brother in the Swan River Colony, he says he can find me work in his shop. Bram's doing well there, sir. That'd be decent, interesting work.'

'Well, your brother does sound to be doing well, I must admit. He and my brother Conn are partners. I had a letter from Bram myself only this week. It's not just the shop, you know. He's set up as a trader and is importing goods from Singapore to the Swan River Colony.'

She frowned. 'Isn't that the same as a shop?'

'Yes. Only bigger.'

She beamed at him. 'Well, there you are. He'll definitely have work for me.'

Julia intervened again. 'You'd go out to your brother, even though it'd upset your mother?'

'She has seven other children living round here, Mrs Largan. And grandchildren. It's not as if there'll be no one left to look after her in her old age.'

Kieran studied her. She spoke passionately, expressing herself well. She looked intelligent, too. Even now, her eyes were sparkling with life when she talked about joining her brother, and the housekeeper said she was a quick learner. 'I think my wife has the best idea, Deagan. We'll let Ismay work here at the big house for a while and think about this whole thing again once we've all calmed down.'

As the man before him opened his mouth, still looking angry, he held up one hand. 'I'm not prepared to argue, Deagan. Your daughter's reached her majority.' He saw the other didn't understand this and explained. 'She's past twenty-one, so she has the legal right to make her own choices.'

'She's still my daughter and always will be.'

Julia interrupted quietly but firmly, 'Mrs Jamieson, will you please take Ismay to the maids' quarters.'

Such a sensible woman, his wife, Kieran thought. He thanked heaven he'd met her.

Deagan took a step forward as if to prevent Ismay leaving. Kieran moved quickly round the desk to stand between them. For a moment all hung in the balance, then the man stepped back again.

But the expression on his face worried Kieran, and he saw the girl shiver as she moved past her father, keeping as far away from him as she could. Kieran could understand that. He too had been afraid of his father, another violent and unreasonable man.

No, let the poor girl have her chance of a better life. Rory Flynn could find himself another wife.

When they were up in the servants' area of the attics, Mrs Jamieson asked quietly, 'Is it worth all the fuss, Ismay? Is it worth losing your family for?'

She bowed her head, not wanting to upset the housekeeper.

'Well?'

Pulling her courage together, she looked up. 'I

don't want to lose my family, Mrs Jamieson, but I won't marry that Rory Flynn, whatever anyone says or does. I've known him since we were children and never liked him. He was always following me around, staring, and he was the worst bully in the village. He's grown into a rough brute without two thoughts in his head apart from cows and having a drink with the other men. What sort of life would I have with him?'

The housekeeper surprised her by patting her on the shoulder. 'Well, then, you seem to know your own mind. We'll have to find you something else to do with your life. We aren't in the dark ages, after all, though I sometimes wonder, I do indeed.' She sighed then said more briskly, 'Right, let's be finding you some clothes. Before you change into them, Ginny will need to check you for lice.'

Oh, the humiliation of being led out to the laundry, immersed in a tub in a small room to one side, used by the servants for their weekly baths, then having her hair gone through with a fine-tooth comb by the senior laundry maid. She couldn't help sobbing at that.

Ginny patted her damp shoulder, laughing. 'Oh, get away with you, Ismay! You're not the first girl to come here lousy and need cleaning up.'

'But I've tried so hard to keep myself clean.'

The other woman patted her again, more gently, a comforting touch. 'You've been living crowded together with your family. It's not your fault you're lousy. Now stop weeping, for glory's sake.'

Her father, Ismay thought bitterly. It'd be him. He was always scratching himself and Ma had to nag him to change his clothes every month.

That must have been why she'd been kept to the most mundane of tasks when she helped in the laundry, fetching and carrying for the other maids, not let go near the clean clothes or the ironing. The shame of it!

When she was clean and dry, she was given underclothes. They were hand-me-downs, but finer than she'd ever worn before. She'd seen the frilled and lace-decked garments of the family when they were being washed. The family and upper servants had so many clothes it made your head spin.

Now, she was the proud owner of three chemises made of soft cotton, with no holes in them at all – well, maybe just a little one, which had been skilfully darned – three petticoats, one of yellowed flannel for warmth, two of cotton and oh, oh, one had a narrow row of lace round the bottom. She touched that gently with her fingertip.

And as well, there were two skirts and three bodices, with a jacket to cover them, and a big fine shawl too.

She put her head in her hands and wept for sheer joy at being so decently dressed.

'What's wrong now?'

'I'm so h-happy.'

'You silly girl!' But Ginny smiled and patted her back again.

★　★　★

When Ismay had left, Deagan shuffled his feet and muttered something. Julia looked at her husband. 'I'll leave you to settle matters here.'

Kieran gave her a pleading look. 'Stay for a moment or two. Deagan may have questions to ask.'

The man looked at them both truculently, bottom lip jutting. 'I still want her to marry Flynn. It's the sensible thing to do.'

'Not if she's taken a dislike to him, surely?' Kieran said.

'Dislike, indeed! It's for me to tell her what to do. Father Patrick is standing ready to marry them. *He* approves of the match.'

'Does he know she doesn't want to marry Flynn?'

'Of course he does, but he says it's up to me to say what she does. Your father wouldn't have let her get away with defying me . . . sir.'

It was the wrong thing to say. If there was one thing Kieran was determined about, it was that his father's arrogant ways should be replaced by kindliness towards those who depended on him. 'Your daughter isn't obliged to obey you in this matter, as I've already explained.'

'She will if she knows what's good for her. You don't know the girl, Mr Kieran. She's a wild one.'

'Then we'll be relieving you of a burden by taking her off your hands. No! No more arguments. She's to stay here as maid and you'll get half her wages each quarter day. And don't worry, we'll make sure she stays respectable.'

Deagan scowled even more blackly. '*Half* her wages? They should all come to me by rights.'

Kieran bit back an even sharper response. Would the man never be satisfied? 'She'll need to keep some of the money to clothe herself decently.'

'But sir—'

'Enough! If you value your job and your cottage, you'll accept my decision. My wife needs another maid and your daughter isn't prepared to marry Flynn, whatever you say or do. Get back to your work now.'

When Deagan had gone, he turned to his wife. 'You'll keep an eye on her?'

'I will.'

'She'd better stay away from her family till they've accepted my decision.'

Julia leaned across to kiss his cheek. 'It was the right one, Kieran darling. I don't believe in forcing young women to marry men they dislike. It happens in our class too. I'm so lucky I met you – and that you had your own money, so your father couldn't meddle, as he did with your brother, forcing poor Conn to marry that dreadful woman.'

Kieran smiled at her. 'I'm also lucky Father didn't want me living too near and interfering in what he was doing. But I'll never forgive him for falsifying the evidence that got my brother transported. How a man could do that to his own flesh and blood, I'll never understand. What Conn must have suffered!'

She squeezed his hand in a mute sign of sympathy and it lifted his spirits, as it always did, to have her by his side. He had a long way to go to repair the damage his father had done to the family estate, but with her by his side, he'd bring it back to prosperity and gradually replace those dreadful tumbledown cottages.

2

Adam Tregear sent his luggage on to the house in Liverpool which he'd come to consider home, then walked to the family lawyer's office. He was delighted to stretch his legs after the days on the ship travelling from New York and, by the time he arrived, he felt ready to do battle.

The lawyer's clerk gaped at him. 'Oh. We didn't expect . . . I'll tell Mr Saxby you're here, Mr Adam.'

'Don't bother. I'll tell him myself.'

He walked along the corridor before the elderly clerk could say another word. He wanted to get this over with, whatever it was. He'd been summoned here many times and never for any good reason – though that wasn't usually Mr Saxby's fault. The lawyer was only acting as a mouthpiece for Adam's father.

He banged on the door, opened it and strode inside the office. 'Well? What's the old devil thought up now to torment me? It must be something particularly nasty to justify the expense of a transatlantic telegram to summon me back.' Only then did he see that the lawyer wasn't alone. 'Oh, sorry.'

Quentin Saxby gave him a stern look then turned to the elderly lady sitting there looking nervously at the intruder. 'I think we've finished our business for today, Miss Carter. As you can see, I've an urgent matter to deal with for my impetuous young friend, so if you'll excuse me now, I'll make sure my clerk lets you know when the new will is ready for you to sign.'

Adam held the door open for her. 'Sorry, ma'am.'

Only when she'd edged past him and disappeared down the corridor did he turn back to smile ruefully at the lawyer.

'Check whether I'm engaged next time, Adam, if you please.'

He nodded, wondering why the mere sight of Mr Saxby always calmed him down.

'Do you intend to sit down to talk, or are you going to stay by the door and glower at me?'

Adam pushed the door shut behind him with one foot and flung himself down in the ruby velvet armchair. Folding his arms, he waited for the lawyer to speak.

Silence hovered between them for a few moments, then with a sigh, Quentin steepled his hands in front of him. 'I'm sorry to tell you that your father died two weeks ago.'

'Did he? And is the unwanted bastard son supposed to care about that?'

'No, I suppose not. But you still need to know. We buried him last Thursday.'

'Which made sure I wasn't able to attend the funeral, eh?'

'Would you have wanted to?'

'To face more snubs? I doubt it. Though a man ought to attend his father's funeral, don't you think?' It was yet another of the normal family things he'd been deprived of since his mother's death when he was ten.

'After the funeral we had the reading of the will, and you were not forgotten, hence my summons.'

'Now, that I hadn't expected.'

'It surprised me when we were making the will last year. It's . . . um, an unusual bequest.'

'Hedged about with *if* and *but* and *unless*, no doubt. He liked to make threats and keep people under control.'

Quentin nodded. He didn't blame Adam for a lack of feeling towards his father. John Joseph Harbisher had been a harsh, unyielding man, whose only act of youthful defiance had created a bastard son. Once he'd repented of this, his family had provided for the child, giving the mother a small allowance to enable her to rear Adam decently, as long as she was frugal.

The family had married their heir off quickly to a woman of their choice, on the principle that it was better to marry than to burn. Cornelia, a very pious woman, had made sure that her husband became an unyielding pillar of the established church.

Unfortunately, Harbisher had later found himself entirely responsible for the bastard son, because

Adam's mother died suddenly when he was ten. Since Harbisher hadn't been able to reconcile it with his Christian conscience to abandon his own flesh and blood to a pauper's life, he'd made sure Adam Tregear went to a modest boarding school and was suitably lodged with a respectable woman during the holidays.

The fact that she'd also grown to love the child was a coincidence that Quentin hadn't brought to his client's attention. If he had, he was sure another woman would have been found, one who'd treat the lad more harshly.

It had been the lawyer's job to oversee these arrangements, and he'd occasionally taken the boy out to tea, because there were some things a sailor's widow couldn't explain to a youth. Quentin had found the lad intelligent, ready to learn, and Adam had grown into the sort of man any normal father would be proud of, bastard or not.

Apart from that, Harbisher had contented himself with a brief annual interview with his son at the lawyer's office, and quarterly reports from the school. Once Adam turned fifteen, a place had been found for him with the East India Company and he'd been told he was to go to India to work as a clerk. That had prompted the lad to run away.

Well, there was never a lad less likely to settle down to a life as a clerk. Whether he had gypsy blood as well as the Cornish family background, Quentin didn't know, but he wouldn't have been surprised. Adam was swarthy-skinned, with black curly hair and dark eyes; the sort of person who was only truly happy outdoors. Ironically, he'd have made an excellent landowner, better than his fool of a half-brother, who was already giving his lawyer a lot of unnecessary trouble with lavish plans to remodel the house, plans which would rapidly bankrupt the estate.

Adam's voice grew softer. 'I shan't blame you for it, Mr Saxby, whatever the will says. You've stood my friend many times. Tell me.'

'Very well. Your father has left you several properties and a half-share in a schooner.'

Other men's faces would have lit up at this news, but Adam's became even tighter with suspicion. 'And?'

'And there are, as you've guessed, certain conditions, which is why I sent the telegram. The properties and schooner are in Australia and it's a condition of the inheritance that you leave the country and go straight there within a month of his death, or as soon thereafter as practicable, given sailing times.' He didn't need to tell Adam that Harbisher had made it his business to buy properties so far away to get rid of this unwanted son.

Adam closed his eyes, sighing as he opened them. 'And if I refuse to go?'

'Then you get nothing. The properties will be sold and the proceeds will go to your half-brother Godfrey.'

'Who hates me and would be glad to see me

get nothing.' Adam looked at the lawyer. 'Did *you* pay for the telegram you sent me?'

'Yes.'

'Thank you. I might not have got back in time otherwise.' He leaned back, chewing one corner of his mouth, then shrugged. 'I've never visited Australia. Tell me more. Of what do these properties consist? Are they worth making such a long voyage for?'

'I have very little information about them, beyond a list of addresses for a public house and two houses in a town called Fremantle in the Swan River Colony, which is on the western coast of Australia. Your father made the arrangements himself through the son of an acquaintance, who is a lawyer out there.'

'And the schooner?'

'Is called the *Hannah Grey* and is based in the port of Fremantle. It sails to the Far East – mostly Singapore, I gather – for trading purposes, but to other ports as well. Recently, I believe, the vessel has been visiting Galle and Suez. I'm afraid I know very little about these places, though, or what the trade is there. In fact, apart from the name of the lawyer in Perth who is handling matters for you, that's all the information I have for you about the whole inheritance.'

He gazed approvingly at his young visitor. Who'd have thought running away to sea would be the making of the lad? Adam had taken to the life and risen quickly in the nautical world. He'd showed himself a good sailor and later risen to officer, where he'd also done well, thus proving his father's predictions wrong.

'If I accept the bequest, my dear father gets his own way again, and will have disposed of me very neatly.'

'Yes.'

'On the other hand, there's a chance, just a chance, that it'll be worth it.' He slapped his hand down on the table. 'I'll do it. He's sugared the pill well enough.'

'In that case, there are further conditions to fulfil. You must promise to get married within the year and to stay away from England for ten years.'

Adam stiffened visibly. 'The old devil! Couldn't he leave me any freedom at all? Couldn't he be content with marrying off my half-brother and -sister young, to keep them from the sin he saw everywhere he looked, whether it existed or not?'

Mr Saxby shuffled the papers, staring down at them for a moment. 'If it's any consolation, he seemed quite certain you'd keep your word once given. He said he had never known you lie or cheat. And at least I prevailed on him to allow you to choose your own bride.'

'I'd have refused to marry anyone of his choosing.'

'Yes. I managed to convince him of that, so he allowed it as the lesser of two evils.'

'Well, I'm twenty-eight now and with a share in a schooner and some properties, I dare say I can manage to find someone reasonable to marry.

Though I'm not staying in Australia if the schooner is worthless, and to hell with his conditions.'

'I don't think he'd cheat you.'

'No. He might have been a narrow-minded bigot, but he was honest, at least. I'd not go if I thought he was trying to cheat me. But I do think there will be unpleasant surprises. He could never give a gift freely.' He looked across at the older man with a wry smile. 'Did you have any doubt that I'd accept his offer?'

'No. Not unless you'd earned a fortune in America in the meantime.'

'I'm not penniless – I'm better with money than *he* ever gave me credit for – but you couldn't call it a fortune, not nearly enough to buy a half-share in a schooner. It's not a steamship, but it's . . . something.'

'Then I'll need you to sign these papers. You may, if you wish, employ your own lawyer to go through them first.'

'No need. I trust you, Mr Saxby, after your kindness towards me over the years, for which I'm grateful. If I need legal help in England, I hope I can continue to ask it of you?'

'It's always been my pleasure to help you. Indeed, I hope you'll continue to keep me informed of what you're doing and visit me if you ever come back to England. I should be sorry not to see you again.'

As Adam gave him one of those rare smiles that transformed his dark features into nearly handsome, Mr Saxby allowed himself the thought that, if he'd had a son, he'd have wanted one as sturdily independent as this fine young man. But his wife had never quickened with child, which was a sorrow to them both.

He took out the papers, which Adam read from beginning to end, before signing them neatly and carefully.

'Are you still staying at Mrs Seaton's?'

'Yes, of course.'

'She's very fond of you.'

'And I of her. Why do you think I call her Aunt? You chose well when you found her to look after me all those years ago.'

'I knew her husband. We were lads together. And I knew she needed someone to love.'

They were both silent for a moment or two, thinking of the kindly woman who had mothered Adam, then he looked at the lawyer. 'Is that all for today?'

'Yes.'

'Then I'll go and celebrate my unexpected inheritance in a fitting way.'

Mr Saxby raised one eyebrow.

Adam chuckled. 'I'm past the age of getting roaring drunk and, to tell you the truth, I never did have a good head for drink, so it's not one of my favourite activities. Besides, Harriet Seaton would never let a drunken man into her house.'

Adam walked slowly home, stopping to buy a bunch of flowers from a street seller. He couldn't help wondering if he'd done the right thing in accepting the bequest. He'd vowed never to take another penny from his father, and he could perfectly well have managed without it. But still, a half-share in a schooner was something he'd dreamed of, something he could only have achieved on his own after years of stringent economies. As for the marriage, he longed for a family. It wouldn't be a penance, not if he chose wisely, a good-natured woman not a mean-spirited one, however wealthy.

He rapped on the front door and poked his head inside. 'It's me.'

'I'm in the kitchen,' she called.

He went to join her, handing her the flowers with a flourish.

She took them with a smile. 'Even in winter, you always seem to find something for me. Thank you, Adam dear.'

'Did my luggage arrive safely?'

'Never mind the luggage, give me a hug! It's nearly two months since I've seen you.' She smacked a kiss on his cheek, the same sort of kiss that had brought tears to his eyes the first time she hugged the grieving ten-year-old lad handed into her keeping.

The greetings over, he sat down in her small but spotless kitchen and watched her take a cake out of a pretty storage tin and cut them both a generous slice as she waited for the tea to brew. There was always a cake in that tin, and always a big hug and kiss to welcome him back. 'Did you know Mr Saxby had sent for me to come back early?'

'Yes. He came to see me, to ask when you'd be back. There's an inheritance, he said. Is it worth having, Adam love?'

'It may be. You know what my father is . . . *was* like.' He explained the conditions and she whisked out a handkerchief to blow her nose as she struggled against tears.

'I'll not see you again if you go so far away.' She had to mop her eyes because the tears wouldn't be held back.

'I've been thinking about that as I walked back. Why don't you come with me to Australia, Aunt Harriet?' He chuckled. 'The old devil never thought of that, or he'd have made leaving you here a condition.'

She gaped at him, then dumped the teapot so abruptly on the table that hot brown liquid spurted out of its spout. '*Go with you to Australia?*'

'Why not? You've no close family left in England now that your cousin's died.' He picked up the teapot and poured her a cup, understanding how agitated the idea of this had made her. He added milk, sweetened it and pushed the cup towards her.

Her hands were shaking as she lifted it to her lips. 'My Jamie would have suggested something like that. He was so like you, love.'

Adam closed his eyes, feeling near tears himself

now, because he knew she was going to come with him. If it was something her husband would have approved of, she'd do it. That was always her rule, even twenty years after James Seaton's death at sea. 'This calls for a glass of brandy in celebration, don't you think?'

'Purely for medicinal purposes, because I'm a bit . . . shocked at the idea.'

'Of course.' He went to find the bottle and pour them both a small tot in the fine crystal glasses she kept for this occasional weakness. Only ever the one glass, sipped delicately, when life upset her.

Raising his glass, he clinked it against hers. 'Here's to Australia! To a new life for both of us.'

Ismay had never been so happy in her whole life. She was clean, well fed and decently clad. She was learning so much in her new job that the hours flew past. The other servants treated her kindly, not mocking her ignorance, and even the mistress stopped to speak to her sometimes to ask how things were going.

One day, the kitchen maid was ill, so Cook asked Ismay to walk across to the home farm for some more eggs.

It being a sunny day, Ismay was delighted at the chance of some fresh air and set off with the big basket in one hand. She hurried past the field where her father was working, not wanting another confrontation.

On the way back she cried out in shock as a

man stepped out from behind some bushes. She tried to walk past him, but Rory moved to block her path, catching hold of her arm and swinging her round to face him.

'Let go of me! You nearly broke these eggs I'm fetching for the mistress.'

For answer he took the basket from her hand, still keeping hold of her other arm, and set it on the ground.

Fear set her stomach churning.

'I'm asking you now to change your mind and marry me,' Rory said. 'You know I've always wanted you. Your father and the priest both say you should.'

'I don't want to marry anyone.'

'You're saying no again?'

She nearly said yes just to get away from him, then something stiffened her spine and she spoke her piece firmly. 'I won't be changing my mind, Rory. I'm enjoying working at the big house and I'm going to live in Australia when my brother sends me the money.'

He looked at her, his eyes resting on her breasts, then her belly. 'Then I'll have to make you marry me.'

She screamed then, guessing what he intended to do, screamed and screamed. But no one came to help and he had her pinned down within the minute, flipping up her skirts and fumbling for his trouser buttons.

Ismay couldn't believe this was happening,

couldn't believe no one had heard her screams. She fought him every inch of the way, but he was so much bigger than her she didn't have a chance. And he hurt her. Oh, he hurt her so much.

But she didn't stop screaming, biting, scratching and spitting in his face. Wouldn't give in, even though he slapped her hard across the face once or twice. He couldn't hold her down and cover her mouth, so she continued to scream and sob.

'*What the hell do you think you're doing?*' a voice yelled suddenly.

Rory grunted and rolled off her. 'She's just agreed to marry me.'

Ismay tried to move away but he kept hold of her arm. 'I've not agreed to anything, sir. He forced me to . . . to do that. Said he'd make me marry him. But I *won't*, whatever he does.' She couldn't help weeping then, because she felt dirty and sick with disgust and shame.

Mr Kieran dismounted and used his riding crop on Rory. 'Let go of her, damn you!'

Only then did the grip on Ismay's arm slacken.

Rory stepped aside, fists bunching as he scowled at the landowner. For a moment all hung in the balance and she thought he was going to attack the master, so furious did he look.

Mr Kieran spoke very softly, but there was the tone of command in his voice. 'Touch me and I'll have you in front of the magistrate and in jail before nightfall.'

Rory spat on the ground to one side to show

his contempt. 'Whatever you say, she'll have to marry me now. No one can change what I've done. She could even be carrying my child. We both come from fertile stock. It only takes one mounting by a good bull to get a cow in calf.'

Ismay moved away quickly, terrified of him grabbing her again. Once she was out of his reach, she adjusted her skirt with hands that shook. 'I hate you so much now, Rory Flynn, that I'd rather kill myself than marry you.'

She wiped the tears away with her sleeve, but was unable to stop the weeping. Only it felt as if there weren't enough tears in the whole world to wash her clean again.

Kieran looked at his cowman, sickened by what the fellow had done. He'd seen and heard for himself that Flynn had forced the girl, who was a sorry, battered little figure. She must have fought back bravely because she was in a terrible state.

'You're dismissed from my employ, Flynn, and I want you off my land before nightfall. If you're not gone, I'll have you before the magistrate for this. If you go anywhere near Ismay again, I'll hire someone to geld you.' The words were shocking in his own ears, for he wasn't a violent man, but he meant them because he loathed this type of crime.

For the first time, the man showed a sign of fear, his hand going instinctively to protect his private parts at the threat, stilling for a moment, then finishing buttoning his trousers.

Kieran moved to stand next to the girl, not sure how best to comfort her.

Flynn was looking at her now. 'Your da will send you to me, wherever I go. You'll see.' With a final scowl, he strode off.

'Surely your father won't do that, not after he hears what's happened?' Kieran exclaimed.

As she looked at him, more tears rolled down her cheeks. 'Oh, but he will. Da's set on me marrying him, whatever it takes. I'll have to get away from here, Mr Kieran. If I stay, I'll never be safe. Never.'

She turned her attention to her clothes and he saw her blushing as she tried to pull her torn bodice across her breasts. They couldn't walk back like this. Taking off his coat, he handed it to her. 'Put that round you, lass. I'll walk back to the house with you.'

'Thank you, sir.' She huddled into his coat, though it was far too big for such a small, slender woman.

At the kitchen door she hung back. 'They'll all say I egged him on. Even Mrs Jamieson asked me if it was worth it, defying my father to come here.'

'I can bear witness that he forced you.' Unable to bear the sight of her anguish without reaching out to her, Kieran put an arm round her shoulders and guided her into the kitchen.

Everyone turned, someone gasped and Cook dropped her ladle on the floor.

Kieran told the simple truth. 'Ismay was attacked

by Rory Flynn. I caught him doing it. He's to be off my land by nightfall and if any of you see him here after today, you're to tell me. Someone fetch my wife and Mrs Jamieson. Tell them to hurry.'

He continued to support the trembling, sobbing girl as he led her through the kitchen and along to his wife's private sitting room.

The sound of running footsteps heralded the arrival of the housekeeper, with Julia close behind her. They both stopped dead in the doorway.

'Dear God, what's happened?' his wife asked.

Ismay had stopped sobbing but was still huddled under his coat and didn't seem able to string two words together, so he explained for her.

The two women exchanged shocked glances, then the housekeeper stepped forward. 'I'd better take her to change her clothes. Pull yourself together, Ismay. You're safe now.'

He didn't like this brusque way of treating the girl and was glad when Julia intervened. She took his place beside Ismay and, unlike the housekeeper, she put an arm round the girl.

'We'll take her to my dressing room and give her a bath. Then you can take these clothes away and burn them, Mrs Jamieson. Ask them to send up plenty of hot water.'

Kieran looked at his poor little maid, angry all over again at the sight of her bruised face as she huddled against his wife, trying not to weep. 'I'll speak to you later, Ismay.'

He looked across at Julia and mouthed 'Thank you' before adjourning to the library. But he couldn't settle to his correspondence, could only pace up and down, furious that this had happened on his estate.

Ismay could tell what Mrs Jamieson was thinking from the disapproving expression on her face, so as soon as the master had gone, she said, 'I didn't egg him on. I didn't. He jumped out from behind some bushes and grabbed me. I hate him.'

'I believe you,' Mrs Julia said. 'If you'd egged him on, he'd not have had to thump you.' She looked sideways at the housekeeper.

'There's usually something that sets a man off,' Mrs Jamieson said stubbornly.

'My husband said she was screaming and fighting,' Mrs Julia told her.

'It's what people will say in the village, though, that she egged him on, and their sympathy will be with him more than her because he's lost his home and livelihood. I'm sorry, ma'am, but I have to tell you the truth.'

'Rory said Da will send me to him as soon as he can,' Ismay said. 'He said they'll make me marry him.'

And then Ismay realised something and began to sob even more bitterly. 'Da must have seen me going for the eggs. I saw him working in the field. *He* must have told Rory where to find me.' This betrayal was nearly as bad as the attack.

Mrs Julia gaped at her. 'Surely your father wasn't part of this?'

'Why would your father do that?' Mrs Jamieson asked, looking equally shocked.

'To force me to marry Rory.'

'Deagan has a reputation for ruling his family with a rod of iron,' the housekeeper explained. 'It doesn't hurt to keep children in order, but he's been an unhappy man since his oldest son was sent away by Mr Conn's wife, and he's been harsher with the younger ones, saying he wasn't having another one sent away for impudence like Bram. Everyone's noticed it.'

There was a knock on the door and Mrs Jamieson opened it to let the kitchen maid bring in a ewer of hot water. Mary glanced across at Ismay, wide-eyed, then went to fetch up other ewers till the bath was full.

Shutting the door firmly again, the housekeeper said to Ismay, 'Give me the master's coat and get your clothes off. The water's nice and hot, and you'll feel better once you're clean.'

With the coat removed, Ismay stood there blushing, ashamed for them to see her bruised body.

Even the housekeeper was convinced. 'Dear God, is he an animal to attack you like that? Look at the bruises where he's held her down. I'm sorry, Ismay. I didn't realise it was this bad.'

'I think she'll feel more comfortable if she's private.' Mrs Kieran pulled a screen round the bath.

Ismay was relieved to be out of their sight and couldn't wait to sink into that lovely clean water. But, as she settled into the warmth, she couldn't help hearing what they were saying and that was so bad it froze the tears on her cheeks.

'What if she's with child, Mrs Julia?'

Silence, then, 'Oh, dear. I hadn't thought of that.'

'They fall for children soon as look at them, those Deagans do – the Flynns as well.'

'Surely she can't be, not after just once!'

'It's possible.'

More silence. Ismay slid down into the water, letting it cover her face, coming up spluttering. She wished she could drown herself here and now and be done with it all. She hadn't let herself think of that dreadful possibility, but now she couldn't avoid it. If she was carrying a child – *his child!* – she would have to kill herself. She would so.

She realised Mrs Jamieson was shaking her arm. 'Finish washing your hair before the water grows cold.'

Ismay did as she was told, then got out and dried herself on the clean towel. She put on the clothes someone had brought, but the thought pounding through her brain was making it hard to listen to what they were saying. She wanted to scream at the top of her voice for the sheer terror of it.

What if she was carrying Rory Flynn's child? How would she escape him then?

★　　★　　★

Downstairs in the estate office, Kieran was speaking to Ismay's father. He'd sent someone to fetch the man and forbidden them to say anything about what had happened today, because he wanted to make sure he heard the truth from him.

But when Deagan came into the office, he had a gleam in his eyes and a strut in his step. He looked like a man who'd just received some good news.

Kieran watched him carefully as he spoke. 'Rory Flynn caught your daughter on the way back from an errand today and he – well, there's no way of dressing this up in fancy words – he raped her.'

Deagan smiled; he actually smiled. Kieran looked at him in shock. 'Do you find that amusing?'

'No, sir. But it's justice, that's what it is, for her disobedience. She'll have to marry him now, won't she? No one else will have her.'

'Are you mad? I saw him forcing her and she's badly battered as well as . . . the other. I'm certainly not going to compel her to marry such a brute.'

'You don't need to, sir. I'll do what's necessary.'

'Oh no, you won't. I've dismissed Flynn and told him to get off my land before nightfall.'

Deagan's smug look vanished. 'But how will he provide for Ismay if he's not got a job?'

'He's not going to provide for her.'

'If you send him away, it'll be too late to do the right thing once her belly's big. No, she has to marry him. Please sir, give him another chance. He's a good worker and he'll see her right.'

'The right thing, Deagan, is to keep your daughter safe and not give her to a man who'll beat her for the rest of her life.'

'Ach, what're a few taps? You have to keep women in order, specially ones like her. She's cheeky and wild.'

'This was more than a few taps. She's battered, that's the only word for it. And she's never been cheeky to us. My wife and I find her quiet and hard-working, quick to learn.'

Deagan's scowl deepened. 'She's only been working here a few days. You'll find out what she's like.' He folded his arms and delivered an ultimatum. 'If you send him away, I'm not having her back. I've enough *obedient* children to provide for.'

Kieran stood up. 'I wouldn't send her back to you, any more than I'd hand her over to him. I feel sorry for the rest of your children, I do indeed, if that's how you treat them. Get back to your work. If it wasn't for those children, I'd be dismissing you as well. I don't care to employ a man who condones rape. And you don't need to worry. I'll provide for your daughter . . . whatever happens.'

When his wife joined him, Kieran said simply, 'Her father's disowned her. He wanted to force her to marry that brute. He actually smiled and said it was a good thing it'd happened.'

Julia looked at him in shock. 'She said her father must have seen her going for the eggs and sent to tell Flynn. I didn't know whether to believe her or not.'

'He knew before he came here, from the look on his face, so that's what must have happened.'

'Some men are brutes.'

'I told him I'd look after her from now on.'

'I knew you would.' She came to stand by him and take his hand, raising it to her cheek. 'You're the prince of men.'

Half an hour later, the butler came into the library. 'Father Patrick is here, sir.'

Kieran looked up from his accounts. 'I suppose I'd better see him. What does he want today?'

'I couldn't say, sir.'

The priest came in, his belly jutting out, in contrast to the thin people who inhabited this village. Kieran didn't like the fellow; found him lazy and old-fashioned.

'Do sit down. How can I help you, Father?'

'I'm here about Ismay Deagan.'

'Oh?'

'Her father came to see me in great distress. What Flynn did was wrong, and I'll be sure to set him a heavy penance, but the girl must marry him.'

'Why?'

The priest blinked in surprise. 'Well, surely it's obvious. In case there's a child.'

'And you'd condemn her to spend her whole life with such a brute?'

'It's women's lot to marry and have children, to suffer for the sins of Eve.'

Kieran stood up. 'I'm making other arrangements for this young woman. Father.'

The priest stayed where he was, shaking his head, so Kieran walked across to the door and opened it. 'I'm afraid I'm busy.'

'My son, you must listen to wiser counsel.'

'I've made my decision. Now, please leave.'

'This is a bad mistake you're making, Mr Kieran.'

'Mistake! Flynn raped the girl.'

'These young men are a bit impetuous. He'll be all right with her once he's married. Think of the child, sir.'

'There is no child.'

'There could be. We have to make sure it's not born a bastard, but to a union sanctified by the church and—'

Kieran was disgusted by this attitude, but since the priest was obviously determined to stay and try to wear him down, he walked out of the room.

'Show Father Patrick out when he's ready,' he said to the butler, then lowered his voice. 'I can't get him to leave willingly.'

His butler, who was English and not a Catholic, had come with them when they inherited the house. He inclined his head. 'Leave it to me, sir.'

The priest was still muttering to himself in annoyance at not being able to change Mr Kieran's mind as he went out of the gates of the big house. He found Deagan waiting for him and stopped to talk.

'Did you arrange it all, Father?'

'No. It was as you said. He wouldn't listen to me. I shall have to write to the bishop. I'll do that at once.'

He went back to his house and wrote a letter, telling his housekeeper to put it into the post at once. She sent a boy to the big house with it, because there was no post office in the village, and the Largans sent their letters into Enniskillen every day or two. The priest had been so agitated, she told the lad to say it was urgent.

Kieran went to find his wife and tell her what had just happened. 'What do you think we should do with her, Julia? Keep her here till we find out whether she's expecting a child?'

Julia stood thinking, then shook her head. 'No. I doubt she'll feel safe here unless she never leaves the house. Which is no way to live. She's already been attacked on our land. We'll have to find somewhere else for her to live.'

'I hate to admit it, but you're right. Her father resents her getting away with what he calls disobedience. And if he's got that damned priest on his side, there will be more trouble brewing.'

Julia looked at him, head on one side. 'From the look on your face, you've got an idea.'

He went to pick up an envelope from his desk and brandished it at her. 'Coincidentally, I heard yesterday that the money had come through from Bram, who's a very different man from his father. Why don't we use it to send Ismay to her brother? I'll take great pleasure in telling old Deagan we've done that with the money instead of giving it to him. He only got drunk on the last lot. His wife and children saw precious little of it.'

Her face lit up. 'What a clever idea.'

'And since my brother Conn is out in Australia,' he went on, 'I'll ask him to keep an eye on her as well. She'll be going to people who'll care for her.'

'Do we not wait to see if she's with child?'

'No. We send a grieving young widow on the first available ship, complete with a letter from you, giving her a character reference and wishing her well after her sad loss. If there is a baby, it'll come as a surprise to her and people will be very sympathetic. Only we'll have to set off straight away to catch the next ship. I have the shipping schedule so that I can write to my brother Conn at the proper times, and I've just been checking it.'

'Will she be willing to go straight away?'

'I think so.'

An hour later, the butler came to find his master. 'They've just brought up a letter from the village to go with the post, sir. It's from the priest to the bishop.' He held it out.

Kieran stared at the envelope. 'We can guess what it's about, can't we?'

'Yes, sir. Shall I send it off today with the rest of the mail?'

'No. Send the rest and don't do anything with this one until I've had time to think.' The cheek of the fellow. He was definitely going to ask for a different priest to be assigned to the village. This man was so reactionary he was holding up Julia's plans to educate the girls at every step.

3

Once his adopted aunt had made the decision to come with him to Australia, Adam set to work. He went to a shipping agency and found there was a ship leaving from Southampton in a few days' time. It didn't give them very long to get ready, but he had to be out of the country soon to meet the conditions of the will, so he authorised the spending of two shillings to send a telegram to make sure two cabin berths were available, then hurried home.

To his surprise he found he would also have to prove that he and Harriet wouldn't be a charge on the public purse once they got there.

Harriet stared at him in shock when he told her how soon they had to leave, then pulled herself together and began packing.

Adam heard her weeping one night after she'd gone to bed and taxed her with it in the morning. 'Am I asking too much of you? I heard you crying last night.'

She bowed her head for a moment, then looked at him sadly. 'It's hard to leave my home, but it'd be harder still not to see you again. You're like a

son to me, Adam, and I'm not going to be parted
from you now. He was a nasty fellow, your father,
for all his churchgoing, and you'll not convince
me otherwise.'

Adam was in complete agreement about that.
His brother was almost as bad as his father, but
lazier, so presented less of a threat. His half-sister
Joanne hadn't seemed as hostile on the couple of
occasions he'd met her, but he'd mostly been kept
away from her, so that was only a feeling, not a
certainty. No, Harriet was his real family.

She looked at him anxiously. 'Are you sure you
want to be burdened with me?'

'You couldn't be a burden. I don't want you to
regret it, though, so I think you should rent out
your house until we're certain we'll be staying
there; then, if you're unhappy, you can always
come back.'

'I agree. I'd already decided to do that. We might
find this is a trick your father's playing on you.
For all we know, he's arranged for you to be
murdered when you get there.'

'Oh, I don't think he'd do that. It's against the
sixth commandment, after all. Though he'd not
have grieved if anything had happened to me.'

She reached out to grasp his hand for a moment.
'He was a cruel man.'

Adam shrugged and silence fell for a moment
or two, then he patted her hand as it still lay on
his. 'I'm sure his main reason was to get me out
of England and away from his family for good.'

He didn't add that he was also sure there would be some trickery involved to make his life more difficult. Struggle, according to his father's annual lectures, was good for the immortal soul.

'So, my dear aunt, let's get on with our arrangements and plan for a happy life together. We'll ask Mr Saxby to look after your house. His clerk will find a tenant and send the rent and your quarterly money to a bank in Australia.'

'You make it sound so easy, Adam love.'

He gave her a quick hug. 'It's not easy, exactly, but we'll make it work. Now, let me take you to buy a ship's kit and a good cabin trunk with drawers. Once we reach Southampton, we'll buy some extra treats for the journey – though I'm told people eat well on P&O ships, unlike on my last voyage to America, when our new cook proved unable to cook.'

Adam was glad there was so much to do from then on, because it kept his aunt's mind off her anxieties. To travel all that way at the age of fifty-six wasn't something to be undertaken lightly. It wasn't an easy journey for anyone, being over two months long, unlike his two-week trips across the Atlantic to America.

He'd look after her, he vowed, cherish her all the days of her life and make sure she didn't regret coming with him. And he'd not take to wife any woman who didn't feel the same about his aunt.

Excitement was starting to bubble up inside him. He'd always wanted to see the world and now he'd be visiting Malta, Alexandria, Suez, Ceylon and Australia.

And he'd not be on his own.

The following morning, Ismay woke feeling heavy-headed after a nearly sleepless night. There was no avoiding joining the other servants for breakfast, because she was sure Mrs Jamieson would want her to get on with her work as usual today.

When she took her place, she felt as if they were all staring at her. Since she wasn't hungry, she pushed the food round her plate, trying to eat, because you shouldn't waste good food, but not managing to swallow much. She knew how bad her face looked: swollen and puffy. She'd been shocked to see herself in the mirror on the servants' landing.

The kitchen maid was sitting next to her. She leaned sideways to whisper, 'That fellow ought to be taken out and shot like a mad dog for doing that to you.'

Ismay thought she'd misheard, and it was a few moments before the words sank in and she realised it was kindness and sympathy speaking, not scorn. 'Thank you.'

'Sure, we're all angry at him.'

Ismay risked a quick glance round the table and a couple of people nodded and smiled at her as they caught her eyes. 'I thought people would – you know, think I'd egged him on and blame me somehow.'

Her companion snorted scornfully. 'Your face

is so battered, anyone can see you tried to fight him off.'

As the others finished eating and went to start their day's work, they came over to her one by one, murmuring how sorry they were and wishing her well.

She was left weeping desperately into her pinafore.

Cook came to sit beside her. 'What's got you weeping, lass? What did they say to you? I'll make sure they regret upsetting you.' She took Ismay's hand and patted it.

'They said . . . they were sorry it happened. I thought they'd be . . . scornful.'

'Aah, I see. So that's why you didn't eat your breakfast. Stay where you are. I'll find you something to eat and you'll get it down you, even if I have to stand over you. You hardly ate a thing yesterday.'

When Mrs Jamieson came to find out where Ismay was, Cook had a word with her.

Ismay forced some food down, then stood up. 'I can't eat any more, truly I can't. Will I start work now, Mrs Jamieson?' Anything would be better than sitting thinking, remembering.

'Yes, but don't overstrain yourself today.'

She heard Cook's voice floating down the corridor after her. 'I'd like to take my big knife to him where it hurts a man most, so that he couldn't do that to any other girl.'

Too late for that now, she thought. He's already

done it to me. She shuddered, as she did every time she thought of *that*.

Later in the morning, Ismay was sweeping out the servants' quarters when Mrs Jamieson came up to the attics. She looked at the housekeeper anxiously, wondering what was wrong now.

'The master wants to see you. Go and tidy yourself up quickly.'

Ismay knew better than to ask what Mr Kieran wanted, so hurried to check her appearance, straighten that stupid cap, which would slip down over one ear, and put on a clean pinafore.

Mrs Jamieson tapped on the door of the library, then waved her to go in first and followed, staying near the door, hands folded across her lace-trimmed cream taffeta apron.

Mr Kieran was sitting in one of the big leather armchairs and his wife was next to him in another. 'Come and sit down, Ismay. You too, Mrs Jamieson, please.'

Ismay sat opposite them on the sofa he'd indicated, worrying what was going to happen now.

'You said you wanted to join your brother in Australia,' the master said.

'Yes, sir. I do.'

'My wife and I think that might be the best thing for you now. It'd get you right away from . . . any more trouble here.'

'I don't have any money to pay my fare, sir, or I'd have gone already.'

'Your brother's money has just arrived. I'm going to use that to send you to Australia. Your father doesn't deserve it after what he's done.'

She immediately felt guilty. 'But Mam needs it for the children. They get hungry sometimes and they're needing new clothes.'

'I'll make sure the children don't want,' Mrs Julia promised. 'Your father is a different matter.'

'If we give him money, he spends most of it on drink,' Mr Kieran said, scorn burring his voice. 'So, as I said, we'll use it to send you to Australia.'

She stared at them, unable to believe what she'd heard. Both smiled at her encouragingly.

'To Australia?' she whispered, still unable to believe it.

'Yes, Ismay. To your brother Bram.'

She had to close her eyes for a moment or two as the news sank in; the idea of it was so dazzling and shiny. When she opened them, she could only say, 'I can't believe what I'm hearing, but thank you, sir, madam. I'd really like to go. Only – I'm not quite sure how you do it.'

'You travel to Southampton, in the south of England, and get on a ship there. You have to change ships on the way, but I'll write all that down for you.'

She couldn't form a word. The thought of doing all that was so terrifying – and yet so exciting.

'Very fortunately, my wife and I were intending to visit friends in London, so we'll take you to Southampton and see you on a ship first. We've just time to get you there for the next ship that sails.'

Mrs Jamieson shuffled uneasily. 'Sir – what if she's with child?'

Ismay shuddered. No, she couldn't be, she couldn't! God couldn't be so cruel.

Mr Kieran looked at his wife and she made a gesture with one hand for him to continue explaining. 'We've been discussing that. You'll need to tell people you've recently been widowed, just in case. Say you're going out to join your brother to make a new life for yourself. Can you do that?'

'Yes, sir.' She could do anything to get to Australia, though the thought of travelling all that way alone made her feel shaky inside. Surely God wouldn't blame her for telling a little lie or two?

Mr Kieran explained the arrangements he had in mind and took out a piece of paper, holding it out to the housekeeper. 'My wife and I have written down what she'll need. Do you think you can find these clothes for her, Mrs Jamieson?'

The housekeeper looked at the list and gasped. 'There's a lot here. I don't think we have enough in the servants' chest, sir. What we do have . . . well, she's so small, most of it won't fit her and there isn't time to alter them.'

'Are you any good at sewing, Ismay?' Mrs Julia asked.

She shook her head. 'No, ma'am. I did a bit at

school, but only sewing plain seams and putting
buttons on. I don't think I could alter a dress. I'd
not know where to start. Ginny from the laundry
was going to teach me more, so that I could help
mend the clothes and linen.' She'd been looking
forward to that. She loved learning new things.

Mrs Julia studied her thoughtfully. 'Stand up,
Ismay.' She went across to stand next to her. 'See!
Just as I thought. She's about the same size as me.
She can have some of my old clothes. They've
been stored in the attic because they don't fit many
other people.'

Ismay stared at her in shock. She couldn't
imagine herself wearing such beautiful clothes.

'We'll go up and look through them after we've
finished here, Mrs Jamieson, if you have the time.'

Mr Kieran smiled at his wife and Ismay sighed.
It was lovely to see the way those two cared for
each other.

He took over again. 'We have to leave tomorrow
if we're to get you to Southampton in time. The
P&O ships going to the Far East don't set off from
Liverpool, you see.' He looked at Ismay. 'If you
don't want to go, you have only to say, and we'll
work out something else for you.'

It was the only thing she was certain of. 'I do
want to go, sir. Really I do. And I know Bram will
welcome me. He's my favourite brother.'

Mrs Julia stood up. 'Then let's sort out some
clothes for you.'

After that it was a whirl of preparations. Mrs

Jamieson, Mrs Julia and her maid whisked Ismay off to the attics where the three women went through several trunks of discarded clothing.

'We don't even have time to air them,' Mrs Jamieson said regretfully as the piles mounted.

Ismay felt shocked rigid at how many clothes they were giving her. 'It's too much,' she whispered.

'You'll need them to change into on the journey,' Mrs Julia said firmly. 'Not much chance to do any washing there. And anyway, they're only lying around in trunks here. It's good to see them put to use again.'

Ismay stroked the braid on the skirt and matching bodice she was trying on, lost for words at how beautiful it was; such a soft blue in colour, and not worn or damaged anywhere that she could see.

Her head was spinning by the time they brought the clothes down to one of the spare family bedrooms, where a scratched old tin trunk was standing with its lid open.

'That's your trunk now,' the housekeeper said. 'And you'll need this leather suitcase as well, plus this.' She held out a bag made of soft leather, gathered at the top. 'Keep this handbag on you at all times with your money, and any odds and ends, like a handkerchief, that you may need during the day. Fashionable ladies don't carry such things, but it's different for folk like us.'

'Mrs Julia carries a handbag sometimes when she's travelling,' the lady's maid said.

*   *   *

When they came down to the servants' hall from packing the things, they got a message that Mr Kieran wanted to see Ismay again in the library.

He looked up as she went in. 'Ah, there you are. My wife's reminded me that you'll need something to do on the ship because the journey will take more than two months. Books. Writing materials. Keeping a diary, perhaps? How good are you at reading and writing, Ismay?'

Here was one thing at least of which she could be proud. 'I was top of the class at school, sir. I love to read. The teacher would have lent me some books even after I left school, only Da wouldn't let us have them in the house.'

'Your father is going to have to change quite a few of his ways if he wants to stay here,' Mr Kieran said grimly. 'In this modern world, people need to be able to read and write, and that's true for women as well as men.'

Ismay saw a chance to help her younger brothers and sisters. 'Da keeps the children home from school whenever he can.'

'That too will change. My wife's going to take an interest in the village school. She has a passion for education.'

Mrs Julia was looking at her thoughtfully again. 'Since your face is still badly bruised, I think we'd better tell people your husband was killed in an accident with the gig and you were injured in the same accident. What married name do you want to use? I'll have your initials painted on your luggage.'

Ismay stared at them both, then it came to her. 'Hope, sir. Ismay Catherine Hope.' Because that was what they'd given her: hope for a decent future.

They smiled as if they understood this. 'Good choice,' Mrs Julia said. 'And Ismay, I wish you well. Write to us when you can.'

'I will, ma'am.'

She had to stop on the way back to the servants' hall to stare at herself in the mirror. Her face still looked terrible, but the new clothes were lovely. She stroked the cloth, staring at herself in the mirror.

'You're going to Australia,' she whispered. 'You really are, Ismay Deagan.' Then she corrected herself, trying out the new name. 'Ismay Hope.' She liked the sound of it.

Crossing herself she whispered quickly, 'Please, God, forgive me for lying.'

Ismay was exhausted by the time she went to bed. In spite of the fact that going to her brother in Australia was something she'd been wanting to do for a while, she hardly slept a wink, because she was terrified of travelling so far on her own.

All too soon, Ginny was shaking her awake. 'Come on, sleepy-head. Get yourself dressed.'

When she was ready, Ismay went down for the final time to have breakfast in the servants' hall. Two of the grooms were waiting at the foot of the stairs.

'Are your trunk and bag ready?' one asked. 'Only we have to tie them on the carriage.'

'Yes.' She went back up to show them where, then lingered to watch them carry the scuffed tin trunk down the stairs. She brought down the shabby leather suitcase herself. It held the clothes for the first stage of the journey. Other sets of clothes were in the trunk, wrapped in old sheets, each set ready to be brought up at intervals en route and the dirty ones stored in the trunk.

By that time she was late for breakfast and could hear the others gathered in the servants' hall already. She stopped in surprise when she found all the indoor servants were there, instead of taking the meal in two sessions as was usual.

When Cook waved her to the head of the table, she guessed this was a way of saying goodbye and tried to smile at them. But it was an effort, because leaving everything and everyone she'd ever known had set fear shivering inside her belly.

Someone put a bowl of porridge in front of her and she stared down at it, not feeling in the least like eating. She looked up in surprise as someone started tapping a spoon against a cup and saw that the butler had come in and was standing at the other end of the table. Everyone stopped eating and turned to face him.

'We're here to say goodbye to Ismay and to wish her well in her new life,' he said.

As they applauded, Ismay could feel herself blushing.

'She hasn't been here with us for long, but she's shown herself to be a hard worker, and I'm sure you all agree that it's a shame she has to leave.'

Cries of agreement greeted this, and their smiles brought tears to Ismay's eyes.

When the room was silent again, Mrs Jamieson picked up an envelope and walked round the table to hand it to Ismay. 'We held a collection because we thought you'd feel better to have a little money behind you.' She held the envelope out.

Ismay was surprised to find how heavy it was. The coins clinked as she took hold of it, more money than she'd ever had in the whole of her life before, because Da had always taken any wages she earned, only occasionally giving her a penny or two for herself.

They waited expectantly, faces turned towards her, and she knew she'd have to speak. Well, she'd be a poor sort of person if she didn't say thank you. 'You've all been so kind to me. I would have been happy to stay here.' She had to stop to swallow hard. She mustn't cry again; didn't want them to remember her weeping.

'But since I can't stay, I'll just be telling you thank you for thinking of me, and you can be sure I'll not waste a penny of this. Thank you so much.' She couldn't speak another word and looked pleadingly at the housekeeper.

'We all wish you well, Ismay.'

They applauded again, then everyone started eating and somehow she managed to get most of the porridge down her.

When the other servants left to get on with their work, Cook came to pat her on the back then went through into the kitchen, which left only Ismay and Mrs Jamieson.

'You've got ten minutes, then you're to meet the master and mistress in the hall.' The housekeeper held out a parcel wrapped in brown paper. 'I thought you'd find this useful on the long journey. It's a novel.' She thrust it into Ismay's hands, took out a handkerchief and blew her nose vigorously, then said, 'Ten minutes. Make sure you've not left anything in your bedroom.' At the door she turned. 'Good luck.'

Ismay stood for a moment on her own, then took a deep, shaky breath and went to use the necessary out the back, vomiting up the porridge she'd forced down, then wiped her mouth and rinsed it out with drinking water.

Then she went upstairs, though she didn't really need to check the bedroom. What she really wanted to do was stand by the attic window at the end of the corridor to take a last look at the village. She could see the rooftops of some of the cottages but she couldn't see her own home from here. It wasn't her home any more, but still, she'd have liked to see it one last time.

What were the villages like in Australia? Bram said the weather was much warmer there, with far less rain, and he lived in a port town called Fremantle. She felt so ignorant about everything.

Picking up her drawstring bag of bits and pieces, she walked down to the entrance hall which the family and their friends used and stood quietly in the corner near the front door, waiting.

There was the sound of voices upstairs and the butler came out from his little room at the back of the hall, nodding to her as he opened the front door.

The voices came closer and the master and mistress walked down the stairs. They were a fine-looking couple; not handsome or beautiful, but healthy and smiling. Ismay was sure they'd never gone hungry in their whole lives.

'Ah, there you are!' Mr Kieran said. 'Ready for your great adventure, Mrs Hope?'

She wondered who he was talking to for a moment, then realised he was using her new name. She must get used to that. 'Yes, sir.'

As she followed them outside, it began to rain, a light, sifting veil of moisture that she hoped would hide the tears on her cheeks.

Rory Flynn was hiding in the woods, still waiting for the priest to fix things up for him to marry Ismay. When he saw the carriage setting off from the big house, he was close enough to see Ismay sitting in the back of it. What was she doing there? Where were they taking her?

He ran across to the stables, where a cousin of his worked, and asked him what was happening.

Pleased to show off his superior knowledge, his
cousin told him about Ismay going to Australia.

'She's on her way to Liverpool?' Rory exclaimed
in shock.

'No. Further than that. I heard the master
telling Peters they were going to Southampton.
That's where the ships leave from, not Liverpool.
And they have to hurry, because the next one is
leaving soon.' The cousin grinned, adding slyly,
'So you won't be able to marry her now, will
you?'

Rory set off running. He had to tell the priest,
had to find a way to bring her back. From being
a boy, he'd set his mind on marrying Ismay, and
he was going to do that, whatever it took. She was
his now; he'd made her his.

Father Patrick listened to his breathless explanation and stared at him in shock. 'They've
already left for Southampton? You're sure it's
Southampton?'

'So my cousin says.'

'Then there's nothing we can do. It's too late.'

'There must be something.'

'The bishop's reply will be too late. No, Rory,
you'll have to find someone else to marry.'

He left the priest's house, scowling and went to
find Sean Deagan. He wasn't going to give up,
whatever anyone said.

Adam woke early. Everything was ready, so he
could have stayed in bed, only he didn't want to

do that. He went downstairs and, to his surprise, found Aunt Harriet sitting in the kitchen.

'Have you been up long?'

'An hour or two. I couldn't sleep. You were snoring as I passed your room.'

'I was not.' When he was younger, it had been a joke between them to pretend the other snored, but now his reply was as feeble as her attempt to smile.

'It's not too late to stay here,' he said gently.

'It was too late the minute your father wrote that will.' She held up one hand to prevent him speaking. 'I've not changed my mind about going to Australia with you, Adam love, but it's only natural I'd feel sad to leave my little home.'

'You'll never regret it,' he assured her.

She nodded and stood up. 'I'll get you a cup of tea, shall I?'

When they were ready to leave, he went to summon a cab, which left her with a few minutes on her own to say goodbye to the shade of her dead husband and the pieces of furniture, which would soon be put into storage.

She walked out to the cab with head held high and lashes still wet with tears.

'It's a pity they don't sail all the way from Liverpool to Australia,' he said as they got on the train for London, where they would change for Southampton. 'That'd have been much easier. It'll be better when they finish the Suez Canal. Just imagine it, cutting a great canal right through from the Mediterranean to the Gulf of Suez. A hundred and twenty miles of it, deep enough for big ships! Passengers will be able to stay on board the same ship and not have to cross the isthmus by rail, as we'll be doing!'

She nodded, but he could see she didn't really care, so he left her to her thoughts and stared out of the window instead. He'd rather have been on a ship. This rattling, rocking train made him feel uncomfortable. Give him the soft rolling of a ship any time.

4

Ismay couldn't tear her eyes away from the carriage window. There was so much to see as they jolted along the rough roads that she felt as if her head was bursting with new images. They went first to Enniskillen, where they were to catch a train to Dublin. They stopped at an inn, where they took refreshments, then went outside to stretch their legs.

She walked behind her employers, who were arm in arm. She stopped when they did, staring at the lough, much bigger than the little one near the village. She loved the way the huge stretch of water glinted in the sunlight and oh, there was the castle she'd heard about at school, with its twin towers. She turned at the sound of tramping feet and saw a group of soldiers march by, looking fine and manly in their uniforms. One of them winked at her but she didn't show she'd noticed. She wanted nothing more to do with men.

She twisted to and fro as they strolled along, not wanting to miss a single thing.

'Have you never been here before?' Mrs Julia

asked with a smile as they stopped at a corner and waited for her to catch up.

'No, ma'am.'

The mistress turned to her husband. 'I must organise an excursion for the children at the school. It's shameful that in the age of railways and travel they've never been more than five miles away from their home. What do you think?'

'I think they'll adore you even more if you give them such treats.'

Mrs Julia turned back to Ismay. 'I wish there was time to take a longer walk round the town than this, but we have to catch the train soon.'

'I've never been on a train before, either, ma'am.'

'Then you're going to have an exciting time. By the time we get to Southampton tomorrow, you'll have been on several trains, as well as a ferry across the Irish Sea.' She looked at her husband. 'I think Ismay had better ride with us on the train, so that we can keep an eye on her.'

He nodded and explained, 'There are different classes of seat, you see.'

'It won't be right for me to ride with you.' She'd never relax for a minute, worrying about doing something wrong.

'It's right if we say so,' he said firmly.

So she sat on a comfortable seat in the middle of the row of three, terrified of speaking out of turn. She left them to chat to one another or to the old lady and gentleman who were sharing their compartment. Avidly, she watched the new world they were passing through, looking first to one side, then to the other: towns, villages, farms, cottages, animals in fields. They didn't seem at all frightened of the train roaring past them. Ah, she was so ignorant! Even the cows had seen more trains than she had.

It felt strange to be shut up like this till the next station. What if you felt sick or wanted to use the necessary? You'd not be able to.

In the middle of the day, the train stopped at a station where they were selling hampers of food for the passengers. There were also necessaries on the station. Even they were very fine, with comfortable water closets, and water coming out of taps to wash your hands and face in. Ismay was so glad she was wearing a matching skirt and bodice that had belonged to Mrs Julia, a soft green with darker green braid on it, because her own clothes had been nothing but rags in comparison to what her fellow travellers were wearing, even those not in the first class.

When the train set off again, she felt shy to be eating in the company of the master and his wife, but she was ravenously hungry by now, so did justice to what she was offered from the hamper. Wouldn't Ma stare to see such food! What was Ma doing now? Ismay took a deep breath and turned her thoughts elsewhere. She'd not be seeing her mother again, or her brothers and sister, but if she wept about that, she'd do it in private.

The master and his wife were so kind. They

kept explaining things, making sure she knew where they were going on Mr Kieran's map. She'd seen maps at school but never before had the time to study one in detail, let alone travel to the places on it. He let her keep it on her knee and trace their journey across Ireland on it.

Then they got onto the ferry, which was nothing like a ferry across a river, but was a huge ship.

It took them across the Irish Sea to England, its engines making the deck throb beneath her feet. She didn't feel at all sick, though Mrs Julia turned a bit pale.

Just fancy that! Ismay Deagan travelling across the sea.

Best of all, she'd got away from *him* now. It seemed as if Rory had been hovering nearby all her life, staring at her, touching her as she got older, making her feel uneasy.

Oh, it was such a relief! Such a wonderful relief! She couldn't help feeling more cheerful, even though her face still hurt a bit when she smiled.

Sean Deagan listened to Rory's tale and anger filled him when he heard they'd taken his daughter away. The rage was so burning hot, he felt as if his head would burst. He had to sit down for a minute because he came over dizzy.

When the blood had stopped pounding through his head, he drew a deep breath. 'You'll have to go after her, then.' He waited a minute, then added, 'Stop staring like a fool. We have to get her back.'

'How can I go after them? I don't have any money.'

'We'll go and see Father Patrick. He'll let us have some when he hears why.'

'He said there was nothing to be done.'

'Leave him to me.'

So forcefully did Sean speak that the priest handed over some money.

'It's all I can spare and it won't be nearly enough,' he said.

'It'll get Rory started on his way. He'll need a letter as well, Father, one he can show to other priests as he travels and get them to help him.'

'I'm not sure I can—'

'Think of that poor fatherless child!'

'We're not sure there is a child.'

'Oh, there will be. Us Deagans fall easily for children and so do the Flynns.'

'Well, yes, you do both have rather large families.'

'Think of the child's soul, Father. Who knows where Ismay will end up? Why, it might even be raised a heathen.'

The priest shook his head, but got out his writing materials. 'Go and pack a bag, Rory. You'll need as many clothes as you can find.'

So Rory went round to all his cousins to borrow clothes, and finished with more clothes than he'd ever had in his life. After making him swear not to tell the master, the farmer at the home farm gave him a wicker box with a lid to put the clothes in, because he had daughters and didn't like the example Ismay Deagan had set of disobeying a father.

Of course the butler overheard the servants talking, but it was a while before he put the various snippets of information together and realised what was going on. When he did confront the male servants, Rory's cousin from the stables sent word to get away quickly before anyone from the big house tried to stop him.

Rory left for Enniskillen on the peddler's cart. He sat there in amazement as the horse clopped along, his head spinning from all he'd done, let alone all he was trying to do.

That'd learn the master not to interfere in other people's families!

Rory found his way to the railway station in Enniskillen and, when he discovered that the train didn't leave for another two hours, he asked the way to the presbytery, cursing the trunk, which was heavy to carry around. He stopped to buy some rope and made a pair of handles to slip his shoulders into. That way he could carry it on his back.

After he'd shown Father Patrick's letter to the priest, he was given another guinea to help him on his way.

When Rory got off the train he found that he'd missed the last ferry to Liverpool but he made his way to the nearest church and got another priest to help him by letting him sleep in one of the pews.

His blood was up now and he wasn't going to stop until he caught up with Ismay. She'd see then that she had to marry him; see the trouble he'd taken to follow her.

And after they were wed, he'd be able to have his way with her any time he liked. No one could interfere between husband and wife.

Not even Mr Kieran Largan himself.

By the time Adam and Aunt Harriet reached Southampton, it was evening and they were both exhausted.

They'd had to change trains several times on the way, because of the different widths of track used by the various railway companies, which put him in a bad mood. 'Why don't the railways organise things better?' he complained. 'All of them should use the same gauge of track. It's only common sense. It's a lot easier travelling by ship.'

'It'd cost a lot of money to change the tracks.'

'The money would be well spent. I'm glad to be done with trains. Once we get on board ship, we'll not be disembarking until we get to Alexandria.'

His aunt gave him a faint smile, but she'd been very quiet all day and he was still worried about her. For two pins he'd turn round, take her home and to hell with his inheritance. But that would mean the schooner and houses going to his brother. If there *was* any schooner called the *Hannah Grey*. If this wasn't all a trick. He still found it hard to believe his father would leave him anything worthwhile.

They found a hotel near the railway station and took two rooms for a night or maybe longer, since he didn't know when they'd be allowed to board. They were just in time to have a meal before the dining room closed.

He watched his aunt pick at her food. 'You need to eat properly.'

She put down her spoon and pushed the plate of apple pie and custard away from her. 'I think travelling upsets my stomach a little, and I need to sleep more than anything, dear. I hardly closed my eyes last night. I'm sure I'll sleep like a baby tonight, even in a strange bed.'

'I'm tired too,' he admitted, then smiled. 'But not too tired to finish off your apple pie, if it's going to waste.'

'You always were a hearty eater, but you never got fat on it because you never stopped doing things.'

'I still like to keep busy.' He wasn't looking forward to being a passenger on a ship, with nothing to do all day but lounge around idly.

Morning saw the start of an extremely busy day. Adam left his aunt sitting in the ladies' lounge at the hotel reading the newspaper, and went to the shipping office. Here, a very obliging clerk explained exactly when they'd be allowed to go on board and what formalities they'd have to undergo before they'd be allowed to leave the country, such as a medical check.

He smiled. 'Though I doubt you'll have any problems with that, sir. It's mainly to catch people with infectious diseases.'

Adam went back to have luncheon with his aunt, then they set off to do some shopping. He knew exactly what treats would be welcome on board ship, and helped her choose dried fruit and nuts, plus jars of chutney and preserves.

'Now. You'll need something to pass the time. Books, maybe?'

'I'd love to buy some books, but I'd also like to start an embroidery if you don't mind finding me a shop. I'll be quick and you can wait outside. I know gentlemen don't like such places.'

'I'm coming inside to help you choose. I'm not letting you out of my sight for a moment.' He didn't tell her that prices were sometimes raised to catch the unwary traveller and he intended to make it clear he was a ship's officer. It was one thing to spend money, another to waste it.

They passed another day idling away their time, strolling round the town until his aunt got tired, after which he went out for a brisk walk alone, ending up at the harbour, staring at the ships, so many of them making their way up or down Southampton Water.

He got into conversation with an old sailor, who told him that much of the waterfront had been

reclaimed over the years so that the port could
handle the larger ships.

'Gateway to the Empire, we are,' he said proudly.
'And a'course we get two high tides a day, so that
makes things easier.'

Adam slipped him sixpence and he tipped his
hat. 'Thank'ee, sir. I'll drink to a safe voyage for
you.'

The following morning they were able to go on
board, to Adam's relief. He was looking forward
to being on a ship again and watching how their
ship was run. It was a hybrid, of course, with steam
as well as sails. Wind was still free, but with coal
and steam they were no longer at the mercy of
the weather, thank goodness.

It was all bustle as they approached the ship,
with a steady stream of people moving up the
gangways, followed by porters carrying their
luggage.

Their cabins were small, but adequate. They'd
paid extra not to share these with strangers, but
hadn't taken the most expensive cabins, whose
cost made his aunt shudder.

The trunks had been taken down to the hold,
but the items for the first part of the voyage went
with them to their cabins. Adam took out his night
things, put a book under his pillow, then stowed
his suitcase under the lower bunk bed. He then
went next door to check that his aunt was all right.

'Let's go on deck and watch people boarding

the ship.' He studied her as they moved into the sunshine and felt the benefit of a light sea breeze. 'You look a little better this morning.'

'I feel better to know it's too late to do anything now but make the best of it. Does that sound foolish?'

'Not at all.' In fact, it sounded just like her. She always found a reason for making the best of things.

He was so glad she'd come with him, but he hoped he never saw another Harbisher as long as he lived.

Liverpool terrified Ismay at first, because it was so much bigger than anywhere she'd ever been before. The pavements were so full of people hurrying about their business, she was terrified of being separated from her employers. Where did all these people come from? Why were they in such a hurry?

The roads were equally crowded, and there were many sorts of vehicles she'd never even seen before. As she walked behind the Largans, she heard people speaking to one another, but had trouble understanding most of them. How strangely they spoke.

Yet again she thanked God she'd been given decent clothes to wear. Even the beggars here were better dressed than she'd been before she went to work at the big house.

Mr Kieran had warned her to keep her valuables safe, so she'd put her money inside her chemise, laboriously sewing a crude little pocket for it from a handkerchief. It was marked not only with uneven stitches but with a few drops of blood, and she'd shed a few tears over it, too, though they didn't show, of course.

She followed her employers from the cab into the Great North Western Hotel, which looked more like a cathedral to her. She was immediately separated from them by a man in a fancy uniform who'd opened the door for them. He jerked his head at her and somehow she found herself moving to one side.

'Can you find someone to keep an eye on our maid?' Mrs Julia asked him. 'She's from our Irish estate and has never been to a hotel before.'

'Certainly, madam.' He turned to Ismay, staring in disapproval at her bruised face. 'Stand over there till someone comes for you, and keep that side of your face out of sight,' he said in a low voice, then turned back to fuss over the Largans.

She saw Mr Kieran give him some money. What was that for? He'd done nothing but talk.

Shaky with fear, she watched them walk away and waited where she'd been told for someone to come for her. To her relief it was a cheerful middle-aged maid, who took one look at her and asked, 'First time away from the country?'

She nodded. 'Yes, ma'am.'

'I'll make sure someone comes to fetch you down to the servants' dining room for your meal, then. We don't want you getting lost or straying into the gentry's part of the hotel. Here. This is your room. The necessary is at the end of the corridor.' She marched along and flung open a door to show a room with a water closet in it, demonstrating how to flush it afterwards.

Ismay didn't dare say she knew that already.

'You can get a jug of water for washing from this sink here. This tap is for hot water and this for cold. Afterwards, you must empty your dirty water here too. All right?'

'Yes, ma'am.'

The woman hesitated. 'What happened to your face?'

'I was in an accident. My husband was killed.' There. She'd told the lie without hesitating. But she still didn't like lying to kind people.

'Oh dear. I'm so sorry.'

Once the door of her room had closed behind the other woman, Ismay stood very still, breathing slowly and letting the silence wash over her. Then she walked three paces to the tiny dormer window where, by standing on a chair, she could stare down at the busy street.

It didn't matter that the bedroom was tiny, with barely space for her to stand upright next to the bed. This would be the first time in her whole life that she'd slept in a room all alone.

She didn't know how long she'd stood there, but suddenly she panicked, wondering what time it was. What if they came for her and she wasn't ready? She put the chair back in place and hurried to use the necessary, fetching a jug of water. It felt good to wash her hands and face and tidy her hair, but the bruises still looked terrible.

She wondered what the servants' dining room would be like. Two worlds again, just like at the hall. Well, it'd be easier to eat there, she was sure, than try to mind her manners and conversation while sharing a meal with Mr Kieran and Mrs Julia.

She sat on the bed, bouncing gently as she waited. It was wonderfully soft and smooth. No straw mattresses here. She stroked the clean, fresh-smelling sheet and fingered the thickness of the soft blankets. On a sudden thought she got out her nightdress and placed it ready under her pillow.

Mr Kieran said they'd come over two hundred miles already, and that she'd be travelling about nine thousand miles more to join her brother in Australia, which would take over two months. She couldn't even imagine what a distance so great looked like.

People went to Australia all the time, though. No need to be afraid. Travelling was very interesting, as she'd found today. But she'd be on her own once she was on the ship and that would be much harder. Still, once she was on it, the captain and sailors would know the way to go. And once they arrived in Australia, she had a tongue in her head, didn't she, to ask for directions to her brother's shop . . . no, Deagan's Bazaar, he called it.

By the time a young chambermaid came to fetch her down to a meal, she was feeling calmer.

'Don't forget to lock your door,' the maid told her. 'There are strangers coming and going all the time.'

Ismay looked at the lock in puzzlement.

'The key's on the inside.' Impatiently, the other woman opened the door, shut it again and turned the key in the outside lock before handing it to Ismay.

She stared at the heavy iron key. 'I've nowhere to put it.'

'Don't you have a pocket? Or a bag?'

'Sure, and I left the bag on the bed.' She unlocked the door again, ignoring the loud sigh next to her, got the drawstring bag and locked the door again, putting her key in it. As Mrs Jamieson had said, it was a useful thing to have when travelling. 'There. I'm ready now.'

'Thank goodness for that!'

The servants' dining room was busy, with older people – dressed as finely as ladies and gentlemen – occupying one table, and speaking like gentry too. They didn't even turn to see who'd come in.

'Upper servants sit there,' her guide whispered. 'You'll sit over here.'

There were younger servants at two other tables and she took a seat next to a cheerful lass who said she 'looked after' an old lady. She was obviously used to travelling around the country.

'Miss has friends and relatives everywhere. I'm

lucky to have this post. I'm learning ever such a lot and I'm really enjoying myself. She's so kind. It's your first time travelling, isn't it?'

'How did you know?' That was the second time someone had guessed immediately.

'You look stiff and nervous.'

'Oh.'

'No offence intended. I can't help noticing things.'

'I'm not offended. I'd never even been out of the village before, let alone out of the country.'

'And now you've escaped the village.'

Ismay considered that, head on one side, and decided it was a good way to describe it. 'I have, yes.'

'What happened to your face?'

Ismay felt tears well in her eyes. She hated being reminded of what had happened. Remembering her story, she stumbled through an explanation. Lies, more lies! What a way to go on. 'My husband and I were in an accident. He was killed.'

'Oh, you poor thing! How long had you been married?'

'Just a few months.'

'How sad! So where are you going now?'

'Australia.' Ismay had the satisfaction of seeing her companion's mouth drop open in surprise. 'I'm going to join my brother who lives there. The master and his wife are taking me to the ship.'

'They sound kind. Not many would do that for a servant.'

'They are kind, yes.'

'I hope you'll be happy in Australia.'

'Thank you.'

The others at the table had been listening unashamedly and several of them nodded, as if telling her the same thing.

It was a sin to lie, but she didn't care. She wasn't going to tell anyone what had really happened, not till she saw Bram again, and perhaps not even him. She must remember her story. And her new name. She kept forgetting.

By the time the master told her they were nearing Southampton, Ismay had seen so many new things, she felt her head was overflowing with pictures. Villages, towns – some pretty, some ugly – farms, fields, woods and then more fields.

Mrs Julia still insisted on her travelling first class with them. While Mr Kieran was talking to another gentleman, Ismay ventured to say, 'I'm really grateful for your help, ma'am. I don't know what I'd have done without you, how I'd have managed.'

'That's all right. People should help one another, don't you think?'

'Yes, ma'am.' But Ismay couldn't imagine herself able to help someone like Mrs Julia. Soon the mistress turned back to the lady next to her and Ismay was free to stare out of the window again at the outskirts of the town.

This time, the way things were arranged at the

hotel wasn't quite as bewildering. She didn't have time to rest, though, because Mrs Julia whisked her out to buy more things for the ship while Mr Kieran checked up on the boarding time. Ismay couldn't believe how much money they were spending on her.

It began to rain while they were out, but most of the time they were inside shops, so they didn't get wet, and then they took a cab back to the hotel. She felt like a queen riding in a cab.

Ismay went to her room, sinking on her bed, feeling exhausted as she listened to the rain pelting against the small window in her room. But within minutes someone knocked on her door and told her she was wanted by her master.

She was taken to the big entrance hall, where Mr Kieran was waiting for her.

'Good news, Ismay. You can board the ship tomorrow morning. We'll see you on to it, then go back to London.'

She'd been feeling a bit braver, but now terror filled her because she'd be truly on her own then, wouldn't she? But she managed to force out a 'Thank you, sir.'

He smiled that gentle smile of his. 'Don't worry. You'll be all right, Ismay. They're used to people not knowing what to do on ships. And always remember, if you need help, ask someone. You won't be the only person sailing for the first time.'

'Yes, sir.'

'You can go now. Be ready to leave at ten o'clock tomorrow morning.'

She didn't see them again until then.

That evening there was no friendly chambermaid to show her where to go, but she found her way to the servants' hall. The other servants took one look at her bruised face and avoided sitting next to her.

Then a rough-looking girl sat opposite her. 'Get into a fight, did you?'

Ismay drew herself up and said indignantly, 'No, I did not. I was in an accident. My husband was killed.'

There was dead silence at the table.

'Oh. Sorry.'

But still no one spoke to her. They just stared.

As soon as she'd eaten, Ismay made her way back to her bedroom, and was relieved when she didn't get lost. She tried to look out of the window, but it was dusk now and she could only see the dark shadows of other rooftops and hear the faint pitter-patter of rain.

She couldn't help having a little cry. She'd never felt so alone in her life and it was terrifying.

But not as terrifying as the thought of being married to Rory Flynn. Thank goodness she'd never have to see him again.

A man let himself down from the back of the goods train on which he'd travelled from London. He fell lucky and found out which train was going

to Southampton, managing to get himself and his
trunk into one of the wagons without being
noticed, because it was pouring down with rain
and most people were trying to shelter from it. He
shoved some crates to one side and made a narrow
space for himself and his wicker trunk.

As the train set off, he crossed himself quickly
and thanked God for looking after him.

He had a narrow escape – was nearly seen – but
managed to get out of the railway station by
climbing a wall. He stopped the first man walking
past to ask the way to the nearest Catholic church.
He had trouble understanding what the man told
him, but it got him started on his way. He had to
ask twice more before he found it and felt irritated
by the way these people spoke.

Again, the letter from the priest back home
ensured that he was given somewhere to sleep.
The letter was looking worn at the edges now and
felt a bit damp, so the younger priest found him
a cover called an envelope for it.

The following morning, he was summoned to
see the older of the two priests.

'I've been thinking about your problem, Flynn.
It'll be hard to get you a berth at this late stage,
but what do you think of working your passage?
I'm sure I can get you taken on. They're often
short of a man or two at the last minute. It'll be
menial work, shovelling coal or cleaning, but I
daresay you won't mind that.'

'I'll do whatever work the Lord sends my way, Father.' Rory bowed his head to hide his smile as the thought followed that, if he worked his passage, he'd be able to keep the money he'd been given and use it later in Australia.

'Before we do anything, I want you to swear on this Bible that you're not wanted for any crime.'

He placed his hand on the Bible. 'I swear that, Father. All I want is to find the girl I was to marry, the girl they took away from me.'

He went on board the ship at six o'clock in the morning the next day, accompanied by the younger priest, who turned to him at the top of the gangway to say, 'Don't let us down, now, Flynn. Work hard.'

'I will, Father, I will.' He turned to face a large man in uniform who looked him up and down as if he was a piece of muck.

'Well, you look strong enough, anyway, Flynn. What was your job before?'

Rory knew better than to trifle with this man. 'I was a cowman, sir.'

'Well, here you'll be stoking the engines and scrubbing the decks. And you'll be doing it well or I'll put you off the ship at Malta.' He nodded to the priest. 'I'll see to him now, Father. Come this way, Flynn.'

'Yes, sir.' He followed the man down into the stinking depths of the ship, scowling at this dark, stuffy place. He didn't like it, not at all.

She'd pay for this later. Stupid bitch. But he wasn't having anyone else marrying his girl, nor was he having his child raised by others. And if there wasn't a child now, he'd get one on her very quickly.

5

Ismay walked up the gangway on to the ship with Mr Kieran, feeling so nervous she wanted to clutch his coat, but of course she couldn't do that. She listened to him explain who she was to the stewardess.

He turned back to her, laying his hand lightly on her shoulder for a moment. 'I wish you well, Ismay. In every way. Give my regards to your brother – tell him we're all very proud of how well he's doing. My brother says he's made a fine start as a trader. And give my regards to Conn as well, if you see him.'

'Thank you, sir. I will. I'm grateful to you and the mistress for all your kindness.'

'We were glad to help. You didn't deserve what happened.'

She watched him walk back to the quay.

'Come this way,' the stewardess said. 'You'll be in the single women's quarters, though I gather you've been recently widowed.'

'Yes.' She touched her face. 'In an accident.'

The stewardess's voice grew gentler. 'That must be hard.'

Ismay could only nod.

The woman stopped beside a steep set of steps that were more like a ladder. 'Don't look so worried. You'll soon get used to going up and down the companionways.'

'Is that what they're called? They look more like stepladders to me.' Ismay climbed carefully down and found it wasn't too difficult, though it must be hard for older people. She looked round.

'This is the day area, where we have our meals and sit sometimes.'

'Don't we go up on deck at all?'

'If it's fine. And on Sundays, of course, there's a service on deck. The captain likes everyone to attend, whatever their denomination.'

Ismay didn't feel at all inclined to attend church after the way the priest had taken Rory's side, but she didn't say so.

'And there will be classes as well. We'll put a list of them on the wall and you can sign your name for any you fancy.'

'You mean – like school?'

'Much more interesting than school.' She smiled. 'And no one canes you. What we offer depends on what the passengers volunteer to do, but there are always sewing and reading classes.'

'Oh, I'd like that! I love learning new things.'

The woman consulted a list on the wall near the companionway and walked across to one of the many doors that lined the big space. 'This is your cabin. You can have one of those drawers for your clothes and your suitcase has to fit in the end space with the others' luggage.'

Ismay stared round the small cabin, wondering how four women would manage in it if they all tried to get dressed at once. Still, they had their own beds, at least, narrow as the bunks were. She was growing to like that luxury.

'Since you're the first to arrive, you can choose which bunk you want,' the stewardess said. 'After you've unpacked, you can sit in the day area, but you can't come on deck till after we've sailed, and even then there are places that are reserved for the cabin passengers.' She saw Ismay's puzzlement and said, 'Richer people have better accommodation than ours and have their own areas of the deck.'

'Oh, I see.'

'There's too much going on up there at the moment to let people loose. Matron's on board ship already and I daresay she'll be down soon. This is her cabin, at the entrance to the area. She keeps an eye on the single women – this captain's very strict about how people behave, so watch your step. If you have any problems, go to her.'

When the stewardess had gone, Ismay peeped outside and shivered at the big, echoing space. It wasn't full daylight down here but there was enough light coming in to read by if you sat in the central area. She turned back to the cabin, deciding on the top drawer and one of the bottom bunks. She didn't fancy sleeping up in the air.

What if you rolled right out of bed while you were asleep?

As she wandered out into the day area, she wished there was someone to talk to. She wasn't used to being completely alone.

Matron came down some time later and looked surprised to see her. 'Passengers are not supposed to be boarding until this afternoon.'

'Mr Kieran and his wife brought me here – they were my employers till my . . . my husband was killed, but they had to travel on, so they arranged for me to come on board early.'

'What happened to your face?'

'I was hurt in the accident when my husband was killed. The cart overturned.'

'I see. I'm sorry. Well then, have you seen the list of rules?'

'No, ma'am.'

'Call me Matron. I'll get you a list and you can study it. The captain's very strict. I'll make sure they bring you something to eat, but it'll only be bread and cheese or something like that.'

'Thank you, Matron. That'll be fine.' This was the second person to comment on how strict the captain was. He must be a terrible fellow.

The list of rules was long and Ismay pulled a face at it. It sounded as if they expected every single woman to go running after the men. That was the last thing she wanted to do.

As the hours passed, she tried not to feel anxious or sad, telling herself it was exciting to sail round the world to her brother, but she was glad when other women started to arrive.

By teatime, however, she was wishing there were fewer people here, because she felt overwhelmed. Single women of all ages were crammed in – talking, laughing, weeping, complaining. They'd all been given the list of rules and regulations, and warned about being alone with any of the men. Some laughed about it, others complained.

To her disappointment, three women who were much older than her had the other bunks in her cabin. One of them was a widow, and the other two were spinsters who seemed to look down their noses at her.

The food they were served at teatime was more than adequate. Bread, butter and jam, followed by fruit cake. Ismay was amazed to hear some of the women complain about this. It was good bread, fresh and crusty, and the jam was made from strawberries – such a treat. You could have as much as you wanted, as well.

The evening seemed to go on for ever, shut below decks, though Ismay talked to one or two people. A tall woman said, 'Oh, you're Irish!' and turned away at once to speak to someone else. What was wrong with being Irish? Ismay wondered.

She felt exhausted now, because she hadn't slept well at the hotel, but didn't like to be the first to go to bed. She was glad when Matron rang a bell and said it was bedtime.

'I'm not sleepy yet,' someone called.

'We all go to bed at the same time and we get up at the same time, too,' Matron said firmly.

She had a very carrying voice, Ismay thought as she went to use the water closet. This emptied into the sea. So convenient, water closets. They made life so much more comfortable. She giggled as she adjusted her skirt. Fancy getting happy about something like a water closet!

Ah, it was such a relief to be going to bed.

She wriggled about in the narrow bunk, trying to get comfortable, hearing the other women moving and the two spinsters, who had the top bunks, whispering to one another. Did they think she was deaf?

All in all, things hadn't gone too badly. She didn't feel as frightened now. After all, you couldn't get lost on a ship, could you? Especially not one with so many rules about what you could and could not do.

As the voyage started, Adam was pleased that the weather was fairly calm, though how long this would last, he couldn't tell, not knowing these waters. His aunt seemed to be settling down nicely on the ship. He wished he found it as easy to make friends as she did. Within a couple of days, she seemed to know all the cabin passengers.

He was less pleased with the captain, who seemed an autocratic fellow. You got them like that sometimes, kings of their own small worlds. The crew were clearly afraid of him.

He was also rather concerned that this was a screw-driven vessel. They might be faster than paddle steamers, but they rolled about more. He did hope his aunt wouldn't be seasick.

Catching her eye, Adam signalled that he'd be across by the rail and she nodded. He loved watching the other ships pass by. There had been quite a lot of shipping in the English Channel but there was less now they were heading for the Bay of Biscay. There was a much bigger swell today, and it was likely to get choppier if he read the signs correctly.

On the lower deck he caught a glimpse of the young woman he'd noticed yesterday, the one with the bruised face. She seemed unaffected by the weather and was obviously fascinated by the sea and the passing ships. He'd first noticed her because she'd been standing alone by the rail, her head thrown back, breathing deeply as if enjoying the taste of the salty air. Then he'd seen the bruises and wondered what had happened to her.

She was pretty, or she would be when the marks had faded, and better dressed than the other steerage passengers. There was an intelligent look to her. He couldn't help wondering who she was and what had happened to her, but she was travelling steerage and the only time the two groups of passengers met was at some of the classes that were being held. Not many of the cabin passengers attended them, though.

He turned back to glance at his aunt. She looked

a bit pale this morning, but hadn't shown signs of nausea so far. With a bit of luck, the fresh air would make her feel better. Some of the other ladies were already feeling the effects and had retired to their cabins.

He lost himself in his thoughts, but after a while a particularly big wave threw him sideways. The young woman below laughed and clutched the rail. He smiled too as he watched.

Next to him, someone cleared their throat. 'Excuse me, Mr Tregear, but your aunt isn't feeling well.'

Adam forgot everything as he hurried across the deck.

'Sorry to be such a nuisance.' His aunt clapped one hand to her mouth. 'Oh, dear.'

'Let me help you back to your cabin.'

When he got her settled, he obtained a bucket from the stewardess, who smiled grimly.

'I'm afraid we're in for some rough weather, Mr Tregear.'

'It doesn't feel as if a storm's brewing.'

She shook her head, 'No, but we often get heavy seas in this part of the world. Though you can never guarantee anything with the sea, can you? I'll have my hands full even if it gets no worse.'

'I'll see to my aunt for you, but perhaps you could check occasionally to see whether the bucket needs emptying.'

'Oh, someone will be bringing clean buckets regularly, don't worry. We have plenty of them.'

His aunt was very sick, but after a while stopped vomiting and lay down on the bed again, her face chalk white. He got her a glass of water, but she only took a sip.

'Try to sleep. It's the best thing you can do.'

'I need a woman's help, Adam. There are some things a man can't do. Is the stewardess free?'

'She's very busy. I'll see if I can find someone else to help you.'

There were only a few people still on deck. The young woman was one of them, looking as rosy as ever. Even as he watched, Matron went across to her and gestured towards the companionway. He could see the disappointment on the young woman's face and that gave him an idea.

He hurried down to join them. 'Excuse me, but I was wondering, Matron, if one of your charges could help me look after my aunt. She's very unwell and the stewardess has her hands full. There are some things a man can't help with, you understand.'

'Oh, I'd be happy to help the poor lady,' the stranger said without being asked.

He should have guessed she was Irish. She had a beautiful complexion. How had she got the bruises, though? He turned to Matron. 'Would you allow that?'

'I'll come and check on your aunt myself first, if you don't mind.'

'I don't mind at all. I'd be careful too, in your position.' He held out his hand. 'Adam Tregear. I was first mate on the *Silvero* for a year or two, running to and from New York. My aunt's never been on a ship before, though.'

He led the way to her cabin, knocking on the door. A groan was the only answer.

'Let me.' Matron went inside and stood looking round, nodding as if satisfied with what she'd found. 'Would you like some help, ma'am?'

'Yes, please.'

'Mrs Hope has offered to stay with you for a while.'

So the stranger was married. Adam was surprised at how disappointed he felt about that. He moved inside the cabin to join them. 'My aunt's name is Mrs Seaton. She's a widow.'

'So is Mrs Hope,' Matron added with a stern glance his way. 'A very recent widow.'

'I'm sorry to hear that.' He addressed himself to Matron rather than the younger woman. 'She'll not come to any harm at my hands, I promise you.'

She studied him, then nodded. 'Very well. Leave it to us now.'

He went back on deck and stood watching the sea, grey-brown in colour now, not the soft blue you got in warmer climates. But still he loved it.

Shortly afterwards, Matron came to join him briefly. 'I think your aunt is in good hands. Mrs Hope has been quiet and well-behaved so far and doesn't seem affected by the rough weather. We've agreed that she'll stay the night. I'll get someone to bring up her mattress and she can sleep on the floor.'

'Thank you. You'll keep an eye on the situation?'

'The stewardess will. I have several sick women to look after in my own area.'

'Sorry, yes. Of course you do. Thank you for helping me.'

As the weather grew calmer, Harriet began to recover from her seasickness, though she still felt very weak. She chatted to her helper, who seemed reluctant to talk about herself, but would listen for hours to Harriet's tales. Perhaps that was because she came from a poor family and didn't want to talk about the life she'd escaped? Yes, that'd be it.

The following morning, Harriet felt well enough to go on deck again, so sent Ismay back to her classes. 'Would you mind sleeping in the cabin for a night or two longer, though, just in case I'm taken ill again during the night?'

Her companion gave her a sunny smile. 'I'd not mind at all, Mrs Seaton. It's a lot quieter up here. There are so many people in the single women's quarters, there's always some sort of noise, if it's only the snoring. And quite a few of them are still being violently ill.'

'They're probably too cheerful for a recent widow, as well. It must have been a bad accident to leave your face so bruised still.'

Ismay flushed, opened her mouth as if to say something, then clamped her mouth shut again.

That child is hiding something, Harriet thought, and she's not happy about whatever it is. Wanting to help the young woman in return for her assistance, she bided her time. She'd find out what it was. People often confided in her, once they grew to trust her, and she'd never betrayed a trust yet.

'How did the classes go today?' she asked the next afternoon.

'Oh, it was wonderful! I'm not in the beginners' class, and we're reading such an interesting book, taking it in turns, so that we can improve our reading. The teacher explains the new words. There are so many interesting words I never knew existed.'

'Indeed there are.'

'Everyone in the class wants to improve themselves, so we all work hard and help one another. And see,' she held out a linen bag which obviously contained a book, sighing blissfully, 'they've lent us a book each to practise on.' The hand with which she stroked it was tender, her eyes soft with pleasure.

'I'm happy for you, dear. And the sewing class?'

Ismay shrugged, some of the pleasure fading from her face. 'I'm in the beginners' class there and it's not very interesting. I can sew a seam, but not neatly enough. The teacher made me take my stitches out three times and start again. She's from Glasgow and it's a bit hard to understand her, but she told us about a man called Mr Singer who's invented a machine for sewing seams. It does them much more quickly – just imagine that! Our teacher's aunt, who lives in Glasgow, is a seamstress, and was one of the first people to buy one. But you still have to be able to sew by hand because all the sewing machine can do is straight seams.'

Harriet was surprised by how clearly Ismay remembered every detail. 'I'd heard about sewing machines, but I enjoy hand sewing.'

'I don't enjoy it, to tell the truth, but I'll be happy to be able to make my own clothes. And just imagine, some kind ladies have sent material for us girls who're taking sewing classes, for us to make up into undergarments. I'm making a chemise for myself, then, if there's time, I'll make some drawers. The teacher said more women are wearing them now, in case their crinolines blow up and show their legs.' She giggled suddenly. 'As if I'd ever be wearing one of them silly things.'

'I think they're silly too, and am content with my three petticoats.'

Once she'd finished talking about the classes, Ismay fell silent, and it was again obvious that something was continuing to worry her. And she didn't seem like a woman grieving for her husband. Harriet knew only too well what that felt like.

That evening, as they were getting ready for bed, each with her back to the other for modesty, Harriet said quietly, 'If you have anything troubling you, Ismay, you can always confide in me. I'd keep your secret.'

There was dead silence in the cabin, then a sob. 'I thought I'd hidden my troubles.'

'Perhaps from others, but I've been spending more time with you.' She turned in time to see Ismay press one hand against her lips as if to hold back more sobs.

'Oh, my dear!' Harriet pulled the girl to sit next to her on the bed, putting an arm round her shoulders. 'Tell me.'

'I daren't.'

'Is it so bad?'

'Yes. Dreadful.' More sobs.

'Then let me guess. You're not really a widow, are you?'

The slender body stiffened against her. 'How did you guess?'

'You're not grieving. It's been done before. A family sends a young woman who's expecting a child out to Australia or America, or anywhere far away, pretending she's newly widowed.'

'I don't know if I'm expecting a child. I pray not.' But she had no feelings that she was getting her monthly and she should have done by now. She was usually very regular.

'But you could be with child?'

Ismay sobbed again. 'There was a man. He forced me. My da wanted me to marry him, so *he* told Rory where I was and then . . . then Rory caught me and . . .' She broke down, weeping uncontrollably.

'Your own father did that? Dear heaven, how wicked! Shh now. Shh.' She rocked the sobbing girl.

After a moment or two, Ismay continued speaking. 'The master found us and stopped it, but he was too late. Afterwards I had to get away, because Da and the priest kept saying I should marry Rory and I was frightened he'd catch me again. The master and his wife brought me all the way to the ship. They were so kind to me. And I really am going out to my brother in Australia. But now . . . I'm on my own for two months, and I don't know what I'll do if I'm having *his* baby.'

'You're not on your own now, dear. I've been helping girls in trouble for many years, especially the ones like you, who deserve help. The women of my chapel in Liverpool bought a house for the poor girls to live in till they'd had their babies. I never had any children of my own, because I didn't want to marry anyone else after my James died, but I'm godmother to a whole tribe of babies. So you see, I'll be happy to help you in any way I can.'

'You won't tell anyone, not even Mr Tregear? If the captain heard, he'd lock me up for immorality, I know he would. He frightens me.'

'Of course I won't tell.' She hugged Ismay suddenly. 'Why don't you stay in this cabin with me for the rest of the voyage? We can say I've hired you as my maid. If you don't mind sleeping on the floor, that is?'

'I'd love to stay. Are you sure, Mrs Seaton?'

'Oh, yes. Very sure. I'll be able to help you with

your reading and sewing. It's not all straight seams. There's embroidery, too. That's more fun to do.'

'You're very kind.'

'It'll give me something to do. I like to keep busy and I was rather bored till you came to help me. Such a long journey, and some of those other ladies are rather foolish and talk only of clothes and jewellery, or how rich their husbands are.'

'How can you get bored? Why, they're going to have concerts and poetry readings and all sorts of things. I've never even been to a concert. There won't be time to be bored.' Only time to worry . . .

'I'll tell you a secret.' Harriet smiled. 'I'm tone deaf and the music all sounds the same to me; and, as for poetry, I've no patience with men sighing over ladies' eyes.'

Ismay giggled, then yawned suddenly. 'Thank you for listening tonight.'

'Let's go to sleep now. I think we're both tired.'

Ismay lay down feeling better than she had since *it* happened. She wasn't feeling sick in the mornings, as her mother always had when she was expecting, so she was hoping there wouldn't be any unwanted results, even if she was a little late with her monthly. And she'd found help from a kindly lady who didn't blame her for anything. She'd been so lucky.

She'd not seen much of Mrs Seaton's nephew, but he seemed a lovely person too – at least his aunt thought so. He was very good-looking and he had such a kind smile. At least, Ismay thought he was good-looking, though some of the other young women said he had too dark a complexion. That didn't stop them from smiling at him, though he never seemed to notice.

Perhaps he already had a young lady. If so, she was a very lucky person. No, he'd have married her and brought her to Australia if he had someone. So why wasn't he married at the age of twenty-eight? All the young men in the village had married long before that.

Ismay had always hoped she'd meet a nice fellow one day and get married, but she'd changed her mind now. If you had to do *that* with your husband regularly, she couldn't think why women ever married. She shuddered to remember it: the pain, the feeling of helplessness. She still had nightmares that Rory had caught her again.

Well, she'd never have to look at his lumpy old face again, or hear his hoarse voice whispering horrid things to her. He'd been doing that for years and she'd pretended to ignore it, but it'd upset her. It wasn't decent to talk like that.

6

Captain Dougal McBride hired a woman to act as companion to his elderly mother in her new home in Fremantle. She was growing very forgetful and needed someone with her at all times. Miss Gunson was a highly respectable lady who had excellent references.

He was satisfied he'd done his duty and went to sea again, but didn't want anything to do with his mother when he came back, not after what she'd done to his sister. He still grew angry every time he remembered how she'd tried to blacken Flora's name to ensure no one would associate with his sister, who would never then dare leave home and open a boarding house as she's planned.

And when his sister left anyway, his mother had become even more outrageous in what she said or hinted to others about her daughter's morals. Of course, they didn't know then that his mother was becoming bewildered and forgetful, gradually losing touch with reality. But even now there were people who were cool with Flora, who didn't invite her into their homes because they felt there must have been some truth in rumours confirmed by her own mother.

He'd continue to support Flora, to whom he was very close. And he'd continue to do his duty by his mother.

He was longing to go back to sea, though. Things were so much more straightforward there. You fought the elements, you carried trade goods, you supervised your men.

And if you were a little lonely, well, you were a captain and had to keep your distance.

One Tuesday, Ann Gunson opened the door to the curate, who came to visit them every week. 'Oh, I'm so relieved to see you, Mr Howarth! I need to ask your advice.'

'What's wrong, Miss Gunson?'

She lowered her voice. 'Mrs McBride has been even more difficult than usual today. Listen to her.'

They both fell silent to hear the old woman's voice raised to a shrill tone, pausing, then saying something else.

'Is someone with her? Should I call later?'

'No. She's talking to herself. First she wanted to go for a walk, but once we were both dressed for that, she changed her mind.' A peal of laughter from the sitting room made her pause for a moment. 'I don't know what to do.'

'Who is it?' the voice called suddenly.

'It's Mr Howarth, the curate.'

'Well, why are you keeping him on the doorstep? Bring him in. He's come to see *me*, not you.'

Mrs McBride greeted the curate warmly and turned to scowl at her companion. 'Leave us alone. I wish to speak to my visitor in confidence.'

Although it went against Ann's principles to eavesdrop, she'd learned the hard way recently that it was necessary to check what her charge was doing at all times. This job might pay double the usual wages, but she more than earned them. There was no minute of the day that she wasn't on edge and she woke in the night worrying, too, thinking she'd heard something.

She went outside and walked quietly along the veranda to stand near the open window of the sitting room. And if anyone walked past in the street and saw her eavesdropping, she didn't care.

Mrs McBride was still talking non-stop, not allowing the curate to say anything. 'That woman doesn't look after me as she should, Mr Howarth. Why my son hired her, I don't know. She says such cruel things. She keeps the good food for herself and gives me only bread and jam to eat. I went to bed hungry last night. Hungry! And my son is a captain. I should be treated better.'

There was a pause, where the voice was too low to be heard, then, 'I'm sure she's had men in her room. I can hear them laughing sometimes or making night noises. *You* know what I mean.'

Another pause, during which the curate didn't speak, but she continued as if answering him.

'Oh, I couldn't do that. I'm frightened to confront her. She's stronger than I am and she slaps me sometimes.'

A peep through the side of the window showed the curate sitting open-mouthed opposite his hostess.

He isn't going to be much use, Ann thought. He's a stuffed shirt at the best of times. And suddenly, it was all too much. She'd been in the job for a few months, and it had never been pleasant, but it had become unbearable. Mrs McBride was enough to try the patience of a saint, even at her best, but lately she'd become very strange and sometimes frightening. Good money or not, Ann was going to find another job, a normal job with normal people.

She walked slowly back into the house to look at the calendar on the kitchen wall and study the list scribbled on the side of it. As if it'd tell her anything different from what she'd read this morning! It would be at least five days until Captain McBride's ship came back from Singapore, and possibly more. She didn't think she could manage that long.

She walked back along the central corridor, which acted as a breezeway for the house in hot weather. Not that it was hot now. June was the beginning of winter and the rains had started.

As she opened the sitting-room door, the curate looked at her warily, but she was sure it wasn't her imagination that he also looked relieved to see her.

'Mrs McBride imagines things,' she said bluntly, tired of trying to conceal the truth about her employer's mother. 'As old people sometimes do.'

'How dare you say that, you lying wretch!' Mrs McBride shrieked. Surging from her seat, she attacked her hired companion physically, the first time she'd done that.

If the curate hadn't been there, Ann didn't know how she'd have defended herself, because Mrs McBride seemed possessed of extra strength and the housemaid was a skinny young woman.

It took both of them a few minutes to subdue Mrs McBride.

'I had no idea,' he said shakily once they had her tied to a chair. He raised his voice to speak above the yelling, shouting and drumming of heels. 'Is she often like this?'

'She usually calms down after I've given her the morning dose of cordial, but she's been getting worse recently.'

'She's trying to poison me!' Mrs McBride said and screamed. 'Help me, Mr Howarth, before she kills me. Help me!'

Ann moved back a little to whisper, 'The cordial contains laudanum to calm her down. She must have spat out her dose this morning.'

It took them five minutes to force more cordial down Mrs McBride's throat, a double dose, and then they had to wait another fifteen minutes before it did its work and she stopped thrashing around and wailing.

'I'll get you a cloth to wipe your hands, Mr Howarth,' Ann said quietly. 'The cordial is rather sticky.'

She was back in a few minutes, because the maid had had to be persuaded not to give notice.

'How long will she sleep for?' he asked.

'She may not sleep, but that much will calm her for a few hours, I hope. She's never attacked me physically before, but she's been making wild accusations for a week or two now.' Ann bowed her head, then admitted, 'I can't go on like this, Mr Howarth, I just can't. Could you please stay with me until her daughter can come?'

'I thought she and her daughter weren't speaking to one another.'

'They aren't, but this is a crisis and with Captain McBride away, who else is there to call? Someone will have to decide what to do about her. I'm not staying here on my own for another night. She's started to wander round the house at all hours. I've found her in the garden in her nightdress once or twice recently.' She lowered her voice to add, 'Last time she was about to remove her clothing.'

He made a shocked, tutting noise. 'I'd better stay, then. Is there someone who can take a message to her daughter?'

'Yes. There's a very obliging lad next door, who's always glad to earn a penny. I'll just write a quick note.'

She wrote hastily and sent the folded note off, after which they settled down to wait.

On the sofa, Mrs McBride was now snoring gently, looking like the peaceful old lady she hadn't been for some time.

Over an hour passed.

'Perhaps Miss McBride wasn't at home,' the curate suggested, taking out his pocket watch and shaking his head.

Ann said bluntly, 'If you leave, so shall I.'

He sighed. 'I'll not leave you on your own.'

'Thank you. Would you like a cup of tea?'

'If it's not too much trouble, I'd love one.'

But when she came back with the tray, he was looking at his watch again.

Flora McBride read the scrawled note in shock. Not Ann Gunson's usual neat handwriting and the message couldn't be ignored.

> *Your mother is becoming violent and irrational. I can't go on like this. Your brother isn't due back for several days and I need help urgently.*
> *Ann Gunson*

Flora had vowed never to go near her mother again; had still not forgiven her for blackening her reputation so that people ostracised her. This had gone on for weeks, until her brother came home from a trading voyage to Singapore and set matters right. But even so, some people were still rather stiff with her. She'd heard more than one person say she was neglecting her duty by abandoning her mother to a stranger's care, remarks that were meant to be heard.

What should she do about this? Dougal wouldn't be back for a few more days. She sighed. She had no choice but to step in; she couldn't leave poor Miss Gunson in such distress. But oh, she didn't want to see her mother again!

What trouble could there be now? The apothecary said that the daily dose of cordial was strong enough to keep her mother calm.

Flora went to put on her bonnet and outdoor mantle, telling her maid where she was going. But she walked slowly through the streets of central Fremantle towards the neat wooden house where her mother now lived. She was dreading this confrontation, absolutely dreading it.

When she knocked on the front door, she heard footsteps hurry towards it and Miss Gunson opened it.

'Thank goodness you're here!'

Flora could see that the poor woman was struggling not to weep, so reached out to grasp her upper arm for a moment. 'Has it been so bad?'

'It was all right for the first month or two, and one or two of her old friends used to come and see her, but she's been getting worse rapidly and they no longer call.' Miss Gunson took out her handkerchief and blew her nose, then straightened her shoulders. 'Sorry.'

'Tell me everything.'

Flora listened in horror. You heard of old people losing their wits and needing to be restrained, but to have it happen to your own mother was a dreadful shock. And she'd gone downhill so quickly, too. She realised Miss Gunson had finished her tale and was looking at her expectantly, as if waiting for an answer. 'Sorry. What did you just say?'

'You need to hire a very strong person to control her. I'm not nearly strong enough. And I'm afraid you need to lock her up, too, for her own safety. I found her trying to set light to the woodpile one day.' She took a deep breath. 'I'm sorry, Miss McBride, but I shall have to give notice. I simply can't manage any longer.'

Flora looked at Miss Gunson, who was smaller than her, about the same size as her mother. 'I do understand. We'll give you an excellent reference, of course, but I'd be very obliged if you'd stay until we can find someone else to take over.'

'I only dare stay if you can find a strong woman to stay with me and if you have locks put on her bedroom door and windows.'

Flora thought rapidly. 'I'll go and ask Mrs Hollins. She knows a lot of people in Fremantle. Those pensioner guards and their families certainly stick together. It must be as a result of being in the army. If I go straight away, will you be all right while I'm gone?'

Miss Gunson hesitated. 'The curate's already late for an appointment.'

'We'll give her an extra dose of cordial. That should keep her quiet.'

Her mother, even though she was still drowsy, spat and struggled so much that two spoonfuls of the thick brown liquid were scattered all over them. In the end, Flora managed to pinch her mother's nose tightly for long enough to do the job. As her mother opened her mouth to gasp in air, Miss Gunson tipped the cordial down her throat.

'I'll have to go now,' the curate said. 'I'm already late.' He scuttled out without his usual flourishes and civilities.

Flora waited until her mother had settled into sleep and said quietly, 'We'll keep her tied up, then you'll be all right. I'll be as quick as I can. The maid is here as well.'

'She's talking of giving notice, too.'

'Tell her we'll pay her extra.'

Mrs Hollins knew a strong woman who'd come in to help look after Mrs McBride but, though Rhoda was a cheerful widow of forty or so, she was a rough sort and she wouldn't be able to manage the household on her own if Miss Gunson left.

The maid agreed to stay on, as long as she didn't have to deal with Mrs McBride. To make sure of this, her wages were raised, which sent her away beaming.

Flora discussed the matter with Miss Gunson. 'I thought I'd put an advertisement in *The Perth*

Gazette and Western Australian Times for a companion to an elderly lady.'

'You should say she needs careful supervision because she's becoming forgetful. I've seen it done before. People know what that means.'

There was silence, then Flora sighed. 'I suppose so. In the meantime, I'm going to hire Rhoda. She is, as you saw, very strong, and I'm sure she'll cope easily with my mother. The thing is, I'd be most grateful if you'd stay on until we find another lady companion.'

Miss Gunson's reluctance showed clearly on her face, though she didn't refuse outright.

'I know you want to leave, but my mother is always worse when I'm around, so I can't deal with this.' She could see the other woman starting to shake her head and added hastily, 'If you stay till we find a replacement, I'll pay you five guineas as a bonus when you leave, on top of your wages, as well as giving you excellent references.'

'Oh. Well . . . we could try it for a week or two.'

Flora closed her eyes in sheer relief. 'Right then. Rhoda can be here within the hour.'

'And you'll stay till she arrives?'

'Of course.'

Miss Gunson nodded. 'I'll need to put an advertisement for employment in the newspaper myself, Miss McBride, but perhaps not quite yet. As long as you don't throw me on the street if you find a replacement quickly.'

Since Fremantle was a small town, with only

about three thousand inhabitants, it'd probably take time to find someone suitable, given the distances involved in the Swan River Colony. Flora guessed someone from the country would apply for the position, or perhaps someone newly arrived in Western Australia.

'If we find someone before you've obtained a new position, you can either stay here or come and live in my brother's house till you do.' It was a rash offer, but Flora was desperate. And she could see from the relief on Miss Gunson's face that it made a big difference. How terrible to be on your own with no income but what you yourself could earn.

She walked back to her own home, lost in thought. She was going to offer to pay the new companion more than Miss Gunson, which made it an excellent wage for a woman. Why women were paid so much less than men she could never understand. Food and clothing cost the same for them as for men, after all, and some women had children to feed and raise without a man's help.

Surely the higher wage she was offering would attract a suitable applicant?

Flora's steps faltered and, with a sinking heart, she faced the fact that if Miss Gunson left, in spite of all the inducements, she would have to take over for a while, a dreadful thought. Her mother had not only made her life a misery for a very long time, but – a few years earlier – had parted Flora from the only man she'd ever loved, just to make sure she had an unmarried daughter with no choice but to look after her in her old age. Losing Joss wasn't something Flora could ever forgive. She still dreamed about him occasionally.

Well, there was nothing else she could do now. She prayed Dougal's ship would return on time and she could hand over this distasteful task to him. She just . . . prayed. For patience and for someone to apply for the position quickly.

And also for something worthwhile in her life, because she still felt at a loss about what to do with herself. Dougal was bound to marry one day and she didn't want to be the spinster aunt everyone felt sorry for.

Bram went round the Bazaar with the young man he'd recently hired as an assistant, checking that all tidying and stocking up was done exactly the way he wanted. He'd had to hire Freddie Spooner because business had been so much better than expected and Isabella couldn't help him as she used to, with a baby to look after. He sometimes had to call in Mrs Hollins as well to help with selling, though most people preferred to deal with a man.

As they finished their morning tour, he looked round the Bazaar with pride. This had once been a series of tumbledown sheds, but wooden buildings were easy to repair and improve. They'd put in new doors and a proper wooden floor, painted the window frames, and brightened the inside with shelves and displays, as well as trestle tables full of goods. He was considering whitewashing the other walls to brighten things up still further.

He was considering all sorts of things.

Of course Isabella was still in charge of selling and ordering dress materials, mainly silk, which Mr Lee and his daughter supplied, as well as the other items. Isabella had lived with the Lee family in Singapore for two years, teaching them English, especially Mr Lee, who was becoming a very rich businessman. She'd been treated as a member of the family and still wrote to them whenever Dougal sailed there.

She'd insisted on hanging a length of silk in a bright colour where people could see it as soon as they entered. It was hung between two poles attached to the ceiling. It was rolled and put away carefully each evening, because they didn't want insects or, worse still, mice, crawling over it during the night. He was going to find a cat to keep the mice down.

The women who came shopping here always commented on the silk and, more often than not, the material on display sold within a day or two, so another piece had to be found. Isabella wouldn't put out more than one piece, though. She said it was best to tantalise customers and make them wonder what else she had in her boxes, not give them a free view of everything. She wanted him to get some boxes with glass fronts made to store the silks. She said Mr Lee would know someone able to do it in Singapore.

What a wife she was! Such a clever head on her shoulders.

Bram left Freddie to deal with any early customers. His new assistant was an unprepossessing fellow, of medium height like Bram himself, thin and weedy, with such bad eyesight he needed to wear thick-lensed spectacles, which made his eyes look too big, like a frog's. But people seemed to like him and he was a hard worker, grateful for an interesting job that didn't require huge physical strength.

It was time to start making a new stock list for Dougal's next trading voyage to Singapore, and for that Bram needed Isabella's help. Of course they noted down the items that sold well as they went along, and kept an eye on stocks, but even with what they owed Mr Lee, they could afford to order far more this time and extend their range of goods. There was such a shortage of manufactured goods in the colony.

Bram felt shaky sometimes when he thought how much profit they were making already and how well things were going. Was this how men started to get rich? He'd only thought to make a comfortable life for himself and his family if he worked hard; hadn't been able to believe in more.

Dare he believe it now? Or was Fate waiting to catch him out and ruin his business? That happened to people sometimes. When you'd grown up dirt poor, as Bram had, you found it difficult to trust in good luck lasting. Which was why he was setting money aside regularly, just in case. He hadn't even told his wife about that.

When he got to the house, which was just down the slope from the Bazaar, he stopped in the doorway of the kitchen, not making his presence known but enjoying the sight of Isabella sitting with their young maid, Sally, drinking a cup of tea. The two of them were laughing about something. A shaft of sunlight had set fire to his wife's glorious auburn hair and his breath caught in his throat at how lovely she looked. That hair had first caught his eye on a street in Singapore and he sometimes thought he'd fallen in love with her on sight.

Their baby son Arlen was asleep in one corner, looking angelic, and little Louisa was playing with her doll under the table. He watched them for a moment or two, then said loudly, 'Would there be another cup of tea in that pot for a thirsty man?'

Sally jumped to her feet with her usual cheerful smile. 'Oh, sir, I didn't see you there. It's only just been brewed.'

'Perhaps you could take a cup up to Freddie in the Bazaar as well? That young man's worked very hard this morning.'

When he was alone with his wife, Bram pulled her to her feet and gave her a lingering kiss that made her sag against him. He grinned, loving the way he could do that to her. 'I'm looking forward to tonight,' he whispered in her ear.

She blushed and smiled, nestling easily against him.

'But we'll continue to be careful. We don't want too many babies.'

She raised one hand to caress the side of his face and he turned his head to kiss it, then took a step back, already breathing deeply. There were times when he wished they didn't have servants – not just Sally, but also a woman who came in three times a week to scrub and do the washing. It was hard keeping their loving quiet, hoping Sally didn't hear them. They surely had the best-oiled bed frame in the port of Fremantle!

'Perhaps we can have a talk about the accounts now. Or, if you're busy, perhaps we should get help doing them,' Bram suggested.

'I don't want anyone else doing the accounts! That's my job. I'm feeling well and energetic again, and Sally's good with Arlen. What we need is to find another permanent maid to help out with the housework, if I'm to spend more time in the Bazaar. *If* we can find one. There's a shortage of good maids.'

'That'd mean finding a bigger house. We couldn't squeeze another person into the smaller bedroom.'

'I don't want to move yet. I love this place. We've been so happy here.'

She stretched like a lazy cat and his breath caught in his throat at the sheer loveliness of her. 'Yes, we have. But things change.'

'Stop staring at me and sit down, Bram. We can make a start on the accounts now.'

'Will I pour us another cup of tea first?'

She smiled. 'No more for me. I've never met a man who can drink as much tea as you.'

'I don't have a head for wine and even one glass of beer is enough for me, but I love my tea. Now, let's start with the silks . . . Tell me what you want to order next time.'

'Twice as much as last time.'

He stared at her. 'That much? Are you sure?'

'Oh, yes.' She reached out to hold his hand. 'The money's not going to vanish, Bram, and if we keep bringing goods in from Singapore, we'll make a lot more.'

He closed his eyes. 'I can't believe it'll last.'

'I can. You're a born trader. You have a knack for choosing things people want. And I'm good with silks, thanks to Xiu Mei's training. I do miss her. She was like a sister to me.'

Then Sally came back and they moved apart, settling to work on the accounts at the kitchen table. Sally took Louisa to play outside, cuddling the baby.

When they'd finished the accounts, Bram went to check on the livery stables next door, which were also part of this business that Conn Largan had funded.

But Les Harding, who now ran it for them, had everything in apple-pie order, as usual.

What a different man Les looked, now that he

was happy! And how capable he was. Bram remembered the haggard ex-convict his partner Conn had helped. Les had been released on a ticket of leave but was fleeing from a brutal master whom he wasn't allowed to leave without official permission. Yet Les had still found time to care for neglected animals in the livery stable where he'd found a hiding place.

Given half a chance, Les had proved himself an excellent worker, reliable and knowledgeable about horses, eager to learn new skills, making friends easily.

But some people still treated him as an inferior, because he'd been a convict. It seemed sometimes as if there were two worlds in the Swan River Colony, and though they'd served their time and proved themselves useful citizens again, people like Les could never be accepted by the free settlers.

Bram had a sympathy for Les, because he was sure things were said about himself as well. The Irish weren't liked by many people, and were not welcome in some circles. But he was successful enough that no one ever said that – to his face, at least.

He smiled. Imagine him, Bram Deagan, a rich man. Who would ever have thought of that? Well, he wasn't rich yet, but he was making money so fast it terrified him.

The ship was due to stop in Gibraltar, but only for a few hours as they didn't need to coal the ship here, so Ismay studied the isthmus (another new word she'd learned) on the map and was up on deck early that morning to catch a glimpse of it. She couldn't have come up on deck if she'd still been in the single women's quarters, because Matron didn't allow them out until after breakfast. She'd have to go down to join them for the meal soon, though.

The sea was quite calm that day and the huge rock looked mysterious and romantic in the hazy dawn light. She was fascinated by the way it jutted up from the sea. She'd never seen anything like it.

Later on, a few of the cabin passengers went ashore, including Mr Tregear, but Mrs Seaton said she didn't feel it was worth clambering in and out of boats for just a few hours on dry land. Besides, it was hot again, and she'd rather sit in the shade under the canvas awning rigged up on the spar deck. Perhaps there would be a cooling breeze off the water later.

The steerage passengers weren't given the opportunity to go ashore, nor were they invited up on to the spar deck, but, like many others, Ismay spent a lot of time near the rail that day, fascinated by the way the town clung to the lower slopes of the rock. The place seemed to be nothing but layers of stone on stone, with no real greenery in the town itself and only scrubby-looking vegetation nearby. There wasn't any vegetation higher up. She'd not like to live here. Ah, she missed the green of Ireland sometimes, and the soft, cool rain.

'Will you just look at it,' she murmured. 'You couldn't farm that land, now could you? How do they grow their food here?'

'Who'd want to farm anything?' one of the girls asked. 'Give me a town any day.'

Ismay heard her add something about the Irish and bogs, which made the young women nearby titter. She was getting tired of pointed remarks about the Irish, so wandered along the deck, going further away from the others than usual, because no one tried to stop her today.

She needed to find somewhere more peaceful to sit; somewhere she could be on her own for a little while. Her monthlies still hadn't started. What would she do if—

As she rounded a corner, she saw a man straighten from his scrubbing and stare at her. It looked like . . . It couldn't be . . .

She froze where she stood, unable to believe her own eyes. It couldn't be Rory Flynn. *It couldn't!*

He smiled. 'Hello, Ismay.'

It was him! She tried to turn and run, but everything seemed to whirl around her.

She regained consciousness to find herself lying on the deck with one of the officers kneeling beside her. She glanced beyond him, but there was no sign of Rory.

'Are you all right?' he asked. 'One of my men found you lying here. You must have fainted. Let me help you up.'

As she sat up, she felt dizzy, but took a few

deep breaths and waited. Gradually, everything settled down and she stood up slowly, waving away his help. 'Thank you. I'm all right now.' She could see him looking doubtful so she forced more words out. 'I need to get out of the sun, though.'

'I'll walk you back to the others, just to be sure you're all right. And you should stay in your own area from now on, miss, not go walking round the ship.'

She couldn't help peering behind them a couple of times to see if she could spot Rory, but there was no sign of him.

How had he got on to this ship?

She closed her eyes, shuddering. *How was she going to escape from him now?*

'Are you all right, miss?'

'What? Oh, sorry. Yes, I'm feeling a bit better now.'

When they got back to the other young women, he stopped. She looked up to where the ladies were sitting. 'I sleep up in my mistress's cabin. I'm working as maid to Mrs Seaton. I need to go and lie down.'

'Which one is she? I'd better tell her what happened.'

Ismay couldn't keep calm a minute longer and hurried along to the cabin. Inside she stood rigid, her back pressed against the closed door, terrified Rory might have followed her here.

The door rattled behind her. 'Ismay? Are you in there?'

It was Mrs Seaton. 'Yes, ma'am. I just need to rest a little.'

'Let me in, Ismay.'

She moved away from the door reluctantly.

Harriet studied Ismay's face, still decorated by yellowish stains from the bruises. 'The officer said you fainted.'

'Yes. I'm sorry.'

'You didn't do it on purpose, child. You still look pale, so sit down on the bed before you faint again. I'll get you a drink of water.'

She looked so terrified, Harriet said softly, 'Tell me what happened. Something's obviously frightened you.'

The girl looked down, fiddling with her skirt, then blurted out suddenly, 'I saw him, ma'am. That's what upset me.'

'Saw who, dear?'

'Rory Flynn. The man who attacked me. He's on this ship, working on it.'

There was silence. Harriet couldn't see how that was possible. 'I think you must be mistaken.'

'I'm not.' She shuddered. 'I could never mistake that man. Never. Besides, he spoke to me.'

'But why would he pursue you this far?'

'I don't know. Maybe he's run mad. He's always followed me around, stared, said things. But I meant what I said. I'll kill myself rather than marry him.'

There was a hysterical edge to Ismay's voice, so Harriet spoke calmly, 'There will never be a need to go to such lengths. Never. No one can force you to marry him or anyone else.'

Suddenly, Ismay rushed to the washstand and was sick into the basin.

Harriet watched in dismay. *Not that! Dear heaven, not that!* She waited, and when Ismay didn't say it, she did, because the possibility had to be faced. 'Could you be carrying his child?'

Ismay stared at her blankly. 'I'm not sick in the mornings. Ma always was. I thought that was the first sign.'

It always surprised Harriet how ignorant of the facts most girls were, even those who'd grown up in the country. 'There are other signs to watch out for.' She explained and watched tears well in the girl's eyes.

'I am a bit sore here.' Ismay stared down at her breasts in horror, then looked up pleadingly. 'No. Please, no! I can't *bear* it.' Sobs racked her suddenly, so heart-rending that Harriet couldn't keep her distance any longer. She gathered Ismay into her arms and let her weep. The poor girl's body shook with the violence of her fear.

As she calmed down a little, she said in a small voice, 'If that's what it is . . . it's not fair.'

'No. It's not. But a child is a gift, however it's got.'

'Not *his* child! And what'll Bram say about it? If Rory gets to Australia and my brother finds out about the baby, he'll want me to marry the father. They all will.'

'No one can force you to marry him,' Harriet repeated patiently.

But Ismay didn't seem to believe this, and continued to sob for a while longer. Harriet couldn't blame her for being upset. People treated girls in that sort of trouble very scornfully, and the ones who kept their babies had a hard time of it with a bastard child to support, as Adam knew only too well.

And why should the innocent victim have to pay the price for that man's attack? She'd like to rid the world of him and every man like him. She'd seen so many lives ruined by their lusts, seen girls commit suicide rather than face the shame. Which was why she and her friends had bought the house and tried to help them.

She sat on in silence, not forcing conversation on the poor girl. When she heard the ship's boat come alongside and voices calling out on deck, she looked down at her little fob watch, surprised at how much time had passed. 'I'll go and see if Adam's back. We need to tell him what you saw. No, don't argue. We can't manage without his help, not with that Flynn fellow running loose on the ship.'

Ismay stared at her dully, then closed her eyes. 'If you say so.' A tear leaked out and trickled down her cheek.

Harriet leaned forward and kissed her. 'I won't let them hurt you, dear. I promise.'

But she could see the girl didn't believe her.

* * *

Rory got on with his work, smiling. He'd shocked Ismay today. Oh, yes. And she deserved it. He'd have found a way to speak to her sooner if she'd stayed in the steerage area, where she belonged, but she'd moved in with that old lady and he'd not been able to get near her.

Best thing he'd ever done, leaving Ireland and heading for Australia. He'd never eaten so well and the work was no harder than what he was used to. He hadn't liked the rough seas, but he hadn't been as seasick as some, just a bit queasy. Best of all, working his passage meant he could save the money the various priests had given him. What fools they were!

Now that it was getting warmer, he was even better pleased with his new life. He loved to feel the warmth on his back as he worked.

He frowned as he thought about the recent meeting. Ismay didn't look as if she was carrying a child, was as slender as ever. You couldn't always tell at first. But look at the way she'd fainted when she saw him. What did that say, eh? She wasn't one to faint or he'd have known about it in such a small village.

He'd stay out of her way mostly till they reached Australia, but he was glad she knew he was here. In the meantime, he'd continue to work hard, because he wanted that sod Jed, who was in charge of the men like him who did the rough work, to help him get a job on the next ship going from Suez to Australia.

He'd thought at first that he'd be able to work his way right through to Australia on this ship. They'd laughed at him when he said that. He scowled at the memory of the ongoing mockery about it. He didn't know how he'd kept his hands off his two chief tormenters, but he wanted that precious bit of paper saying he was a good worker, so he had to bottle up his rage.

Even if he got taken on by the next ship Ismay was sailing on, it'd be a month or more after that till they got to Australia. They had to go across Egypt by train to a place called Suez, so he'd have to spend some of his money on his ticket. He was sure he'd got that right in his head now. One of the men had shown it to him on a map. He hadn't thought much of maps until now; hadn't realised how useful they could be.

If there was a baby, it'd be showing by then. He'd seen his sister's belly in the early stages and he was sure he'd be able to tell if he could only catch Ismay for a quick feel of her. He could afford to wait. After all, she couldn't escape from a ship, now could she?

Her brother was in Australia and Bram would surely want her to marry Rory and give the child a name. The menfolk in a family always did because, if not, they'd be lumbered with supporting the mother and child.

And if there wasn't a child, then he could try again, couldn't he? He licked his lips at the thought of her soft, slender body. She hadn't been hard to catch the first time. He'd keep her locked up if he had to, until he was sure she was expecting.

She was his and always had been. It was as simple as that. Whistling softly, Rory mopped his way along the deck.

'You're doing a good job there,' a voice said behind him.

'Thank you, sir.'

Jed nodded and walked on.

Rory smiled and bent to his work again. He knew how to keep things clean. You had to learn that with cows if you wanted to avoid them getting sick.

Here on a ship, you had to keep yourself cleaner too, because you were living close to others. He was getting used to that, liked it even.

On deck Harriet saw that her nephew had indeed returned to the ship. He was talking to another gentleman, but she didn't want to wait, so made her way across to them. With her standing there, letting her impatience show, the other man soon moved away.

'I need to talk to you privately, Adam love. Right away. Could we go to your cabin so that we can be private?'

He looked at her sharply. 'Is something wrong?'

'Yes. Oh, don't look so worried. It's not me but poor Ismay who needs our help.' She turned and led the way towards their cabins, not prepared to say more in public.

He gestured to the only chair and she sat down in it, wondering how best to tell him. In the end, she stopped trying to soften the tale and, as soon as he was settled on the bed, she explained exactly what had happened to poor little Ismay.

His face reflected shock and disgust. 'Well, I'm sorry for her, of course I am, but what do you expect me to do about it?'

'There's more. The man who did it is on the ship, working his passage. She saw him today and fainted in shock. He must have followed her.'

'Are you sure it's him?'

'She's certain. I doubt she'd mistake him after what happened.'

'Well, that's not good, but it isn't really our business, aunt. I don't want you getting hurt.'

'You surely don't expect her to marry him?'

He stared at her, then scowled. 'No, of course not. She's a nice lass. I'd not have her tied to a brute.'

'I'm going to help her and I hope you will too.'

He opened his mouth as if to protest, and she said firmly, 'When I needed help, she gave it, and generously too. She never once made me feel embarrassed about the disgusting messes I made, just cleared up after me, fetching and carrying cheerfully.'

Harriet waited, but he continued to scowl at her, a reaction that surprised her. 'You know I was involved in a ladies' charity group that helped girls in trouble?'

'You did mention it once or twice. Look, you're sure she's carrying his child?'

'I think it's likely. There are signs.'

'She'll need a husband, then.'

'Yes, but not one who thumps her. Remember the bruises on her face when she first came on board? There was no accident. He beat her hard when he was forcing her.'

'What a brute!'

She could see anger sparking in his eyes and was pleased. 'I want you to find out for us if it is Rory Flynn working on the ship, and what's going to happen to him at Alexandria.'

'And if it *is* him?'

'Then we must protect her until she reaches her brother.'

'He may think it best if she marries the father.'

'In that case, I'll look after her myself.' She looked him firmly in the eye. 'With or without your help, dear boy. That sort of thing matters a lot to me. Helping such girls means my life hasn't been wasted.'

Adam smiled, a smile he kept for her alone, and she sagged in relief. He was going to help her, she could tell.

'So you've found another waif to look after, then. I wondered how long it'd be. You seem to collect them wherever you go.'

'Do you mind?'

'How can I? You took me in when I needed help. And, as you said, she helped you in your hour of need. Besides . . . Ismay's a nice lass.' He enjoyed her company himself, because she was always so cheerful.

'She is nice, very nice indeed, and she doesn't deserve this. I'll go back to her now. She'll be worrying about what you'll say. I'll offer to keep her on as my maid once we get to Australia and assure her she can keep the job even after the child's born. And if that brother of hers is like the father and wants her to marry this Flynn fellow, I'll make him understand that she's not going to do that.' She looked at him challengingly.

'Very well. You've persuaded me.' Memories came flooding back, things he usually managed to avoid thinking about. 'I know what it's like to be helpless and afraid. I was only ten when I first came to you.'

'And had been beaten at that dreadful school. Where would you have been without Quentin Saxby's extra help?'

'In a very different place. It's all right. I'm convinced. I'll help you – and her.'

When his aunt had gone back to join Ismay in her cabin, Adam went on deck, but he did nothing about Flynn, because he kept seeing the bruises on Ismay's face. He'd been bruised himself a few times, and it hurt more than just physically. Oh, yes, this had brought it all back.

Bad enough to think she'd been in an accident, but to know someone had beaten her so hard it left bruises that lasted a couple of weeks . . . Well, that made his blood boil.

She was a pretty little thing when she smiled, but there was much more to her than that: steel beneath the softness. Look at the way she was avid to learn. She never forgot what you told her; had surprised him a few times with that.

He strolled along the deck and, when he saw one of the officers with whom he was friendly, he went to chat, asking if there was a fellow called Rory Flynn working on the ship.

'I don't have much to do with that side of things, but I can find out. Is it important?'

'It is to my aunt's maid. If it's him, then he's following her and she could be in danger. I'd rather not explain further, but you can take my word for it.'

'I'll find out and let you know.'

After the evening meal, the officer came to find Adam as they filed out of the dining saloon. 'The chappie you were asking about, Flynn, he is working on the ship. But he's well thought of, a hard worker.'

'Damn. I was hoping she'd been mistaken.'

'Anything we should know about him?'

'Nothing to do with his job. It's his private life that sticks in my gullet. My aunt and I will just have to make sure she's not left alone till we can hand her over to her brother in Australia.'

'Oh, if it's just about a woman, it's definitely not our business. Treading on your preserves, is he?'

Adam nearly said no, then decided it'd be better

for Ismay if people thought he was interested in her, so nodded.

It needed no urging to persuade Ismay not to go anywhere on her own. She was now pale and anxious, jumping in shock if she hadn't heard someone coming up to her before they spoke. And she had a tendency to go into his aunt's cabin when she had no classes to attend, instead of sitting on the lower deck with the other young women, enjoying the balmy weather.

It seemed such a shame for her to miss the pleasures of a sea voyage.

To his surprise, Adam continued to worry about her at odd moments throughout the day. Life was going to be hard for her, as it had been for his mother. She seemed fond of her brother, but she wasn't sure Bram was the sort of man to support her against Flynn, not once he found out about the baby.

But what was the alternative? A woman needed a breadwinner and a child needed a father's name. Adam's mother had suffered for years after bearing an illegitimate child. His father had given her barely enough money to survive on, and even that had been hedged about with restrictions over what she could and could not do.

The main one was that the money would cease immediately if she married, which had always seemed unfair to Adam. But she'd never complained, never made him feel anything but loved and wanted.

Even so, he'd suffered from being a bastard in many ways. People hadn't always been kind, and he'd not wish that sort of treatment on any child. He owed so much to his aunt Harriet. All bastard children should have someone like her in their lives. And people like Ismay should have such help, too.

He'd be turning into a damned philanthropist if he didn't watch out – only how could you not want to help someone you liked?

He discussed the matter with his aunt. 'When we disembark, if we want to go sightseeing as we've agreed, we must make sure Ismay comes with us. We can't leave her on the ship with him.'

'You're a kind lad.'

'Well, this trip is a once-in-a-lifetime experience for all of us. It's already broadening Ismay's horizons. She's changed a lot since we set out.'

'That girl will surprise everyone one day. She's not just sitting in my cabin, she's reading voraciously – something she was never allowed to do at home. Imagine stopping a child reading! Even with the sewing, which she doesn't enjoy, she can see the value of it and works hard to improve her stitchery.'

'You're growing very fond of her.'

His aunt laughed. 'Yes. When you live with someone, you either fall out with them or you grow closer.'

'It's agreed then. We'll all go to see this new shipping canal they're building. I'm eager to see it,

I must admit. It's such a major undertaking, and will make a big difference to travel to the Orient.'

'Do you think it'll make that much difference? The P&O people say their system of railways and hotels on the isthmus will hold its own and the canal will soon silt up. Why, they've only just opened a new hotel. The captain was mentioning it to me last night at dinner.'

Adam shook his head. 'I don't agree with that. If travellers get the choice of continuing on the same ship, not having to pack up their bags and move in and out of hotels, most of them will take it. Mr Thomas Cook will soon be running excursions to Australia as well as to Europe.'

'I doubt it. Not many people would come on such a long journey for pleasure.' She sighed.

He didn't comment on that, knowing how tedious she was finding the journey already. His aunt liked to keep busy and this enforced idleness was fretting her, though she didn't complain.

It was a good thing she had Ismay to look after. It kept her occupied.

He wished he had more to occupy him.

7

Flora was surprised to receive a response to her advertisement within two days. She wrote back at once, suggesting this Mrs Southerham come to see her the following afternoon – any time would do – or the next afternoon if that wasn't suitable. She hoped the reply would reach the woman quickly so that she could get this matter settled. It was an address in Perth, which lay just a few miles up the Swan River from Fremantle, so there shouldn't be any delays.

To her relief, there was a knock on the door the following afternoon and, when she went to answer it, she found a lady of about her own age. She guessed who it was even before her visitor spoke. 'Mrs Southerham? Please come in. I'm Flora McBride and I'm delighted to meet you.'

When they were seated, she asked, 'Do you live permanently in Perth?'

'No. I'm staying in a lodging house while I do some shopping. For the past few years I've been living in the country to the south of the capital, about thirty miles down the road to Albany. I saw your advertisement in the newspaper and thought I'd find out more about the job.'

Flora felt it only fair to explain the circumstances frankly. She didn't want someone starting work and then leaving within the week.

Mrs Southerham nodded, not seeming put off by this. 'For a while I cared for another lady who was . . . not herself, so I do have some experience in that area. If you can find someone strong to manage your mother physically, I'd be willing to take charge of the household and keep her company. Is that what you're looking for? Oh, good. I'm definitely not strong enough to manage a physically difficult person on my own.'

'We have someone to do that, and Rhoda's doing very well with my mother, because she's cheerful and always agrees, even when she's not going to do what my mother wants. Um, do you have references?'

'I can give you the name of the gentleman whose wife I looked after for a time, a Mr Largan—'

'Not Conn Largan?'

'Yes. I knew his wife and her sisters in England and I live near Cassandra at the moment.'

Flora relaxed. 'We know Conn and his wife. It's a small place, the Swan River Colony, isn't it?'

Livia looked sad for a moment. 'Yes, a very small place. We came here for my husband's health, because he had consumption, but we were misled about the possibilities here. It was hoped that a warmer climate would help, and we bought a farm where he could breed horses. He seemed a little better for a time, but then he grew worse quickly and died.'

'I'm sorry.'

'It's not just the remuneration you're offering that matters to me, Miss McBride, though such a generous salary is very tempting. I'd like the opportunity to live in Fremantle or Perth because I'm going to sell the farm and buy a house. I want to live among people. You can't hold an intelligent conversation with trees.'

Flora nodded. She'd heard other ladies say how starved they were for companionship in the country, however busy their family lives.

'A position like this would give me the chance to look around and decide where I want to settle.'

Flora didn't need to think about it. She'd taken a liking to Mrs Southerham, who was an elegant woman of her own age. 'How soon can you start?'

'You're offering me the job?'

'Yes.' She could see the other struggling not to weep and pretended to fiddle with a nearby ornament to give her guest time to calm down.

'Thank you. Um . . . there's just one other thing. My maid, Orla. Could she stay with me for a few weeks? She'll help out as much as she can, in return for her keep. I'm hoping to find some way to keep her on so that she can work for me when I buy a place of my own.'

'Of course she can come with you.' Flora would

let Mrs Southerham bring the devil himself if it got her someone decent to care for her mother.

'Then I accept gladly. It'll take me a week, perhaps a little longer, to make the necessary arrangements. I have to go back to the farm and check that the neighbour who's leased the land still wants to buy it. Reece Gregory is married to one of Mrs Largan's sisters, Cassandra. I'll also need to find somewhere to store my furniture in Perth. I don't want to lose it.'

'We have a large attic here, mainly empty. There's plenty of room for your things up there.'

Her visitor looked at her in surprise. 'You're very kind.'

'I'm desperate. My mother becomes hysterical at the mere sight of me and I . . . well, I don't enjoy her company.'

'Don't you want me to meet your mother first, Miss McBride?'

'Not unless you'd prefer that. If *I* introduce you to her, she'll take an instant dislike to you. By the time you get back from the country, my brother will have returned from Singapore – he's a ship's captain – and he can say he's hired you as her companion. Though I warn you, she may change her mind about having you, and then you'll just have to stay on anyway. She doesn't always remember what she's done the day before, I'm afraid.'

Flora could see a look of warm understanding in Livia Southerham's eyes and dared to hope that she might have found a friend for herself, as well as a companion for her mother.

In the evening, as usual, Harriet and her nephew went to have their meal in the dining saloon and Ismay went below to join the steerage passengers for her meal. It was a short distance, and there were plenty of people around, so she felt quite safe crossing the deck. But she had no appetite, was too worried about the future.

'Ain't you feeling well, girl?' a woman from London asked. 'You've been looking real peaky this last day or two and you've hardly touched your food.'

'Oh, I'm just a bit under the weather.'

The woman looked at her, eyes narrowing suddenly and going straight to her stomach. 'You're not expecting, are you?'

'Of course not!'

But she could see that the girl didn't believe her, and later, she saw the same girl whispering to another one, then both of them staring at her.

Thank goodness she'd pretended to be a widow! And she had the letter from Mrs Julia to back up her claim, for lack of marriage lines.

She told Mrs Seaton what had happened.

'They can't prove anything, dear. Just ignore them. You won't even be showing by the time we arrive in Australia, and fortunately you're not sick in the mornings.'

★　★　★

The following afternoon, however, Matron came up to Harriet, where she was sitting on deck helping Ismay with her sewing. 'Could I speak to you privately, Mrs Seaton?' She threw a disapproving glance at Ismay as she spoke.

Harriet's heart sank. Someone must have spread the gossip from yesterday's incident. Why couldn't people mind their own business? She decided to fight whatever this was on her own territory. 'We'll go to my cabin. Get on with that seam, dear. Your sewing is much improved.' She turned to lead the way without waiting for agreement.

Terrified, Ismay watched the two women walk away. She turned as Adam came across the deck to join her and said in a low voice, 'Matron's come to speak to your aunt about me, I know she has. You should have seen the disapproving look she gave me.'

'How would she have found out?'

'Last night some of the other girls said I wasn't looking well and started to tease me, asking if I was expecting, even though I denied it. They weren't very nice about it, either, because they're jealous of me being with your aunt.' She turned to stare out over the water. 'When Matron tells him, the captain will send me back to the steerage quarters, I know he will. He's so strict about morals. And if I'm down there all the time, Rory will find it easier to get to me.'

'They won't take you away from my aunt if she

needs you. Come and sit down with me while we wait for her.'

'It'd be better if I stand by the rail, Mr Tregear. The other ladies don't like me sitting down near them and to sit with you on our own would be frowned on. They don't approve of me being on this deck at all.'

'Very well.'

He hated to see that anxious expression on her face. It reminded him of how his mother had looked sometimes when the money didn't stretch and they were short of food. Strange how being with Ismay kept reminding him of his boyhood.

Matron waited till they were both seated and cleared her throat. 'It's about Ismay Hope. I fear she's expecting a child.'

'Well, that's no surprise, is it?' Harriet was pleased to see the shock on Matron's face at this response.

'What do you mean, "no surprise"?'

'She's only recently been widowed, a matter of about three weeks, I believe. She's already told me what she suspects, though I don't know how anyone else has found out, because she wants to keep it to herself till she joins her brother in Australia. It's very hard for the poor girl to lose a husband then carry the burden of rearing a child alone.'

'If there *was* a husband. Does she have her marriage lines with her?'

'I believe they were mislaid and it wasn't possible to get another copy, because she had to leave in a hurry to catch the ship, otherwise she'd have had to wait weeks for the next ship to Western Australia from Ceylon.' Harriet allowed her voice to become sharper and more emphatic because this was the weak spot in their tale. 'She has a letter from her employer, however, who was worried this might happen.'

'You've seen the letter?'

'Of course I have.'

'It could be a forgery.'

'If so, then someone else did it, not Ismay. She's still learning to write fluently, and her handwriting's rather childish. Nor does she have the vocabulary of an educated person. No, she couldn't possibly have written that letter. And besides, not only is the paper embossed with the name and address of her master, but I saw Mr and Mrs Largan bring her to the ship. They came down from London specially. That says something about the esteem in which they hold her, don't you think?'

The latter was a lie, because Harriet hadn't seen them, but she didn't care about lying if it'd help that poor girl.

'Her employers brought her right to the ship?'

'Yes. All the way from Ireland. I believe they spoke to one of the stewards, so you can check that out if you doubt my word.'

Matron flushed slightly. 'It's not that I doubt

your word, but rather that the captain likes things to be checked carefully. You must admit it's rather unusual for employers to do such a thing. So I'd like to see the letter for myself, if you don't mind. I'm responsible for the morals of the single women on this ship and, not only do I take my duties very seriously, but the captain is meticulous about them, too.'

Interfering old biddy, Harriet thought. You're enjoying this. 'I'll remind you that Mrs Hope is not a single woman, but a widow, before I ask her to join us and get the letter out. I won't be long.'

Harriet went on deck and saw Ismay standing with Adam by the rail, looking terrified. She walked swiftly across to them.

'You'll need to show Matron Mrs Largan's letter, my dear. And for goodness' sake, don't look so guilty. You've done nothing wrong.'

'I'll come with you,' Adam said.

'Better not. This really is women's business. Anyway, I can handle it. Chin up, Ismay. Don't let me down.'

Adam watched the girl look at his aunt with sheer adoration in her eyes and immediately start to hold herself more confidently. His aunt could do that to people. What a wonderful woman she was!

He wished he could be with them for this confrontation. He didn't like bullying and Matron reminded him of the woman who'd overseen the boys' dormitories at his school. She'd enjoyed finding fault with them and punishing them. He'd had many a caning from her – still resented that.

In the cabin Harriet said calmly, 'Get your letter out, dear.'

Matron studied the letter, then looked at them.

She's still not sure, Harriet thought. Well, she can prove nothing. 'As you can see, the Largans thought highly of dear Ismay. As do I.'

That brought an even sourer look to Matron's face. 'I'll rely on you, then, Mrs Seaton, to make sure this young woman behaves herself.'

'I wasn't aware she'd done anything except behave herself on this ship. I certainly don't know what I'd have done without her help, and I've heard she's working very hard at her classes, wanting to improve herself. In any case, we have only another two days before we get to Alexandria. I think I can manage to keep her out of your way till then.' She stared challengingly at Matron to make sure the woman understood how strongly she supported Ismay.

'As you say, only another two days.' The other woman looked openly at Ismay's stomach, then nodded to Mrs Seaton and left.

'Don't cry!' Harriet said fiercely. 'We're going right out on deck again to face them. If you act guilty, they'll assume the rumours are correct. Chin up and smile!'

That evening Rory heard the gossip and felt himself swell with pride. He'd done it, then, created a child. Every man wanted to know he was capable of that.

Best of all, this was his chance to make sure of her. He'd claim the child as his and offer to marry her on the spot. Mrs Hope, indeed! She was no more married than he was, and so he'd tell them.

After some thought he went to see Jed and told him about the problem, ending, 'I want to marry her but she won't have me.'

'She'll be forced to marry you now. Our captain will make sure of that. He's very much against fornication. I'd better tell the first mate about it straight away. Stay here.'

The first mate came down and questioned Rory, then went off to inform the captain.

'I was right to tell them,' Jed told Rory. 'Cabin passengers can get away with murder, but they like to keep an eye on those single women.'

Rory nodded and tried to look interested, but he was listening for footsteps, waiting to see her face when she found she had to marry him.

One of the stewards turned up. 'You're wanted by the captain, Flynn.'

Rory looked at Jed, who waved one hand. 'Don't keep him waiting.'

It was the first time Rory had been in the captain's cabin, and he was amazed at how big and comfortably furnished it was. Looked like the rooms at the big house, though he'd only seen them through the windows. He stood very upright, as he'd seen the crew members do, and waited for the captain to speak first.

'Is it true? Is this young woman carrying your child?'

'Yes, sir. We were courting, but when she got the chance to go to Australia, she changed her mind. I wanted to marry her but she ran off, pretending to be a widow. Only she isn't a widow.'

'Has she been *lying* to us?'

'Yes, sir.'

'And are you still willing to marry her, give the baby a name?'

'Oh yes, sir.'

'Hmm. It's the right thing to do now, though you shouldn't have touched her before marriage. Go and wait for me on deck.'

Harriet was taking an evening stroll with her nephew, enjoying the cooler evening air, when the first mate came up to them.

'Oh. I thought I'd seen Mrs Hope with you.'

'She was tired and went back to the cabin. Is it important?'

'Yes. The captain wants to see her.'

Harriet shot a quick glance at Adam, then said firmly, 'In that case, I'm coming with her. I'm not having anyone trying to bully that poor young woman, captain or not.'

'It's not bullying, ma'am, to want her to marry the father of her child, surely?'

She stopped walking for a moment. 'I don't

understand you. She was married to the father of her child, but he's dead now.'

'We have someone who says differently. And she did faint at the sight of him. Rather suspicious, that, don't you think?'

'It would be if she hadn't fainted a couple of times before in my cabin, as some women do when they're expecting.'

He frowned at that, then shrugged and led the way to the cabin.

'I'll go in first and give her your message,' Harriet said. 'She's probably gone to bed and will want to get dressed before she sees the captain.'

'I'll wait here with you,' Adam said easily to the first mate.

When his aunt had shut the door on them, he shook his head. 'I don't know what that fellow Flynn is trying to do, telling all these lies, but I think he's a bit unhinged – where she's concerned, at least.'

'But if he *is* the father of her child, he should surely marry her.'

'Even if he were the father, it'd be no one's concern but hers whether she marries him or not.'

'The captain thinks differently. He's very strong against fornication.'

'I shan't allow them to bully her into doing something so ludicrous.'

The first mate rolled his eyes. 'Got an interest there yourself, have you? Better not let the captain find out.'

'I have an interest in justice.'

'For a maid?'

'For anyone.'

He sniggered. 'Excuse me if I don't believe you. Mrs Hope's pretty, I grant you, but I'd not have thought she's pretty enough to attract a gentleman's attention.' He winked. 'Unless she's a very willing lass.'

'She's a decent young woman, who is devoted to my aunt, and I'll thank you not to blacken her name.' But Adam could see the first mate wasn't convinced of Ismay's innocence.

Ismay stared at Mrs Seaton in horror when told why the captain wanted to see her.

'Better get dressed quickly, dear. And wear that dark blue dress.'

Harriet studied her appearance then nodded. 'That's it. You look nice and demure in that. Now remember: no one can force you to marry him.'

'But it's the captain. Everyone's terrified of him, even the officers.'

'What can he do to you? We're leaving the ship for good in two days.'

'He can lock me up until then and stop me going to the other ship.'

'Nonsense! Of course he can't. He's not a judge and jury. You've committed no crime.'

'I sometimes feel as if I have.'

'Oh, my dear, of course you haven't. It was that man who committed the crime. Pull yourself together. You're about to fight for your freedom. Do you want to spend the rest of your life with Rory Flynn?'

Ismay shuddered.

'If necessary, we'll tell lies. I've already told the captain that I saw your employers bring you to the ship.'

That made Ismay feel warm inside. 'You're so kind.'

When they appeared outside the cabin, the first mate said, 'You took long enough.'

'I couldn't go and see the captain in my night-dress,' Ismay said. 'It wouldn't be decent.'

Mr Tregear mouthed the word 'courage' at her as he turned to follow them.

The first mate stopped when he realised he had two extra people with him. 'The captain only sent for Mrs Hope.'

'We're her friends as well as her employers.' Mrs Seaton gave her maid's hand a quick squeeze as she spoke.

With all the support, something inside Ismay grew warm and she even felt ready to face *him*.

The captain was sitting writing at his desk and, to her relief, there was no sign of Rory. He looked up as they entered and frowned. 'I only asked to see Mrs Hope.'

Mrs Seaton spoke. 'I'm sure you'll understand, Captain, that your summons worried us all. Ismay is a grieving widow and, from what your first mate said, there are some ridiculous rumours going round about her condition. We felt she needed our support.'

'Hmm.' He turned to Ismay, studying her stomach openly. 'Is Rory Flynn the father of your child?'

She stared back at him and found that by thinking of how much she hated Rory, she could lie quite easily. 'No, sir. He isn't.'

'But you do know him?'

'Unfortunately, yes.'

'Oh? Why do you say unfortunately?

'Because, almost as soon as my husband was dead, he started following me round and pestering me. I thought I'd got away from all that when I boarded this ship. It was such a shock to see him here. That's why I fainted.'

He looked at her sourly and she wasn't sure he believed her, but she managed to stare back at him steadily.

'Fetch Flynn in,' the captain said.

She hoped she'd hidden her shudder.

As the first mate went to the door and sent someone off to fetch him, Ismay edged a little closer to Mrs Seaton.

Rory came in, looking at her triumphantly.

'Mrs Hope denies that you're the father,' the captain said.

'She's lying. I can't abide women who lie. Once we're married, I'll teach her not to lie, sir.'

'How will you do that?' Adam asked.

Flynn scowled at him. 'The usual way. Wives

have to be learned to behave, like animals do. A few slaps usually sorts out who's master.'

Harriet put her arm round Ismay's shoulders. 'Do you approve of men who beat women into submission, Captain?'

'A little judicious chastisement can sometimes be necessary.'

'Then it's a good thing there's no reason for Ismay to marry this man. I do not approve of brutal behaviour to women.'

'There's the child to think of,' Flynn said. 'It needs a father and I'm a good provider.'

'I'd rather throw myself overboard than marry a man like you, Rory Flynn,' Ismay said. 'You have no connection to my husband's child.'

Adam decided to distract the captain's attention. What a bigot the man was! He moved closer, took her hand, and gave it a hard squeeze to warn her. 'Ismay, my dear, excuse me for speaking out without asking your permission first.' He turned back to the captain. 'If it's a provider you're looking for, I'll make a far better one than this fellow.'

Ismay quickly looked down, hoping she hadn't given away her shock. But Adam was still holding her hand and he squeezed it again. She guessed he was saying this to free her, so gave him a squeeze in return.

'I'm waiting to start courting Mrs Hope,' he went on, 'because I respect her grief, though my aunt knows my feelings and approves.'

Harriet nodded.

'But, given the circumstances, I'll tell you now, Captain, that I intend to start courting Ismay once we arrive in Australia, where I can meet her brother and gain his permission – do things the proper way.'

'I find that hard to believe. There's another man's baby involved, and she's hardly of your class. You can't have known her for long.'

'It took only one day for me to fall in love with her.'

The captain's snort said what he thought of this.

'And as for her being of my class, what is that? I'm a bastard, so women from the better classes would look askance at me once they found out about my parentage.'

He waited a moment, but the captain only continued to look at him sourly. 'I have my way to make in the world, so what I really need is a clever wife. I'm sure the various teachers here can tell you that Ismay is very quick to learn, and a hard worker.'

Ismay let out a long, slow breath, not knowing how to answer this, but Adam went on speaking and kept hold of her hand, so she held on to his. It made her feel strong, that hand did. She suddenly realised that she wished what he'd said was true. Oh, she did!

Don't be stupid! she told herself. As if a man like him would look twice at a person like her when seeking a wife! He was just being kind. For his aunt's sake.

There was a further silence, then the captain said, 'In that case, as long as she behaves herself, we'll leave it at that.' He looked at Ismay. 'You may go.'

Rory moved to bar her way. 'But it's not true! Captain, sir, none of it's true. That *is* my baby. And it's me she should be marrying.'

'It seems she's found herself another man to father the child. That's her choice. I can only be glad she's not continuing on my ship.' Disgust burred his voice.

Rory still didn't step out of the way, and Ismay moved closer to Adam, frightened now. Rory had *that* look on his face, the one he'd had when he attacked her.

'I won't give her up,' he told the captain, then turned to stare at her. 'No matter what they say, I won't give you up, Ismay Deagan. My son isn't going to be raised by someone else.'

'That's enough, Flynn!'

He turned to face the captain again. 'I won't let her—'

'Quiet!'

The captain's voice was so full with power, Ismay wasn't surprised when Rory fell silent. But he didn't stop watching her as Adam and Mrs Seaton shepherded her out, and the anger in his eyes made her shudder and stumble.

Ismay let them lead her where they would. Her head was spinning and she was feeling shaken to the core by the interview.

She'd had one experience of the violence lurking in Rory Flynn; didn't want him turning it on her friends. But how could she stop him? How could she make Mr Tregear and his aunt understand that he was as dangerous as a mad bull.

In the cabin, Harriet let out her breath in a whoosh and went to sit on the bed, patting the space beside her for Ismay. She'd never sat on her bed as often as she had since coming on board. She missed her old sofa. 'Are you sure it was wise to say that, Adam?'

'It stopped that farce, didn't it? Better speak more quietly, Aunt. You never know who's listening.' He pulled the chair closer to them before he sat down and leaned towards them.

Harriet sighed. 'You've put Ismay in a difficult position now.'

'I hope not. Until we get to the Swan River Colony, she'll have the protection of my name. Once we get there, we can end our so-called engagement and she'll be free to make a new life with her brother's help.'

'I'm grateful for your kindness,' Ismay murmured. And she was. But she wished she didn't have to be. You could even grow tired of being grateful, she'd found.

'I couldn't bear to see you being hounded to marry a brute who talked of beating you into submission. Or listen to the captain approving of *chastisement*.' He hesitated, then admitted, 'It was one of my father's favourite words and he too had a heavy hand.'

Harriet watched the two of them staring at one another and wondered suddenly if Adam was genuinely attracted to Ismay. Or was he making these extraordinary efforts to help her because the poor girl was in the same position as his mother had been? Who knew why people did things sometimes? They often didn't even know themselves, but acted simply on instinct.

She changed the focus of the conversation, carefully turning it away from Ismay. 'We're less than two days from Alexandria. Once we're off this ship, we'll be away from that captain. Are men like him usually so autocratic, Adam?'

'Some are. This one is a religious bigot and uses the power of his position to force his personal views on others. I'm surprised the company puts up with it. I've heard the officers muttering, and you saw how long the religious service was last Sunday. And look at how he forbade any classes to be held or games to be played on the Lord's Day.'

He yawned suddenly. 'Sorry. I'm getting tired now. Perhaps I'd better go to bed. Will you and Ismay be all right now, Aunt?'

'Yes, of course.' She turned to Ismay. 'You'd better call my nephew Adam from now on, and you should call me Aunt Harriet.'

Ismay cast a doubtful glance at them both. 'It wouldn't be fitting.'

Harriet laughed. 'It would if I say so.'

Adam stood up. 'That's a good idea. Now, let's get to bed. Oh, and be sure to lock this door tonight. Don't go out on your own tomorrow, Ismay.'

'I still have to eat in the single women's quarters.'

'I'll ask the stewardess if you can have something to eat here,' Mrs Seaton said.

'Let me do that,' Adam said. 'It'll look better if I slip her some money as a thank you.'

'But I didn't mean to cost you money!' Ismay said.

'A few shillings won't break the bank.'

'I think on the next leg of our journey, we'll book you in as my maid,' Harriet said. 'And ask for quarters near me.'

'Won't that cost you even more money?'

She smiled, such a warm smile. 'I can spend my money as I choose, and I prefer to spend it on those I'm fond of.'

'Oh.'

'Let's get ready for bed now.'

As she lay on her mattress on the floor, Ismay heard Mrs Seaton's breathing slow down almost immediately, but she found it hard to get to sleep.

It was always quite noisy at night on the ship, and it seemed worse tonight. If it was in use, the creaking of the screw turning as it moved the ship forward went on and on. Otherwise, sailors were on deck still, obeying orders to take in sail or let it out.

The animals penned on deck, mainly sheep and fowls, were clearly not happy either, judging from the pitiful noises they made as the ship rolled around.

In the quieter moments she could hear a little whiffling noise from the bed. Ismay smiled. Mrs Seaton made that noise sometimes during the night.

How kind she and her nephew had been! They'd saved Ismay from a dreadful situation today. The captain terrified her and, as for Rory, she wished she need never see or hear of him again. She hated him. He and her father were the only two people she'd ever truly hated.

She snuggled down, feeling sleepy now. If only all that they'd said was true. If only she really was engaged to Adam Tregear! He made her heart beat faster just by being near.

Oh, she was a fool! She shouldn't even be thinking of him in that way. As if a gentleman like him would ever care about an ignorant Irish lass like her, whether he was bastard born or not.

8

Dougal returned home from Singapore a few days later than Flora had expected, but then you could never be sure exactly when a ship would arrive, except for the P&O vessels, which called in at Albany to bring the colony's mail. She'd heard that you could almost set your watch by them, because they carried Her Majesty's mail and that must get through on time. Apparently they left passengers behind rather than fail to keep to the timetables.

She went down to the harbour to watch the *Bonny Mary* unloading its cargo into the lighters from where it was anchored just off shore, and met Bram, who was staring out at the ship hungrily.

'Are you looking forward to seeing your new trade goods, Mr Deagan?'

'I am, yes. There'll be more than last time, too, Miss McBride.' He watched the lighter set off for the South Jetty, loaded with goods. 'They need a proper, deep-water harbour here, don't you think?'

'They argue about it regularly. Some people are afraid that if larger ships can sail straight up the river to Perth, it'll take trade away from Fremantle.'

Her brother said the Fremantle authorities were a bunch of short-sighted fools, but she didn't repeat that.

Bram hesitated, then asked, 'How is your mother keeping?'

She didn't need to pretend with a good friend like him. 'She's getting worse by the day, I'm afraid. She throws a fit of hysterics if I go near her, so I've hired someone to look after her, a Mrs Southerham. You may have met the lady while you were staying with Conn in the country.'

'I didn't meet her, but I heard of her. They buried her husband while we were down there and the family went to the funeral. Will Mrs Southerham be able to cope with your mother? Is she a strong woman?'

'No, but she's a lady, and my mother thinks that's the most important thing in a companion. She wouldn't have anything to do with Mrs Southerham otherwise. I've hired a strong, cheerful woman to help out as well and we shall just have to take each day as it comes. My mother isn't looking well, won't eat sometimes, frets and fusses over nothing.'

''Tis sad that some lives end that way. We had a neighbour the same. But her family couldn't afford help to look after her. They had to tie her to a chair during the day, then towards the end she just lay on her bed, refusing to eat.'

Flora nodded, and it was a few moments before she spoke again, changing the subject to something more cheerful. 'How are your wife and little son?'

He beamed at her. 'Ah, they're thriving, bless them.'

She smiled encouragingly and he started telling her about baby Arlen.

After a while, he said, 'Well, I can't stand here all day, pleasant as it is to chat to you. You must come round and take tea with us one day. You're right next door when you go to visit your mother.'

'I'll do that.' It was bitter-sweet to see how much Bram and his wife loved one another, and it always hurt to see another woman's joy in her baby. Flora wondered sometimes if she'd ever get over this longing for a child of her own.

They both turned, walking together for part of the way then separating to go to their own homes.

Flora made sure Dougal's bedroom was ready and that there was plenty to eat. She and her maid, Linny, lived quite simply while he was away, but men always seemed to need more food than women.

He came breezing in just as it was getting dark and, as she ran to greet him, he swung her up into his arms, twirling her round the hall.

'Put me down, you fool!'

For answer he twirled her again, till she was helpless with laughter. 'Can't I give my little sister a swing?' He set her on her feet, but still held her by the shoulders as he studied her face. 'You look strained, Flora. What's gone wrong now?'

She hadn't intended to tell him until after tea, but, since he'd asked, she explained how their mother's condition had worsened rapidly while he was away in Singapore.

He sighed. 'I'll go and see her in the morning after I've been out to the ship.'

'She'll probably behave herself for you. You always were the favourite.'

'For what that's worth. She was never easy to deal with. Let's forget about her now. Tell me what you've been doing. Have you started taking in paying guests again?'

'I decided not to. I may open a boarding house when I find somewhere of my own to live, but I'll not do that in your house, not any more. We needed the money when you first got your own ship, then it was a way of giving me something to do other than run round after Mother.'

'It's your home as well as mine. You can do what you want here.'

'I know. For the moment. But you keep talking about finding a wife and no woman will want to find the place full of strangers coming and going. As soon as you marry, I'll find somewhere of my own.' She could feel herself colouring in embarrassment. 'Though I'll have to ask you for some money to help set things up, I'm afraid.'

'I'd not throw you out, even if I did get married.'

She gave him a serious look. 'I'd throw myself out. But how you are to find a woman to marry if you're always away, I don't know.'

'We'll have to do some entertaining while I'm at home and you can introduce me to all the current eligibles. Are there any new ladies in the colony whom I should inspect?'

She pretended to slap his arm. 'What a way to talk! As if I just have to line them up for you to pick one.' Though that would likely be more or less what happened, even with the shortage of women in the colony, because he was very eligible himself. He was not only doing well with the schooner and trading, but was also a fine figure of a man.

Ah, but it was good to have him home, to joke together, to know he cared about her. She missed him when he went away. She didn't miss living with her mother at all.

As he was finishing a second slice of apple pie, he said suddenly, 'You're looking a bit peaky. Maybe you should come with me on my next trip. What do you think?'

She nearly said yes straight away, but then practicality took over. 'I don't think I can. There's Mother to think of.'

'You've found a woman to look after her and we could appoint someone to act as her guardian – my lawyer, perhaps. Wouldn't you like to visit Singapore?'

'I don't know. I've never seriously considered it, but yes . . . I think I would like to visit it, once at least. Bram's wife makes it sound so exotic and interesting. Isabella still misses some things about living there, especially Mr Lee and his family.'

'Then you'll come?'

'I think I ought to see how Mrs Southerham manages first, so perhaps next trip.'

He clasped her hand tightly and gave it a little shake. 'No, come this trip. I think you need a rest from worrying about our dear mother. I'll make sure I don't leave till you've got this Mrs Southerham started.'

Flora felt excited for the rest of the evening as they discussed what she'd need to take on a trip like that, but when she went to bed, she started having second thoughts. How could she possibly leave? Some people in the town already thought badly of her, thanks to her mother's lies. They'd say she'd abandoned her duty. But the idea of seeing Singapore wouldn't be dismissed. Dougal and Bram said it was a vibrant city, growing all the time, though Dougal would have preferred it not to be so hot.

She hadn't been on a ship since her arrival in Australia, because her mother had been very seasick on the journey out from England. But Flora had thoroughly enjoyed the voyage, in spite of the discomforts. Dougal said ships were much more modern and comfortable these days, and she'd have her own cabin this time, not have to share with her mother.

She stared at the dark shapes of furniture, outlined in the faint moonlight leaking round the edges of the badly fitting curtains. She'd vowed to change her life, to take charge of her own future, and how would she do that successfully if she was afraid to travel, even under her brother's protection?

She'd only be away for a few weeks, so perhaps if Mrs Southerham was good at looking after her mother . . . Did she dare do it? Yes, she did.

On that thought, Flora fell asleep with a smile on her face.

The harbour at Alexandria fascinated Ismay. She stayed at the ship's rail for as long as she could, comparing it in her mind to the harbours she'd seen at Southampton and Malta. It seemed larger and more exotic – more crowded, too, with vessels of all shapes and sizes positively jostling for position.

As the ship moved slowly towards its mooring in the West Harbour, she studied the long wall running the whole length of it. It gradually became clear that there were inner and outer mooring areas, also walled. Everything was built of stone. How long had those huge walls taken to build? How had they moved such massive stones into position in the water?

Every new place she saw brought so many questions, and she had so few answers. She hated being ignorant.

And the sun shone so brightly, hot upon her skin. She'd never felt sun like that before. It was so different from the cool, damp air of Ireland.

Then it was time to get her things together and

follow Aunt Harriet off the ship. How easy it was to call her that. If only she really was an aunt. She was such a lovely woman.

Ismay kept her eyes open for Rory, and was relieved to leave without any further encounters. The trouble was, he might find a job working his passage on the next ship. Oh, stop worrying! she told herself. You can face that when it happens. You're not alone now, and you won't be travelling steerage.

She gave a little skip of excitement, then glanced quickly sideways, hoping they hadn't noticed. But Adam was smiling at her. He must think her a fool. Today they were going to the company's hotel, then they would explore Alexandria a little. Excitement bubbled up inside her again as she peered out of the cab, not wanting to miss a single thing.

Adam smiled across at her. 'Don't worry, Ismay. You'll have time to do some sightseeing today.'

'Ismay's not the only one to feel excited.' His aunt beamed at them. 'Oh, how lovely it is to get off that ship! I'd like a good long walk on ground that doesn't move beneath my feet.'

The hotel was spacious, with fans moving the hot air, and a manager with darker skin than theirs who spoke excellent English.

'I'll go and see the local P&O agent to try to change our bookings to Galle,' Adam said, once he'd made sure there were rooms for them. 'That shouldn't take too long. Can you see that my luggage is taken up, Aunt?'

Their rooms were so spacious that Ismay stared round hers in surprise, because it was exactly the same as Aunt Harriet's. 'This is too expensive for me,' she whispered.

'No, it isn't. Anyway, it's much more convenient for you to be next to me, with Adam just across the corridor. Let's go down to that guests' sitting room the manager pointed out, and get a nice cup of tea.'

Ismay would rather have gone to the hotel door to stare down the street, but didn't say so.

Adam returned to the hotel in time to drink tea with them before they set out to do some sight-seeing. 'It's hot outside. Are you sure you'll be all right?'

'I don't care if it's like a furnace,' his aunt said. 'I want to go for a walk.'

Once they'd been served, Ismay could hold back her main worry no longer. 'What about Rory? Will he follow us to Galle, do you think?'

'He may find work on the next ship or he may travel steerage, if he has the money, but he'll be disappointed, because we're not leaving straight away. I've arranged with the shipping agent for us to take the following ship to Galle, not this one.' Adam took a long gulp of tea and held out his cup to his aunt for more.

'Since we aren't going on to the Orient, like

most of the other passengers, we need to connect with the mail ship to Australia. It stops at Albany in the Swan River Colony and then we have to travel by land or coastal steamer to Fremantle, where your brother lives. That ship won't arrive at Galle for another week, apparently. I decided it'd be more interesting for us to stay here than in Galle, which is quite a small place. I hope you don't mind.'

A load seemed to slide off Ismay's shoulders, and she couldn't speak for sheer relief.

His aunt leaned across to kiss his cheek. 'How clever of you, Adam dear. So, what is there to see?'

'I'm told they're working very hard to get the new ship canal finished by next year. I'd love to see that, though it'll mean a long day's journey. It's one of the wonders of the modern world. Apparently there are parties made up regularly to inspect the workings, so I thought we'd join one.'

He laughed. 'I had to arrange that at the hotel, because the shipping agent turned up his nose at the idea. He told me a canal would never replace the comfort of their company's system, with their own railway across the isthmus to Suez, and hotels; not to mention farms to provide good food for their passengers.'

'Do you think he's right?'

'No. I'm quite certain he's wrong. The people in charge of the P&O must have their noses buried in the sand, they understand so little of how people feel when they're travelling. It'll be much easier to stay on the same ship and do any sightseeing from its comfort. It should be cooler on the water, too.' He grimaced. 'I'd not like to live permanently in a place this hot.'

Ismay agreed with him. She couldn't believe how warm it was outside. She let them talk, not really caring what they did today, as long as she was included.

In spite of the heat, she enjoyed every minute of the afternoon's sight-seeing. Adam and his aunt admired the beautiful buildings, especially the ancient lighthouse, and yes, the buildings were wonderful. But it was the small things that Ismay enjoyed most, especially the people who talked in a language of which she understood not one word and wore strange clothes. Many of the women had flowing garments that covered them completely – they must be so hot underneath all those layers! – while some of the men had very baggy trousers and funny little hats called fezzes with tassels on the top.

She saw real camels for the first time in her life and forgot to move as she stared in wonderment at a group of them walking in single file through the streets, taller than she'd expected, loaded with boxes and bundles, which swayed from side to side as the animals walked.

Aunt Harriet might smile at her excitement, but Ismay couldn't stay calm and quiet. Was she really standing in a street next to camels? Her teacher had talked to them about other countries, including

Egypt because it was in the Bible. But it was much more colourful in real life than she'd expected, with many delightful little differences.

They spent the next day walking round the city with a guide, who took them to visit the souks. These turned out to be huge markets selling everything on earth. Aunt Harriet bought a few bits and pieces, especially some filmy shawls, but Ismay had no money to spare, so pretended she didn't find anything she wanted.

The following day they were to go on the trip to the canal diggings, and that was much less interesting to her. She got more pleasure from watching Adam's enjoyment of a lengthy discussion with one of the engineers about what was being done, but she wasn't really interested in the details of what the huge pieces of equipment could do. The ground was very sandy and they were using dredging machinery to dig it out, then gradually filling up each section with water.

She didn't bother to go near the machinery. She was a little tired today and was afraid of stumbling and falling over the edge because the soft sand shifted under your feet. If only it wasn't so hot here! Sweat was trickling down the backs of her legs, under her skirt, and she was sure her face was as red as her father's when he got drunk.

After a while, Aunt Harriet suggested they follow the example of the other ladies in their party and seek shelter in the shade, leaving further exploration to the men.

By the end of the day, Ismay was feeling so weary she could hardly put one foot in front of the other and her head was throbbing. She wasn't at all hungry when they got back to the hotel, just wanted to drink several cups of tea then go to sleep. She hoped it wouldn't be this hot in Australia.

Perhaps she'd eaten something that disagreed with her, because she continued to feel under the weather and left the other two to go out on their own the next day, insisting all she wanted was to sleep. But it was hard to get to sleep when the air was so still and warm, and sweat kept trickling down your face.

She felt so terrible she must have eaten something bad.

As they got ready to take the train to Suez the following morning, Aunt Harriet laid one hand on her forehead. 'You're still feeling unwell, aren't you, dear? You feel a bit feverish to me. The trouble is, we have to leave today if we're to catch the next ship to Galle.'

'I'll be fine, really I will. All I have to do is sit quietly on the train.' She tried to look more alert, but it was hard to keep up the pretence.

By the time they reached Suez, Ismay was feeling so dizzy that, when she stood up to leave the train, she had to clutch Aunt Harriet or she'd have fallen. Then pain stabbed through her and she gasped, clutching her stomach.

'Ismay? What's wrong?'

'It hurts! Oh, it hurts so much!'

The pain subsided a little and she tried to move on, but couldn't. Everything seemed to waver around her and she felt herself falling. Adam caught her but she couldn't make out what he was saying to Aunt Harriet. All the sounds were jumbling together and the light hurt her eyes, so that she had to close them.

He laid her down gently and someone took her hand. 'I'm here, dear.'

'Aunt Harriet, I—' But the pain had started again, worse this time, and all she could do was groan.

She was vaguely aware of being lifted into a vehicle that jolted her badly. It was hard to speak but she managed to say, 'Sorry for . . . trouble.'

'We're only sorry you're not feeling well, dear,' Aunt Harriet said. 'We're taking you to a hotel and we'll ask them to call a doctor straight away.'

Ismay gave up trying to speak because the pain had taken over, pulsing and stabbing into her.

Harriet looked at her nephew and whispered, 'I think she may be losing the baby.'

He nodded. 'Poor girl. She looks so white.'

His aunt was desperately worried, but didn't want to say so in case Ismay heard her. Bearing children was a dangerous thing for women. Many years ago she'd lost a good friend to puerperal fever after childbirth.

They arrived at the hotel just then and the manager was very helpful. Two men were summoned with a snap of the fingers to carry Ismay up to her room. He promised to send for a doctor immediately.

'The best doctor you can find, one who speaks English.'

'Yes, Mr Tregear. We have very good doctor for our visitors.'

Worried sick about the poor girl, Harriet followed the men upstairs, stopping briefly at the door as her nephew hurried to join her. 'You'd better wait in your own room, Adam.'

The manager had come up with them. 'This way, sir. This is your room and this one is for Mrs Seaton.'

Harriet nodded, her mind still on Ismay. Inside, she shooed the gaping men out and closed the door behind them. Going back to the bed, she loosened Ismay's clothing, but the poor girl wasn't fully conscious. Harriet sat beside her, not knowing what else to do.

To her relief, the doctor arrived soon afterwards, bringing a woman to help him. He spoke poor English with a heavy accent, but it was good enough for her to understand.

'She's expecting a baby,' she told them.

'Ah.' He beckoned the woman forward.

To Harriet's relief, he was clean and seemed very confident, and it was the woman who examined Ismay intimately.

Harriet averted her eyes while this was going

on, wishing she understood what they were saying to one another.

The doctor turned to her. 'She's losing baby. Must keep her still afterwards. Very still. Keep her to lie down. Not to get up. Not to walk about.'

He indicated the woman. 'Fatima look after her. Very good nurse.' He showed Harriet a small jar of powder, then handed it to Fatima. 'This keep her asleep afterwards. Good thing to sleep and lie still.'

He stared down again at Ismay, whose face was flushed; he touched her forehead. 'Too much sun also. No more sun. Drink much water.'

Soon after that it was all over. The baby had been lost.

Once he was sure his patient wasn't bleeding, the doctor left and Fatima took charge. She seemed to know what she was doing, but her English was worse than the doctor's, so sometimes she had to pantomime what she wanted. Harriet watched her give Ismay some of the powder mixed in a big glass of water and it did seem to calm her down and make her sleep.

Someone tapped on the door and she went to open it.

'How is she?' Adam asked.

'She's lost the baby. It's quite early on, so that's not too bad. She should recover from it quite quickly, but if I understood the doctor correctly, she's also been too much in the sun and that's making her ill too.'

'Will she be well enough to board the ship tomorrow morning?'

'I don't know. We may have to arrange to have her carried on board. She's sleeping quietly now.'

But when Harriet went to see Ismay early the next morning, she still looked very pale, and Fatima said firmly that she must not be moved.

Harriet went to knock on her nephew's bedroom door. He opened it so quickly she guessed he'd been waiting for her. 'Ismay can't leave today, or for a few more days. She has to lie still.'

He looked puzzled and she blushed as she explained about her losing too much blood. 'Fatima is going to stay and look after her, thank goodness. She's an excellent nurse.'

He stared at his aunt in consternation. 'The ship won't wait for anyone because of the mails.'

'I know. But I won't risk moving her.' She gave him a very firm look. 'Nor will I leave her here in a strange country, sick and on her own.'

'No, of course not. We'll both stay.' He thought for a moment or two. 'Luckily, my father's will says nothing about how quickly I have to get to the Swan River Colony once I've left England, so it won't matter if we stay here, though it could be a while before we're able to link up with the next ship to Australia.'

'Can you get our things taken off the ship before it leaves?'

'I'll go and see what I can do.'

She went back to the bedroom. 'How is she, Fatima?'

'Sleeping. Good to sleep. She be all right soon.' She held up her fingers. 'Two, three day, lie still. Then move gently.'

'Shall I stay with her?'

She shook her head. 'No need. You rest. Eat. Keep strong. I here today, all day, come every day after.'

And so reliable did Fatima seem that Harriet decided to trust her to care for Ismay. The worry had tired her out.

Adam hurried to the ship and explained about Ismay being ill. The first mate came to see him as he was supervising their cabin luggage being brought up on deck.

'Can we get our trunks from the hold as well?'

'No time to hunt for them, I'm afraid. There are a lot of trunks down there and we can't delay our departure. The mail must go through on time.'

'Hell! What am I going to do?'

'Is there someone you can have the trunks sent to at the other end?'

Adam gave him Bram's address and scribbled a note to go with the trunks. He could only hope they'd not go astray. He had a lot of things he valued in his, and knew it was the same for his aunt.

Rory had been worrying when he saw no sign of Ismay coming on board as it got closer and closer to sailing time. Had they changed their minds? No, where else could they go but on to Australia?

Then a cab drew up and Tregear came hurrying on to the ship without the two women, looking anxious. They were so close to sailing, Rory guessed something was wrong. He tried to get closer to find out, but was told to be smart about his work or he'd be off the ship before he'd even started the journey.

After a moment's hesitation, he did as he was told. Since this was an unofficial 'job' dependent on the supervisor's good will, he didn't dare argue.

Before the end of the day, he'd found out what had happened, because he overheard one of the stewards grumbling about the tips he wouldn't get now that two cabins were empty. Someone had fallen ill, one of the two women apparently, and the cabin luggage had been taken off the ship, but their trunks were still in the hold.

Probably the old lady. Old folk often fell ill. Serve her right too for interfering in Rory's affairs.

He thought about it as he worked. He came to the conclusion that, even if Ismay hadn't got on this particular ship, she and her companions would still be going to the same destination as he was. He'd probably catch up with them at this Galle place, or if not there, in Australia. That had puzzled him for a while because they sometimes called it Western Australia and sometimes the Swan River Colony. Then someone explained it was the same place, which had started out as the

Swan River Colony, but was gradually changing its name.

He worked hard, but found it more difficult to get on good terms with the man in charge here, who made it plain he didn't think much of the Irish. The other men he worked with followed that example.

When they got to Galle, Rory had to wait a couple of days for the ship to the Swan River Colony. This time he wasn't able to get a job working his passage, because the chief steward didn't believe in taking on unofficial help, so Rory had to waste his precious money on a place in steerage.

Should he stay here in Galle till the others arrived? No, it cost money to stay here and he didn't like foreign places where he couldn't understand what people were saying. As for the food in these heathen countries, he didn't like that at all. He'd be better going on to the Swan River Colony and getting a job.

He'd find out where Bram Deagan lived, though he'd not approach him at first. They'd not got on very well as lads and he didn't suppose they'd get on now. But she'd join her brother eventually and, when she did, Rory would be waiting.

He dreamed of Ismay. Often. She was so pretty, so soft. And she was his; had never belonged to a man before him and never would belong to another man, either. He'd make sure of that. He wasn't letting her go.

He talked to other passengers and most seemed

so certain they were going to make a better life for themselves and their families in Australia, it made him think. Why should he not do the same? He wasn't frightened of hard work.

It was probably a good thing he'd come chasing after her. He'd never have done anything but look after cows if he'd stayed in Ireland.

Once things were settled, life would be good. He'd have Ismay to share his bed, look after his house and bear him lots of children. What more could a man want?

When Ismay woke the following morning, she was drowsy and not fully aware of what was happening. Fatima checked her carefully and said she must lie still for another day or two. 'I go home now, come back later to see her.'

Harriet had breakfast sent up to the room and, when she'd finished hers, she went to sit by Ismay, who was getting restless. She stroked the damp hair back from her sweaty forehead. 'You're going to be all right, dear.'

'What happened?'

'You lost the baby.'

'It's gone? It's really gone?'

'Yes. But you also have sunstroke. The doctor says you must lie still and rest for a while.'

Ismay was quiet for so long, Harriet thought she'd gone to sleep again; then she saw the tears and the poor girl started sobbing – such harsh, distressing sounds. 'Shh now, shh.'

But Ismay continued to weep. 'I'm bad, wicked.'
Harriet was puzzled. 'Why do you say that?'

'Because I'm glad I lost the baby. Only it wasn't
the baby's fault, was it? Will I go to hell now for
being glad it's dead?'

'No, of course not. You didn't do anything to
cause its death.'

Ismay clutched her hand and gradually stopped
weeping. After a while her breathing slowed down
again. Whatever was in the potion was making her
sleep a lot. Which was probably a good thing.

Even after her young friend had fallen asleep,
Harriet sat on. She too was glad the baby had
gone. Raising it would have been a heavy burden
for the girl, and perhaps she'd never have been
able to love a child created in such a dreadful way.
No one need ever know what had happened. Ismay
could make a good life for herself with her brother
Bram's help.

Perhaps in the Swan River Colony, Harriet
could find some like-minded ladies and continue
to help young women in trouble. She'd find that
very satisfying.

She was sure she and Ismay would stay friends.
She didn't know why she liked this particular girl
so much, she just did. Ismay had such a vivid
personality, was so interested in the world. Her
whole face lit up when she was excited about
something and she made you feel excited too.

Adam also liked Ismay. More than he should,
Harriet suspected, given their different backgrounds.

Was it possible he might start courting her? Who knew? Harriet wouldn't interfere if he did. Of course, he had a new life to make for himself in the colony as well, and that would keep him busy for a while.

But her nephew had never looked at other young women in quite the way he looked at Ismay. And Harriet had introduced him to quite a few suitable young ladies over the years, those whose families could accept his lack of a father.

Oh, why did life have to be so complicated? She went to stand by the window for a while, then answered a knock on the door and found Adam outside.

'Would you like to go out for a walk?'

'No, thank you. I think it's better if I stay with Ismay, just in case she needs me.'

'You won't mind if I go out for a while?'

'Of course not.'

Harriet would be glad when they arrived in Australia. She wasn't made for sitting around being waited on. She enjoyed having her own house and possessions around her, meeting friends, going to concerts, even baking cakes to serve to her friends when they called – all the small joys of daily life.

Whatever happened there, she would still be with Adam, so it was worth this boring journey. His properties were in Fremantle and they'd probably settle there. She liked living in a port city, a legacy of her time married to a sailor, and didn't think she could settle inland.

Oh, her thoughts were wandering, like so many butterflies. Would this long day never end?

She turned at a sound from the bed and saw Ismay pull herself up.

'I feel a lot better now.'

'Are you sure?'

'Yes. I'd like to get up.'

'They said you were to rest.'

Ismay smiled. 'I don't want to go for a walk, just move around the hotel a bit.'

'We'll ask Fatima when she comes to check on you and, if she says it's all right, I'll help you get dressed.'

Fatima came, studied Ismay and said she could get up. 'No long walks. Little walk. Sit and rest. Little walk again.'

They laughed at how wobbly Ismay still was, but she insisted on going down to the foyer of the hotel, where she sat for a while, then came back up to rest.

'I'm coming to eat dinner with you,' she announced.

'Are you sure?'

'Oh, yes. I'm feeling very hungry now.' She looked at Aunt Harriet. 'Thank you for staying with me.'

'As if we'd leave you here, ill and alone!'

'You're a lovely woman. I wish you were really my aunt. Though I do have one aunt I like. Maura's my father's youngest sister and she's only ten years older than me. She went away, though, when she got a job in England as a maid. I missed her. We all did. Even Da said she was his favourite sister.'

'There sound to be a lot of Deagans.'

'Too many.' Ismay yawned and stretched, falling asleep a few seconds later. She dozed for a short time and woke up looking much brighter. She was well enough to join them for dinner, Harriet was sure.

9

Adam paced up and down the hotel's sitting room for a few moments, encountering disapproving looks from an elderly gentleman sitting reading in a corner. Should he leave his aunt and go for a walk? He'd go mad if he had to stay here. Oh, why not? He needn't be away from the hotel for too long.

As he stood at the door, wondering which way to go, he took a deep breath of the hot, dry air. The small town of Suez was surrounded by desert, some of it disturbed by the unattractive workings of the canal and the heaps of spoil from the excavations left lying near the town. He doubted it'd be worth thinking of further trips into the countryside to while away the time. Best to explore the town itself, so that he could take the ladies for walks when they were able to go out.

He sighed. He was as bad as his aunt, much preferred to keep busy. Then he brightened. Mr Saxby had said his schooner traded to this port from time to time. It wouldn't hurt to get to know the harbour a little, see what facilities there were.

Strolling along the narrow streets meant threading

his way past vendors of food and other items, beggars and stray children, women muffled from head to toe in dark cloth, men talking and gesticulating. Ismay would love to see this, he was sure.

He moved to one side as a line of camels came towards him, laden with goods. They seemed docile enough, but to his mind, they had sneering expressions on their faces. How excited Ismay had been to see these creatures in Alexandria!

There he went again, thinking of her. This had to stop.

Ah, here was the harbour at last! The tide was out and the larger fishing boats were grounded, lying on their sides as if having a nap. He looked out to sea and saw a schooner at anchor. Its rigging was bare of sails and its decks were deserted, so it was clearly not going anywhere soon. He couldn't see its name from here.

For the hundredth time, he wondered what his own schooner would be like. Well, his half-schooner. It apparently carried cargo all over the Orient, but mainly to Singapore. It'd be exciting to visit new ports.

There was a man in European clothing standing at one end of the harbour, staring blindly at the water, looking rather sad. His suntanned skin suggested he'd spent a lot of time in the open air, and Adam wondered if he was from the schooner, one of the officers perhaps, so went towards him.

When he stopped and nodded a greeting, the

man looked up and gave a half-smile and nod, acknowledging his presence.

'Hot, isn't it?' Adam offered, hoping to strike up a conversation. 'Do you ever get used to it?'

'You change your habits and your clothing somewhat.' The man grinned. 'If you've just come from Britain, you're probably wearing woollen underwear. It's better to use cotton.'

'I'll make a note of that for future reference.' Fancy talking about underwear to a stranger! But it did seem like sound advice.

'If you feel like some refreshments and a sit-down in the shade, I know a place where we can get strong coffee with a fan above us to stir the air? You can give me the latest news from Britain.' The stranger cocked his head enquiringly.

'That sounds an excellent idea to me. The ladies of my party are incapacitated and I'm going mad sitting in the hotel on my own.' Perhaps this man would know about the *Hannah Grey*, have seen her, even?

They chatted about ships as they walked along and, after they'd sat down, the stranger looked at Adam. 'You sound like a nautical man yourself.'

'I am. I used to be second mate on a ship on the Liverpool–America run.'

'Joss Rutherford. Captain of the *Hannah Grey*.' He offered his hand.

Adam stared at him in shock over their clasped hands as he heard the ship's name. 'What port are you out of?'

'Fremantle, in the Swan River Colony.'

He let go of the hand. There couldn't be two schooners with the same name from one port, just couldn't. 'My name's Adam Tregear and I've just inherited a half-share in a schooner called the *Hannah Grey*. It's why I'm travelling to Australia. My lawyer said it sometimes visited Suez, but I didn't dare hope it'd be here now.' He wasn't usually so lucky.

The man stiffened, giving him a searching look. 'What's the name of your lawyer in England?'

'Quentin Saxby.'

'Good lord! I didn't believe in coincidences, but it seems they do happen and fate has brought us together. I'm your co-owner. Didn't you recognise my name?'

'Mr Saxby didn't know it. An Australian lawyer has been handling my inheritance on behalf of my late father and I only found out about it recently. I've apparently been left three houses in Fremantle as well, but I know nothing about them, either. My father was . . . a strange man.'

'Did you know I'd be here?' Joss answered his own question. 'No, how could you? I didn't know myself till I got a profitable cargo for Suez out of Galle. I prefer the Singapore run, though. I've made a few friends up there.'

'So you don't come to Suez as frequently?'

Joss grinned. 'No. Though I'll trade anywhere in the region that I can see a profit. I've been trying to pick up another cargo going back to

Australia, or at least to Galle, but it looks as if I'll have to go to Singapore from here first. I'm waiting to hear about it later this afternoon.'

'Have you always owned a half-share in the ship? Or did it have another owner?'

The unhappy look returned to Joss's face. 'I used to be full owner. It was my first vessel, but I had some bad luck – we ran into a severe tropical storm. There was a lot of damage to the ship and I had to jettison some of the cargo to stay afloat, so I'd that to repay as well. If she hadn't been such a sound vessel, she'd have sunk, but somehow we managed to limp back to Fremantle under a jury rig. I was trading out of Sydney before that, but I couldn't have made it back there and I have no real ties with Sydney anyway, not now, so I've decided to base myself in Fremantle. Till I see how certain other things go, anyway.'

He fell silent for a moment or two, sighing and staring down at his hands. 'I was short of money after buying the *Hannah Grey*, so I was risking one trip without insurance. Just the one. I should have known better but I was upset about something and wasn't thinking clearly. The only way to pay my debts and get my *Hannah* seaworthy was to sell a half-share. I've had a couple of decent trips since then, but I don't have enough money to buy you out yet.'

'I don't want to be bought out. I want my own vessel. Half will do for a start.'

'Well, it's not quite a half-share. You own forty-nine per cent to my fifty-one per cent. So I still have the deciding vote if we disagree, wouldn't you say?'

'What?' Adam felt anger rise in him as this information sank in. His damned father had cheated him again. He wasn't half-owner but the junior owner, even if it was only by 2 per cent. 'The lawyer didn't tell me that. He said I owned half.' And Mr Saxby had probably been told 'half' deliberately.

There was silence for a while until Adam felt compelled to bring everything out into the open. If he was to work with this man, it was better to understand one another, so Adam explained about his birth and his father's manipulative will.

Joss listened without interrupting, let a moment or two pass then said quietly, 'Difficult situation for you. But Australia's a good place to live, and most people there aren't as hidebound as in Britain – the ordinary people, anyway – so your birth won't be nearly as important. Unless the *Hannah* hits more storms, you should do quite well out of your forty-nine per cent. Would you be prepared to sail under me as first mate, or do you intend to be a sleeping partner only?'

'I'd go mad if I had to live ashore all the time. I'd be happy to give working together a try once I've got my aunt settled in Fremantle.' Adam pulled out his watch and checked the time. 'Talking of my aunt, I've been away for longer than I said. She'll be worrying.'

Joss glanced at his own watch. 'And I have to meet the agent arranging the cargo to Singapore. Do you want to get together again later and continue this discussion? I'll have to leave in a couple of days, so the sooner we settle matters the better. And of course you'll want to come out and see the ship properly, whatever else we do.'

'Definitely. Look, why don't you join us for a meal at the hotel after your meeting?'

'I'd be happy to.' He grinned. 'Apart from anything else, my cook isn't back on board yet.'

They shook hands and Joss strode away.

Adam walked more slowly, still finding the heat enervating. He had a great deal to think about. He looked out at the schooner, wishing he could see it more clearly. Well, he'd look it over tomorrow.

As he left the harbour, the town seemed to close around him like a prison. So many people pushing and shoving. Give him fresh sea breezes and a far horizon any day.

Ismay was feeling a lot better. Her face had lost the worst of its redness, though the skin on her nose and forehead was peeling. The thumping headache was completely gone, thank goodness. Oh, she'd still needed a nap, but only a short one. In fact, she was well enough to feel bored.

Best of all, she was no longer carrying Rory's

baby. She kept hugging that thought to her, feeling like a prisoner reprieved from hanging at the last minute.

'What should I wear for dinner tonight, Aunt Harriet? It seems quite a . . . a fancy hotel.' She'd noticed on the ship that the cabin passengers changed their clothes for their evening meal, which seemed a silly thing to do, as if they'd have dirtied the garments by wearing them for a few hours and doing no work.

'The pale green.' Harriet studied Ismay thoughtfully. 'And you'll need something for your hair.'

Ismay looked at her in surprise. 'Wear a bonnet to dinner, do you mean?'

'No. Since you're supposed to be a widow, a silly bit of lace not big enough to be called a cap. Mine's always sliding sideways, however carefully I pin it, my hair's so soft and fine. Yours ought to have black ribbons, but we'll ignore that.'

'I don't have anything like that.'

'You can borrow one of mine.'

When they were both ready, she looked at Ismay and nodded approvingly. 'You look beautiful.'

'Me?'

'Yes, you. I've excelled myself with your hair tonight. Look.' She turned the young woman round to face herself in the mirror. The dark hair was gleaming now, polished with a piece of silk. It was parted in the middle, with the side hair turned back and puffed out over the ears, then drawn into a high chignon. The froth of lace and ribbon perched on it was small and flattering.

'Is that really me?' Ismay hardly recognised herself looking so elegant. She lifted one hand to touch the lace of the cap, then stroked the silk of her short sleeve, which was also edged in lace. How could Mrs Julia bear to give away clothes as pretty as this?

There was a knock on the door and Harriet went to open it. 'Ah, Adam. I was beginning to worry that you'd got lost, you were so late back. Did you have a nice walk?'

'It was hot and dusty. It might be a smaller city than Alexandria, but the streets were just as crowded. It was good to get out, though, and—' He looked across at Ismay for the first time and gaped. 'You look . . . very nice tonight.'

She flushed. 'Thank you.'

As he continued to stare and Ismay's blush deepened, Aunt Harriet intervened, 'Did you see anything interesting on your walk, dear?'

'What? Oh, yes. You won't believe this, but I met the fellow who owns the other half of my schooner. It's my ship, the one that's anchored just off shore. I've invited him to join us for dinner tonight.'

'That'll be nice. What a lovely coincidence for you. Is it a sound modern ship?'

'It looks very trim, but I can't see it in detail. I'm going out to inspect it properly tomorrow.'

Ismay wasn't so sure about the stranger joining

them. It was one thing to practise her new manners in front of her two kind friends, but what if she made a fool of herself with the knives and forks in front of the stranger? That would embarrass them as well as her. She'd sneaked out of her room while Aunt Harriet was changing to walk as far as the front door of the hotel and on the way back had peeped into the dining room. It looked very fine, with white tablecloths and lots of knives and forks. 'Perhaps I should have my meal up here and leave you to talk to your new friend?'

Aunt Harriet looked at her shrewdly. 'There's nothing to be nervous of. Your table manners are perfectly acceptable.'

'But when I get to this Fremantle place, I'll have to look for a maid's job again. It won't look good to put myself forward.' She had to keep reminding herself of that. This life was like a dream, so comfortable was it. She wished it would go on for ever now that she was free to enjoy it. But it couldn't last. Good things never did.

They ignored her protests and escorted her down to the dining room, sitting on either side of her. She caught Adam glancing at her several times and wondered if her hair had come loose. Before she could ask Aunt Harriet, a tall man appeared in the doorway and scanned the room.

'There he is.' Adam stood up and raised one hand to attract the newcomer's attention; the man strode across to join them, a waiter scurrying behind him. He looking cramped by the narrow spaces and bumped into a chair, sending it sideways but catching it easily with one hand before it fell.

Something about him reassured Ismay. He didn't seem the sort of person to look down his nose at her. Even though he was taller than Adam, he had the same air of freedom about him. Perhaps it was being a sailor that did it.

She left it to the others to do most of the talking, but she listened carefully to what they were saying. For the moment, they had her future in their hands. For the moment, she was more than content to let them guide her.

Livia Southerham arrived in Fremantle one windy day, anxiety about her new position making her heart beat faster. Clouds were racing across the sky, as if they too were unsettled.

Reece Gregory, the neighbour who'd bought her farm, had driven her and her possessions up from the country in his cart. She'd become good friends with him and his wife Cassandra since the death of her husband, and neither would hear of her struggling up to Perth and on to Fremantle with all her luggage and furniture on a stranger's cart – a stranger who might or might not take good care of her.

When Conn Largan heard where they were going, he decided to accompany them on horseback. For all his love for his wife Maia and his little son, he grew restless at times, Livia knew.

He'd been waiting so long for final proof to come from Britain that his conviction had been quashed. Until it did, he was still treated as an ex-convict by most people and she wondered if the taint would ever leave him. There was such a big division between people who'd come here of their own free will and those who'd been transported. Even the children of ex-convicts were looked at askance. So unfair, Livia always thought.

Conn wanted to visit the Bazaar, of which he was part-owner, and discuss business with Bram, and Livia was looking forward to seeing it, too. Since coming to Australia nearly five years ago, she'd been living an isolated life in the country and had had to make do with the clothing she'd brought.

It had shocked her and Francis how unlike the English countryside it was – not only the look of the land itself, burnt and straw-coloured in summer; but also how hot those summers were. And the winters were so rainy; it was pounding rain that speared down and kept you penned indoors.

As for the lack of other people living nearby, that hurt most of all. There were no cosy villages with churches nearby to visit or stroll round; only one shop, half an hour's ride away from their farm, where you had to order most things apart from basic foodstuffs. As for concerts, lantern shows or lectures, she'd not been to a single one since her arrival here. She'd read and re-read the books she'd brought and was fretting for something more to feed her mind.

The trouble was, she didn't know what to expect or look for from the future. She couldn't see herself marrying again. She'd never been pretty, never attracted attention from men, except for dear Francis. It was terrifying sometimes to realise she was dependent on herself alone for her survival.

Orla, who had been her maid until now, had come to Fremantle with them, because unless Livia could find a way to offer her employment she'd have to find another job. Livia still felt guilty that she'd paid Orla such low wages for the past year. She'd been short of money because her husband had been hopeless at managing, and they'd not had much to start with.

She'd not been much better at managing herself at first, and had been very ignorant about the details of housekeeping. But necessity had made her learn to be more practical as Francis grew unwell, even though housewifery didn't come as naturally to her as it seemed to do to other women.

Since her husband's death she'd been terrified of spending a penny that wasn't necessary because he hadn't left her as much as she'd expected. And though she'd now got the money from selling the farm and horses, she had to find somewhere to live and some way of earning a living for the rest of her life. That thought was terrifying.

'I'd come with you,' Cassandra said as she got ready to leave, 'but the baby's too small yet to travel with comfortably, and Sofia would be getting into mischief. Two is a difficult age, old enough to run around, not old enough to have much sense.'

'She's a clever little girl, pretty too. Speaks so well for her age.'

Cassandra smiled down at her daughter, bending to give her a quick hug. 'Nonetheless, we'll stay here. Leo will keep an eye on us and the animals. He's settled in so well here now.'

'He's a dear fellow.'

Leo was slow-witted, but was a positive genius with animals. His stepfather had sent him to Australia to get rid of him, but he'd settled down with Reece and Cassandra, who would probably look after him for life.

Reece was bringing some of the cheese he and Cassandra had started making, to see if people would like to buy it regularly. Livia had been invited to test it as they experimented. She thought it very tasty now, though it did go off more quickly in the hotter weather than it would have done in England. 'I think your cheese will do well. The last batch you made is the best yet.'

'The cellar we built into the hillside keeps it nice and cool,' Cassandra said with satisfaction. She laughed. 'Who'd have thought that someone like me, who grew up in a mill town in Lancashire, would so enjoy being a farmer's wife?'

Silence fell and lingered. It was hard for the two women to say goodbye to one another. They'd been so close and now Cassandra would be left without a woman friend, and was an hour's drive away from her sister.

Life was hard, Livia had decided. Very hard. Some people might find things easy, but she never had and she knew Cassandra hadn't either.

They arrived in Fremantle the following day, having camped overnight by the roadside, something Reece was used to now, though the two women found it more difficult. The roads in this part of the colony had been improved over recent years by convict labour, but were still only rough tracks that twisted and turned as they detoured round large trees or other obstacles.

'How lovely to see so many people!' Orla said as they entered Fremantle.

Livia nodded, suddenly feeling sure she was doing the right thing in moving, even though it'd been a wrench to leave her husband's grave behind.

Flora was supposed to be waiting for them at her house, so that they could leave Livia's furniture there and then let her introduce Livia to her mother since they couldn't wait for Dougal's return. But the maid who came to the door gave them the news that Miss McBride had been summoned urgently to her mother's house.

'Is Mrs McBride not well?' Livia asked.

'She's . . . um, a little upset.'

Conn rolled his eyes. 'I'd guess that dreadful woman's been making one of her fusses over nothing. She's led poor Flora a dog's life in recent years. Let's drive across and see if we can help. Surely your arrival will distract her? We can unload these things later. It's not far away.'

They arrived to find the modest wooden house in uproar. Rhoda, the strong woman who helped control Flora's mother, came to the door, glancing over her shoulder.

'I'm sorry we're in a mess, Mr Largan, but that flibbertigibbet of a maid has just packed her bags and left. She says she's not coming back, however much Miss McBride pays her.'

'Why did she do that?'

'The old lady attacked her. But the maid wasn't hurt apart from a couple of slaps. I think she was looking for an excuse to give notice. She's met a young man and is going to marry him. Well, she'll soon find out what hard work is,' she boomed in her cheerful loud voice. 'It's not easy looking after a husband, especially when the children start coming.'

She still hadn't moved back to let them inside, but Miss Gunson came hurrying out to join them at that moment. 'Take the water in to Mrs McBride, Rhoda. I'll deal with our visitors. Do come inside out of the sun, Mr Largan.'

He introduced his companions quickly.

Miss Gunson beamed at Livia. 'I'm so glad to

meet you, Mrs Southerham. I'm afraid Mrs McBride is in a very agitated mood today.' She lowered her voice. 'She's getting harder to manage. She overturned the tea tray this morning on purpose and broke the best teapot, just because the tray wasn't set to her liking. Then she attacked the maid.'

At that moment Flora came to the door of the sitting room, pausing for a moment with a look of relief. 'I'm so glad to see you, Mrs Southerham. Conn and Reece, too.'

An old woman with her hair straggling down and her face twisted with anger came up behind her and shoved her daughter out of the way. 'What are you all whispering about?' She glared at her daughter then looked across at Livia. 'Is that my new companion? Well, thank goodness for that. If *you* can't do your duty and look after your poor old mother in her old age, Flora McBride, you can just stay away from me. But I'm not having that maid back. She was a slut. Not the right sort of maid for a lady of my station. And who are these other people?'

Flora looked at her mother in shock. She ought to know who Conn was, because she'd met him several times, and she'd met Reece too, though not as often.

Livia had been watching them with a sinking heart. Mrs McBride was going to be even harder to look after than she'd expected when she took the position. The old woman looked as if she'd just woken from a nightmare and thrown her clothes on anyhow, but her accent was that of a lady.

Flora introduced Livia properly and she at once moved forward, holding out her hand, hoping to make a good impression. She'd been told that genteel manners mattered to her charge.

Mrs McBride shook it and studied her. 'Well, at least *you* look like a lady, not a scraggy mouse.' She cast a look of dislike at poor Miss Gunson.

'I should hope I do,' Livia said cheerfully. 'My late father was a parson, after all.'

Mrs McBride brightened a little. 'Well, that's very nice to hear. Parsons are always respectable. Do come in, my dear Mrs Southerham. Are you a widow, did they say?'

'Sadly, yes.'

'So am I. We shall have that in common at least. And your husband was a gentleman, too?'

Livia didn't usually boast, but for the sake of her future peace, she said airily, 'He was one of the Southerhams of Outham. His family has an estate in Lancashire, but he was a younger son.'

Mrs McBride seized her arm and pulled her back into the room, calling, 'We'd like some tea,' over her shoulder.

Once they were inside the room, Flora sagged against the wall for a moment in sheer relief that her mother's new companion hadn't run away at the sight of her in one of her moods. 'I think my mother's taken to Mrs Southerham. For the time being, at least. But what am I going to do about finding another maid? They're very scarce.'

Orla stepped forward. 'I can do the job, Miss McBride and I'm looking for another position. How much would you be offering as wages?'

'Since it's not always an easy job, I'm offering a higher wage than usual.'

Orla beamed at the amount named. 'You can ask Mrs Southerham what I'm like. She said she'd be giving me references. It'll be wonderful to stay with her.'

At the sight of Orla's pleasure, not to mention Flora's relief, Conn winked at Reece. 'Come on. I think things are going to settle down again now. Flora, we'll go and fetch the ladies' luggage, then take Livia's furniture up to your attic.'

'I'll wait for you in the kitchen, ma'am,' Orla said, moving towards the only door at the back of the hall.

'Your bedroom is just off the kitchen. You can't miss it.'

'I'll show her where things are and help get a tea tray.' Ann Gunson stepped forward.

Flora showed the men where to put Livia's luggage. 'When Miss Gunson moves out, Mrs Southerham can take over the front bedroom, but I think she'll be comfortable enough here in the meantime.' She threw an irritated look in the direction of the sitting room, whose door was still open showing the two ladies sitting opposite one another. 'My mother's not stopped talking since she sat down, though she loses track regularly and moves on to something else. Mrs Southerham just smiles at her and nods. I hope she has a lot of patience.'

'Livia's glad to be earning money while she looks for somewhere to live, and this job won't go on for ever, will it?' Conn said gently, not offering false hope.

'No. The doctor's explained it all. In the end my mother will refuse to eat or drink or speak.' Flora's voice thickened as she spoke. 'I don't feel any affection for her after what she's done to me, but I wouldn't wish this terrible affliction on anyone.' She took out her handkerchief and blew her nose.

'Shall we take Mrs Southerham's furniture round to store at your house now, or do you need our help here?' Conn asked.

'I'll be fine. Linny will show you where to put the furniture. I'd better go through Orla's duties with her. Rhoda's gone out shopping. She'll be back soon, then she can help Orla find her way around the kitchen.'

The two men looked at one another as they walked out to the cart. 'Poor woman!' Conn said.

'Flora or her mother?'

'Both. Probably Livia as well, now. She's taken on a difficult job, but at least it pays well. Come on, let's get rid of this furniture, then we can go and talk to Bram. That'll cheer us up. I can see the Bazaar from here and it looks even more splendid than last time. I'm eager to go inside and see what else he's done.'

Bram went to stand at the doorway of the Bazaar, watching people pass by in the street, a hundred yards away down the slope. It was his favourite way of relaxing in quiet moments and, as an added treat, he sometimes strolled down to see his wife and son in their little house, which was down near the livery stables.

He saw Conn and Reece turn into the yard of the livery stables in their cart and hurried down the slope, beaming at them. 'Welcome, welcome! Did you have a good journey, then?'

Conn swung down and clasped his friend's hand. 'No problems at all. We're hoping you can put us up for the night.'

'I certainly can. In fact . . .' He hesitated, then shared his thoughts in his usual breathless rush of words, 'I was wondering whether to build on simple lodgings at the side of the stables. Not for ladies, you understand, but for men on their own who want to stable their horses and leave early next morning. What do you think?'

Conn grinned at him. 'I think I never come to see you but you offer me another idea for making money. Mind you, that sounds to be a good one, as long as you keep it simple.' He looked beyond Bram. 'Isabella! You look to be blooming.' He strode across to kiss her cheek and then admire little Arlen.

'No news about your status?' she asked softly, for his ears alone.

'Not yet. Why they have to take so long to inform me officially that I didn't commit a crime, when it's already been decided, I don't understand.' He took a deep breath. 'But we won't let that spoil our evening, will we?'

10

The next morning Adam went out to the ship with Joss, who was supervising the loading of the new cargo. Trying to hide his excitement, he followed the other man around, looking at everything and listening carefully to how Joss spoke about the ship. He obviously cared about the *Hannah*, speaking of her affectionately, as if she were a living creature.

The two of them had a lot in common, both young still and making their way in the world. Adam hoped they would become good friends. Joss was only a little further ahead in this sort of life than he was: owning his first vessel, proud of it, wanting to make a success of it all. But Adam wasn't minded to lose his most important asset, so he intended to make certain they didn't put out to sea again without insurance.

When they came back on deck after visiting every corner, from the bilge to the cook's rather cramped domain, he glanced sideways and found Joss doing the same, as if trying to assess his reactions. Suddenly Adam's sense of the ridiculous took over and he let out a crack of laughter.

'Let's stop eyeing one another up and down like a pair of dogs about to fight, and give our partnership a really good try. You keep a tidy ship and I like the way you speak to your men.' He held out his hand and they shook to cement a step forward in their relationship. If men could laugh together, they could usually work together, he thought with satisfaction.

'So you'll be coming on board as first mate for this voyage?'

'Only if we can take my aunt and Ismay to Singapore with us. Oh, and I'm hoping you've insured the vessel this time.'

Joss shuddered. 'I most certainly have. I'll not make the same mistake twice; not gamble on my only asset by not insuring it. I'd not have done it at all if I hadn't been . . . upset about something else.' He frowned. 'I'm not used to carrying lady passengers, though, and don't have any fancy facilities, let alone a stewardess. Would they not do better to wait for the next P&O steamer? They'd be much more comfortable on that.'

'I don't care to leave my aunt to travel on her own. It's her first time overseas, you see, and she's come specially to be with me. And Ismay grew up in a small village in Ireland, so she knows even less about travelling.'

'She's a strange friend for your aunt to have.'

'She was a maid before she left Ireland, as must be fairly obvious. On the ship, she looked after my aunt, who was very seasick in the Bay of Biscay, and has stayed with her ever since. She's a good lass and a hard worker.'

'She's pretty, too.' But Joss said it absently, not as someone who was attracted to her.

Adam was relieved about that. He was still puzzling out how he thought of Ismay; hadn't expected to be so attracted to any woman, let alone a former maid. But she was so bright and cheerful, such a pleasure to be with.

And his father's will had specified that he was to marry within the year. He'd signed a promise to do this. The promise he'd made mattered much more to him than his father's wishes or the piece of paper. He didn't give his word lightly.

Would Ismay make a good wife? How did you know? Or did you just follow your instinct. He smiled wryly as he added mentally, and your desires.

Would she even want to marry after what she'd experienced? And if she did, would she want a rather serious fellow like him?

But at least she'd get on with his aunt if they all lived together, and that was very important indeed.

So many questions in his life at the moment. He brought his attention back firmly to the present. The answers would come in time, as fate willed.

When Joss moved away from him, it seemed to Adam that his companion had moved both physically and mentally, going to lean on the rail, with his back turned.

As he stared out to sea, Joss said quietly, 'Just so that you know what upset me and made me take foolish decisions, I'm a widower. I lost my wife and our unborn child last year.'

'I'm sorry.' That explained the sadness.

He sighed and stared at the horizon.

'Men talk when they sail together,' Adam said quietly. And other men often confided in him, he didn't know why. He tried to help them when he could, because he knew what it was like to need help.

Joss nodded and changed the subject firmly. 'You're sure your aunt and Mrs Hope will want to detour to Singapore?'

'I'm sure of nothing at the moment, except that I want to sail on this ship and get to know her. I think they'll be happy to join us. When exactly do you plan to leave?'

'The sooner the better. We should finish loading the rest of the cargo late this evening. If you're joining the crew, we could set off tomorrow with the first tide. That'd mean you coming on board this evening.' His eyes went back to the men carrying bundles down into the hold. 'Strong chaps, those, but I'd better go and check how things are stowed, given my first mate's defection.'

'I'll go and look over the cabins again, then go and check that my aunt and Ismay will be happy to come with us. I'll send a note to the ship as soon as I've spoken to them.'

Joss nodded and hurried away, not waiting to

see him off the ship into the small boat that had been patiently waiting alongside.

Once ashore, Adam stopped and looked across the water, smiling proudly. His own ship – well forty-nine per cent of it was his – and a fine vessel it was too. This was a big chance to make something of himself, bastard son or not. He wondered what his father had expected. Success or failure? Both were possible, however hard he worked. He could lose everything, his life included. The sea was a harsh mistress. But if he failed, it'd not be for lack of hard work and effort.

He liked what he'd seen of Joss Rutherford, felt comfortable with him. Big fellow, must be over six foot tall, with light-coloured hair, greying at the temples. He had a rather solemn expression most of the time. They'd get to know each other better at sea, as men usually did, because there would be times when their lives depended on one another, as well as their livelihoods.

The crew seemed decent enough: some Australian, some darker-skinned lascars. He couldn't imagine Joss Rutherford employing vicious men or ill-treating them, any more than Adam himself would have done.

He just hoped his aunt and Ismay would fit in on board. You could never tell with women. He knew some who sailed with husbands and had the whole crew devoted to them, others who rarely saw their husbands and didn't seem bothered about being left behind.

If he ever married, he'd not want his wife sailing with him. He was quite sure of that. It'd add another layer of anxiety. Besides, he wanted children, three or four of them, and wanted them brought up in a loving home where they felt secure.

With a part-share in the *Hannah*, he could afford to marry. He didn't need his father prodding him into it. Apart from anything else, his body had its own needs.

Was it just them being together that had made him think of Ismay, or was she the woman for him? He could imagine her as a mother. She'd been good with the children on the first ship.

How could you be sure, though, about marrying? It was such a big step to take.

Ismay stared around wide-eyed as the boat was rowed out to the ship. She rather liked the rocking movement and it felt a little cooler on the water, but she was glad the sea was calm. Aunt Harriet gestured to her to go first, so she climbed up the rope netting that had been let down the side of the ship. It was fun, reminded her of climbing trees as a little child – and being smacked for it.

At the top, Adam stood waiting to help her on to the deck. 'Are you all right?'

She laughed aloud for sheer pleasure at this adventure. 'I enjoyed climbing up.'

But when she turned, she saw Aunt Harriet moving very slowly up the net, her face pale and anxious, her hands clamped round the knots in the netting so tightly that her knuckles showed white, even from here, whenever she stopped for a moment.

'I should have noticed,' Adam muttered and clambered nimbly down, staying beside his aunt and encouraging her as she managed the last few feet on to the deck.

After that he hugged her close. 'Well done, love. I know it wasn't easy for you, but you won't have to do that again in Singapore. Joss says there's a proper harbour there.'

She gave them a shaky smile. 'I never did like heights.'

Ismay went to give her a hug as well. 'I'm sorry. I should have come up more slowly and helped you.'

'You weren't to know, and anyway, you're a bit small to hold me if I'm falling.'

Ismay looked down at herself and grimaced. 'I've always wished I was taller.'

'You are what you are. Worry about things you can change, not things you can't.' Harriet looked beyond her nephew to Joss. 'Well, here we are, Captain Rutherford.'

He moved forward, hand outstretched. 'Welcome on board, ma'am. We've given you and Mrs Hope a cabin each. We have no other passengers this trip, so it'll be very quiet, I'm afraid. I do have a few books you may enjoy.'

Ismay's face lit up. 'I love reading.'

Adam, watching her, was delighted to see that

she'd regained her former sparkling joy in life. He
knew his aunt enjoyed her cheerfulness and he did
too. Somehow Ismay made everything seem bright
and full of hope. That she could do so with her
background spoke wonders for her resilience.

The ladies settled quickly into their cabins, then
came back up on deck to find Joss looking furiously angry.

'Is something wrong?' Harriet whispered to her
nephew.

'The cook hasn't turned up.'

Joss pulled out his watch again, then snapped
the lid shut and came across to join them. 'I'm
afraid I'll have to set off without the cook, ladies.
We do have a fellow who helps him, and he makes
good bread, but I'm afraid the meals won't be very
palatable because Dan's still learning to cook.'

Harriet's face lit up. 'Then let me help him. I'm
a good cook.'

He stared at her in shock. 'I can't ask a lady like
you to do that. It's hard work feeding the whole
crew, and in uncomfortable conditions.'

'You didn't ask, I offered. I'll enjoy it, because
I don't like being idle.'

Ismay ranged herself next to Aunt Harriet. 'I'd
like to help too. I don't know much about cooking,
but I can do what I'm told.'

Joss pulled out his watch again, stared at the
shore, then spread his hands in a gesture of helplessness. 'Then all I can say is, I'm grateful and I
accept your offer. Danny will make the bread and

do any heavy lifting, as well as the clearing up. If you can teach him to cook a few simple things, he'll take over gradually. I'll also assign a lad to help you.'

He hesitated, then added, 'I'd better explain: Danny's too old to run the rigging up and down or go aloft now, but he's been with this ship for years, since well before I bought it, so I don't like to dismiss him.' He looked at Adam, as if challenging him to object.

'I'd not dismiss him, either, as long as he can do something to earn his keep.'

The two men nodded at one another, then Joss bellowed, 'Tell Danny he's wanted!'

The man who came up on deck was scrawny and suntanned after years in the tropics, with sparse hair and a mouth lacking many teeth. He smiled and nodded at the ladies when his captain explained the situation. 'I'll do my best, Mrs Seaton. I like cooking.'

Joss left the old man to show them the galley in more detail and discuss meals, then went to supervise the ship's departure.

With Bram and Conn both promising to keep an eye on Mrs McBride, Flora allowed herself to be persuaded to go to Singapore with her brother Dougal. She felt guilty and yet enormously relieved as she walked on to the ship. It was as though she'd left all her troubles behind for the first time in many years.

Dougal greeted her with a hug. She was a tall woman, but he was taller, and here on the ship, he seemed a much more impressive figure than the loving brother at home. The men jumped to obey him, his officers spoke respectfully to him, and he gave the impression of someone who was aware of every puff of air that twitched the edges of the still-furled sails.

She went down to her cabin and it felt more cramped than she'd expected, though it was the biggest one, apart from the captain's. Her cabin trunk was there already, fixed to the wall. When opened, it was like a chest of drawers on one side, so there was nothing to unpack. Her books and writing materials would be safe in the box they'd come aboard in, which was also fastened in place.

She sat on the bed, wondering what to do with herself till they sailed. She'd be in the way if she went back on deck, but she didn't feel like reading a book, so she leaned back and let her thoughts drift where they would.

Was she doing the right thing in leaving Fremantle for this holiday? There was still time to go back.

No, she couldn't face the embarrassment of that and, anyway, she'd been leading a very unsettled life for the past few months. She was only going away for a few weeks and it'd do her good to get away from all her troubles.

Wouldn't it?

Or would it make her quiet life in Fremantle

seem even quieter once she got back? Her former ambition to run a lodging house for the better class of person seemed unappealing now, but what else was an unmarried woman of her age to do? She didn't have an income of her own to live on.

She knew she could find herself a husband if she wanted. Indeed, she'd had a proposal of marriage recently. Perhaps she should have accepted Mitchell Nash's offer? No. He was a friend, and a good one, but she wasn't drawn to him in that way.

When you'd once tasted the heady brew of love, it spoiled you for anything less. Her mother had interfered in that and driven away the man Flora loved. She'd never heard from him again.

After this voyage she had to find something interesting to do with her life. Keeping house for her brother Dougal wasn't enough.

'I'll be sorry when we get to Galle,' Ismay said a week later. 'I've enjoyed helping in the galley. It isn't only Danny who's learned a lot about cooking from you, Aunt Harriet.'

'Didn't your mother teach you to cook?'

'There wasn't much cooking to be done. We lived mostly on boiled potatoes and cabbage. If there was an egg or bit of meat, Da got most of it and Ma had a mouthful or two, but that wasn't often. Bram ate well when he went to work at the big house as a groom, and sometimes he brought us children leftovers from the kitchen. He was a good brother, Bram, always thinking of us. We had some hard times when he got sent away.'

'Then I'm glad I can help you learn. But I'll tell you a secret: fond as I am of cooking, I don't enjoy baking bread. I'm so glad Danny has a knack for that. I always used to buy mine from the baker's.'

Judging by the thanks they received from the sailors, not to mention Joss, the ladies' cooking efforts were greatly appreciated.

'I'm glad Sim didn't come back on board,' Danny said one day. 'He wasn't near as good a cook as you, ma'am.'

'You'll be a good cook yourself by the time I'm finished with you,' Aunt Harriet said. 'You have the touch.'

He beamed at her. 'Do you really think so?'

'I'm certain.'

'I'm grateful. That should get me a berth on the *Hannah* for a few more years. It's the only real home I've ever had. When I can't work, I'll have to go into the poorhouse, I suppose. I'd rather die on the job, though. The sea's in my blood now. But you never know what will happen to you when you get old.'

She sighed. 'No. You don't.'

As the days passed, Danny gradually took over most of the cooking, not managing to hide his pride in having a lad as an assistant. Aunt Harriet still supervised everything, and occasionally made cakes or other treats, because they had some live fowls in cages on the deck to give them fresh eggs and meat, as a change from the usual sailors' fare of salt beef and ham. The fowls were scrawny things, though, producing only small eggs.

Once they had some free time, the two ladies sat and read or sewed under an awning on deck, which also protected them from the almost daily tropical downpours.

Joss continued to be friendly, but distant. Adam said he was a good sailor and knew these waters, which could be dangerous at other times of year.

'That young man's sad underneath,' Harriet said quietly one day. 'It's as if he's been sad for a long time.'

'It was lucky you met him that day, Adam, wasn't it?' Ismay said. 'Otherwise we'd still be in Suez.'

'Fate must have been on my side, for once, sending the *Hannah* there. I shall be interested to find out what the three houses I've been left in Fremantle are like. I'm sure there will be surprises there, too. My father wasn't . . . generous.'

Adam felt a gentle touch and looked down to see that Ismay had laid one hand on his.

'We've both been unlucky in our fathers, haven't we?'

He turned his hand to clasp hers. 'But not in our friends.' It was as if something tingled between them, some invisible link that kept tightening, drawing them closer together. He could see she felt it too.

It was a few moments before he realised he was

still holding her hand and let go of it. This wasn't
setting a good example to the men.

And he shouldn't lead her on unless he felt
certain they had a future together.

As if he could help enjoying her company,
seeking her out! She drew him like a moth to a
flame.

Ismay tried not to let her disappointment show
when Adam let go of her hand and changed the
subject abruptly. She'd liked holding his hand. It
felt . . . right. Oh, she was a fool!

'Joss and I think it only fair that you receive
some wages for all the hard work you've done,' he
told her.

She shook her head. 'I won't take anything.
Helping out is a small return for what you and
your aunt have done for me.'

Aunt Harriet had come across to join them in
time to hear this. 'You'd better not offer me money,
either. We're both happy to have something to do.
Anyway, Danny has more or less taken over the
cooking now. I just help him here and there. I'm
still showing him and Ismay how to bake cakes
and puddings.'

'What am I to do with the pair of you? Such
stubborn women.'

Ismay looked away from his dear, laughing face,
afraid of betraying her feelings, but she saw that
Aunt Harriet had noticed her reaction to Adam
and hoped it wouldn't make her angry.

To her surprise, the older woman said nothing at all about it.

All too soon they reached Galle, which was very beautiful when approached from the sea. It stood on a rocky promontory, with a fort overlooking the harbour to guard it, and behind the town some low hills. It looked wonderfully green and fertile after the desert near Suez.

Two of the largest buildings in the town were an old church and a mosque. Joss spared a moment to explain what a mosque was, because neither Ismay nor Aunt Harriet had even heard the word before.

A P&O steamer with a funnel and three masts was coaling nearby, and for a few moments Ismay watched it nervously, afraid Rory might be on it, afraid he might see her.

Adam stopped beside her. 'What's the matter?'

When she confessed her fears, he explained that this steamer was a different one, on its way to England, not Australia, and she let out a long, shuddering sigh of relief. She couldn't quite shake off her dread of meeting Rory again in Australia. He was known to be pig-headed when he wanted something, and he'd always wanted her.

Since both ladies again spurned the idea of waiting there for a P&O ship to Australia, they spent only a few hours at Galle. There was enough time for them to take a pleasant stroll round the town, in the care of a guide Joss found for them, who had shown him round before.

Danny went with another guide to buy more fresh food from a list Aunt Harriet had helped him make. He wasn't a good reader, but he'd perused the list earnestly, repeating the words several times as he tapped each of them with his forefinger.

The guide explained to the ladies in fractured English, which sometimes made them hide a smile, how many big ships now stopped to coal here. He seemed very proud of that.

Joss and his crew had brought a small consignment of goods to Galle and, once the boxes had been unloaded, Joss introduced Adam to an agent he was dealing with. He was glad to pick up some small batches of cargo bound for Singapore, but the main load was for one man.

'We'll leave at daybreak tomorrow,' he told the ladies as they ate their evening meal together, enjoying the tropical fruits that only Joss had ever tasted before.

Ismay closed her eyes in ecstasy as she tried an orangey-yellow fruit. 'Mangoes must be the most delicious things in the whole world.'

'You said that about dates,' Adam teased.

'Well, I've changed my mind. Mangoes are better.'

'What about bananas?'

She licked some juice from the corner of her mouth and laughed at him. 'I give up. They're all equally good, so they are.'

'Is it likely to be stormy in this region?' Aunt Harriet asked once the meal had ended.

'We should be all right at this time of year,' Joss said in his usual quiet way. 'It can be treacherous at other times, given the prevailing winds. I avoid the area then. If I had a ship with a steam engine, it'd be different. We'll be going across the Bay of Bengal, then the Andaman Sea and finally down through the Strait of Malacca to Singapore.'

'Such exotic names!' Ismay's eyes were aglow with excitement. 'I can't wait to see Singapore. Can you show me on the map where we are each day?'

'Of course.' Joss smiled at her enthusiasm but soon fell quiet again, and it was left to Adam to carry on the conversation, explaining how maps at sea were always called charts.

Time passed slowly in steerage for Rory. He'd rather have worked his passage, not only because it would have saved him paying out good money to sit around doing nothing, but also because it'd have filled the time.

Out of sheer boredom, he joined a reading class. He'd learned to read at school – well, more or less – but hadn't been interested, because it didn't help you earn a living in Shilmara, but he reckoned a bit of extra learning might come in useful in a strange country. It was years since he'd even looked at a book because there were so few of them in the village.

The man teaching them reading was also offering a course in simple accounting and he was letting women attend this, which annoyed Rory. What use were such things to females? Their place was in the home. When he incautiously said as much one day, everyone looked at him as if he was a pile of dung. He scowled back defiantly.

As everyone left, the teacher called him back. Rory stood quietly. This man might be a fool, but he was giving up his time to teach them, and for nothing, so it was only fair to be polite to him, even if he did have some stupid ideas.

'Mr Flynn, I'd be grateful if you'd keep your views about a woman's place to yourself in my classes from now on.'

Rory breathed deeply.

'I can assure you that in my experience some women are better than men at figures.'

Rory's disbelief must have shown on his face, because the man smiled. 'I promise you, it's true.'

'Even if they are, who's going to look after their husbands or raise their children if they go out to work.'

'What about widows? What about those who aren't married? What about those whose husbands need their help with the accounts for the family shop?'

Rory didn't know what to say to that, because he had never thought of women as anything but wives and daughters before. So he said nothing.

'Shall you be coming back to the next class, Mr Flynn?'

It was the polite form of address that settled it

for Rory. No one had ever called him Mr Flynn before, in the quiet respectful tone. 'Yes. If you don't mind, sir.'

'As long as you're polite to the women, you're welcome.'

Rory went to stand by the rail and stare out across the ocean. Stupid ideas some people had! But it was either go to the class, or stand here and stare at nothing but water all day long.

He wondered where Ismay was. She was bound to come to the Swan River Colony some time, because her brother was there and Rory had found out that she hadn't been able to get her luggage off the ship. Sean Deagan kept boasting that their Bram was doing well for himself there, making a lot of money. If he could do it, so could Rory. By hell he'd give it a good go, at least!

And when Ismay did arrive in Australia, Rory would be waiting for her. He wasn't letting her get away from him and he'd be raising his own child, thank you very much. He'd not be leaving it to a woman to spoil and pet his sons.

But it was taking a hell of a long time to get to Australia, and they said there were still a couple of weeks to go.

And they didn't arrive in Australia near this Fremantle place, oh no, but somewhere on the south coast called Albany, so they had to get on another smaller coastal steamer to travel up to Fremantle.

He hadn't realised how far away Australia was;

hadn't had even the faintest idea of that when he set out. Or how big it was.

He'd better look at one of those damned maps again and fix it in his mind where Fremantle was, because whatever happened, he'd not be going back to Ireland. Even on this ship he was eating and feeling better than he had in his whole life before.

For the first time, he wondered what he'd do if he didn't find Ismay and make her marry him. Marry some other woman?

No. He was going to marry her. He'd always been going to marry her, because she was the prettiest girl in the village.

But he still couldn't help looking at the other women on the ship. They might not be as pretty as Ismay, but they weren't a bad lot. They didn't look half-starved, as many of the village girls did back in Ireland. Well, a few had when they got on the first ship, but they'd soon fattened up, because there was as much food as you could eat.

He'd never had thoughts like this in the whole of his life before.

It just showed what travel did for you. Made you think.

He wasn't sure that was always a good thing, but it was too late to change things now.

No storms chased the *Hannah Grey* across the ocean on this trip, though there were a couple of windy days that made Aunt Harriet turn pale and refuse anything but dry toast and cups of tea.

'Another two or three days should get us there,' Joss told them over dinner one evening. 'Then you ladies can enjoy your visit to a fascinating city. I'm certain the ladies who live there permanently will make you welcome, Mrs Seaton. They're very kind to visitors and newcomers.'

'They'll not welcome me,' Ismay said bluntly.

'Perhaps not, but their maids will. Or we can hire a guide to take you sightseeing.'

'I would like to see the city,' she said wistfully. 'It sounds so interesting.'

Aunt Harriet cleared her throat. 'I'd rather go sightseeing with Ismay, to tell you the truth. I'm not exactly a lady myself, as they'll soon find out. My father was a shopkeeper, and it was just a small shop, a haberdasher's.'

Adam looked at her in surprise. 'You never said that before.'

'What did it matter? He died when I was twenty and the shop was failing for a couple of years before that. But I was married to my Herbert by then, thank goodness, and we'd moved to Liverpool. My mother died a year later and I lost touch with my cousins when they moved away.'

'My brother calls his shop in Australia a bazaar. I don't know the difference. Have you ever visited it, Captain? It's in Fremantle. Deagan's Bazaar.'

'I've heard about it. It's very popular and quite a big place. But I was too busy visiting the banks in Perth, trying to raise money for repairs to my ship to bother with shopping.'

He had that grim look on his face, which he got whenever she mentioned Fremantle. It must have bad memories for him; or perhaps he didn't like the town – except that he'd settled there now. Most people seemed to have secrets, as she had herself.

But there was no need now to pretend to be married. She'd ask Aunt Harriet if she could take her real name back. If anyone asked, she could say it had been thought safer for her to travel as a married woman.

She was looking forward to seeing Bram and his shop. And to seeing an oriental city. She had so many things to look forward to now.

11

When Singapore showed on the horizon, Adam pointed it out as a darker smudge ahead of them. They'd been sailing past land all day, but this was different. They were going to stop here.

Ismay was so thrilled to be going to another new country, she stayed on deck all day watching. As they drew closer to their destination, she was surprised to see large junks – such a strange name for a sailing ship – sailing along in the same direction as them or coming away from Singapore.

Aunt Harriet sat in the shade, declining to join her at the rail because of the heat. 'You'll turn brown as a berry if you spend so much time in the sun,' she called out after a while. 'Or bright red, which is worse.'

With a sigh, Ismay joined her and sat fidgeting with her sewing. She was getting better at it, but still didn't enjoy the activity, even though she could see the need to learn it. She couldn't settle, though, and when her companion dozed off, she went to lean against the rail again.

They were to berth in the New Harbour, Joss

said. As they got to Singapore and moved towards it, the water was so crowded with boats, large and small, Ismay wondered how anyone ever found their way around. She didn't know which way to look first, fascinated not so much by the various craft as by the people on them and their exotic cargoes: their darker or yellowish skins, their slanting eyes and different clothing. She wondered if they were fascinated by the differences they saw in Europeans. That was another new word that Joss had taught her: what the locals called people from Britain and Europe.

The second mate paused for a moment beside her. 'Many families live completely on the water. Look, you can see their cooking facilities, their washing hanging up to dry and their children playing.'

'Aren't they afraid of the children falling overboard?'

He laughed. 'You'd have to ask them. I've never spoken to any of them.'

She watched nervously as the ship eased into place gradually and tied up at the dock. How clever Joss was to edge the *Hannah* into place so neatly!

He was very much the captain now, yelling to his second mate to send that message to the owner of the cargo at once. He seemed to be watching everything, tossing out orders, and Adam was the same. Ropes were coiled, sails furled, the deck made tidy as always.

Officials came on board briefly, then gave permission for the unloading.

'Where does the cargo go now?' Ismay asked as Joss paused for a moment nearby after seeing the officials off his ship.

'To the godowns – that's the word for warehouses. Most of our cargo is for a man called Lee Kar Ho. They say their surname first, so we call him Mr Lee. I don't know whether he'll come down to the quay in person or send one of his clerks. I've not met him before.'

An hour later, Ismay watched in fascination as a Chinese man, taller than most of the others, came towards the *Hannah* and stopped beside it. From the way people moved out of his path, she knew he must be an important person.

'Mr Lee?' Joss called down.

The man bowed.

Joss went hurrying down the gangway to greet him. He'd already told the others that a man who sent for large cargoes like this was worth getting to know.

There was much bowing of the head by both gentlemen in turn, then Adam was summoned to join them.

She wished she could hear what they were saying.

'It's rude to stare,' Aunt Harriet said. 'Do come away from the rail.'

'I can't help staring. Everything is so interesting.' For the first time Ismay didn't do as she was told. She didn't want to miss a single thing.

A man walked past the ship selling something to eat, which he carried on a tray slung round his neck. Some of the workers crowded round him, taking away their purchases wrapped in big leaves. She wished she could taste whatever it was, because it smelled delicious.

Another man passed by, sitting in a sort of wheeled chair with handles, pulled by a scrawny man with bare, muscular legs.

'That's called a rickshaw, miss,' one of the sailors said as he walked past. 'People hire them to get around in, like cabs.'

'Rickshaw,' she mouthed. Another new word to learn.

Adam bowed his head when introduced to the Chinese man, having seen Joss do the same thing, but he couldn't help feeling silly, because he knew Ismay was watching him from the ship.

'Do you speak English, sir?' Joss asked. 'Or do we need an interpreter?'

Mr Lee gave them a gentle smile. 'I learn English many year now, do my humble best.' His expression was anything but humble and his clothing said he was a wealthy man, as did the presence of two strong men waiting patiently a few paces behind him, arms folded.

'Your cargo is in the hold, sir, ready to be unloaded.' Joss held out a piece of paper, holding it with both hands. 'This is from your agent in

Suez. We can find some coolies to unload it, if you'll tell us where to send it.'

Mr Lee studied the paper, clearly able to read as well as speak English. 'I send my own coolies.'

When he lifted a finger, a third man stepped forward. After one short command, he bowed and ran off.

'Would you like to come on board ship and wait while they unload?' Adam asked. 'We could offer you a cup of tea.'

Mr Lee inclined his head. 'Thank you but no. Another time, perhaps. Came to see this ship, see cargo arrive safely.'

'There's been no tampering with your goods on the way here, sir,' Joss said at once.

Another bow was the only comment on that. Clearly Mr Lee was taking nothing for granted. 'Your ship come to Singapore before, Captain. I hear of all ships trading here from Australia. You go back to Sydney after?'

'No, I'm sailing out of Fremantle for the present.'

'Ah. I have much trade with Fremantle. Maybe give you new cargo.'

'I'm looking for one.'

The man who had run to fetch coolies came and waited for his master's attention. Behind him, muscular men wearing knee-length breeches were waiting on the quay.

'We speak another time. Unload cargo now.' With a bow to each of them, Mr Lee walked away, followed by the two servants – or were they bodyguards?

'He seems an important man,' Adam said in a low voice.

'I'll make enquiries about him.'

'He has an air of command. You can't mistake it.'

'And he speaks English better than most people here, too.'

Joss and Adam left the ship, promising to take Ismay to explore the city the following day.

Aunt Harriet went to her cabin to take her usual afternoon nap, saying she'd slept badly last night. 'Stay on deck, don't go on the quay,' she said in parting.

Ismay fidgeted about. There was much less to watch because suddenly the sky had clouded over and it began to rain hard. She was bored and didn't want to go to her cabin. In fact, she was just about bursting with unspent energy, now that she'd recovered her health and lost her worries.

Once the rain had passed, she was down at the foot of the gangway before she'd come to a conscious decision to disobey Aunt Harriet. The sailor on duty asked, 'Are you all right, ma'am?'

'Yes. I'll just walk up and down the quay to stretch my legs.'

He looked as if he wanted to stop her, so she set off without giving him the chance.

She meant to do no more than walk about a little, but there was a narrow street full of the most fascinating shops. She looked down it with a sigh, then glanced back at the ship. She'd just walk a little way along the street. She'd only be out of sight for a few minutes.

And oh, the goods for sale were so interesting! She didn't know what half of them were for, and couldn't ask, but she could look and wonder, watch people buying. Everyone seemed very polite and she soon lost her nervousness at being the only European.

There were piles of fruit and vegetables in one part of the row of shops and her mouth watered as she saw them. She didn't dare spend her money, though, and anyway, she didn't have any local coins.

At the end of the street was another, just as interesting, so she turned into it, just for a short distance. Then another corner led her to some clothing shops, tunics and trousers made of bright fabrics that she longed to stroke. Women wore baggy trousers here, with tunics over them. She giggled at the thought of how people would stare if she wore something like that in the village.

After a while she decided she'd better go back to the ship. She thought she'd kept count of the turns, but at the fourth corner she stopped, because it didn't look right. Groaning softly at her own stupidity, she turned back. Soon she knew herself completely lost and she didn't have the slightest idea which way to try next.

She wondered whether anyone spoke English,

but when she said, 'Excuse me,' to a Chinese woman, the other shook her head and hurried past. Ismay didn't dare ask a foreign man for help, but she'd seen one or two Europeans in the distance and was hoping desperately that one would come past again.

She waited, but there was no sight of any. Wasn't it always like that when you were desperate to see someone?

A little frightened now, she walked along slowly, stopping every now and then. But nothing looked familiar. A woman came past and she tried again to ask for help. 'Excuse me, please. Can you tell me the way to the harbour?'

She thought the woman would have helped her if only she'd understood the words, but in the end, the stranger shrugged in a sort of apology and walked on.

Twice more this happened and Ismay was beginning to feel more than a little afraid.

Then suddenly she remembered the name of the man who owned the cargo. He was an important person and he spoke English. Perhaps they'd be able to direct her to him? Surely he wouldn't refuse to help her?

The next time she stopped a woman, she bowed her head, as they had done, and said, 'Lee Kar Ho?'

That got the woman's attention straight away, so Ismay looked round, tried to show she was bewildered and repeated his name again.

The woman made a beckoning gesture with one hand.

Hoping this wouldn't lead her into worse trouble, Ismay followed.

When Adam and Joss came back to the ship, Aunt Harriet was on deck looking anxious.

'Isn't Ismay with you?' she asked.

'No. We haven't seen her since we left the ship.'

'She went down to the quay to stretch her legs. A sailor saw her go but she didn't come back. We hoped she'd met you.'

'When was this?'

'Nearly two hours ago.'

Adam felt his heart turn over suddenly, at the thought of Ismay, lost and alone in a strange city whose language she didn't speak. He couldn't bear the thought of her in danger or, at best, frightened. He just . . . couldn't bear it.

It was then that he knew how much he cared about her. He turned to Joss. 'How do we set about finding her?'

'We find some guides and send them out. Most likely they'll soon find her. She surely won't have gone far and she'll be easy to recognise.'

'And if they don't find her?'

'I'm sure they will. But, at worst, Mr Lee will probably be able to help us.'

The woman guiding Ismay stopped outside a shop selling beautiful silks. She beckoned again and went inside to speak to the young woman standing there.

Together they came back to Ismay and she asked, 'Do you speak English?'

'Yes, I do.'

'Oh, thank goodness for that! I'm lost and I can't find my way back to the ship.'

'Ah. First time in Singapore?'

'Yes. I'm sorry to trouble you, but when I tried to ask directions, no one understood me, so I asked for the man whose cargo arrived on our ship. Lee Kar Ho. He spoke good English, you see.'

'He's my brother. I'm Xiu Mei.'

'I'm Ismay Deagan.'

The young woman stared at her in surprise. 'Deagan? Your name is Deagan?'

'Yes.' She'd forgotten to give her false name but, whatever Aunt Harriet said, she was tired of pretending to be married.

'We meet man call Bram Deagan. Come here trading.'

Ismay gaped at her. 'Bram's been here? He's my brother. I'm on my way to join him in Fremantle.'

'Ah.' Xiu Mei beamed at her. 'He marry Isabella, who live with us, teach us English.'

She pronounced the words 'Isberra' and 'Ingris' but it was clear what she meant.

'I've not met Bram's wife yet. I'm going to live with them in Fremantle.' Ismay stared round the shop, fascinated by the beauty of the materials. 'I got lost. It was so interesting. Could you please tell me how to get back to the ship?'

Just then Mr Lee came walking along the street. He turned into the shop and stopped in surprise at the sight of Ismay. The young woman spoke to him in their language, which Ismay supposed was Chinese.

He turned to her. 'You are Bram's sister?'

'Yes.'

'Happy to help. Very happy. We take you back to ship.'

'Thank you so much, Mr Lee. I'm sorry to be a trouble to you.'

'No trouble. You wife of captain?'

She laughed. 'No, sir. I'm a friend of Mrs Seaton. She's the aunt of Adam Tregear, the first mate. I'm Ismay Deagan.'

Another quick exchange between him and his sister sent her hurrying down a corridor at the back of the shop.

'Stay for cup of tea. You look tired. We send message to ship quickly.'

'Well . . . if you're sure it's not too much trouble, I'd love a cup of tea.'

'No trouble. Please come.' He gestured with one hand and led the way down the corridor.

She was delighted to have the opportunity to see inside a Chinese house, and he seemed to understand, stopping to smile and say, 'We call this shop-house.'

'Do you now. Shop-house.'

They passed a couple of rooms which seemed to be used for storing goods and one which had a table being used as a desk. Mr Lee stopped here. 'You write message for Captain.'

She sat down and wrote that she had got lost and was with Mr Lee.

He didn't hesitate to look at what she'd written. 'Say I send you back to ship soon.'

She added. 'They're giving me a cup of tea, then will send me back. They're so kind.'

He studied her message, smiled and folded it in half, taking it with him.

The corridor came out in a large room at the rear of the house, much brighter than the others because it had big windows and an open door. It had a cooking area in one corner and a large table, behind which stood an older lady wearing the same sort of trousers and tunic as Mr Lee's sister, but in black.

They must be very comfortable garments, Ismay thought wistfully.

A girl who looked like a maid was standing in the cooking corner, watching them with great interest.

'This is my mother, Lee Bo Jun.'

The old lady bowed her head, so Ismay didn't hold out her hand but bobbed her own head in reply. 'I'm pleased to meet you, Mrs Lee.'

'I must go back to shop,' the younger woman said.

Mr Lee handed her the piece of paper and spoke

in Chinese again. She nodded, then smiled at their guest and left.

A gesture from the older lady towards a chair sent Ismay to the table, but she waited for the other woman to sit down first, as she would have done at the big house. That earned her a slight nod, which seemed to express approval.

Tea was served without milk in tiny bowls, which were so pretty Ismay couldn't resist touching the flower on the side of hers before she had a drink. Not sure what to do, she watched her hosts, and noticed that Mr Lee waited for his mother to drink before sipping from his cup. So she waited too.

'You come from Ireland, like Bram?' he asked.

'Yes, from Ireland.'

'Long way for girl to go without family.'

'I'm travelling with Mrs Seaton, and her nephew.'

'Adam Tregear.' He made a good try at the name.

'Yes, Adam. He owns half the ship and he's first mate.'

She drank the rest of the tea and, without being asked, the maid came to pour her another tiny cupful.

'This is good.'

'You not need milk?'

'No. My family are poor. We couldn't afford milk – couldn't afford tea a lot of the time.'

'Not poor now. Bram do well with bazaar, send for more goods each time ship of Captain McBride come here.'

She couldn't help beaming at him. 'That's wonderful. He's always been clever, our Bram has.'

The maid brought a plate of tiny dainties to the table.

Ismay looked at it in fascination. 'How pretty they look! What are they, please?'

Mr Lee did most of the talking, but his mother obviously understood English.

Ismay tasted first one, then the other, delighted with the new flavours.

Suddenly there were footsteps in the corridor and Adam followed Xiu Mei into the room. He stared across at Ismay. 'Are you all right?'

'Yes. I got lost.' She introduced him to Mr Lee's mother, then explained how she'd found her way to their house.

Adam couldn't conceal his anger. 'Why did you leave the ship? It's not *safe* to go wandering in a strange city.'

'It was so interesting, I forgot where I was.' He looked so furious she felt tears come into her eyes. 'I'm sorry.'

Mr Lee interrupted. 'Have cup of tea now.'

Ismay could tell that Adam was about to refuse, so said hurriedly, 'Yes, do. Mr Lee and his mother have been so kind to me and the food is delicious.'

Adam hesitated, still frowning, then took a deep breath and turned to his host. 'I'm sorry. I'm not being polite. I was worried about her, you see.'

Mr Lee nodded and, with a smile, gestured to a chair. Adam had no choice but to sit down.

Fresh tea was brought. Another plate of snacks.

Conversation turned to cargoes and Ismay noticed that Mrs Lee listened with as much interest as she felt herself. She couldn't help being glad she'd got lost, because she was enjoying the visit and the food.

When they took their leave, a man was waiting to guide them back to the ship.

Adam said very little as they walked. When they got to the ship, he gave the man a coin, then turned to grab her arm before she could start up the gangway. He gave her a shake. 'Don't you *ever* go off on your own again. My aunt was worried sick about you.'

She rubbed her arm, because he'd hurt her. 'I won't.' She wished he'd said he was worried about her, but no, just his aunt.

She ran up to the deck and found Aunt Harriet waiting for her, arms open wide. It was so rare to have someone worry about her and offer her a hug, she flung herself into the older woman's arms and burst into tears.

When Aunt Harriet led her towards the cabins, she whispered, 'Adam's so angry with me.'

'He was worried sick about you. Weren't you afraid?'

'A bit. But people were very polite and I had such an interesting time.' She described her visit to the Lee family.

★   ★   ★

That evening the captain and second mate dined with the ladies, both seeming very relaxed now they were in port. Ismay had to go over the details of her outing again.

After the meal, Aunt Harriet excused herself, saying she was tired, and Ismay went to stand by the rail, staring down at the quay, which still had plenty of people moving to and fro, selling and buying things.

Someone came to stand beside her and she could sense it was Adam. 'Look at them, making their living in so many ways. I'd love to taste some more of those foods.'

'We have to be careful what we eat. We don't want to fall sick.'

He was so close, her heart started beating faster. 'The food we ate at the Lees' house didn't make me sick. It was lovely.'

'Yes, it was. And I suppose if you landed in hell, you'd make friends with the devil.'

She looked at him, puzzled by this remark and, as her sleeve fell back, it revealed the bruise on her arm in the light of a nearby lantern.

Adam stared at it and she hurriedly lowered her arm, but he took hold of it gently. 'Did I do that to you?'

She shrugged. 'I bruise easily. You weren't to know.'

'I was angry because I'd been worrying myself sick about you.'

'Oh.'

The air around them seemed suddenly charged with tension. She stared out at the water, but he took her gently in his arms and pulled her close. 'I care about you, Ismay. Surely you must realise that.'

She didn't feel afraid of him because he was nothing like Rory, who was a big bull of a man. Adam was neat and of medium height only, rather like her brother Bram. And, anyway, he was . . . Adam. She looked up at him sadly and raised one hand to touch his cheek. 'You mustn't care about me in that way. I'm only a maid. You're gentry.'

'I'm not. I'm neither fish nor fowl, and most folk would look down their noses at me for being a bastard.'

'They'll not be doing that now. You've a half-share in a ship, so you're a man of substance, and . . . you need a wife who can help you get on, not an ignorant girl like me. And I won't go to any man's bed without being married, in spite of what happened.'

'I understand that. And I don't care about what happened.'

'How can you not? I still have nightmares about it.'

'I'm sorry.' He had her in the circle of his arms still, and she loved the warmth and strength of him. She was so close to him that if she stood on tiptoe she could kiss him. Only she mustn't. It could lead nowhere.

On that thought, she pushed at his arms and he let her go at once.

'It can't be,' she repeated. 'If you won't be wise, I must, for I'm not losing my second chance to stay respectable.' She looked at him yearningly, then fled for her cabin, ignoring his call to her to wait.

Locking the door, she leaned against it, tears streaming down her face. Adam might care about her now but, once he was back in his world, he'd soon start to scorn her ignorance. And she couldn't bear to hold him back.

For both those reasons she had to keep her distance from him. However much it hurt. Ruining his life would be no way to repay their kindness to her.

Adam watched her go. He couldn't hold her back by force, because he wasn't sure whether he wanted to marry her or anyone yet. He certainly didn't want to make her his mistress; he respected her too much for that. In fact, his thoughts and emotions were in turmoil.

He'd never particularly wanted to be married because, from what he'd seen, it was difficult for both partners, even at the best of times. And a sailor's wife had a harder life than most.

Aunt Harriet insisted hers had been a truly happy relationship, but would the happiness have lasted if her husband hadn't been killed? Adam didn't think so.

His mother had often told him not to trust in love, and though he'd been too young to understand it at the time, he still remembered her words, and her unhappiness about how his father had treated her. She'd said love was a deceiver and tricked you into behaving foolishly. She'd begged him many a time not to get a girl into trouble, because it was always the woman who paid.

Joss came to join him, standing by the rail in a companionable silence.

Adam surprised himself by saying, 'I don't know what to do.'

'About Ismay?'

'Yes.'

'I'm not the best person to ask. I made a mess of it and lost the woman I loved. That was well before I met my wife.'

'Do you wish you'd married the first woman?'

'Yes. Every single day.'

Another pause, then Joss said, 'I can't tell you what would be best for you. But if you feel Ismay is necessary to your happiness, then don't pay any heed to what other people say. Marry her. Because marrying someone you don't really care about can be hell.'

'You were . . . unhappy in your marriage?'

'Very. I'd rather not have lost Lottie in such a final manner, poor girl, but I grieve more for the shortness of her life than because I cared deeply about her. She married me because she wanted children, rather than because she wanted me in particular. She knew I still cared about someone else, someone I couldn't marry. I was just a good provider and a father as far as she was concerned.

Only she lost two babies, each at a few months, and grew very shrewish. I'd begun to regret marrying her, to be sorry I'd have to spend the rest of my life with her.'

With that he turned and walked away, and Adam wondered if he regretted his brusque confidence.

Was Ismay necessary to his happiness?

How could you tell for sure?

'Bram darling, you should go out for a stroll,' Isabella said. 'You can't spend every hour of the day in the Bazaar.'

'I like my shop.'

'And I want my husband healthy, not dead of overwork and pale for lack of sunlight on his skin.' Her voice became coaxing. 'Look at what a beautiful spring day it is. I'll be taking little Arlen out for a walk later. That baby loves to look at the world. Come with us.'

As he strolled along High Street with her, enjoying the sunshine on his face and the pleasure of her company, Bram saw a man in the distance. He frowned and stopped walking. He looked familiar, but Bram couldn't place him.

Who was it?

Someone from Ireland?

It looked like – no, it couldn't be . . . It was! How could Rory Flynn possibly be in the Swan River Colony?

'What's the matter?'

He turned to Isabella. 'I think I know that fellow.'

'Which one?'

Bram squinted against the sun. His eyes must be playing tricks on him. It was just another burly fellow taking the air. 'No, it's not him after all.'

They stopped to look in the baker's window and decide on a cake for tea. When they came out, he looked round, but there was no sign of the man.

With a sniff of annoyance at himself for being so fanciful, Bram turned back to his wife, who was glowing with health and whose love for him shone in her eyes. Life was so good. At the Bazaar they were selling more things than he'd thought possible. It seemed he had the trick of choosing things people wanted to buy.

When he went back to the shop, he decided he'd done right to divide it into two, placing the new goods at the front and the secondhand items at the rear. The latter weren't rubbish, but pieces of furniture or household linen like quilts that had a lot of life in them still. Even some good-quality outer clothing, though that was discreetly placed behind a screen.

He'd never accept rubbish in his shop, even if it'd make him money. But in a town where there was a lack of goods, secondhand items were not scorned as they might have been back in Britain.

Then a customer claimed his attention and he turned to smile and listen to what she wanted.

Just before closing time, Bram saw two men with a cart draw up at the cottage and start to pull something off it. The fools. They should be delivering goods to his shop, not his home.

'Keep an eye on things, Freddie.' He hurried down the slope just as the men disappeared inside the cottage, carrying what looked like a trunk. He followed them.

'What's happening?'

Isabella beckoned him across and held out a letter. 'It's your sister's luggage, and that of some friends of hers.'

He read the letter. 'I've never heard of this Adam Tregear. Why should he be sending me his luggage to look after?'

'And Ismay's,' she reminded him.

'I didn't even know she was on her way. Wait, please!'

The men looked at him in surprise.

'There isn't room for all that stuff here. It'll have to go in the stables.' He took out a coin and they were suddenly very obliging.

When they'd gone, he and Isabella both re-read the brief letter.

'He says Ismay's ill and they have to stay in Aden till she recovers; they can't get their luggage off the ship in time.'

'If she's ill, it's lucky she found some friends.'

'But I didn't send her the money to come here. I didn't think Da would let her come on her own.'

'Well, there's nothing you can do about it until she arrives and explains what's going on.'

Was Ismay really on her way to join him? He

did hope so. But he couldn't help worrying about her, hoping she'd recovered from whatever was wrong with her. The letter was dated a month ago. There wasn't another mail ship due in the colony for another two months. So he'd have to wait for his answers.

She was young and healthy. She must be all right, surely?

12

Flora stood by the rail of the *Bonny Mary*, relishing the wind on her face and even enjoying today's rougher seas, which filled her with exhilaration. She was glad she'd proved to be a good sailor. She waved to Dougal, who grinned at her from his position near the helm, then she turned back to the water and the horizon . . . and her thoughts.

Not long till they got to Singapore now, and she'd be glad. At first she'd found it healing to be alone for most of the day, had needed that after the long, dreary years at her mother's beck and call. Now she wanted to be with people, had such a hunger for a normal life. She wanted to chat and laugh, make friends, go visiting. Dougal said they'd be invited out in Singapore, because the Europeans there were very hospitable. Good.

Her brother was insisting on buying her a couple of dress lengths in Singapore. He said the Lees sold beautiful silks, cheaper than the prices Bram was asking. You could have garments made up quickly and at small cost by local dressmakers.

She looked down at herself with a wry grimace.

Dull, sensible clothes. She was tired of them, wanted to wear brighter colours and fuller skirts, even perhaps a crinoline. Not one as ridiculously wide as some she'd seen in Perth. You could hardly get through a door in one of those. But she did like the way the skirts swayed tantalisingly around you as you walked, wanted to show people she still had a trim waist.

Her face wasn't beautiful, but it wasn't ugly either. Her skin was still good and her hair had only the occasional grey thread. In fact, she probably looked better now than she had as a girl. Hers had never been a girlish face.

She'd brought along a fashion magazine to show the dressmaker and had picked out styles she thought would suit her. Nothing too frilly or fussy. And there would be no one now to make sharp remarks that made her ashamed to be even considering brighter colours, 'suitable only for younger, prettier women' her mother had always said.

Why had she obeyed her mother so meekly, though? That was something she still didn't understand.

A strand of hair blew loose and, as she twisted it back in place, a sudden memory sent a pang through her. *He* had loved her hair; said it was the colour of honey not 'straw'.

She forced that memory to the back of her mind, but it wouldn't stay there and she had to ask herself if she was just an old fool of a spinster trying to look young again.

She threw back her head and laughed into the wind. Fool or not, she was going to dress well from now on, if only to please herself.

The following morning, quite early, Mr Lee sent a message to *Hannah Grey* to say he knew a guide who would take the ladies out and show them the sights.

Joss showed the note to Aunt Harriet. 'What do you think?'

'I think I'd love to go and explore. Ismay hasn't stopped talking about her outing and I'm quite jealous.'

'You could buy some material from his sister and each have a dress made up.'

She clapped her hands. 'What a wonderful idea! Ismay, come over here. Mr Lee is sending us a guide and Joss says we should choose some material from his sister's shop and have dresses made up.'

'I'd love to go out again and help you choose yours, but I don't need a new dress. Mrs Largan gave me several of her old ones.'

'Silk dresses?'

'No, of course not. That wouldn't be suitable.'

Aunt Harriet looked at her with her head on one side. 'I should have made it plain that this will be a present from me. Every girl needs a brand-new dress for parties.'

Ismay opened her mouth to protest, but couldn't. Instead she said wistfully, 'I've never been to a party. I've never had a brand-new dress, either.'

Joss, who was standing to one side, looked at her sympathetically. It was obvious this poor girl had led a very limited life. Perhaps that was why she did things with such gusto, sweeping everyone else up in her pleasure.

After noticing that Adam was watching her with an unguarded fondness, Joss gave in to a sudden impulse to interfere. 'Well, I'll be giving a party on board the ship, to return people's hospitality, so you'll be going to at least one here.'

She gaped at him. 'Me? But—'

'Don't tell me you're only a maid. You *were* a maid. You're a companion to Mrs Seaton now.'

She gave him a look that made her suddenly seem very old and knowing. 'And when we get to Fremantle, I'll have to look for work and be a maid again.'

'More likely, you'll get married. They're short of women in the Swan River Colony and you're very pretty. You'll have fellows chasing you from the very first week.' He smiled as she blushed, then saw Adam's indignant expression. Don't deny your love for her, he thought. It's too rare and precious.

'Are you sure people won't mind me being there?' Ismay asked.

'You're Bram Deagan's sister and he's the owner of a large shop, so you've gone up in the world. You should definitely use your own name from now on, though. It's becoming a respected one in the colony. Your brother will probably have visited the Wallaces when he came here. All the officers do, and he'd count as that level of person.'

'So it's agreed, then,' Aunt Harriet said firmly. 'Ismay and I will go and choose some material and we'll all attend your party. Thank you, Joss.'

He knew she was thanking him for more than the party. 'My pleasure. Now, if you're ready, Adam, I'll take you to call on some people I've met here a time or two. After that we'll see if there are any other Australian ships in port and visit them too.'

Joss took Adam first to call on the Wallaces, ignoring the other man's protests that he wasn't good at social chitchat.

Mrs Wallace, a lady of comfortable proportions and amiable disposition, at once invited them to come and dine with her one evening.

'We'd love to. Um – my friend's aunt and her companion are travelling with us,' Joss said. 'Did you meet Bram Deagan when he was here?'

'Yes, we did. A very shrewd young man. We attended his wedding.'

'Did you really? Well, his sister is Mrs Seaton's companion. She's going out to live with him and his wife. I'm sure she'd love to hear about the wedding.'

'You must bring them with you to dine, then. We keep open house here.' She chuckled. 'We residents see the same old faces day in, day out, so we all love to meet new people.'

A date was agreed on, then Joss took Adam out and insisted he too have some new clothes made.

Adam was very quiet on the way back. 'Ismay's brother seems to be well liked,' he said at last.

'He is. I've not met him myself, but everyone speaks well of him. Oh, look!' He pointed.

Another schooner had anchored just along the quay from them, so naturally they went towards it.

As they got closer, Joss started frowning then stopped dead. 'I know the man who owns the *Bonny Mary*. I'd rather not meet him again.'

He gave no explanation for this, even though he could see the surprise on Adam's face, but turned round and strode swiftly back to his own ship.

The guide Mr Lee sent was an older Chinese woman whose English was quite good. Naturally, when the ladies explained that they wished to buy some dress material and have it made up, she took them to Mr Lee's shop.

Ismay introduced Mrs Seaton, before explaining what they wanted.

Xiu Mei immediately began pulling out rolls of silk.

'I can't have silk,' Ismay whispered. 'It wouldn't be right and, anyway, I'll never get a chance to wear it again.'

Aunt Harriet tossed her head. 'You can't tell me what to buy you for a present.'

'But—'

'Oh, look at this one! It'd really suit you. The blue exactly matches your eyes, and with your dark hair it'd look lovely.'

They held it to her and Ismay couldn't help stroking the lustrous material with one fingertip, a finger that wasn't rough and red these days, but soft like a lady's.

'It's perfect,' Aunt Harriet said. 'He'll love you in this.' She chuckled. 'Don't blush. If you think I'm not aware of how you two feel about one another, you're fooling yourself.'

'But I'm not good enough for him. It wouldn't be right.'

Aunt Harriet gave her a hug. 'You're good enough for anyone. And even if nothing comes of your feelings for Adam, you must do your brother credit. Thank you, Miss Lee.'

'Not cut silk till we decide on dress style.'

'Very sensible. Now, will you please help me choose a material for myself, Ismay?'

But it was Xiu Mei who did that, seeing how overwhelmed her younger customer was. She stood back, studied Aunt Harriet, then climbed on a little ladder to pull down a roll of moiré silk. The subdued magenta added warmth to Aunt Harriet's complexion, and they decided to have an under-dress made in a darker shade of the same colour.

To their surprise, Xiu Mei seemed quite up to date with the fashions they showed her and said she knew excellent dressmakers used to making up garments for European ladies. She sent for one immediately and invited her customers to sit down and wait.

'Many European ladies come here,' she explained, seeing their surprise. 'Show me pictures, talk. I need bigger shop now. Find one soon. My brother want bigger house, not shop-house.'

The dressmaker arrived within five minutes, had a quick discussion in Chinese with Xiu Mei, then let her translate for the two ladies. She studied the pictures they showed her, pulled out paper and a piece of charcoal and swiftly sketched a garment with the modifications they'd asked for.

'That's it exactly,' Aunt Harriet said in delight.

The dressmaker measured them and took their height, then she and Xiu Mei decided how much material to cut.

As they walked away, Aunt Harriet whispered, 'Our dresses will be ready in two days. How can that dressmaker possibly manage to do that?'

'Some poor souls will be working all night.'

'Well, I daresay they'll be glad of the extra money.' Harriet looked thoughtfully into the distance, her steps slowing. 'I'm going to ask Joss how long we'll be staying here. I might have another dress made, or even two. Just simple day dresses, you know.'

'I've plenty of those,' Ismay said hastily.

'But you might like her to alter yours and make them more fashionable.'

'We-ell.' She couldn't refuse, but she sometimes felt overwhelmed by the older woman's kindness.

And by her feelings for Adam. She couldn't help wondering what he would think when he saw her dressed up so finely.

Back at the ship, Joss gave them a note from Mrs Wallace, inviting them all to have dinner at her house in two evenings' time.

'I can't do that!' Ismay gasped, clasping her hands to her mouth in an age-old gesture of holding in worry.

'Persuade her, Adam.' Harriet walked away towards their cabins.

'Of course you can go,' Adam said quietly. 'If you listen more than you talk and make sure to agree with your hostess's views, you won't go wrong. It's what I do when I go out in new company.'

She looked at him uncertainly. It felt as if the two of them were alone, even though there were sailors working a few paces away.

'I mean it. You'll do well, I'm sure.' He smiled at her and saw her cheeks colour as she continued to look at him. 'Ismay, I—'

What he was going to say was lost as Joss called for him to do something.

And perhaps that was a good thing, Adam thought as he went about his work. He might have said something he regretted.

But would he have regretted it?

Later he saw Ismay speaking to his aunt, gesticulating, her face alight as she pointed something out in the harbour. How could you regret knowing a woman as special as Ismay?

She had spoiled him for anyone else.

But he still didn't know what was waiting for him in Fremantle. His father had left him three properties, but what sort of places were they? Until he found out, he didn't know whether he'd have anywhere for his aunt to live.

Or a wife.

There might even be some nasty twist to the inheritance, as there had been with the ship being less than half his. He didn't want anything affecting Ismay.

Another note was delivered to the ship in the late afternoon, just after a short, thundery shower. This time it was from Mr Lee, inviting them for a meal at his house the following evening.

'We like to enjoy the company of Bram's sister and friends,' it concluded. 'Give you Bram's favourite dishes. Good food for Europeans to try.'

Her brother must be doing even better than she'd thought, Ismay decided when she was shown the note. Just a mention of his name had caused everyone to invite her out to parties. Thank goodness she'd learned to handle her knife and fork properly when she was working for the Largans and since becoming Aunt Harriet's companion.

Only . . . Joss said Chinese people didn't eat with knives and forks, but with two little sticks. How on earth did you balance food on those?

If she spilled any down herself, she'd die of embarrassment.

Dougal invited his sister Flora to come and explore Singapore with him during the afternoon. They took shelter under the long walkways in front of the shops when it began to rain and watched the rain pour down, while thunder rumbled across the sky and lightning stabbed down at the city. But the storm was over quite quickly and it certainly didn't stop people going about their business.

He took Flora to the Lees' shop and insisted on buying her some dress materials.

To his surprise she didn't even attempt to argue, and to his delight she chose flattering colours and styles this time.

As they were returning, they passed a young woman in the street who was yelling at an older woman, trying to tug her along. The old one had a mindless look on her face and the younger one seemed exhausted.

Flora stopped with a shudder. 'The poor thing is like our mother.'

Dougal nodded. He didn't like to think about that.

She walked on a bit, then murmured, as if speaking her thoughts aloud. 'I hope Mrs Southerham isn't having too much trouble with Mother.'

'She's got plenty of help, so I'm sure she'll be coping perfectly well. Rhoda is a strong woman and can easily handle Mother.' He stopped for a moment, taking her hand and saying, 'Forget about them, Flora. Enjoy your freedom while you can.'

They both knew that once they returned to Australia, he would continue to go away and Flora would be the one to keep an eye on their mother's care.

'I'm sorry,' he said, and knew from her expression that he didn't have to explain what he was sorry for. All the years she'd wasted, and he had to take some blame for that. He should have noticed what his mother was doing.

When they got back to the ship, he stopped at the foot of the gangway to stare along the quay. Who owned the *Hannah Grey*? It was a trim vessel, well kept. He'd go along and introduce himself later, as a matter of courtesy – but also to satisfy his curiosity. He'd seen her being repaired in Fremantle a couple of months ago, but hadn't caught up with the captain then.

He liked to know his colleagues, especially the few who sailed out of Fremantle. Sometimes you needed help. Or they did. And anyway, it was good to make friends who understood your way of life.

He was a little surprised that the captain hadn't already come to visit him and introduce himself. The fellow must know they shared a home port. And, since the *Hannah Grey* had been here longer than Dougal had, her captain must have finished dealing with his cargo.

There were no signs that the other vessel was

preparing to go back to sea; no signs of any cargo being loaded. Strange, that.

Since her new dress wouldn't be ready until the following day, Ismay put on the best of the ones Mrs Largan had given her for the dinner at the Lees'. It was a soft cotton with long sleeves, too warm for Singapore, of course, but the lightest she had.

Would it be this warm in the Swan River Colony, she wondered, fanning her face as she waited to set off. It was so humid that sweat was already trickling down her face and between her breasts.

'I'd not like to live here,' she said to Aunt Harriet.

'Me neither. But it's very interesting to visit it and I'm looking forward to trying the different food.'

Again, Mr Lee sent a guide and two men to escort them.

Ismay was puzzled by this. 'It didn't seem dangerous to walk round the streets. Why do we need guards?'

'That was in the daytime,' Joss said. 'If he hadn't sent men to look after us, I'd have taken a couple of crew members along. There are tongs, secret societies, and I've heard that sometimes violence breaks out between them.'

The shop was still open; the family had obviously drafted in someone to sell the dress materials while they dined. The woman inclined her head to them as they arrived and called out in Chinese, before gesturing towards the narrow corridor, which was well illuminated by lamps tonight.

Mr Lee appeared at the other end and there was a lot of bowing to one another.

Inside, Mrs Lee and Xiu Mei were waiting for them, again clad in tunics and trousers, which seemed to be standard wear for Chinese women, but this time the garments were made of rich silky material that gleamed in the candlelight. There were two maids preparing food in the back corner.

The older woman was in black again, but with delicate coloured embroidery around the hem and neck of the tunic. Xiu Mei was wearing a vivid rose colour, with black embroidery, which had occasional gold threads in it.

After a few words of greeting, they were shown straight to the table and a small bowl was placed in front of each of them. Ismay looked uncertainly at Adam, but he shook his head to indicate that he didn't know the correct manners, either.

Mr Lee smiled at them benignly. 'You eat Chinese way tonight?'

'We'd love to, but you'll have to tell us how,' Joss replied. 'And I hope you'll forgive us if we do things wrongly.'

The older man's smile broadened. 'Not give you chopsticks. Use spoons. But we eat in our way, with bowl.' He offered the big bowl. 'Put in rice first, take mouthful of just rice.'

'But wait till after my mother eats,' Xiu Mei whispered.

The first course was vegetables in a delicate sauce, just that, and they all took a small serving.

Adam watched Ismay lift the blue and white china spoon to her lips and taste the food.

She closed her eyelids with a blissful expression, then opened them and exclaimed, 'I never had anything as delicious as this!'

Oh, she was a delight, with her beaming smile and enthusiasm! Mr Lee seemed to think so too, and Joss noticed Adam watching her with a fond smile.

'I like your way of eating,' she said to Mrs Lee when the bowls were at last taken away. 'That was the best meal I've ever had. I'd like to learn to cook like that.'

'Not hard,' Mrs Lee said. 'Come here tomorrow and I show you some things.'

'Would you really? Oh, I'd love that!'

Adam wanted to hug her because, though she didn't know it, she'd captivated the Lees. Which could be very helpful. Why had he not realised what an asset she would be as a wife?

After they'd finished eating, they all chatted for a while, and continued to drink pale tea from tiny bowls. Eventually Joss looked at his pocket watch. 'We must be going now or we'll all be too late to bed.'

He seemed to know exactly how to deal with people here, Adam thought. But then, he'd been trading with the Orient for a while. Still, there were men who traded all over the world and refused to do things in any way but their own. Hidebound. Like his father. He was relieved not to be partnered with one of those.

On the way back, Joss offered his arm to Aunt Harriet and Adam found himself walking with Ismay. She held his arm for a while, then let go to stop and examine some delicate carvings in a shop that was still open. The others pulled ahead of them but he didn't call them back, because it was nice to be alone with Ismay.

Two shops along the street, it was crockery she had to comment on, small bowls like the ones the Lee family had used to drink tea, slightly larger bowls for eating from.

He suddenly realised that the others were out of sight and soon afterwards he became aware that they were being followed. He stopped, saying, 'Shh!'

She stopped talking, looking up at him uncertainly.

Two men came to a halt when they did, staring at them from a few yards back, not hiding their interest. He remembered seeing them a few streets back.

Their faces were expressionless, but somehow he knew they offered some sort of threat.

'Stay behind me, Ismay,' he said quietly. 'I think we're in for trouble.'

'If they try to hurt you, I'll hit them with this.' She bent and picked up a small piece of rock from the gutter.

As the men took a step forward, Adam felt her

bend again, but didn't dare take his eyes off their pursuers. People nearby began to sidle away and that only confirmed that he was right: they were in danger.

'Take this,' she whispered.

He felt her thrust a piece of rock in his hand and grinned suddenly. Any other woman would be screaming and fainting. Not Ismay.

He was expecting the rush forward of the attack, but even so it took him by surprise that the men were so fast. One of them lunged at him with a knife and he leaped sideways, praying that Ismay would move with him.

She did. But because of her he couldn't act as nimbly as he needed and the edge of the knife had caught his arm just above the wrist. He cursed as blood began to drip down his hand.

'Are you badly hurt?' she cried.

'No. Watch out!'

The man made another lunge forward, but Adam was better prepared this time and, as he swung the rock at the same time, he arched his body away.

Ismay let out a banshee yell and there was an answering cry that was a curse by the sound of it.

Then yells from down the street made their two attackers freeze.

The shouts that followed were from several men and had people moving forward from among bystanders to place themselves protectively beside Adam and Ismay.

The two attackers had already taken to their

heels, but the men sent to escort Mr Lee's visitors caught them before they reached the corner. From the sound of it, one of them was yelling orders.

Another two men moved out from the crowd and helped them subdue the attackers.

There was no sign of Joss or Aunt Harriet. Adam pulled Ismay close to him, praying that his aunt was safe.

'Where are the others, do you think?' she whispered.

'Safe, I hope. Joss is no fool.'

Adam asked the guard where the others were, but got no answer and saw no understanding of his words in the man's eyes. But there was a watchfulness as the other kept checking anyone standing nearby, his eyes moving to and fro, never still.

'Where is my aunt?' he yelled again, terrified that she'd been hurt. He turned in the direction the others had taken, but one of the guards put out one hand to bar his way, shaking his head vigorously and repeating some word several times.

'He can't understand you,' Ismay said.

Only then did Adam realise how closely he was holding her. 'You're all right, though.'

'I am, yes. But if you've a handkerchief, we'd better wrap it round your arm.'

By the time this had been accomplished, the crowd had parted respectfully and Mr Lee came striding through it, face grim.

'Are you badly hurt, Mr Tregear?'

'No. Just a scratch. I can't find out where my

aunt and Captain Rutherford are. They were ahead
of us.'

Mr Lee turned, tossed one curt phrase at the
nearest man, and got an equally short response.
He turned back to say, 'They're safe. We find them
afterwards.'

'I don't understand why we were attacked.'

'My fault. Some people . . .' he stared at Adam
as if weighing his words, then finished, 'want me
gone. They've failed. Time to show my strength
now.'

'Enemies?' Joss hazarded.

'Tongs,' Mr Lee said. 'Groups. I belong one,
these belong another. Stupid to attack Europeans.
Very stupid.'

Several more men slipped through the crowd
to range themselves around Mr Lee and his
companions. If this was a show of strength, Adam
thought, it was impressive.

Mr Lee nodded in satisfaction. 'You can go back
to ship now. Safe to move about alone in daytime.
Not at night. Not yet. I send rickshaws for
tomorrow night. Take you to Mr Wallace. Bring
you back.'

'Thank you.'

He gestured with one hand and four men
stepped forward. 'Should go back now. Take Bram's
sister to ship. I finish dealing with things here.'

As they walked through the streets, Adam kept
his arm round Ismay, and she pressed against him.

'It seemed so safe in daytime,' she said suddenly.

'It probably was. We got in between two groups tonight, I think. They were trying to use us.'

'Mr Lee will win,' she said confidently.

'You can't be sure of that.'

'He's a very clever man. You can see it in his face.'

She was right. But Mr Lee had a ruthless side, too, Adam was sure, and he was glad not to be his enemy.

As the ship came into sight, Adam breathed a sigh of relief to see Joss standing on the quay beside it, with three members of the crew, each holding a belaying pin.

Joss ran towards them. 'Thank God you're safe!'

'Thank Mr Lee's men, rather,' Adam said as he let go of Ismay and gestured to her to walk ahead of him on to the ship.

His aunt was waiting on the deck, out of sight from the quay.

'I'm all right,' he called.

She rushed across to hug him, but stopped at the sight of the makeshift bandage. 'There's blood on you.'

'It's just a cut on his arm,' Ismay said. 'Not deep. They attacked us with knives.'

'It needs washing.' Harriet turned to call, 'Fetch me some boiled water. Adam, come and sit down in the main cabin, where I can see to look after you.'

He grinned and winked at Ismay. All the tension was suddenly gone and he felt like a child again, a boy whose cuts had been bathed and bandaged by his aunt many times. She'd always given him a kiss afterwards.

But when Harriet set to work, her hands were shaking, and Ismay had to take the strips of bandage out of her hands.

'I'll do that.'

'I'm all right, Aunt Harriet,' Adam tried to reassure her. 'Really I am.'

'I know. But you nearly weren't.'

'If I'd stayed in England, I could have been killed by a runaway horse. Or fallen overboard on one of my voyages, or had my throat cut in a dark alley. Nowhere in the world is completely safe.'

He waited till Ismay had finished tying up what was, really, only a minor cut, then thanked her and leaned across to kiss his aunt's soft, wrinkled cheek, repeating, 'I *am* all right.'

When he went to his cabin that night, he felt exhausted, but sleep eluded him. He kept seeing images of the two men creeping up on himself and Ismay, knives at the ready. Why had they not thrown those knives? They could easily have done so. They could have killed the two of them in a blink. They must have wanted to capture them. He was glad they hadn't.

If they'd hurt Ismay, he didn't know what he'd have done.

He smiled in the darkness. What a woman she was! She'd stood by him without flinching, found them both stones to throw.

And afterwards her hands had been soft on his skin as she bandaged his cut. So very soft.

He was suddenly gloriously sure that no other woman could possibly suit him better.

He'd keep his word to his father and get married – but only because he'd found a very special woman.

He was still going to wait to see his properties in Fremantle before he proposed, though. If they weren't suitable for living in, he'd wait and rent somewhere else for them – all of them; Aunt Harriet as well.

Smiling, satisfied that he'd come to the right decision, he felt himself sink towards sleep.

13

For two weeks Livia Southerham tried to make friends with Mrs McBride, but in vain. The older woman kept trying to order her about, pestering to leave the house. When Livia refused to obey any of her unreasonable orders, Mrs McBride would throw a tantrum and sometimes had to be restrained with Orla or Rhoda's help.

It would be at least ten weeks before the *Bonny Mary* returned, so the responsibility was hers, though of course she could go to Bram or the lawyer for help, if necessary.

Then, almost overnight, the old woman stopped being so arrogant and became much easier to manage. It was as if she was fading. She retreated first into a sullen silence, scowling at the world. Then even the scowls grew less fierce as the days passed.

They treated their charge gently, thinking her harmless now, but one night she went on a destructive rampage in her bedroom. They heard bumps and ran to investigate, but found the door jammed shut.

Rhoda had to go outside and smash the window

to get in, and was confronted by a screaming harpy, who tried to stab her with some scissors. Mrs McBride must have been using them to tear up her sheets into long strips of material. Ironically, they used those same strips to bind her to a chair, by which time Livia and Rhoda were both bruised and scratched.

By then it was dawn. Orla hurried round to the doctor's house to ask him to call urgently, explaining what had happened.

When he saw the damage, he shook his head and prescribed a much stronger dose of laudanum.

'I hope I never degenerate into this state,' Livia said to Rhoda and Orla as they cleared up the bedroom, working round the figure now tied to the bed, snoring gently under the influence of the sedative.

'She wasn't easy to live with even when she had all her wits,' Rhoda said. 'I've talked to Linny, the maid at her old home, and if you knew some of the tricks she used so she could get poor Miss Flora do what she wanted – well, you'd think she deserves this, if anyone does.'

'No one could deserve such an end,' Livia said quietly.

She didn't like giving so much laudanum to her charge because it turned the poor woman into a vegetable, and after a day or two she reduced the dose a little.

She woke a couple of nights later to the smell of smoke. Jerking out of bed, she ran along to the kitchen at the rear. Flames were rising from the top of the wood-burning stove, which had been stoked far too high. It was a wonder the nearby shelf hadn't caught light.

Mrs McBride was standing staring at the flames, as still as a statue now.

Rhoda joined them but, as they tried to get the poor woman away from the blaze, Mrs McBride suddenly went mad, scratching and clawing at them, screaming.

'Orla and I can hold her. You damp that fire down, Mrs Southerham, or the house will catch fire,' Rhoda panted.

Livia managed to put the lid on the stove and close down the damper to cut off the air supply. Gradually the flames began to die down and the heat lessened. All they'd suffered was charring of one corner of a nearby shelf, and damage from smoke and smuts. The ceiling above the blaze was blackened.

'If you hadn't smelled it, the whole house could have been destroyed,' Orla said, shuddering.

After that, they gave their charge the full dose of laudanum and kept her chained to her bed because she gnawed through the rope one day.

A week later, Mrs McBride stopped speaking completely and had to be persuaded to eat.

Then she stopped eating and drinking, and no amount of persuasion would make her.

'It'll do no good to force her,' the doctor said. 'She'll starve anyway. They all do once they've got to this stage. You'll only prolong the process.' He stared down at his patient. 'I doubt it'll be long now. She's nothing but skin and bone. It'll be a merciful release. When does her daughter return?'

'November, I think.'

'It'll probably be too late. She's declining faster than I'd expected.'

'What dreadful things can happen to people.' Livia couldn't help thinking of her previous charge, Conn's first wife, who had also stopped eating and drinking in her final madness.

'When you see the suffering I do, you know to be thankful for each day you live,' he said sombrely. He turned to study Livia. 'You look tired, Mrs Southerham. Don't neglect yourself. And don't blame yourself for anything that happens, either.'

When the rickshaws arrived to take them to the Wallaces, Ismay climbed nimbly into hers, marvelling at how small the man was who pulled it. Still, he had very muscular legs beneath the knee-length baggy breeches he was wearing. She felt excited as well as apprehensive.

Adam saw his aunt into another rickshaw and got into the one behind. As if there had been a signal, they all set off, with Joss's rickshaw in the lead.

The Wallaces had a large house in the European quarter. They weren't on the waterfront but not far from it. The house was like a square box, two storeys high with verandas on both floors. It was surrounded by well-tended gardens with palm trees and other plants she didn't recognise swaying around it in the breeze. The trees were hung with paper lanterns.

Ismay let Adam help her down, though she could have jumped easily enough. After a few paces she stopped to stare at the lanterns, entranced. 'Oh, how pretty!'

'Keep up with the others,' Adam tugged her along.

Once inside the house, he saw Ismay lose her sparkle. She watched the others carefully, saying hardly a word. His heart went out to her, because he could guess how nervous she felt.

Mrs Wallace surged forward to greet them. 'Mrs Seaton, I'm so pleased to meet you. And this must be Mr Deagan's sister. You have a look of your brother, my dear.'

'Thank you.' Ismay hesitated, then added, 'I believe you went to his wedding. I'd love to hear about it.'

'We did go. It was most interesting, too.' She studied Ismay shrewdly. 'I'll tell you about it later. Now do come across and meet the Rowtons. They have a son of about your age.'

The son looked at Ismay so warmly, she felt even more nervous. But she relaxed a little as she found that the young man considered himself a poet and wanted an audience more than anything. He didn't say anything very interesting, and the bits of his own poetry he quoted while staring soulfully at the ceiling were full of words she didn't understand. However, as long as she said yes, or hmm, or no, and asked the occasional question about what he'd said, she found he would continue talking and save her the worry of trying to think what it was safe to say next.

At one stage she caught Aunt Harriet's eye and received a nod to say she was doing well.

It was hard to keep her face straight, however, when she exchanged glances with Adam. He was close enough to hear the poet declaiming, and rolled his eyes so expressively she wanted to chuckle. But she managed not to do that.

Joss was standing chatting to a very elegant lady and seemed to be enjoying her company, but after a while she moved on. Before he could start talking to someone else, two newcomers were shown into the room and his mouth fell open in shock. He jerked as if he wanted to rush across to them, then took a deep breath and got himself under control.

Intrigued at Joss's reaction, Ismay turned her head to study the newcomers. The man was stocky with crinkly hair of a faded gingery colour, and he was accompanied by a lady who resembled him enough to suggest she was a relative. But her hair wasn't crinkly, just had enough curl to frame her face nicely. She had a lovely smile, a low, attractive voice and was well dressed.

In fact, there was something about her that

made Ismay feel she would like to get to know this lady.

Joss clearly knew her already.

Flora smiled as she waited to greet her hostess, then suddenly her brother grasped her arm tightly. She tried to free herself, but he wouldn't let go, shaking it to get her attention.

'Look over there!'

As she followed his gaze, she felt as if all the air had left the room. When her brother said something else, it was only a blur of sound. Oh dear heaven, how she'd hoped for this over the years. And feared it too!

But she hadn't wanted to meet Joss again in such a public place.

Taking a deep, shuddering breath, she pulled herself stiffly upright.

Their hostess noticed that something was wrong and asked, 'Excuse me, but are you feeling unwell, Miss McBride?'

'Just a momentary dizziness. I'm fine now.' But her eyes were drawn across the room again. He'd grown a little older but, other than that, he was still the Joss she remembered so clearly.

'Perhaps if my sister could sit down for a moment or two?' Dougal said.

'No!' She tugged her arm away from his grasp but he wouldn't let go. 'You're hurting me, Dougal.'

'I didn't want you to . . . do anything foolish.'

'I'm old enough to decide for myself what I want to do.'

But when she looked across the room, Joss hadn't moved towards her. He was staring, oh yes, but standing like a figure carved out of stone.

The woman next to him spoke. A young woman with dark hair and a kind face. Was it his wife? Was he married?

Thank goodness she hadn't made a fool of herself by running across the room to him.

As her brother let go, she rubbed her arm and fluffed out the skirt of her new gown. 'Don't interfere, Dougal.'

'What are you going to do?'

'I don't know yet.'

Something. She wasn't going to let this opportunity pass. But first she had to find out who the pretty young woman beside him was.

Ismay didn't even think. She moved to his side. 'Are you all right, Joss? You look as if you've had a shock.'

He blinked and looked at her, then across at the woman he'd been staring at, who was now fussing with her skirt. The man beside her was frowning at them.

'I've just seen a ghost.' Joss tried to laugh, but it was a mere scrape of sound.

'Do you know her?'

'Oh, yes. At least, I used to think I did.'

From the harrowed expression on his face,

Ismay guessed then that he must once have loved the woman. 'Who is she?'

'The sister of Captain Dougal McBride. Who was kind enough to warn me away from courting her some years ago and threaten trouble if I persisted.'

'Oh.'

Joss pulled himself together and turned away. 'Let's go and stand on the veranda for a moment or two. I can't seem to breathe in here.'

So Ismay went outside with him. She didn't try to chat and he didn't, either.

After a few moments, the gong sounded and their host called them to table.

'I pray I'm not sitting near them,' Joss muttered as they went back into the room.

Ismay was praying she wouldn't make a fool of herself.

It was Adam who found himself sitting next to Miss McBride. He too had noticed Joss's reaction to her, and hers to him, but he'd seen Ismay go to Joss so had let her help him, if she could. He didn't think his friend would like them all fussing round him.

He wondered about this strong reaction to one another. His immediate guess was that Joss and Miss McBride had once been lovers, but she didn't look like a loose woman. In love, then: a youthful fancy that hadn't worked out. No, more than a mere fancy, from the stunned expressions on both their faces, and the wistful looks that had followed.

Miss McBride turned to him and started the conversation by asking him where he came from, but he could see it was an effort for her to chat. After he'd explained a little about himself, the gentleman on her other side asked a question and she turned to him.

Adam was left with a fluttery lady who peppered him with questions about where he'd come from and soon found out that he owned half the schooner. After which she started mentioning her daughters so pointedly that he was forced to murmur he was about to become betrothed. That stopped the fussing, thank goodness.

Food was lavish and delicious, solid English fare. But the heat and high humidity seemed to have taken away Adam's appetite. He was now longing for cooler weather. He didn't know how people could bear to live here all the time. But perhaps they didn't have any choice. Thank goodness he did.

There were no Chinese people at the table, only Europeans, and the food was heavy stuff: roast beef, potatoes, pies, small fowl. It seemed very unsuitable for such a climate. He much preferred the meal Mr Lee had given them.

'You're not hungry, Mr Tregear?' the lady beside him asked as he pushed his food around the plate, trying to pile it up to look as if he'd eaten most of it.

'I'm afraid not. The food is delicious but I find the heat takes away my appetite.'

There was a fan above them, presumably being pulled to and fro by a servant, hidden away somewhere, but it only served to stir up the hot, moist air, not to cool him.

'You grow used to it.' But she looked to be wilting as well, and pulled out a handkerchief regularly to dab at her face.

'Do you live here permanently?' He listened to her response, trying to look as if he cared, wishing the meal would end and he could escape from these meaningless civilities. If it had been Ismay beside him, they'd not have been short of something to say.

When Miss McBride was free again, she looked at him then asked abruptly, 'Did I hear you saying you owned half of the *Hannah Grey*?'

'Yes. Joss Rutherford owns the other half.'

'Ah. Yes. I used to know him, but I haven't seen him for years.' She hesitated, then asked in a low voice, 'Is he married? He was with that pretty young woman earlier.'

'No. She's . . . my young lady. Joss is widowed.'

'Oh.'

She was screwing up her table napkin so tightly it was a mess of wrinkles, and had hardly touched her food. He wondered what had happened between the two of them. A sudden thought struck him. Was *she* the reason why Joss had been unable to love his wife?

'Is your aunt coming to live in Australia, Mr Tregear, or just visiting?'

'She's coming to live with me. We have no one but each other . . . till I marry.' He didn't count his half-brother and -sister in England, would probably never see them again.

'Miss Deagan will be going to live with her brother, I suppose?'

He looked across the table at Ismay. 'I suppose so. For the time being, anyway. She's been a wonderful companion to my aunt.'

'I dare say I'll see something of her, then. Dougal and I are friendly with Bram and his wife. And I'll call on your aunt, of course. She'll want to make new friends.'

'That's very kind. I'll introduce you to her after dinner, if you'd like.'

How annoying it was to hold a conversation where both of you clearly wanted to say other things and couldn't, because of manners and polite behaviour.

He would be glad when this evening ended. Doing the pretty to strangers wasn't his idea of having a good time.

What was?

That was easy. Chatting to Ismay, teasing her, explaining things to her. He looked across the table, found her gazing at him and smiled. Her answering smile warmed his heart.

She was definitely the one.

★   ★   ★

When the meal was over, Dougal stayed by her side like a fierce watchdog, so Flora got no chance to speak to Joss. And she didn't know whether to be sad or glad about that. It'd be wise to think about their situation before she did anything . . . and she wanted some sort of sign that he was still interested.

When they got back to the ship, her brother said abruptly, 'We need to talk. Why don't you come to my cabin? The chairs are more comfortable there.'

She did as he asked, in this at least, and waited to see what he would say.

'I'm sorry that fellow's in Singapore. I saw how the sight of him upset you.'

'Joss, you mean?'

'Yes. We'll have to keep our distance. I'm sorry if that spoils your visit.'

Here it came again, her family interfering. 'Why must we keep our distance?'

'Because he's not worthy of you, that's why. I've been thinking about it. If he'd had any guts, he'd have stayed, braved my mother and continued to court you.'

'I still don't know exactly why he left. What she said to him. And she's always refused to tell me, insisted she did nothing but ask the sort of questions any parent would.' Suddenly she knew what she wanted to do, had to do. 'So I intend to ask him now.'

'Flora, no! You'll only get hurt again. I found

out . . . he's been married. So he wasn't exactly pining after you.'

'Yes, Mr Tregear told me.'

'You were wasting your time hankering after him. I wish you'd accepted Mitchell's offer. The two of you got on so well, and you'd have been safe with him.'

'I worked for Mitchell Nash. We weren't courting. How many times do I have to tell you that he only wanted me for a housekeeper and mother for his son? He didn't *care* about me.'

'And how many times do I have to say that liking isn't a bad basis for marriage at your age.'

Her brother always said that. As if your feelings withered as you grew older. 'Mitchell is more like a cousin than a lover. I just can't think of him that way. I've known what love was like and I won't be content with less.'

'I beg you not to reopen old wounds, Flora.'

She smiled, stood up and went to kiss his cheek. 'You're a lovely brother, and I do appreciate how you care for me, but I'm a grown woman and I'll make my own decisions from now on. About Joss. About everything.'

She left him then but didn't go back to her cabin. Standing on deck, where it was cooler, she thought about their discussion.

It was a relief that Dougal didn't follow her, because, for all her brave words, she was still afraid to take the first step.

Don't reopen old wounds, Dougal had said. Only they'd never closed, had they?

What she didn't know, what she had to know, was why Joss hadn't tried to see her. Why had he just left? That had haunted her over the years.

How would she find the courage to ask him?

She couldn't help wondering how Joss felt about her now. He'd looked so grim tonight she feared it was too late for them. But if it wasn't . . . if there was the slightest chance . . .

No, she mustn't let this opportunity go. She needed to *know* why he'd left so suddenly.

14

The following day, Flora waited until the busy time was past on her brother's ship and he'd retired to his cabin to fill in his log and eat his usual mid-morning snack. She put on another of her new dresses and gathered her courage in both hands, praying he'd not come back up on deck until she was out of sight.

'I'm just going for a walk along the quay. I won't go out of sight of the ship,' she said brightly to the sailor on guard at the top of the gangway.

As she hurried away, her heart thudded in case Dougal called after her. But there were no voices, so she made her way along the quay to the *Hannah Grey*, threading her way in and out of the myriad people who always seemed to have business at the docks.

She could see Bram's sister standing by the rail, watching the teeming life on the water and quay, her face alight with interest. Stopping at the foot of the gangway, Flora called, 'Ahoy there! Permission to come aboard?'

'Oh, how lovely to see you! Do come up. I'm

dying to go out and about, and Aunt Harriet is having one of her naps.' Ismay pulled a wry face. 'They've made me promise not to go ashore on my own, you see. I got lost the first time.'

'My brother's as bad, but I just gave him the slip.' Flora hesitated at the top of the gangway, glancing over her shoulder towards the *Bonny Mary*, and moving further on to the deck so that she wasn't visible from it. Though of course the sailor on duty would have seen where she went. 'I need to speak to Joss. It's very important.'

'He's not on board at the moment. He and Adam have gone to discuss a new cargo. They went that way.' She pointed. 'Joss said this morning that it was about time we loaded up and left.'

'Oh.'

One word, but so full of pain. Ismay's heart went out to the other woman. 'It's sorry I'll be to leave Singapore. I love it here. Did you ever in your life see such a bustling place?'

'No, never. It's my first visit here, too, and I was hoping we could stay for a few more days, but from what Dougal says, I suspect we'll be leaving soon as well.'

She saw Ismay open her mouth, then close it again, and decided on frankness. 'I think you must have heard that Joss and I used to . . . see one another. We wanted to marry.'

'I guessed there was something between you. He said he used to know you, but I don't know any details. After we got back last night, he went straight to his cabin.'

'How did he look?'

'Sad. He's always sad underneath. I can't help noticing.'

'My brother had a word with me after we got back. Dougal insisted I should stay away from Joss . . . but I don't agree, so here I am.' She couldn't hold back. 'Oh, Ismay, I need to talk to him. Desperately.'

'Aunt Harriet says not to interfere, but I don't like to see people I care about unhappy. So, if I can help you, I will.'

There was silence, then Flora said, 'Would they think it all right if you came out for a walk with me? We don't need to go far, but we could go in the same direction Joss took.'

Ismay chuckled, feeling very comfortable with this woman. 'We might even run into them coming back.'

'Yes.'

'And if we do, I'll take Adam away with me.'

'That'd be . . . useful. If Joss will stay and talk to me, that is.'

'You won't know if you don't try. I'll leave a message for Aunt Harriet. And you can tell me about my brother as we walk. Bram doesn't write long letters, and I'm dying to know how he is and, oh, all sorts of things. Mrs Wallace told me about his wedding. Just imagine Mr Lee and his family attending, then taking everyone for a Chinese meal.

She seemed surprised at how good it tasted. You'd think she'd know already, living here, but she only has an English cook.'

'I've not tried Chinese food yet. I'd like to, though.'

'We had some at Mr Lee's. He's a splendid man, isn't he? So powerful and yet kind. And Xiu Mei is very pretty. Oh, I'm talking too much. Let me leave the message and we'll be off before anyone can stop us.'

As they set off along the quay, Ismay asked the questions closest to her heart. 'Is Bram happy? Really happy? And what's his wife like?'

'I don't think I've ever met a man as busily happy as your brother, and I like his wife dearly. They love one another very much. It shows.'

'I'm glad to hear that.'

They walked slowly, with Ismay bubbling over about everything they saw. Even now, when she was so apprehensive, it lifted Flora's spirits just to be with her.

Joss and Adam went to see Mr Lee in his godown, at his invitation. They found the warehouse to be much bigger than they'd expected, and were shown to a room at the rear by a beautiful young Asian man who spoke English.

Mr Lee waved them to seats and waited till tea was brought and each man had drunk two bowls.

Setting his empty bowl down, he pushed it away and came straight to the point. 'I have a cargo for your friend, Captain McBride, ordered by Bram Deagan. Have other things to sell as well. Some for Bram, some for Sydney perhaps.' He looked at Joss. 'You know people who buy goods in Sydney?'

'I might. What sort of things? Could you show me?'

Mr Lee led them through to a quieter corner and gestured to some displays of glass and china set out on tables. Beautiful pieces they were too.

'These are expensive,' Joss said.

'Good makers.'

'They're of a quality not often seen in the colony.' Joss felt excitement rising in him. 'I could arrange a sale in Sydney. Sometimes ships come in and advertise goods for sale themselves rather than selling them to shopkeepers. You can make more money that way. But you'd have to trust me about the money because I can't afford to buy the goods from you. My ship was damaged and it took everything I had to get it repaired.'

'And you had to take a partner, too,' Mr Lee said.

Joss looked at him in surprise. How had he found that out?

For a moment, Mr Lee's expression hinted at a smile, then it became impassive again. 'Ship is repaired now, though, and well repaired, more seaworthy than before.'

'How do you know that?'

'I ask about it. I always ask before I do business.

Prefer to do business with people I know. People I choose. People I trust.'

Joss studied the items again. 'Will Bram not be able to sell them for you in Perth?'

'Sell some. Good businessman, Bram. Good husband for Isabella. But not enough people in Swan River Colony. Isabella write me about it.'

'It's much smaller than the other colonies, except for Tasmania.'

'Many more people in Sydney. And Melbourne too, I think.'

'Yes. How big a cargo do you have?'

'Have some good china and glass, not risk a whole shipload. Also have much building material: nails, hinges, locks. Window glass. Can make up full cargo with other things. You help choose if you work with me.' He stopped and studied them both, waiting.

Joss studied the items on show, thinking hard, then looked up. 'It could be very profitable, if it was done right.'

Mr Lee inclined his head in a sort of salute. 'Yes. Need to take great care.'

'And the money?'

'I trust you to bring my share back to me, cost of goods plus eighty per cent of profit.'

'Seventy per cent. I have men to pay and feed.'

Silence, then another nod. 'Very well. I think you not steal from me, Captain Rutherford, or you, Mr Tregear.'

'I'd never steal from anyone.' Joss offered his hand.

The men shook on the bargain.

'Unfortunately there is one problem about me going to Sydney this time,' Adam said. 'I have to take up an inheritance in Fremantle, and I've promised to go straight there. Also, even more important to me, I need to get my aunt and Miss Deagan settled in a house before I go on any more voyages.'

Joss sighed. Wasn't there always some problem to prevent him seizing the moment? 'And I've promised Adam's group passage to Fremantle, so I can't in all conscience add a month or more to the journey by going via Sydney.

There was silence.

'There is another ship sailing to Fremantle soon,' Mr Lee said. 'Mr Tregear could sail back to Fremantle with Captain McBride, if you can manage without a first mate, Captain Rutherford.' He steepled his fingers together and leaned back, watching them again.

Neither man spoke as they thought about this, then Joss said quietly, 'It will need thinking about. Captain McBride might not want to oblige me. We had a few differences some years ago.'

Mr Lee frowned. 'Long time to hold bad feelings. Not good in business.'

'I can't decide straight away.' Could he do it? Could he sink his pride and ask this favour of McBride?

And would Dougal forget his animosity and help out? With any other captain he'd not hesitate.

'I think Captain McBride will help. He's a good man.' Mr Lee picked up some papers, offering them with both hands. 'This is list of goods I think sell in Australia. Read it. If you think of other goods, I can supply.'

Joss decided that Dougal could only say no. He'd go and see him, plead if necessary. Would Flora make sure her brother refused? He couldn't get her face out of his mind. She'd aged well; she looked better as a mature woman – though he'd not loved her for her looks, just for herself.

The profit from this one voyage could be huge, so he had to try. He looked at Mr Lee and suddenly remembered the modest shop-house in which the other man lived. Doubt crept in. 'Excuse me asking, but do you have the money to do this?'

Mr Lee gave them one of his gentle half-smiles. 'Have more money than people think. Going to build new house now. Big one. Time to show some wealth.'

He stood up. 'Talk to Captain McBride. Come back tomorrow. Think very carefully about it. I like to have partners in Australia for long time. Isabella's brother and his friends.'

As the two men walked slowly back towards the ship, Joss said, 'I don't think McBride will take you. He holds a grudge against me.'

'I saw how he scowled at you last night. Because of his sister, I suppose?'

'Mmm.'

'Can the rift not be mended?'

'I don't know. Flora was so . . . unkind. And I was young enough to be hurt and turn away, instead of trying to see her and talk about our differences, even if we had to wait years to marry. I've had a long time to think about it. To wonder. To know I could have handled it better.'

'It's easy to be wise with hindsight and—' Adam grabbed Joss's arm. 'Talk of the devil!'

The two men stopped to watch two European women making their way along the quay, weaving in and out of the hawkers, the piles of goods, the crowds of people bustling around or sitting watching all the activity.

Ismay saw them first and nudged her companion before waving to them.

Flora stared at Joss. It was as if Adam didn't exist, as if nothing existed except Joss.

And he was staring at her with the same intensity.

'Let's walk forward to meet them,' Adam said gently. 'She's not turned away. That shows a certain willingness to talk, don't you think?'

'Yes. You're right.' He took a deep breath, feeling a flutter of hope, praying he wasn't mistaken.

They walked forward, stopping with only three or four feet between them and the two women.

'Hello, Adam. I haven't forgotten my promise not to leave the ship alone, but I didn't think you'd mind me going for a walk with Flora.' Ismay smiled at him, then glanced at the other two. 'I was longing to stretch my legs.' She jerked her head in a signal that they should leave.

He immediately offered her his arm. 'In that case, if you're not too tired, let me escort you a little further. I'd enjoy a brisk walk myself.'

She linked her arm in his and didn't even try to speak to Joss or Flora, because she doubted they'd have heard her. As they walked away, she whispered, 'I do hope they can sort out their problems.'

'What about us? Do you think we can sort out our problems too?'

She looked at him in surprise, then her breath caught in her throat at the warmth of his gaze. 'I don't know. Aren't they . . . too big? I can't change who I am.'

'I don't care how big you think they are, I'd like to try because I like who you are. Joss and Flora must have been very unhappy, you can see that. I don't want to have . . . regrets like theirs.'

Once he and Flora were on their own, Joss said gently, 'We should have talked properly years ago. I'm sorry about that. I was a fool to leave without seeing you.'

Flora nodded. 'I'm sorry, too. I shouldn't have let my mother stop me.'

'Can we talk now?'

'Yes. I'd like that.' She looked round, as if only just aware of the teeming life around them. 'But could we go somewhere quieter to do it?'

A man bumped into Joss and hurried past without apologising.

'I don't know anywhere quiet unless . . . Look, would you come to my cabin? It's the only place I can think of where we definitely won't be interrupted. Will you trust me?'

'Of course.'

'Your brother won't approve.'

'I've let others dictate my behaviour for too long. And regretted it for years.'

The last words, spoken so quietly he had to strain his ears to hear them, gave him a sudden surge of hope that made his breath catch in his throat. He was terrified of saying the wrong thing, so offered his arm, relieved when she took it and began to walk beside him, equally silent.

He couldn't help it. He laid his other hand on hers as it rested lightly on his sleeve, feeling her hand quiver beneath his. But she didn't pull away.

So they walked like that to the ship, not saying anything, just touching, skin to skin.

And hoping. He was beginning to hope again.

As they stepped on to the deck, he said curtly to the man on watch, 'I'll be in my cabin. I'm not to be disturbed for anything less than an emergency. No visitors.' He didn't wait for an answer.

Mrs McBride failed rapidly after the doctor's visit. They offered her water to drink and she turned her head away. If they tried to give her food, she spat it out or let it lie in her mouth.

Rhoda was horrified. 'We can't just leave her to starve to death. It's not right.'

'We can hardly force food down her. She might choke.'

'We should ask someone else about it. It's too heavy a responsibility, Mrs Southerham.'

'Hmm. You're right.'

'How about Mr Deagan? He's a clever man, and not about book learning like that doctor, but about real life.'

Livia stared down at Mrs McBride and nodded. They all turned to her to find out what to do, and half the time she wasn't at all sure she was managing things properly. It was ironic when you thought how impractical she'd been when she arrived in Australia. Was she more practical now? Of course. But oh, she longed to be rid of responsibility for sick people. Surely this couldn't be her life from now on?

'I'll walk down to see him now,' she said abruptly. She needed to get away for a while.

She found Bram inside the Bazaar, working on his accounts at the rear of the store.

He set his pen down when he saw her. 'Is something wrong?'

'Yes. And I'd like to ask your advice about it, if you don't mind. Miss McBride suggested I turn to you if I had any worries.'

'If I can help you in any way, I will. I told you both that before she left.' He put the cap on the inkwell and blotted his figures, before closing the big leather-bound book with a marker at the page. 'We'll go down to the house.'

'Could we . . . Is there somewhere else? It's a difficult subject. I don't mind your wife being there, but you have a maid and . . .'

'If you don't object to one of the new rooms in the stables, that might be better. It looks as if it's going to rain, so we can't go for a walk, or I'd suggest that. There's nothing like a walk for clearing the head.'

It started to pelt down as they went down the slope from the Bazaar, so they ran the last twenty yards to the livery stables, arriving breathless, having to shake the raindrops from their clothing.

She looked round. 'This place looks very prosperous too, which I gather it wasn't when you first moved in. You've a magic touch.'

He smiled. 'It's Les we have to thank for it looking so trim. He's a wonder with horses, that man is, and keeps the stables in immaculate order, too.'

At the sound of his name, Les looked up from where he was murmuring to one of the horses that someone had lodged with them. He smiled at the praise.

Since she wasn't one to scorn men who had put their mistakes behind them and made decent new lives for themselves, Livia waved and called a greeting. He had his conditional pardon now and was free to do anything except leave the colony until the term of his original sentence had been fulfilled.

'I'll just be showing Mrs Southerham the new rooms,' Bram said. 'No need to trouble you.' He didn't wait for an answer, but led her to the rear of the livery stables and opened a new door there that led out into a single-storey wooden structure, still smelling of sawdust and paint. 'We've not quite finished these off, but one or two are ready for use.'

He showed her the row of small rooms, designed for grooms or single men wanting only a night's simple accommodation. 'Why don't you sit on the bed here and I'll bring in a stool?'

He did that, but when she bit her lip and seemed to have trouble starting, he said encouragingly, 'It'll be about Mrs McBride . . .'

'Yes.' Still she hesitated, not sure how to ask him if it was right to leave a woman to starve to death. But that was cowardly, so she looked up and told him about the decision she had to make.

His expression grew sympathetic and, when she'd finished, and was dabbing her eyes with a handkerchief, he said in that soft, lilting voice, 'You can't be making miracles, Livia. No one can.'

'But to let her starve without even *trying* . . .'

'The doctor said it'd be quicker and more merciful not to force her. Did he not?'

'Yes.'

'Is she showing any signs of distress?'

'Only if we try to give her a drink or touch her.'

'Then let the poor creature go in peace. I'll come back with you now to see her, though, so that I can tell people I agreed with your decision.'

He stood up, looking out of the window with a grimace. 'But first we'll make a dash for the house and let Isabella give us a cup of tea and some sympathy. Maybe the rain will have eased off by then. We'll not be getting much more rain, will we? Soon it'll be summer and hot. I'm getting to like the heat.'

Later, as he stood by Mrs McBride's bedside, Bram shook his head sadly. 'She looks almost dead now, no expression on her face at all.'

He took Livia's hand. 'There's nothing you can do, my dear, but tend her body while she's still in it. Keep her clean and comfortable. No one can do more.'

'I wanted to keep her alive till Flora came back.'

'Maybe it'll be easier for her if her mother slips away while she's in Singapore. She's had such a hard time of it over the past few years. I hope fate has something better in store for her now.'

Joss waited till Flora was sitting down before he went to occupy the window seat in his cabin, the place he usually sat when at leisure. He looked across at her and couldn't help asking the question he'd meant to keep until later. 'Why did you write me that final letter? It was very . . . hurtful.'

She looked at him in puzzlement. 'Which letter do you mean?'

'The one where you said you were riven with guilt about neglecting your duty to your family.'

She stiffened. 'I never wrote anything like that, Joss. I wrote saying I'd be prepared to run away with you. Anywhere. And you didn't reply.'

He looked at her in shock. 'I never received such a letter. I'd have snatched you away from that old harpy at once if I had. I have the letter I'm talking about still. And it's in your handwriting, though blurred in parts with what I took to be teardrops.'

'Joss, I swear I've never sent you any letter with those words in it, let alone one covered in teardrops. I've too much pride to do that. And I'd never have put my mother before you. Never.'

She gasped and clasped both hands to her face, hiding for a moment from the dreadful thought that wouldn't be banished. 'You have the letter here? Can I see it?'

'Yes. I could never bear to destroy it.'

But she already knew what they'd find. Oh yes, she knew. Hatred sliced through her, sharp as a knife, and it seemed as if the seconds crawled past slowly while she waited to confirm her suspicions.

He went across to his desk and opened a beautifully inlaid wooden writing slope, lifting the inner lid and fiddling with something to reveal a hidden compartment. From this he pulled out a letter that had clearly been badly crumpled at some time in the past.

She couldn't wait a second longer but went across to join him as he passed the rolled up letter to her without a word. She smoothed it out and stared at it, but the words didn't make sense, and she had to force herself to concentrate and start reading it again.

My dearest Joss, though this is the last time I can allow myself to call you that,

I have lain awake weeping all night, but can only come to the conclusion that I must be loyal to my family.

I have a duty to my poor widowed mother, a duty I have been neglecting sadly of late. I'm riven with guilt about that.

In short, I cannot reconcile it with my conscience to see you again and leave her to live out her days alone. She's already lost her husband. Should she also lose her daughter?

Please do not try to call at the house or write to me, because I shall not read the letters or see you.

There is something else that urges this decision. Whatever our feelings have been, I have been made aware that your birth and breeding are not acceptable to my family and they will disown me if I wed you.

I cannot force the connection upon them and never see them again.

I wish you well.

Flora

She frowned and read it again, then looked up at him. 'The handwriting does look a bit like mine. But the words. No, they're not mine. Joss, when have I ever talked like that? I left such sentimental rubbish to my mo—' Her voice broke then and she began to weep.

He finished the sentence for her. '. . . To your mother. She wrote it.'

'No wonder it's scattered with drops of water. She was hiding the fact that she couldn't imitate my handwriting perfectly.'

'I couldn't believe it when I read it . . . But Flora, your brother said much the same thing when he came to see me.'

'*Dougal came to see you?*'

'Yes. He said I was causing you great unhappiness, and the family were unhappy about our connection. His visit, coming on top of what I took to be your letter . . .'

He paused and sucked in a deep, shuddering breath. 'It had hurt me greatly to read that my birth and breeding were not acceptable because I was aware, always aware, that my father had married beneath him. Their love didn't survive their differences, you see, and my mother was a very unhappy woman, always struggling to do the right thing. She often infuriated him and in the end he treated her with utter contempt. I couldn't bear the thought of you scorning me, looking at me as he'd looked at her.'

Flora studied the letter again. 'There's no doubt

in my mind that my mother wrote this. That's exactly how she does an M. And the flourish after the signature is hers.' She raised one hand to dash away the tears, but more followed.

He put his arm round her shoulders, holding her as she leaned against him, sobbing.

After a few minutes, she managed to control herself. 'How could she? How could she *do* that to her own daughter? When she knew how much I loved you.'

He guided her across to the window seat and sat down, with her leaning against him in the circle of his arms. She didn't sob again, but the tears kept rolling silently down her cheeks, falling on his hands and dampening his shirt front. It was agony to see her like this.

In the end he pulled out his handkerchief and wiped those damp cheeks. 'Shh, my love. Shh, don't cry any more.' Then he kissed her.

For a moment she stiffened against him, then she was kissing him back hungrily, like a woman who'd been starved for years. He rained kisses on her face, felt her kisses on his skin, felt something painful inside him start to melt.

When she pulled away, she looked at him. 'So many years wasted. Such dreadful, tedious years.'

'Has it been bad?'

'Very bad. At first I was numb. Then I found out you'd left the colony and I didn't care enough to fight any longer. I let her have her own way more often than I should have done.'

'But you've got away from her now. You're free to do as you wish, surely?'

'I only escaped because she's ill, losing her mind, as old people sometimes do. I was exhausted by caring for her and Dougal brought me with him to Singapore for a rest.'

He let out a soft whistle of surprise. 'That must be very hard, whatever your feelings about her.'

'Yes, she has to be looked after by a strong woman in case she harms herself or others. She can be violent at times.'

Silence fell for a few moments, then he changed the subject. 'I couldn't believe it was you at Mrs Wallace's.'

'You looked shocked to see me.'

'I was. And yet, delighted.'

'Yet you turned away.'

'I wanted to carry you off, and at the same time was afraid to face your scorn.'

'No scorn for you, ever.'

'Did the voyage help?'

'Yes. I spent most of it recovering my peace of mind. I love standing by the rail, watching the ocean, even watching the men deal with the sails.'

'You must be a good sailor.'

'I think I am.' There was one more thing to be sorted out. 'I heard you'd married.'

'It was a marriage of convenience only, as I told her when I offered. I wanted children, so did she. But she thought she could make me love her.'

'You can never do that.'

'No. And having a child killed her . . . but only after I'd made her very unhappy. I couldn't forget you, you see, Flora. Never, ever.'

She let him pull her towards him again, raising her face for a kiss, and losing herself in it.

When he pulled away, smiling now, she raised one hand to caress his cheek, then push back his hair from his forehead. 'Oh, Joss.'

'I love you, Flora.'

'And I love you.'

'Will you marry me? As soon as possible?'

'Oh, yes. We've wasted far too much of our lives.'

There was a sound outside, men arguing, and when she listened, she recognised one of them. 'That's my brother.'

'Are you ready to face him?'

'Yes. But please, Joss, don't let him make you lose your temper. He was fed lies by our mother too.'

Joss dropped one last kiss on her forehead and went to open the cabin door.

15

Adam and Ismay strolled round the streets, taking their time, enjoying the sights and sounds; most of all enjoying being together. They didn't need to put that into words. Not that they were short of words. They always found something to talk about.

As they turned back towards the harbour, he said abruptly, 'I do want to marry you, Ismay. I haven't changed my mind about that.'

She looked at him, her love showing very clearly, then she bent her head and shook it. 'I'm still the same old Ismay, an Irish peasant, and I'd hold you back. I'm not good enough for you.'

'What about making me happy? Don't you think you can do that?'

'It won't be enough. In your position you need a wife other people can respect, not someone they'll scorn as low Irish. Haven't you seen the signs saying *No Irish need apply*? I never realised till I left home how scornful people are of us.'

'I'm sure it'll be enough for me that you're my Ismay. And you keep forgetting that I'm bastard born. People scorn that too.'

'All the more reason not to marry someone like me. Adam, you own half of a ship, while I—'

He put his fingertip across her lips. 'Let me finish. You learn quickly. If any problems crop up, you'll have my aunt to help you. It'll be fine.'

'I can't believe she approves.'

'Oh, she does. And it's no small thing to me that you get on so well with her. She's come all this way to be with me and I want to offer her a home for as long as she needs it. There are some women who can't live with relatives, but I think you could do so quite happily.'

'Anyone could live with your aunt, she's so pleasant and easy.'

'There you are, then.'

'Oh, Adam, don't be tempting me like this. I'm trying to do what's best for you.'

'The best thing for me – the only thing – is to marry the woman I love. But I'm not getting officially betrothed until I'm certain there are no more nasty surprises waiting for me. My father has left me three properties in Fremantle, but the lawyer didn't have any information about them. Don't you think that's strange? I do. If there's one thing I know about my father, it's that there will be some trickery involved, some bitter pill to swallow if I want to keep these properties.'

'Why are you so sure of that? He left you a share in the *Hannah*.'

'And I had to leave England to get it. He used it as a bribe to send me as far away from his other children as was possible. I dared to dream, to hope that I'd be master of my own ship, that the other owner would be a sleeping partner . . . and he made sure that wasn't to be.'

'But you still own a big share of it.'

'Yes. Forty-nine per cent. Joss has the deciding say in things. *He* is the captain. I had nothing before and you'd think I'd be glad of this, but that loss of control sticks in my gullet.'

'Even with Joss? You and he get on so well.'

'Even so. But my damned father judged one thing rightly. I'm not stupid enough to throw away my share in the schooner. It's still a better chance than I'd have had without the legacy.'

'You sound as if you hate him.'

'I do.'

'It's such a relief to hear you say that. I hate my father too.'

He stopped to clasp her hand. 'I know. And you have every reason to. But at least you came out of that without an extra burden.'

She felt tears rise in her eyes and for the first time dared to tell someone. 'But it's left its mark. I still have nightmares from what happened with Rory.'

Then she shared another fear, one that kept her awake at night sometimes, the fear that Rory had spoiled her for ever for marriage. 'I don't know how I'll feel if a husband touches me in that way. That's another reason for you to find someone who hasn't . . . hasn't . . .'

'Oh, Ismay!' He gave her a quick hug and she didn't pull away. 'If someone who loves you touches you gently and caringly, I'm sure you'll learn to welcome his touch. I'd never hurt you, you know that. And you didn't flinch from my hug just now.'

'I didn't, did I?'

They stared at each other and suddenly she could protest no longer. She wanted so much to be with him. 'If you're sure . . .'

He beamed at her. 'Very sure.'

'Oh, Adam, I'd love to marry you.'

He hugged her again. 'We'll tell Aunt Harriet that we love one another and hope to marry, but we're not going to make our engagement public until I'm certain I can offer you a good name and future.'

She pulled away, face flushed with happiness, and began to tidy her hair.

'We'd better get back to the ship, my love. I do have a few other things to do besides courting my lovely lady.'

Did she dare feel this happy? Ismay wondered.

But as they strolled back together, something made her shiver and clutch his hand even more tightly. For a moment she wondered what had caused that feeling, then she remembered that Rory Flynn had been on his way to Australia.

Would he be waiting for her there?

Would he still insist she should be marrying him? Would he blacken her name and make it impossible for her to marry Adam?

Or would Rory try to hurt him? She couldn't bear that. He was such a big man, and Adam was slight, like her brother Bram.

What was she going to do when they got to Fremantle? But she couldn't bear to spoil this moment by her fears. She'd talk about those another time.

Dougal accepted an invitation to join Joss in the cabin, walking in to see his sister standing there with her hair in disarray. It was quite clear they'd been kissing. 'How could you, Flora? Are you lost to all decency to come to a man's bedroom?'

Joss went to stand beside her. 'Don't you dare speak to her like that!'

'I'll speak to her any way I please. She's my sister and I'm not having you hurting her again.'

'And she's going to be my wife, and knows I'll never hurt her.'

Dougal opened his mouth but no sound came out and Flora seized the opportunity to say, 'Please sit down, Dougal. I . . . we need to talk. I think you've been tricked by Mother as much as Joss and I have.'

She moved back to the window seat and sat down, afraid that her brother would lose his temper and say something he'd regret later. When he was younger, that temper had got Dougal into trouble many a time, and it had taken a lot of effort for him to get it under control.

She watched him open his mouth as if to protest,

then he shut it with a snap and sat on the chair she'd indicated. His scowl deepened as Joss sat down beside her and took hold of her hand.

'For all his fine words, he left you once before, Flora. You can't trust this man to stick by you.'

'He had reason to leave me.'

'No man leaves the woman he loves because her mother tells him to go away. You were over twenty-one at the time, remember?'

'I agree. But what you don't know . . .' She had to pause to stop herself from weeping again and, even so, her voice wobbled as she said, 'Our mother forged a letter and Joss thought it was me who'd written to tell him things had ended. Show him, Joss.'

Dougal took the crumpled paper, read it and looked at her in shock, then read it again. As if it was poisonous, he threw it down on the desk. 'I can't believe she did this.'

'No. I was . . . shocked.' And hurt so deeply, she wished she need never see her mother again.

'You still shouldn't have come to his cabin today, though.'

'He's behaved like a perfect gentleman.'

Her brother let out a snort. 'Then why is your hair coming down and why are your lips swollen?'

Joss jerked forward as if to answer, so she said quickly, 'Because we've been kissing, of course. People usually do when they agree to marry. I'm not ashamed of that.'

Her smile was so radiant that Joss, who'd been

getting increasingly annoyed by what her brother was saying, calmed down a little and smiled tenderly at her.

Dougal looked at them grimly. 'And yet, this loving man got married while you were apart. *He* didn't wait for you. How can you trust him?'

'I know about Joss's marriage and the reasons for it. I don't care about that. But I do care that you're trying to bully me and stop me doing what I want. *I won't have it, Dougal!* I'm free of my mother now and I'm not letting you take over from her and start dictating what I do. I'm going to marry Joss.'

Dougal breathed deeply. 'Can't you see that I'm trying to protect you?'

'I don't need protecting from Joss.'

He sighed, clenched his fists and turned to Joss. 'You'd better make her happy or you'll answer to me.'

'I'll make her as happy as fate allows.'

Flora beamed at them both. 'There. That's settled. And the sooner we get married the better.' But her smile faded as she saw that her brother was not pleased by this statement.

'Now that I definitely won't allow.' Dougal glared at the other man. 'Do you want to make her name a byword, Rutherford? Surely you realise word of her coming to your ship will get out? It always does. I'm sure Singapore is no different from Fremantle in that respect. If you must marry, you need to give people time to get used to the idea, not rush into a hasty marriage, which will look as if you've done something wrong.'

'I don't care what people think or say,' Flora snapped.

'You ought to. Mud always clings. You know that.'

Flora had had enough. She bounced to her feet and let her own temper loose for once. 'I'm marrying him – today if possible – and nothing you say or do will stop me. Nothing.'

Joss stood up too, and if the looks he'd been giving Dougal had grown more and more unfriendly, the expression on his face was now as furious as his visitor's. He took a step forward, breathing deeply.

Flora moved hastily between them. 'Don't you dare start fighting, either of you.' She stretched out her arms to touch each man, as if holding them apart. 'I don't need your permission, Dougal, and Joss, I forbid you to scrap with my brother.'

Both men took a step backwards, but their angry expressions didn't change.

'Remember: least said, soonest mended, Dougal. Unless you want us to be estranged?' Flora let her words sink in, then turned back to Joss. 'Go and find out how quickly we can get married, my darling, then get your new cargo loaded. When you leave, I'm coming with you. I'll go and pack my things straight away.'

She stood on tiptoe to kiss his cheek, ignoring a growl of anger from her brother, then turned and threaded her arm through Dougal's, forcing him to leave the cabin with her.

'Don't do it, Flora,' he pleaded as they walked back along the quay. 'Don't rush into this till you've had time to think.'

'I've wasted years of my life because of our mother. She may even have cost me my chance to have a child. I'm not wasting one more day from now on, even for you. *Not one single day!*'

But he looked unconvinced and she abandoned the attempt to persuade him.

Once back on the ship, she said, 'I'm going to pack my things and, as soon as Joss and I can marry, I'm going to him. I hope you'll come to my wedding, Dougal. If you don't, that really will cause talk.'

Livia was woken by someone hammering on her bedroom door. 'Yes, I'm coming.' She swung out of bed, pulling a shawl round her shoulders. 'What's the matter, Rhoda?'

'I went in to wash Mrs McBride, only . . . I think she's dead.'

'I'd better come and see.' Livia had a sudden memory of her husband dying and, oh, she didn't want to deal with another corpse. But life was full of difficult situations and you just had to brace yourself and get on with it.

They stood looking down at Mrs McBride.

'She's not breathing, is she, Mrs Southerham?' Livia could see no pulse in the neck, but picked up the little hand mirror from the dressing table and held it to the old lady's nose. She had to make sure, absolutely sure. She watched it carefully, but the mirror didn't cloud up at all. 'She's definitely dead.'

'She looks unhappy even in death, doesn't she? Shall I cover her face?'

'Yes, please. I know you're not supposed to speak ill of the dead, but she wasn't a very nice woman, from what I've seen. I'm glad for Flora's sake it's over.'

'I heard a few things about her over the years. Bullied her poor daughter, she did, and acted like she was better than other folk, and her running a boarding house too!' Rhoda paused, then said, 'I could lay her out, if you like. I do that for people sometimes. I'd have to charge you, though. If I'm losing my job, I'm going to need every penny.'

'We'd better not touch her till the doctor's been. But afterwards, yes, I'd be grateful. Perhaps you could go round and ask him to call?'

'All right.' Humming cheerfully, Rhoda clumped along to her room and Livia heard her go into the kitchen and tell Orla what had happened.

She was quite sure Orla was crossing herself and saying a quick prayer. Livia just wished she had the same solace. She hadn't been able to pray for quite a while now.

The house door banged shut and silence reigned again.

Livia looked at the still figure on the bed and

shivered. She didn't want to die so alone and unlamented. Why hadn't she and Francis been blessed with children? This horrible woman had been blessed with two, but look how badly she'd treated her daughter.

Well, it was no use standing here feeling sorry for herself. She went to the kitchen where Orla was setting the table for breakfast.

'Is everything all right, ma'am?'

'Yes. I'm not doing anything until the doctor's seen her.'

'I'll make you a nice pot of tea, shall I? You look a bit pale.'

'Do I? I can't think why. But a pot of tea would be lovely in a few minutes. I'll go and get dressed first, then we'll share the tea with Rhoda.' She went to get ready for what was sure to be a difficult day.

She was glad of the kindness that made Orla bully her to eat something; glad of the company of the other two women; guiltily glad to be done with Mrs McBride.

'Well, I'll have to start looking for a job,' Rhoda said, as she finished a third piece of bread and jam. 'Still, I always seem to find something.'

'Do you ever think of getting married again?'

'Bless you, I'd do it in a minute, but my hubby ain't dead. Not that I know of, anyway.'

'That must be hard for you.'

'Oh, I get by. If you don't have a man living with you, at least you can't get any more children.

Not if you live decently, anyway. Though I ought to be getting past child-bearing soon and at least my four are all employed or married.'

'I suppose we'll have to find somewhere else to live now, won't we, Mrs Southerham?' Orla asked.

'Yes. But I'm sure they'll let us stay on here for a week or two.'

'Or perhaps we could rent this house and open a little school like you once thought of doing?'

'Yes. Perhaps we could.' Though Livia had lost all desire to open a school now. She didn't think she'd be good at keeping other people's children in order. 'I can't think about that until after the funeral and fuss are over.'

When she'd gone, Orla looked at Rhoda and rolled her eyes. 'She's tired out, poor thing. It's a heavy responsibility, looking after someone who's like the old lady was. And the missus didn't have an easy time of it before, what with her husband dying bit by bit. She said I could go on working for her, though, for as long as she can find the money, and I will. I like working for her. She's always polite and she talks to you about things. She's even got me reading those books of hers.'

'I noticed. She isn't like some I've met who treat you like you're not fit to breathe the same air because you're a servant. Is there another cup of tea in that pot?'

'I think I could just squeeze one out, but it'll be very strong.'

'I don't care how strong it is. You can keep your beer and booze. It's tea that keeps me going.'

The doctor arrived half an hour later, pronounced Mrs McBride dead and looked at Livia, leading her across to the window and studying her face. 'You need a rest now, my dear lady. You've been pushing yourself too hard for a long time, from what I hear. We don't want you collapsing.'

'I'll rest once she's buried.'

'I suggest you send a message to Punchley's. They do a decent funeral. I doubt you'll be wanting all the trimmings with her son and daughter away.'

'No, just a simple funeral. I'll send Rhoda to ask the undertaker to call.'

When the doctor had gone, she said, 'I must let Mr Deagan know. Could you take a note to him for me, Rhoda, as well as calling in at Punchley's? Would you mind? I'll just go and write it.'

'See what I mean,' Orla said. 'Polite as you please. You'd think she was asking a favour of you.'

Bram came up to the house as soon as he'd read the note. After one look at Livia, he said, 'We'll have to spoil you a bit now, my dear. You're looking rather peaky.'

'You're the second person to say that to me today.'

'Oh? Who was the other?'

'The doctor. But I daren't get used to being spoilt. I have to make a living somehow.'

'Do you need any help?'

'I've enough money to manage for the time being, thank you, but not enough to live on decently for the rest of my life. And anyway, I can't just sit around all day doing nothing, can I? I must find some purpose in life.'

'Best thing for you would be to find another husband.'

'How do I do that? Wear a sign on my back? Besides, I'm past the age of marrying now.'

'Nonsense. You're a fine-looking woman, or you will be once you've rested a bit.' He grinned at her. 'I'll look into finding a fellow for you.'

'Don't be silly.'

But as he walked away, he smiled. He would definitely look into it. Livia wasn't the most practical of women, however willing. She was meant to be a wife, probably to someone like a clergyman. Bram might mention her situation to one or two of the gossipy ladies who came into his shop, just casually, not suggesting anything outright. There was a shortage of women at all levels in this colonial society, after all. Someone suitable might turn up.

And there was Mitchell Nash, too. He'd asked Flora to marry him, not because he loved her, but because he wanted a wife and mother for his little son. Perhaps he'd be interested in Livia instead.

Yes, there were plenty of men in the colony looking for wives. It was just a matter of finding the right one and— He stopped and gaped as he recognised someone just ahead of him. So he hadn't been mistaken before.

'Hoy! Rory Flynn,' he roared at the top of his voice.

The other man turned round, jerked as if he wanted to run away, then waited for Bram to reach him.

They'd never been friends back home in Ireland, but perhaps Rory would have news.

'What are you doing here, Rory?'

'Same as you. Trying to make my fortune.'

'I wish you luck. How are you going to do that?'

'Haven't decided yet.'

'How were my family when you left?' To his surprise, Rory squirmed. There was no other word for it. He looked uncomfortable and shifted his feet before answering.

'Your da is well. He's missing you.'

'And Ma?'

'Oh, she's the same as always.'

'What about Ismay? She must be a grown woman now. Is she as pretty as she used to be?'

'Very pretty. You'd better know now since you're her brother: I'm going to marry her.'

'You are?' Bram would do anything he could to stop that, knowing how rough Rory could be.

'She wouldn't have me.' Rory hesitated. 'She ran away. I'd expected her to be here by now. But she got off the ship in Aden and she didn't get on again.'

Bram's heart sank. 'Was she in trouble?'

'She was with some lady who needed a maid.' He sucked the corner of his mouth, then said, 'Only remember, I *am* going to marry her, put things right. That's why I came here.'

'But you said she didn't want to marry you.'

'Well, she's got to now, hasn't she?' He made a suggestive movement with one hand to indicate a swollen belly.

Fury rose in Bram. 'You mean, you got her in trouble?'

Rory took a step backwards, eyes careful, standing like a fighter. 'I said I was going to marry her, didn't I? Your father approves. He couldn't think what got into her to refuse me.'

'Where are you staying?'

'Here and there. Look, I've got to go. I'm working for a fellow who won't like it if I'm late.' He turned on his heel and hurried off.

Bram didn't follow him. It'd be easy enough to find him again if he was living in Fremantle.

Besides, it didn't do to be hasty. He'd never liked Rory Flynn, and didn't want him for a brother-in-law; couldn't see him making any woman happy, let alone one as bright and cheerful as Ismay.

She couldn't be pregnant to Rory. She just *couldn't*. She wouldn't let a man like him touch her. Only . . . Rory had seemed so certain she was carrying his child.

He mentioned the encounter to Isabella that evening, but warned her to beware of Rory if he came round.

'I don't trust the fellow. Don't even let him through the door if you're on your own.'

'If you don't like him, then there must be something wrong with him. You're a good judge of character, my darling.'

So he had to take her in his arms and give her a kiss and a cuddle.

It wasn't until he was lying in bed that night that he faced the thought he'd been holding back all day, the thought that made him want to hunt out Rory and smash a fist in his face, even though he knew he'd never get near enough to do that. If Ismay was carrying that man's child, she hadn't got it willingly. She'd always hated him, even when they were all children at school together.

Surely Rory was lying? Saying it to get his own way. Only, why would he do that?

The answer was obvious. Money! To get what he could out of Bram, who was doing well for himself now.

In fact, Bram was making so much from the Bazaar it scared him sometimes. It might seem a modest amount to people used to being rich, but to a man from a poor background, it seemed like a huge fortune. More than enough to move out of this humble cottage. More than enough to bring his family out here from Ireland, as he'd planned. He was going to offer them the chance soon. All of them.

He couldn't get the meeting with Rory out of his mind, though. If that fellow had put Ismay in the family way, Bram wouldn't be answerable. He didn't normally believe in revenge, wasn't a fighting man; usually managed to talk his way out of difficult situations. Only . . . if someone hurt those he loved, he'd make sure they paid for it, one way or another.

No, it couldn't be true. It just . . . couldn't.

But Ismay's luggage had arrived. Why hadn't she come with it? Where was she now? Who was she with? Was she safe?

He turned over again, but the questions kept repeating in his mind. He couldn't afford a sleepless night. He not only had a business to run but a funeral to attend tomorrow.

Only, Ismay was his favourite sister. What if she was in trouble somewhere with no one to help her?

They buried Mrs McBride the following afternoon, with no fuss and no one in attendance except the curate, the three women who'd cared for her, and Bram and his wife.

Afterwards he walked back with them while Isabella went to keep an eye on the Bazaar.

'Won't you come in and have a cup of tea, Bram?' Livia asked.

When they were sitting down, she came straight to the point. 'Will it be all right if Orla and I stay in the house, do you think? And poor Rhoda needs somewhere to stay as well till she finds a new position.'

'You must definitely stay till they get back and I don't see why the two maids shouldn't stay with you. Why not ask Dougal if you can rent the house from him? I know you've been looking for somewhere to live. Unless your experiences have spoiled you for living here, that is?'

'No, of course not. I'll be glad not to move for a while. I think I can afford it.'

'Shall I write to Conn to let him know what's happened, or shall you?'

'I'll write, if you like, Bram. I owe Maia and Cassandra a letter anyway. Goodness, how long ago it seems that we all met in Lancashire. That dreadful Civil War is over in America now, and the mills are getting supplies of cotton again. And we're all here, far away from home.'

She sighed and was silent for a few seconds, then said, 'I'll write them a nice long letter. After all, I'll have plenty of time on my hands now. Captain McBride told me he wasn't going to hurry back. He wanted to give Flora a week or two in Singapore first. He told me he was worried about how exhausted she was looking.'

Bram drank his tea, let her talk for a while, then walked down to the Bazaar, whistling softly.

This evening he'd ask Isabella's advice on how to find Livia a husband. Women knew more about that sort of thing than men did.

And he'd tell her about Rory, and what the fellow had said about Ismay. He should have done that before, only he hadn't liked even to think about what must have happened, let alone bring it out into the open.

There was always something to worry you. He saw his wife standing inside the Bazaar, holding up a piece of silk and talking to a customer. His heart lightened at once, as it always did at the sight of her.

He had enough money to look after Ismay, whatever was involved. And thank heaven for that. But he'd do nothing about sending for the rest of his family until he found out exactly what had happened.

How could any father want his daughter to marry a brute like Rory?

16

When they got back to the ship, Dougal followed Flora to her cabin and went inside without asking her permission. 'I can't let you do it.'

She swung round. 'I thought we'd settled it. You can't stop me marrying him. I'm thirty-one and my own mistress!'

'I intend to stop you marrying him *in a hurry*, though, give you time to think, to be certain you're doing the right thing.'

She set her hands on her hips and glared at him. 'Oh? And how will you do that?'

'Simple. I'll lock you in your cabin till after we sail.'

She hadn't expected that of him, but his expression was grim and he had that dogged look on his face. 'Dougal, no! Surely you'd not do that to me?'

'I would if it was for your own good. I'm not having you make a hasty marriage that you may regret for years.'

'I won't regret it if I marry Joss.'

'How do you know?'

'Because I love him. Because it's as if we've not

been separated for more than a few days. I've always felt like this with him. Comfortable. As if we were meant for one another.'

'Then if you're so sure of your love, you can wait and marry him properly from our home in Fremantle.'

'I don't want to wait. Haven't I lost enough time already? Besides, Joss has to go to Sydney and then come back here to Singapore, because it's his first voyage for Mr Lee. He might not get back to Fremantle for months, a year even. I don't intend to be separated from him for so long.'

And suddenly they were quarrelling, the way they had as children, yelling at one another.

They fell silent just as suddenly, staring at one another.

Dougal spoke more quietly. 'You won't change my mind. I'm still going to make sure you have time to give the matter serious consideration.' He moved backwards. 'I'm doing this because I care about you, Flora.'

Before she could stop him, he'd taken the key from inside her cabin door. As she flung herself towards him, he edged quickly outside and slammed the door shut, so that she bumped into it, tugging vainly at the handle.

She heard the key turn in the lock and could only stare at the door in shock. He couldn't do this, keep her prisoner! He had no *right*!

She began yelling for help and banging on the door with her clenched fist. But she couldn't make enough noise, and anyway that hurt, so she picked up the metal slop bucket and started banging that against the door, yelling at the top of her voice, not caring that she was making gouge marks in the polished wood.

No one came to answer her calls for help, and eventually she stopped banging and stood there panting, trying to think. What could she do?

She went across to the porthole, but it was far too small for her to get through. She laid her head against the wall and tears welled in her eyes. She really was a prisoner here. Somehow, she didn't think even Joss would attack a fellow captain's ship. And would the Singapore authorities care about her? She wasn't even on their land now. What did the law say about that? She had no idea.

Then she took a deep breath and lifted her head. She was *not* going to give in. Opening the porthole, she began to yell through it. Loudly. She'd always had a loud voice.

She could just make out people turning their heads, some stopping, more joining them. Gradually a crowd gathered on the quay, pointing. But no one moved towards the ship. Not a single person.

'Help me! He's locked me in!' she yelled, again and again, till her voice grew hoarse.

When Adam and Ismay returned to the quay, they had to pass the *Bonny Mary*. They saw a group of people gathered near the ship and stopped to find out what was going on. To their amazement, they heard Flora yelling from on board, waving a scarf out of a porthole to attract attention.

'Help! I'm a prisoner here. Fetch the police. Someone get me out!'

Even as they heard this, they saw Joss run up to the other edge of the crowd, looking as astonished as they felt – and obviously getting angrier by the minute as he listened to Flora's pleas for help.

'Mary, mother of God, whatever's going on?' Ismay muttered.

'Whatever it is, I don't like the expression on Joss's face. Men don't think straight when they're that furious.' Adam stepped forward to intercept his captain. 'Where are you going?'

'He's locked her in her cabin. One of my crew heard her shouting and came to fetch me. Listen to her. I have to get her out.'

'Who's locked her in?'

'McBride. It must be because we told him we were going to get married straight away. He came to see me on the ship and we exchanged a few sharp words, but I thought he'd accepted the situation. I never thought he'd try something like this or I'd have kept her with me.'

'Can he do that, lock her up?'

'Some captains think they can do anything on board their own ships. I didn't believe him to be one of those. But I was wrong. Well, I'm not having it.'

He turned as if to storm on board the ship just as two sailors placed themselves at the top of the gangway.

Adam grabbed his arm. 'You can't force your way on to another captain's ship and tell him what to do.'

'Well, I can't leave her like that, can I? What if he sets sail? Besides, if I don't save her, who else is going to?'

'I don't think brute force is the answer and, anyway, you're one man against a whole crew.'

'Something has to be done.'

'You'd not drag the two crews into a fight, surely?'

Joss hesitated, then shook his head. 'No.'

'Let's go and discuss it.'

'Before we do, I'll shout to tell her we'll find a way to rescue her. I don't want her to think I've abandoned her again.'

'That'll put him on his guard.' Adam saw that his words were beginning to sink in. 'We have to do this carefully and keep calm. Anyway, I have an idea.'

'Maybe he'll let *me* go and speak to her in the meantime,' Ismay said.

Adam looked at her thoughtfully. 'Why don't you try that? Look around carefully while you're on board so you can tell us what sort of watch is being kept.'

She nodded and walked up the gangway. 'I'm here to see Miss McBride.'

But as she stood there, she heard someone shut the porthole with a bang and the voice cut off abruptly.

Dougal erupted into Flora's cabin, his face red with fury. 'Stop that yelling this minute. You're making a spectacle of yourself – and me.'

'Then set me free. You have no *right* to keep me prisoner.'

'I keep telling you: I'm doing this for your own good.'

'It seems I've exchanged one tyrant for another. Dougal, please be reasonable.'

A man appeared in the doorway, clearing his throat to attract their attention. 'Did you want me, Captain?'

'Yes. Seal that porthole shut. Just temporarily, till we set sail.'

'No!' Flora tried to stand in front of it and her brother had to pull her away.

'Look sharp, man. Seal it.' He stood between her and the window and when she tried to run out of the door, he yanked her back.

She wasn't going to attempt the impossible. He'd always been a strong man, so she stood with arms folded. 'I'll suffocate in here with that closed.'

'Of course you won't.'

'I'll be very uncomfortable, and well you know it.'

He flushed.

The sailor secured a bolt into the porthole latch

and left without a word, avoiding looking at either of them.

'I'll never forgive you for this,' she said.

'On the contrary. I believe you'll thank me for it one day.'

'*Thank you!* You couldn't be more wrong. But how would you know anything about love? You've never loved a real person. You're in love with the sea. I pity your wife, if you ever take one. And I hate you, Dougal McBride! You're as bad as our mother.'

'Flora, please . . .'

She turned her back on him, shoulders shaking.

He stretched out one hand towards her, hesitated, then let it drop. As he left, he locked the cabin door again. A sailor was waiting for him on deck.

'Begging your pardon, Captain, but there's a lady to see Miss Flora. Says she's arranged to visit her.'

'Oh, hell, what next?'

He marched up on deck to find Ismay Deagan waiting for him. 'I'm afraid my sister is indisposed.'

The look she gave him said she didn't believe this, but he was beyond caring, anger still burning through him.

'Perhaps I could write her a note, then?'

'Is it worth it? I'd not give it to her till after we'd sailed.'

'So it is true. You've locked her in her cabin.'

She gave him a look so full of disgust, he felt uncomfortable. For the first time he regretted what he'd done . . . no, not what he'd done, but how he'd done it. Having started, though, he wasn't going to be seen by his men to back down. 'What I do on board my own ship is my own business. I'll see you to the gangway, Miss Deagan.'

She stopped at the top of the sloping wooden ramp. 'I hadn't thought you a bully, Captain McBride. Or cruel.'

'I'm only stopping my sister rushing into something she'll regret,' he said again, but the words seemed to echo emptily in his brain, as if they had lost all their meaning.

'She won't regret finding the man she loves,' Ismay said quietly. 'What she'll regret is how you're treating her. What sort of brother does that to his sister?'

Her quiet words hit home and he felt a need to clutch the rail tightly as he watched her walk down the gangway and along the dock to the other ship.

The sailor on duty was staring stonily into the distance. People were still gathered below on the dock.

He'd done something he'd vowed never to do again, let his anger carry him away as it had when he was younger. He'd had to learn to control that anger when he went to sea, but sometimes, even now, he could act hastily.

This time he'd accused Flora of doing the same thing. And she was.

Should he let her go?

No, what would it look like to his men if he gave in now?

And anyway, he still didn't trust Joss Rutherford.

He turned and walked briskly to his cabin. But when he got there, he couldn't think what to do next.

'Come on.' Adam tugged Joss's arm.

'Shouldn't we stay here and wait for Ismay? If he tries to sail away, I'm going on board and hang the consequences.'

'We'd know if they were making preparations to sail. Better to wait on our own ship.' To Adam's relief, Joss sighed and started moving, though he kept looking back over his shoulder.

At one point he stopped. 'This is ridiculous: just like one of those damned Gothic romances my wife used to read.'

'It's surprised me that he'd go so far, I must admit. I'd thought him a pleasant enough fellow.'

When they were alone in Joss's cabin, Adam checked that the door was closed before he made his offer. 'Look, I have a few skills you don't know of. One of them is picking locks.' He saw the other man's astonishment and shrugged. 'You learn more things at boarding schools than parents realise. I used to hate being penned up indoors, and if I hadn't been able to get outside every now and then, I'd have gone mad.'

He cocked his head, sure now that he'd caught

Joss's interest. 'If I can get on board the *Bonny Mary* tonight, and if there isn't a guard outside her door, I should be able to let her out before they realise what's happening.'

'And maybe we shouldn't wait for that, but go and see the governor.'

'And cause a worse scandal? Apart from anything else, that'll not be good for us as traders. He won't hurt her physically, I'm sure.'

'That's the one thing holding me back. He does care about her in his own damned arrogant McBride way.' Joss frowned and looked at Adam, as if what he'd offered to do had just sunk in fully. 'You really can pick locks?'

'Yes.'

'Then do it. Tonight.'

'Very well. Once everything's quiet. But I'm not getting into any fights with his crew.'

'What do you need?'

Adam grinned. 'Nothing I haven't got already.' Joss nodded.

Thank heaven Joss wasn't doing something rash, Adam thought. Two furious captains confronting one another could cause a major scandal, which would ruin both their reputations. He was selfish enough not to want his ship and trading future tainted. But he also felt sorry for Flora.

Ismay came back a few minutes later, looking angry and with little to report. 'I didn't get a sight of her and he showed me off the ship, so I can't be much help. Sorry.'

'I've a fair idea where her cabin is,' Adam said. 'I'll find her.'

She gaped at him. 'What do you mean, *you* will find her?'

When he explained, she continued to gape for a minute or two, then slowly started to smile. 'Oh, I do hope you succeed.'

'Given a few uninterrupted minutes, I ought to be able to do it.'

'Be sure to lock the cabin again afterwards, so that he can't figure how she got out.'

Adam gave a snort of laughter, and even Joss's angry expression lightened briefly.

She turned to Joss. 'What you need to do now is arrange a wedding ceremony for after you've rescued her. Surely there's a priest here?'

'There's a cathedral, St Andrew's. Remember, we saw it when we were out walking? I could ask there.'

'The church with the beautiful lawns round it?'

'Damn the lawns! I just need one of their clergyman,' Joss said. 'I'll go and arrange for us to get married.'

'Will they do it in the middle of the night?'

'If it's the only way to keep her, I'll persuade them.' Grim-faced, he set off.

'That should keep him out of the way for a while,' Adam said. 'I thought for a moment back there he was going to try to storm the ship single-handed.'

'I'm a bit angry myself. People think they can treat women any way they want.'

She was silent for a moment or two and he knew she was thinking about herself. He took hold of her hand and, after a few seconds, she looked up again, giving him one of her dazzling smiles.

'So you can pick locks, can you?' she laughed. 'Let's see what you use.'

He took her to his cabin and let her examine his picklocks, slender pieces of metal in various shapes. He hadn't used them for ages, but he'd kept them with him, he didn't know why. Strange, the things you carried through your life. They'd helped him keep sane at a very vulnerable time of his life – he'd grown fond of them, thought of them as his passports to freedom.

He'd also kept the letters Aunt Harriet had sent to him in boarding school, every single one of them. How he'd looked forward to them!

Strange what mattered in life.

Livia wrote to let Conn and his wife know what had happened, then walked to the post office with the letter. On the way back she bought a cake from the baker's.

She felt vaguely disoriented today, as if she ought to be doing something. She hadn't expected her job to be over quite so quickly, had made no preparations for the future.

Back at the house, she insisted on sitting in the kitchen and sharing the cake with Orla and Rhoda. She'd have welcomed a glass of wine, too, but knew the others preferred tea, and anyway, you shouldn't drink alcohol in the daytime. She had done sometimes when looking after her dying husband. A glass of wine had been a small comfort that got her through the worst days. Never more than one glass. It just . . . helped. She had a couple of bottles of port in her room, would open one later.

'What are you going to do now, missus?' Rhoda asked. 'If you need any extra help, I'd be glad to stay on . . .'

'I wish I could hire you, because you're a hard worker, but I haven't the faintest idea what I'm going to do.'

Rhoda chewed thoughtfully for a minute or two, washed the mouthful of cake down with a gulp of tea, then said, 'I reckon you should look for a husband.'

Livia blinked in shock. She was used to Rhoda's blunt speech and what others would have called lack of respect. It wasn't. Rhoda was only offering an honest opinion with her mistress's welfare at heart. Colonials were sometimes much franker than their counterparts in England, a bit like Lancashire mill workers.

She stared down into her cup. 'You can't just conjure up a husband from mid-air.'

'They advertise for wives in the *Gazette* sometimes,' Rhoda said, taking another piece of cake. 'You could look there. Or in the *Inquirer*. You could even put an advert in yourself.'

'Advertise myself in a newspaper, like an object

for sale! Marry a complete stranger! Oh, no. Never!
I just couldn't.'

'Wouldn't hurt to look. It might not be as bad
as you think. You might meet a kind gentleman.'

She shook her head. Definitely not.

Joss came back from his visit to the cathedral
looking angry.

'Wouldn't they agree to marry you?' Ismay
asked, ignoring the way Adam nudged her and
put one finger to his lips.

'The law says you're supposed to get married
only between eight in the morning and six in the
evening.'

'Oh.'

'But in Australia and other colonies we can't
always stick to the letter of the law, or people would
never get married. How can you call the banns
when there isn't a church – only a visiting clergyman who comes every three months?'

'I never thought of that. What are you going to
do then?'

'I managed to persuade them. I had to tell them
why we were doing this secretly and at night. I
could see they disapproved, but the curate said
he'd do it for twice the usual fee, but only to
prevent immorality and because things are more
irregular in the Orient. I don't mind paying the
fee, but I resent the way he looked down his nose
at me. They all promised not to tell anyone, for
Flora's sake. Would you believe it, he's gone off to

bed now and I'm to wake him up once my lady-friend slips away from the ship. It's going to be a shabby sort of wedding. I daresay he'll be yawning all through it.'

Ismay smiled. 'Flora won't be caring about that. She comes to life, positively glows when she's with you.'

'Does she really?'

She could hear the wistful note. 'Definitely. And anyway, Adam and I will be there as witnesses, so you'll have friends to support you.'

She looked at Adam. 'It all depends on you now, doesn't it? If they've got a difficult lock . . .'

'Oh, I'm sure I can deal with the lock. It's the crew I'm worried about.'

A few hours later, just after they'd changed the watch on the *Bonny Mary*, Adam, Ismay and Joss made their way along the quay. There were still people out and about, so Adam didn't think their little group would be noticed.

Ismay was wearing a dark gown and carrying a little leather prayer book that Aunt Harriet had slipped into her hand as she was leaving: 'for the bride'. Joss was neatly dressed in his uniform, but Adam was wearing navy blue trousers and a dark, seaman's jersey, plus rope-soled shoes so that he'd not make a noise. His picklocks were wrapped in a handkerchief to prevent them clinking.

'Wait there,' he told the others, and moved closer to the ship, standing in a patch of shadow. To his annoyance, he saw a sailor standing on guard near the top of the gangway.

What was he going to do now?

He waited a few moments, shifting from one foot to another, glancing back to see Joss and Ismay standing like a pair of lovers, chatting quietly. He wished he were the one talking to Ismay.

When he turned back, the sailor had started moving along the deck, probably to do a circuit. He watched, counting the seconds, till the man came back. About three minutes. That gave him time to get on board.

He waited. Five long minutes later, the sailor set off on his rounds once more. It was now or never.

Adam ran up the gangway, crouching for a moment at the top, just in case there was anyone else on deck. But he could see no one, so he ran across to the entrance to the cabins and slipped into it.

He watched the sailor return from his patrol and take up his position again, back turned towards where Adam stood. With a smile, he moved to the cabin door.

Dougal, who had been standing in the shadows staring out at the many craft anchored nearby, heard a faint sound and turned in time to see a man run across the deck and into the corridor that led to the cabins.

He recognised the intruder instantly and stiffened.

What was the first mate of the *Hannah Grey* doing on his ship at this hour of the night? Not difficult to guess. It could only be for one reason. He must be trying to get a message to Flora.

But why him and not Joss? Was the fellow too cowardly to run his own errands?

Dougal didn't see how they could rescue her, so if it was just a question of a letter, he'd keep out of sight and let Tregear pass the note to her. It might cheer her up a bit.

But minutes passed and his intruder didn't return. The man couldn't be holding a conversation with her through the solid door, so what was he doing?

Dougal waited for the sailor on watch to pass by, then followed Tregear. He could see him fumbling with the lock and realised he was trying to let Flora out.

He wasn't having that. He opened his mouth to shout for help.

Adam had to admit he felt guilty about doing this. But you had to help a friend in trouble, and anyway, what McBride was doing was grossly unfair.

He took out his picklocks. There was nothing he could do about the faint sound they made as they jangled on the big ring. He put the one he thought most likely to do the job into the lock.

He was so on edge he fumbled and dropped the whole bunch. Cursing under his breath, he picked them up and tried again, annoyed to find it was a type of lock he'd not opened before. Stifling his impatience, he tried the picklocks one after the other.

He heard a sound from inside the cabin and made a shushing sound near the keyhole, not certain whether she'd hear it or not.

He fiddled some more and there was a click. 'Ah!' He opened the door slowly, saying 'Shhh!' as soon as a gap appeared.

'Who is it?'

'Adam Tregear.'

He edged inside and shut the door. 'Ready to escape, Miss McBride?'

There was enough moonlight to see her smile. 'Yes. I've got my bags packed and I didn't change into my nightgown because I was hoping Joss would find a way to rescue me.'

'He can't pick locks, so I came in his place. He has a wedding booked. Now, keep very quiet as we leave. When we get outside, we have to wait for the sailor on guard to pass by and then hurry down the gangway as quickly and quietly as we can. Give me the bigger bag.'

Taking a deep breath, he opened the door.

For some reason he didn't understand, Dougal still didn't shout for help. He crept away from the corridor and sought a new hiding place, from which he saw Tregear come out and Flora follow.

She looked so happy in the moonlight. Radiantly happy. He'd not seen his sister look like that for years, not since Joss left the colony.

He watched her and Tregear wait at the end of the corridor, then run across the deck.

He did nothing but watch as they disappeared down the gangway. He didn't even follow them. He couldn't bear the thought of wiping that radiant happiness from her face.

Anyway, as she'd said, he had no right to keep her prisoner. He was *not* a bully, just a man with a temper.

With a sigh, he went into his cabin and poured himself a stiff cognac, taking a big gulp, welcoming the warmth as it slid down his throat.

'I'm a fool,' he muttered, and took another mouthful.

She wouldn't believe him if he told her he'd let her go. She'd probably stay angry at him for years.

What was she doing now? Had she gone to join Rutherford on the *Hannah Grey*? Or were they getting married? No, they couldn't be doing that at this hour of the night.

He'd been wrong to let her go. She'd now be living in sin.

But she'd be happy.

He lifted the glass to his mouth, found it empty and poured another measure. As he raised it, he said aloud, 'I hope you're very happy, Flora, but I hope you get married soon.'

His next toast was, 'I hope you'll forgive me one day.'

*   *   *

As they reached the quay, Flora flew into Joss's arms, pressing herself against him and shuddering in relief.

But Adam couldn't allow them to stay like that. He tugged at Joss's coat. 'We have to leave before McBride finds out she's gone.'

'We'd better take your luggage back to the ship first, my love,' Joss said. 'I'll do it. I won't be long.'

They watched him run along the quay to the *Hannah Grey* and go up the gangway, then come back without the luggage. He held out his hand to Flora. 'Come on, then, my love. Make an honest man of me.'

The four of them hurried through the streets, which were not quite as busy now but were still filled with plenty of people. At this hour of the night, though, there was a rather threatening feel to them.

'We should have brought a couple of crew members,' Adam muttered.

'Too late to worry about that now,' Joss said.

When a man stepped out of the shadows to block their way, the two men tensed.

'Mr Lee say come,' he said.

When they didn't move, he repeated his message. 'Mr Lee say come.'

'I don't think he understands what he's saying,' Adam whispered. 'The question is, do we trust him?'

'I've seen him before outside the back of the

shop,' Ismay said. 'He really is one of Mr Lee's men.'

'Thank goodness for that!' Adam bowed his head to show agreement; when the man set off, they followed. Two other men stepped into place behind them.

'How does Lee find out so much?' Adam whispered to Ismay.

'I don't know, but this could be very helpful for us.'

Their guide led them to the cathedral, where they found a side door open with a faint light shining from inside.

'I have to fetch the curate,' Joss said. 'Stay here, Flora.'

'Have sent for curate,' a voice said, and Mr Lee stepped out of the darkness beside the door. 'Safer to wait inside.'

'How did you know we were coming here?' Adam asked.

'Heard Captain McBride locked sister on ship. Heard other captain went to arrange marriage.' He looked at Flora. 'You want to marry this man? Go against brother? No one forcing you?'

'I very much want to marry him, Mr Lee. My brother wants me to wait. He wasn't stopping me from marrying. But I'm older, and a woman doesn't have time to wait if she wants a home and children.'

He nodded his head slowly as if in agreement, then turned to look across the grass. 'Here is clergyman. I wait for you.' He stepped round a corner and his men followed him.

The curate arrived, breathless and scowling. 'This Chinaman came to fetch me. I was a bit worried, but he wouldn't take no for an answer.'

'We won't keep you out of your bed for long,' Joss said.

The curate turned to Flora. 'Do you really want to get married in this shabby way?'

'Yes, I do.'

'Very well, then. Come inside. It's a good thing you've brought witnesses, because I couldn't find you any at this hour of the night. It's most irregular all the same, and if it weren't for the moral aspect, I'd have refused to do this.'

'I'm grateful to you, sir,' Joss said.

'We both are,' Flora added, giving her betrothed a brilliant smile.

The curate sniffed disapprovingly at the blatant display of affection.

The wedding itself didn't take long, but Adam found the words very moving. The expressions of joy on the faces of bride and groom brought a lump to his throat and made him wish he was marrying Ismay, who was standing by his side, mopping away a happy tear. No, he mustn't wish that till he'd found out what his father had done.

When they came out of the cathedral, complete with marriage lines, Mr Lee and his men were there, waiting to escort them back to the ship.

As they set off walking, Adam stifled a yawn

and smiled at Ismay. 'I shall be glad to get to my bed.'

'So shall I.'

But they found Aunt Harriet waiting for them, dozing by the side of the fixed table on which they dined. On it stood a cake.

She jerked awake. 'Is it done? Are you married?'

Flora sent another beaming smile at Joss. 'Yes.'

Aunt Harriet gave her a big hug. 'Congratulations.' She gestured. 'You can't get married without a wedding cake, so I baked one myself. It's a bit lopsided, I'm afraid, and I had to decorate it with real flowers, because I couldn't make any icing sugar ones in this short time.' She gestured to the table.

'It's beautiful,' Flora said.

Joss laughed. 'We need a bottle of wine, too, to drink to the bride's health.'

It was an hour before they sought their beds.

Only as they went into Joss's cabin did Flora start to feel nervous. 'I've never . . .' she began.

'I didn't think you had. But I know what to do, my love. Let me show you.'

And her fears soon faded in the warmth of his touch, because love showed in everything he did.

The following morning, very early, carts arrived at the *Hannah Grey* with the cargo from Mr Lee.

After barely two hours' sleep, Joss had to get up and deal with it, including answering a summons to see Mr Lee at his godown to finalise details.

The message was written in an angular black script that looked Chinese, for all the words were English.

Joss summoned Adam. 'We need to do our negotiating together as joint owners. Flora's still in bed and I've suggested she remain in my cabin till I return. My men won't allow anyone near her or Ismay, I can guarantee that.'

Together the men went to see Mr Lee, then came back to find the loading well under way.

Standing on the deck of the ship was a trunk.

Flora came out to greet her husband. 'Dougal's just sent my trunk. I need to go through the things in it and repack the stuff that needs to be kept in the hold.'

'I'll have it taken to the cabin. Unfortunately there isn't room to keep it there.' He couldn't hold back a yawn.

'You must be exhausted.'

'I am. But it was well worth it.' He reached out to brush her cheek with his knuckles and she gave him a misty smile.

In the late afternoon, the rest of the garments the ladies had ordered were brought to the ship by the seamstress and a helper. She didn't understand much English, but still managed to insist on them trying on the garments.

She stayed to make some final tiny alterations, then accepted her payment and left.

By nightfall everything had been loaded and the ship cleared for sailing at dawn.

'What are you going to do?' Joss asked Adam, Ismay and Aunt Harriet. 'It might be a while before another ship leaves for the Swan River Colony.'

'The *Bonny Mary* is leaving in a day or two. I'm going to buy passage on it,' Aunt Harriet said crisply.

'Do you think Dougal will take you?'

'Just let him try to refuse. I shall insist he help his fellow Europeans, stranded in Singapore.'

Adam stifled a laugh. He'd seen his aunt get on her high horse about something before and, if he'd been a betting man, he'd have put his money on her winning. 'If anyone can do it, my aunt can.'

She gave them all a nod, as if to say, leave it to me. 'We'll wait until you're almost ready to leave, then place ourselves and our luggage at Captain McBride's mercy.'

As the ship eased its way out of the harbour, Joss and Flora saw a group of figures on the deck of the *Bonny Mary*. At the rail, in the midst of them, was a stocky figure, taller than the others.

'It's my brother,' she said. 'He's let them on his ship. Oh, thank goodness!'

As they moved slowly past, Dougal raised one hand and waved, yelling, 'God speed!' and silently mouthed the words 'Good luck', for Flora's eyes only.

Flora hesitated, then waved back.

'I thought you were never going to forgive him,' Joss teased.

'I thought I wasn't too. But he's my brother, the only relative I have that I care about.'

'Apart from me.'

Flora's smile was a glory. 'Yes. Apart from my brand-new darling of a husband.'

17

Just over three weeks later, the *Bonny Mary* anchored in Gage Roads, just off Fremantle in the Swan River Colony. Ismay stood at the rail with Aunt Harriet, staring at the small port, trying to hide her disappointment. It wasn't at all what she'd expected. They said it was a port so, having seen Liverpool, she'd expected big ships and docks. Why, they couldn't even dock here properly, it seemed, but had to anchor off shore!

As for the town itself, there were some larger buildings dotted about the centre, but they were nothing like the massive stone edifices of Liverpool, which had filled her with awe. She'd remembered the huge hotel they'd stayed in, had thought about it several times because it was so magnificent. And as for Lime Street Station – why, she'd been speechless as she stood beneath its great soaring roof, which had so much glass in it that she was amazed it didn't break in a storm.

Most of the houses in Fremantle looked like a child's building bricks: a lot of them square and simple in form and of one storey only. The sun was shining, there wasn't a cloud in the sky, because this was the start of summer, even though it was winter now in Ireland. The buildings made of stone reflected the light back so strongly it hurt her eyes, so that she had to put up one hand to shade them. She didn't mind that, though, because she liked the bright clear air and the warmth of the sun on her skin. And it wasn't muggy warmth here, like Singapore, thank goodness.

Beside her, Aunt Harriet was also shading her eyes. She hadn't said anything, which was unusual, so Ismay sneaked a glance. If her companion was disappointed with her future home, she wasn't letting it show, and Ismay was sure she'd not complain about it.

'So now we have to climb down the side again,' Aunt Harriet said, sighing.

Ismay suddenly realised what was worrying her companion. Not the town, but getting off the ship. 'Yes. But you'll be all right.'

'I've been dreading it ever since we found out that was how we had to get ashore. It's bad enough climbing *up* the side of a ship, but climbing *down* is much more frightening to me.'

Adam came to join them. 'The town's smaller than I'd expected, but I'm sure we can make a good life for ourselves here. It's people who matter most, after all.'

'Yes, of course, dear. As long as we're together.' Aunt Harriet tried to force a smile, but it wasn't convincing.

'Are you all right?' he asked.

Ismay put her arm round the older woman's shoulders. 'She's worrying about climbing down the side of the ship.'

He looked apologetically at his aunt. 'I'm sorry. Dougal did offer to rig up a sling to get you down. You'd be quite safe in that, I promise.'

She swallowed hard. 'I prefer to climb down under my own steam, but I'd be grateful if you'd climb next to me, in case I find myself in difficulty. I'm not . . . not as nimble as I used to be.'

'You're a brave woman,' he said quietly. 'Of course I'll come down with you, and we can go very slowly, I promise you.'

Dougal stopped briefly beside them. 'Well?'

'She's climbing down.'

'That makes it easier to get on with the unloading. You'll be all right, Mrs Seaton. Nearly everyone does it this way and we've not lost one person yet.'

They watched him stride away. His stiffness with them had lasted only a day or two and they were on good terms now, but he refused to discuss what had happened between himself and his sister, and sometimes he was distinctly lacking in tact.

Ismay squinted at the shore. 'I wonder how long it'll be before Bram gets my message.'

'The note went ashore on the first lighter that took off cargo, so he should have it by now,' Adam said reassuringly.

She couldn't stop a yawn. She was trying to hide it, but she'd slept badly because she had another worry: what if Rory Flynn was waiting for her here? Well, unless he'd fallen overboard, he must be. She didn't mention him; didn't even like to think about him.

But Adam guessed what was upsetting her. 'No one is going to hurt you here, Ismay, especially that man. I won't let him.'

She nodded, but the fear didn't leave her. She loved Adam dearly, but she was just as frightened that Adam might get hurt if it came to a fight as she was of getting hurt herself.

A lad brought a message to the shop and handed it to Bram. 'From the *Bonny Mary*.'

Automatically he gave the lad a penny and took the folded paper, studying the handwriting in surprise. He recognised it at once. 'It's from my sister!' he yelled, unfolding it and scanning the message quickly.

His wife looked up from where she was arranging the piece of silk for today's display.

'Ismay's here at last! In Fremantle. She's arrived on that schooner. I can't wait to see her.'

Isabella came to read the note, then gave him a hug. 'You must go to the jetty at once. Bring her back here. We'll fit her in somehow.'

'She says she's with two good friends, the ones she's travelled out from England with. She doesn't ask, but they'll all be needing somewhere to sleep, won't they now?'

Isabella thought for a moment, then said, 'They could sleep in the stable annexe. It's the only place we have free. And it might be simple but it's clean at least.'

'That settles it. We'll have to find ourselves a bigger house. What's the point of having money if you can't give your friends a bed for a night?'

'I'm fond of our cottage.'

He knew it was the first real home she'd had, given the improvident nature of her parents and the way they'd moved from one place to another all through her childhood. 'So am I. We've started a very happy marriage there. But we have two children and a maid of our own to find beds for, as well as my sister. And anyway, we can easily afford a better place now.'

'Yes. We do need somewhere bigger but . . . we won't spend lavishly, will we?'

He gave her cheek a quick kiss, knowing what was worrying her. 'It's all right, darlin'. I'm not your father, nor am I foolish with our money. Didn't I promise you you'd never again be without something saved for a rainy day? And don't you do the accounts yourself?'

She smiled and clasped his hand for a moment. 'Yes.'

'I doubt I ever could throw money around, because I know only too well what it's like to go short of food.' Bram looked out of the door of the bazaar, down the slope that led to their cottage. 'I was wondering if Conn would sell me a bit of land, so that I could build a house close to the Bazaar. It'd make things easier to be nearby.'

'We can ask him. But now's not the time to discuss that. Off with you. Go and fetch your sister. I'll make sure there's a fine welcome waiting for her and her friends, and that the luggage that arrived before is taken to the annexe.'

He gave her a street urchin's grin and set off running, forgetting his hat. With each stride, his coat flapped about his thin body like a live thing.

She stood watching till he was out of sight, smiling. Oh, but she loved that man!

Rory stopped at the sight of a man running head-long down the street. Bram Deagan. What was that about? His eyes narrowed at the sight of the joy on his old enemy's face, and he abandoned his errand to follow him.

Then he realised what would cause such happiness: Ismay must have arrived! What else would send her brother running towards the water when he could afford to pay a messenger?

Rory stayed out of sight behind some bales when Bram stopped; he watched him jigging about on the jetty, looking out to sea at the lighter pulling away from the ship. There were women on it.

Rory smiled. He'd guessed right, then. She was back.

Well, he'd bide his time, but he'd make sure she didn't get away from him again. Very sure. He became aware of someone tugging at his coat.

'Want a ride out to the ship, mister?' a lad said. 'Only a shillin'.'

Rory shoved him away hard. 'Get away from me, you scabby rat.' When the lad didn't move, he made a threatening gesture with one fist. 'Get away with ye'!'

The lad made a gesture of cutting his throat.

'If that's meant to be a threat, you watch your step with me.'. He took a step forward and the lad held his ground for a minute; then, as Rory got closer, he ran off down the street, turning to stick his tongue out and yell, 'Dirty Irish!'

Rory ignored the insult, which he was getting used to now, though he couldn't work out why people disliked the Irish so much.

'That'll learn the young devil,' he muttered, then turned back to watch the lighter pull alongside the jetty. He gloated over the sight of Ismay, who was as pretty as ever.

He nearly ran out and grabbed her there and then.

But, though her brother couldn't have stopped him, there were sailors and that fellow from the ship with her, not to mention the old lady.

He moved to the side of a building and continued to watch. No need to follow them afterwards. He knew where she'd be going. He could go and get her when he was ready.

Aunt Harriet made it safely down the big rope nets to the lighter, shuddering in relief as she settled beside Ismay. 'I hope that will be the last time I ever have to climb down the side of a ship. Ever.'

'You did very well,' Ismay told her, then turned to look at Adam.

His attention was on the shore, on the town where he hoped to make his home and, if fate was kind, marry the woman he loved.

As they got close to the jetty, Ismay shrieked suddenly. 'Oh, oh! It's Bram. Look, Aunt Harriet, that's my brother, the one jumping up and down like a child. Ah, he's not changed, not our Bram.'

As the boat pulled in, he ran forward and was waiting as Ismay climbed on to the wooden jetty. He dragged her into his arms and waltzed her round, ignoring the way people were smiling.

'Ismay, Ismay! I can't believe you're here. I've been watching out for smaller ships, hoping you'd be on one of them, then today I got your note and came straight down here to meet you.'

Adam and Aunt Harriet joined them and she introduced them, delighted when Bram invited them to stay with him and his wife.

'Are you sure?' Aunt Harriet asked. 'We don't want to be a nuisance.'

'Of course I'm sure. If you're friends of my sister – and it sounds as if you've been good friends, too, helping her when she was sick – then you're friends of mine. We have an annexe to the livery stables with a row of bedrooms for hire. They're very small and simple, but you can have one each and share one for storing your luggage. It's not a palace but it's clean. Besides, there aren't a lot of fine hotels in Fremantle and some of them can be very noisy. As for lodging houses, those places restrict your comings and goings.'

Aunt Harriet smiled at him. 'You're so right. How kind of you to welcome us in this way, Mr Deagan. And how like your sister you are. I'd have known you were related, even if I'd never met either of you before.'

He grinned at Ismay. 'Oh, I think her face is much prettier than my ould phiz. Now, are you able to walk into town, Mrs Seaton? Our place is only ten minutes away and we can have your luggage sent in a handcart once it's unloaded.'

'I'd enjoy a walk very much.'

'How about you take the ladies now while I wait here for the luggage?' Adam suggested. 'Give me your address.'

Bram smiled proudly. 'Oh, you only have to ask for Deagan's Bazaar. Everyone knows my little shop, and my wife and I live next door to it in the cottage.'

Laughing at the way they were still staggering as if they were on board ship, Ismay and Aunt Harriet each took one of Bram's arms and the three of them set off for the Bazaar, with him pointing out the sights.

A few minutes later, he stopped outside some livery stables and pointed to a large wooden building up the slope beyond it. 'There it is. My little shop.' The name Deagan was prominently displayed outside it and Bram didn't try to hide his pride in the place.

Ismay was speechless, then she gave him a mock

punch in the upper arm. 'That's not a *little shop*! It's a very big one. Bram, how wonderful! Are you rich now?'

He hesitated, then said it aloud for the first time. 'Well, I'm comfortable, yes.'

'You deserve it.' Then what Adam had said was really brought home to her – if her brother wasn't a poor man, was a respected businessman, maybe other people wouldn't consider her too far beneath Adam. Once he'd sorted out his own situation with regard to the inheritance from his father, that was.

Bram nudged her. 'Wake up, you. I'll show you round the Bazaar later. Come to the cottage and meet my wife and son first – he's the grandest baby you ever saw – then I'll show you your rooms. Or Isabella will.'

Ismay took to her sister-in-law on sight, mostly because of the warmth of her smile when she looked at Bram. If anyone deserved a loving wife, her favourite brother did. She could remember a thousand kindnesses from him, little things that had made a difference in their hard life.

Aunt Harriet sat down thankfully and accepted the offer of a cup of tea. She leaned her head back with a murmur of appreciation for the comfort of the chair. 'I can usually walk miles without getting tired, but I'm out of practice after months on board ships.'

'You'll be as right as rain in a day or two,' Bram picked up his son and jiggled little Arlen about. 'Say hello to your auntie.'

Ismay smiled and held out her arms for her nephew. 'He's lovely. And who's this?' She gestured with her head towards the child hovering in a corner of the room, wide-eyed.

'This is Louisa. She lives with us now, don't you, darlin'? Her mother's a cousin of my wife's.'

He pulled the little girl forward, treating her so gently that Ismay guessed the child had been hurt in the past. Hadn't Bram always collected animals and people in trouble and tried to make things better for them? She held out one hand to the child. 'I'm pleased to meet you, Miss Louisa.'

After a moment's hesitation, during which she studied Ismay's face, the little girl shook hands solemnly, then stuck one thumb in her mouth and leaned against Bram, clearly confident of safety with him.

A young woman brought in a tea tray and set it on a side table.

'This is Sally,' Isabella said. 'She helps out with the children and anything else that's needed. I don't know what I'd do without her.'

Sally beamed at her and bobbed her head in Ismay's direction. 'Welcome to the colony, miss.'

'Thank you.'

It was all so cosy and homelike that Ismay relaxed and sipped her tea, feeling as if she truly had come home.

Then something that had been niggling at her resurfaced. 'Bram – have you seen Rory Flynn?'

'Yes. He spoke to me in the street the other day; said he was going to marry you.'

Aunt Harriet caught Ismay's cup as it tilted dangerously, and Adam, who had just joined them, was on his knees in front of her before anyone else could move. 'Ismay! Are you all right?'

She shuddered and clung to him. 'Am I never to be free of that man?'

'I won't let him come near you.'

Bram exchanged glances with his wife, waited until his sister had regained a little colour in her cheeks, then asked, 'What has Flynn done to you, Ismay? If he's hurt you in any way, I'll—'

'I'm before you in wanting to give that fellow the beating he deserves,' Adam said, a sharp edge to his voice.

Bram looked at him, and then at his sister, who was still clinging to Adam's hand. Interesting, that – but for explaining another time. 'What did Flynn do to her?'

Ismay buried her face in her hands, feeling utterly humiliated by the mere thought of it.

Adam jerked his head towards the door. 'I could do to stretch my legs. Fancy joining me, Deagan?'

'Yes.' He shot a quick glance at his wife and she nodded imperceptibly.

When the two men had left, Ismay stayed where she was, hunched in the chair.

It was Aunt Harriet who said briskly, 'Sit up straight, Ismay dear. You're not going to fall to pieces now, surely, after being so brave?'

'It was just . . . a shock, to know for certain he was here. I'd tried to tell myself he would be waiting for me, to think what I'd do, but I couldn't help hoping . . .' She sniffed and fumbled for her handkerchief, then turned to her sister-in-law. 'I'd better tell you now, because I'm sure that's what Adam is doing with Bram.'

Haltingly she explained what had happened to her, the reason she'd come to Australia, unable to stop weeping as the tale unfolded.

'Well, at least there is one good thing come of it,' Aunt Harriet said when she'd finished her tale.

The others looked at her in surprise.

'Because of it, we met and became friends. Because of it, Ismay and my nephew met and grew to love one another. Some of the thorniest ground can grow the most beautiful flowers.' She gave Ismay one of her gentle, loving looks. 'We'll try not to dwell on the past, though. It can't be changed, after all.'

Ismay nodded agreement. Such wise words and advice. What would she have done without Aunt Harriet? 'Sorry. It's been so wonderful to be free of him the past few weeks.'

Her sister-in-law patted her hand, stuffed a clean handkerchief into it and said, 'Wipe your eyes. We'll make sure you're safe here.'

But Ismay didn't think anyone could make her feel safe as long as Rory Flynn was living nearby. She still remembered . . . too much.

★   ★   ★

'We'll go somewhere private.' Bram took Adam up to the little storeroom cum office at the back of the Bazaar, a place where they could be private. Neither man so much as glanced at the contents of the shop as they passed through, and when someone tried to speak to Bram, he made a dismissive gesture with one hand.

As soon as he'd shut the door, he said, 'Tell me.'

When Adam had finished, Bram sat with tears running down his cheeks, cursing and thumping the side of one clenched fist hard on the desk till Adam took hold of it.

'It'll do no good to hurt yourself.'

'I never did like the man, but now, I wish him dead. I do. And if that's a mortal sin, I don't care. To hurt Ismay like that! And Da egging him on. Ach, I can't bear the thought of it.'

'Thank God the Largans were there to help her,' Adam said. 'Some employers would have blamed her and dismissed her out of hand. Or forced her to marry him.'

'They're a good family, the Largans. Except for the father. He was a nasty devil and everyone was glad when he died. He arranged for his own son to be accused of treason and transported. Conn Largan's conviction has been quashed now, of course. He's my partner here at the Bazaar. He owns the land and I put the shop together. You'll be meeting him soon. He likes to visit from time to time. We sent a while back to let him know Ismay was coming. I'll tell you his tale in full later, once we've sorted out this . . . other thing. You'll be seeing more of him, no doubt.'

There was silence, during which Bram kept shaking his head and staring down at the floor, still finding it hard to accept what had happened to his little sister.

Adam waited patiently, letting him get used to the bad news.

Eventually Bram sighed and looked up. 'What now? I can see you care for her, but there's a world of difference between the two of you, and don't be pretending there isn't. You're a shipowner, for a start.'

'That's what she says. Not so much difference, though. I'm bastard born, neither fish nor fowl. And if you're asking about my intentions, I want to marry her.'

'She seems fond of you, turned to you in trouble.'

'I'm fond of her. And she's agreed to marry me. But we're waiting until I find out what nasty surprise my father has waiting for me here. It might be something that would affect a wife.'

Bram blinked at him in shock. 'You're expecting your *father* to have planned something to hurt you?'

Adam explained.

'It seems we're neither of us blessed by our fathers, then,' Bram said grimly when his companion had finished the tale. 'I was going to bring my parents out here to live. Now . . .' He shook his head. 'No. If I saw my father, I'd spit in his face. For my mother's sake, I'll go on sending them money, but I'll not have them here.'

'I'll go to Perth and find my father's lawyer tomorrow, see exactly what I've been left. After that, if things are all right, I'll talk to Ismay about when we should marry.'

'And, in the meantime, we'll go back now and I'll give her the biggest hug in the world.'

Which Bram did, his throat too full of tears to say what he was feeling, so he hugged her again.

Back in Ireland, Rory would have lost his job for vanishing during the day. Here, when he came back from following Ismay and her brother, he had to face a tirade of abuse from his employer and the news that he'd be fined a shilling of his pay for that absence.

This didn't put him in a good mood. When he'd got the cows he tended settled for the night, he didn't go to the beer shanty as usual. He didn't feel like idle chat, or even drinking. He wanted to lie on his bed and think about what he'd seen. About her.

She was carrying the child tight in her belly. He'd seen other women do that, not look as if they were expecting for the first few months, then suddenly, towards the end, blow up like pigs' bladders.

She'd have found out now that Rory was in Fremantle. He grinned. That'd start her worrying. So she ought, the hussy. Leading him on, then giving him all this trouble. Still, it was true what they said. You could make a better life here in Australia, so it had maybe been worth it. Already he was saving money from his wages, adding it to his savings, wondering what to do with it.

He'd go and see the priest first. Explain what he'd done, act penitent, and get the man of God on his side to make her marry him.

She was a stubborn bitch, though, and she might not agree, even now. In fact, she probably wouldn't, so he had to work out what he could do to force her. He couldn't beat sense into her, not with her carrying his child. Some men might not care whether they damaged their unborn children, but he wasn't one of those.

There must be some other way of threatening her. Perhaps someone she valued so highly she'd do anything to protect them. The old lady who'd travelled with her? One of the children at Bram's? He'd have to keep an eye on her and work that out.

But it wouldn't hurt to let Ismay know he was there and still of a mind to marry her.

It was how to do it to best effect. He couldn't see his way yet. But he would, if he had to lie awake all night thinking.

18

Dougal didn't go ashore till the day following his arrival at Fremantle. What was the point when Flora wasn't there to welcome him? He hadn't understood until now quite how much he'd looked forward to seeing her after a voyage, sharing all his news, listening to her news, enjoying the comfort of a well-ordered house.

Even his mother's foolish twitterings hadn't upset him too much, with Flora to chat to while his mother was out visiting or receiving visitors, or offering tea to their paying guests. He was glad he was no longer going to have strangers in his home, though.

He didn't want to go and see his mother yet, was worried about being totally responsible for her care. What if she was now a drooling wreck? He shuddered at the idea of seeing her like that. He'd always been proud of how well she looked and dressed.

The thought that followed couldn't be avoided. He really needed a wife now. The doctor had said it was only a matter of time before she died. Only, Dougal hadn't met anyone he could face spending his whole life with.

Maybe Flora was right and he'd been too engrossed with his ship and making sure his business was secure. He'd enjoyed one or two liaisons with women, though sex wasn't such a driving urge with him as it seemed to be with most men. Maybe there was something wrong with him? No, the men in his family were known for marrying late.

Even if he did decide to look for a wife, it wouldn't be easy to find a suitable one. It took a very special woman to face the long separations involved in a sea captain's life. He didn't want *his* wife entertaining other men while he was away.

In the morning, the visit to his mother could not be put off any longer, so after breakfast he got ready, left his ship in his mate's charge and had himself rowed ashore.

Should he go to his own house first? The maid Linny would still be there, surely. She'd agreed to look after it while Flora was away. He could be sure of a welcome and a cup of tea. No, it was better to get his visit to his mother over with straight away. He walked briskly to the house he'd rented for her, to the rear of the Bazaar. He stopped before he went up the path, pleased at how trim the garden looked. It was being well cared for, at least.

When he knocked on the door, Orla answered, not giving him her usual wide smile.

'Welcome back, sir. We heard your boat had dropped anchor. Mrs Southerham is in the sitting room.' Taking it for granted he'd follow, she went across to an open door. 'Captain McBride is here, ma'am.'

He went inside, expecting to see his mother slumped in a chair, her senses dulled by laudanum. But there was only Livia Southerham.

She got to her feet, looking apprehensive. 'Do sit down, Captain.'

He sat and waited for her to speak. Something was wrong, he knew it.

'I'm sorry to tell you that your mother died several weeks ago.'

'Ah.' He tried not to show the relief that was flooding through him. It wasn't right to be relieved when your mother died, but he couldn't help it.

'I can assure you that everything was done to care for her. Everything possible.'

Did she think he suspected her of not doing her job? 'I'm sure it was. And I'm equally sure it was a merciful release for all of us, including you. She wasn't an easy person to deal with, and it's not an easy illness to deal with, either.'

'No, she wasn't . . . easy.'

'How did it happen?'

'She simply stopped eating and drinking, and the doctor said nothing could be done about it. He advised us not to force her to eat or drink, as it would only prolong things unnecessarily. She died quite gently in the end, in her sleep.'

'It's the only time she's ever done anything gently in her life, then.' He saw he'd shocked her. 'I'm not going to pretend I was fond of her, because I wasn't. What she did to Flora made me dislike her intensely at the end.'

Livia nodded acceptance of this.

'Presumably you had her buried?'

'Yes. I can take you to her grave.'

He considered this, then nodded. 'I'd better visit it or I'll give people further reason to gossip about our family. Perhaps this afternoon would suit you? I haven't been home yet.'

'Of course. You'll have to tell your sister.'

'Ah. Well, no. That is . . .' He broke off, not sure how to explain it.

Livia looked at him, head cocked slightly, seeming content to wait for him to gather his thoughts.

'As it happens, Flora didn't come back with me.'

'She's all right, isn't she?'

'Yes. It's just . . . well, we met the man she once loved. My mother had tricked them, kept them apart for years. They still felt the same about each other and decided to get married. So she's gone with him to Sydney. He has a schooner, so she's living with him on the ship, as some wives do.'

Livia clapped her hands together. 'What wonderful news! I'm so happy for her.'

'You are?'

'Didn't you approve of the marriage?'

'Just between ourselves, I was worried about her marrying in haste and then regretting it. Given the gossip there already was about her, thanks to my mother, I was concerned what people would say about a rushed marriage.'

'I see. But I'm sure if *you* approve the marriage and announce it in the usual way in the newspaper, since she can't, people will simply be happy for her.'

'You really think so?'

'Yes, of course.' She clicked her tongue in exasperation. 'Look at me, sitting chatting to you and not even offering you a cup of tea. Perhaps you'd like a piece of cake as well?'

'I would, if you don't mind.' Anything to delay going back to an empty house.

'Could you . . .' He stopped, wondering if he was going too far. 'Could you kindly help me with the announcement for the newspaper?'

'Yes, of course.'

'And . . . could I trespass on your kindness still further by asking you to dispose of my mother's things? You can keep them or give them away. I don't care which.'

'I'm happy to deal with that. When will you want me to vacate the house?'

'Oh. Yes. There's the house too.' He thought furiously. He hadn't considered any of the details. He usually left details to Flora. 'Well, I've taken a lease on it, so you might as well stay here until you decide what you want to do next. There's no hurry for you to leave. In fact, before you go, perhaps you could help me work out what to do with the furniture here? There is more than enough for my needs at home, so I don't want it back.'

He stared at her, realising how much he would miss his sister's unobtrusive and efficient help. Did he dare ask her further help? Then he remembered that Livia needed to earn her living. 'I wonder . . . could I hire you as . . . as a . . .' He couldn't think of a name for it. 'Someone who does all sorts of helpful little jobs.'

She smiled. 'An amanuensis might be the correct term.'

'Yes, that's it. I'll pay you the same as I did when you were supervising my mother's care.'

'I'd be very happy to help. There's no need to pay me if you're letting me stay in the house.'

'I insist. And you should keep the maids on for the time being, too. I'd want the place kept in good order.'

'Are you sure? It'll cost you a lot of money for the two of them. I could manage with one.'

He leaned back, grinning. 'With the cargo I've brought back, I expect to make a lot of money, Mrs Southerham, so keep them both. Though perhaps Rhoda could come and help out at my house as well part of the time? There'll be too much for Linny to do on her own when I'm home. You could manage that arrangement for me, too.'

Tears filled her eyes, so he knew he'd been right to make the offer.

'Thank you, Captain McBride. Working for you

gives me time. I'll not have to rush into anything now.' She dabbed at her eyes. 'Sorry.'

'Don't be. It must be very worrying for you. And your help will be a godsend to me. I wouldn't know where to begin. It's the sort of thing Flora would have dealt with.' He gestured with one hand. 'Now, if I could trouble you for another piece of that delicious cake?.'

She smiled. 'Rhoda has a gift for making cakes. It's the only thing she likes cooking.'

When he'd gone, Livia went into the kitchen. 'Good news. We're to stay here. Captain McBride sister has married and gone to live with her husband, so the captain needs help with all sorts of things.' She explained.

'Well, praise be for that!' Orla said. 'I wasn't looking forward to moving. I was just starting to enjoy living in Fremantle, now that we don't have the old lady to cause upsets.'

'You're sure he still wants me to stay on as well?' Rhoda asked.

'Oh, yes. Working both here and at his house. And he loved your cake.'

Rhoda beamed at her. 'Well, that's a relief. I'll bake him a dozen cakes a week if he'll let me stay. I've never been so comfortable.'

Nor had Livia. She'd loved Francis, but life with him had been filled with upsets and financial worries. But she didn't dare get too used to being comfortable. She still had to find a way long-term to earn her living.

She certainly didn't intend to look for a husband, as Orla had suggested. That would be too embarrassing to bear.

Only what was she going to do with the rest of her life?

The following morning, Adam left the ladies with Bram and his wife, and went to see the lawyer his father had dealt with in Australia. He felt very tense, because his whole future might be ruined by what he found out today. He didn't know why he was so utterly certain he'd find some nasty surprise waiting for him, but he was.

He travelled up the river to Perth on a paddle steamer; a smallish vessel, but it seemed well found and was carrying quite a few other passengers, some in the mood to chat. He watched the land they chugged past with interest. Not beautiful. Scrubby was a better word for it. Small headlands, low-growing vegetation; trees sometimes, sandy foreshores.

It felt strange not to recognise what sort of trees they were, though he'd heard the terms 'gum tree' or 'eucalypt' and seen sketches of them. But black and white sketches were very different from real life. Most of the foliage was a dull greyish-green, making him think wistfully about the brighter green of English vegetation.

There was an occasional house, built of wood usually. Other craft were using the river, none as big as the paddle steamer. Men were fishing in small boats on some stretches, or fishing from the shore. They seemed to be doing well at it, too. He saw several pull in fish.

The river itself was beautiful, wide with big, sweeping curves, and he found the swish of the paddle wheel through the water very soothing. As they arrived at the capital and slowed down to dock at the jetty, the river grew much wider, and one man told him this part was called Perth Water.

The city was another disappointment. It might be the capital of the colony, but it was no more than a small town in size, though there were one or two large buildings, which an obliging gentleman named for him: Government House, with its turrets; the new Town Hall, still unfinished; the Catholic cathedral and the Pensioner Barracks.

The latter was a vaguely Tudor building, built of red brick. It housed the guards who'd come out with the convicts and had then settled here with their families. The government had stopped bringing convicts out to the colony now, but his companion considered that foolish, since there were still a lot of roads and bridges needed. Not to mention railways. It was a crying shame there were none of those in the colony.

'How are we to progress if we do not have the most modern transport, if we're still tied to horses and carts on land?' he demanded.

When they got off the steamer at the William Street Jetty, Adam was amused to find himself trudging along a mere sandy track to get to the

city itself. His talkative travelling companion
walked with him, still pointing out the sights, then
showed him where to find the street in which the
lawyer had his rooms.

Was it the isolation of the colony that made
people more friendly, Adam wondered? Whatever
it was, he liked that attitude.

Outside the house, which bore his lawyer's name
on a shiny brass sign, Adam stopped to take a
deep breath. Why was he hesitating? He needed
to get this over and done with.

An elderly clerk was sitting at a desk in the outer
office, and when Adam had explained who he was
and what he was doing there, the man said, 'Ah,'
and looked at the visitor sympathetically, as if he
knew something unpleasant.

'I'll go and inform Mr Wilford you're here.'

Nerves churning, Adam waited.

'Mr Wilford is fortunately free to see you at
once, sir. This way, if you please.'

Feeling like a man on his way to be executed,
Adam followed him along the corridor.

The lawyer was younger than he'd expected.
After shaking hands, he gestured. 'Please take a
seat, Mr Tregear.' Then he too looked at Adam
assessingly for a moment or two, before saying,
'It's a rather . . . unusual bequest.'

Adam said nothing, just waited.

'Your father asked me to purchase some properties on your behalf.' Pause, sigh.

'Get on with it. I didn't expect them to come

without conditions and probably nasty tricks, too. There was no love lost between him and me. He only bought them and the share in the schooner to get me out of England.'

'Very well. I'll be frank. He wanted properties that were not rented out to respectable businesses. He was most specific about that. I could only do as he asked, so . . . one property is a brothel, another a pub haunted by the lower orders, among them known thieves and villains. It's little more than a grog shop. The third is a rather shabby little house nearby, in which you must live for a year if you want to take up the inheritance.'

'Can he do this? Make conditions like that?'

Wilford pursed his lips. 'He can do what he likes, but at this distance, I'm not sure he, or his heirs I should say, will be able to enforce the conditions.' He smiled. 'Well, who's to tell them that they've not been fulfilled? Your father didn't ask me specifically to inform him of the outcome, and now that he's dead . . .'

'I doubt my half-brother will be interested anyway. As for my damned father, he's achieved what he set out to do.' Adam couldn't finish the sentence; felt himself choking with anger.

'And what was he trying to do?'

'To tarnish my reputation here, destroy any chance I might have to make something of myself.'

'Your own father?'

'He deeply regretted having fathered a bastard son; seemed to blame me for it.'

Mr Wilford shook his head, then said quietly, 'Being born out of wedlock doesn't carry quite the stigma here that it might in Britain, you know. It's much worse to be an ex-convict.'

'It won't help if the bastard owns a brothel, though.'

'You will have more chance to be judged on your own merits in the long term, I'm sure, than you would in England. And you surely don't intend to continue allowing a brothel to be run there?'

There was a pregnant silence. Adam looked at him. If this lawyer didn't despise him, could there be hope? Or had the damage already been done to his reputation? If so, that would affect his ability to earn a living.

'Anyway, there are papers to sign if you wish to retain the properties.'

'If I wish to retain them?'

'He made provision for you refusing to accept them.'

'I see.' And Adam did see. He felt as if he understood the whole picture now. His father had driven him out of the country and wanted to make sure he didn't make a success of his life here. 'Why did he bother to add this final nail to my coffin, I wonder? He'd got me out of England, had he not, away from his two legitimate children? That ought to have been enough, even for him.'

The lawyer hesitated, then said, 'Since you weren't close to him, I don't scruple to say that some people, as they grow older, start to act rather strangely. I see it quite often when drawing up wills. I've never met your father, though I believe he's done business with a relative of mine in Liverpool, which is how he came to contact me. But he can't have been a kind man. And this . . .' He flicked one hand towards the papers. 'Well, it's sheer spite.'

'Yes, it is. The question is, how much do you think it'll have damaged my reputation already to be known as the owner of these properties? I shall be sailing from Fremantle, trading too, I hope. Will people find it acceptable to deal with a brothel owner?'

'It won't be liked, in spite of the freer society here.'

'Even if I close the brothel down straight away?'

'That could help, but I'd guess the stigma will cling until you've proved yourself.'

His father had certainly laid his plans well. Adam sat for a moment longer, sickened by this final blow from the man who should have cared for him and never had. Then he took himself in hand. 'Well, where are these papers I need to sign? Whatever I do with the properties, I'm not refusing to accept them.'

'That would be improvident. I'd do the same thing in your place. And if you like, I'll tell people later that you were shocked to find what your properties were being used for.'

'Thank you.'

Adam walked out of the lawyer's rooms some

time later with a box of papers and deeds. Since he had time to spare before taking the steamer back, he went for a stroll round the town centre, but he couldn't really be bothered with the sights. His mind was too full of his problems, and his anger was simmering dangerously high.

The only thing he was certain of was that he didn't intend to do anything to blacken Ismay's name and reputation. Which meant he couldn't ask her to become his wife yet.

If they waited to marry, perhaps he could improve his reputation somehow. Would she agree to wait a year or two until he'd made sure that nothing from his inheritance would tarnish her name? Or her brother's? Oh, hell, it might hurt Bram too if Adam married Ismay! Scandals and gossip were like skittles: set up in a row, the one ready to bring down the others.

But even if she agreed to wait, she was such a lovely young woman that other men were bound to show an interest.

Misery swept through him. Even here, so far away from England, his birth and his father's spite were hanging like millstones round his neck.

Ismay stayed close to the cottage all day, afraid to go out without Adam to protect her. She and Aunt Harriet went up to the Bazaar and spent a pleasant hour marvelling at the wonderful items for sale. She smiled at the little bowls for drinking tea, remembering her days in Singapore and the kindness of Mr Lee. She ran her fingertips over a panel with a beautiful wooden carving of a forest scene. She eyed the silks enviously. Such lovely, lustrous pieces.

As they were walking back down the slope to their rooms behind the livery stables, she saw a man walking past in the street and stopped dead. It was him, Rory Flynn.

'Don't show that you've so much as noticed him,' Aunt Harriet snapped. 'Let your eyes travel over him as if you're indifferent to him.'

Ismay couldn't do that – just couldn't! The best she could do was look the other way as they walked back to the livery stables.

'You have to learn to stiffen your spine,' the older woman said. 'Face him out. Show him nothing but scornful indifference.'

'I can't. When a man has done *that* to you—' She rushed to the washbasin and retched into it.

'I wish I could kill him myself. Here, child. I asked too much of you. I'm sorry.' Aunt Harriet put an arm round Ismay and they sat together on the bed.

And it was this small gesture, added to yesterday's words, that made something start to change in Ismay, the first flutterings of confidence in herself. She still felt dirtied by what Rory had done to her, but Aunt Harriet could touch her lovingly and stand up for her. And Adam could love her and want to marry her.

Her world hadn't ended because of one act. Her

life contained people who knew about it and loved her anyway. She raised Aunt Harriet's hand to her lips and kissed it. 'I wonder if you realise how much your kindness means to me. I've never known anything like it. It's as if we're really related, as if you really do love me, as if I . . .' She couldn't go on.

'Of course I love you. And I love Adam too. You might not be the children of my body, but you're the children of my heart.' She cupped Ismay's chin with one hand so that the young woman had to look her in the eyes. 'There's something else I need to say. I want you to promise me that, whatever happens today, you won't let Adam delay your marriage. If that dreadful father of his has played another of his nasty tricks, it could make Adam try to wait, for your sake. Don't let him do it. Promise me.'

'I promise. As long as I'm sure it's what he wants.' Ismay leaned forward to kiss Aunt Harriet's rosy cheek and smiled. 'We'll find a house and we'll all live happily together, as families were meant to do. And it's all because of your kindness to both of us. You'll make a wonderful grandmother one day.'

Now it was the older woman's turn to blink away tears.

They sat for a while, holding hands, happy together, and the hard and hurtful lump that had felt to be lodged permanently inside Ismay since *it* happened dissolved still further.

Rory had done his worst, but she wouldn't let it ruin her life. Or Adam's.

Dougal went round to pick up Livia that afternoon to visit the grave. He was now correctly attired in dark clothes with a black armband that Linny insisted he wear.

They walked to the cemetery in Skinner Street, stopping a couple of times to chat to acquaintances, who welcomed him back and offered their condolences. He took the opportunity to mention his sister's marriage and his delight that she'd found such happiness.

He fell silent as they entered the cemetery, but Livia didn't pester him to talk. Leading the way to a new grave that still had no headstone, she said simply, 'This is it. I'll wait for you by the gate.'

'No, don't! Please. Stay with me.'

'Very well.'

He tried to say a prayer, but couldn't, so he stood there with head bowed for a few moments because it was the right thing to do.

Livia cleared her throat. 'You'll need to order a headstone of some sort.'

'I suppose so. Can you help me with that?'

'Of course. We could visit a stonemason on the way back, if you like. Or perhaps you wish to consider the design first?'

His voice came out more harshly than he'd intended. 'I want the simplest of headstones, with no flowery words on it. Simply her name and my father's.'

'Then we can place an order quite easily.'

He took her arm to stop her moving on. 'Thank you.'

She looked at him questioningly. 'What for, particularly?'

'Being here today, helping. Understanding how I really feel.'

'I'm just doing my job.'

'You're doing it well. Not intruding, but helping.' He offered her his arm and they walked out of the cemetery. He didn't intend to come back again if he could help it.

Adam didn't get back till late that afternoon, and he didn't feel like looking at his properties yet so made no detours as he walked through Fremantle. When he got to the livery stables, he saw Ismay and his aunt going into the cottage and held back until the door had shut behind them, not ready to face them yet. He was still no nearer to working out what to do and he knew Ismay wouldn't care for her reputation.

But he did. He must. For her sake.

He stared up at the Bazaar, where someone had lit lanterns on either side of the entrance, and it looked so welcoming in the dusk that, on impulse, he went up. He had to talk to someone about his situation and who better than Ismay's brother? Bram had been here for a while and was an astute businessman. Perhaps he could advise Adam?

Bram was attending to a customer, laughing with him as he took the money.

The man who kept watch at night was locking a door at the rear of the Bazaar, starting the nightly ritual of shutting up, probably.

As Bram walked to the door with the lady, he smiled at Adam and waited until she'd gone to ask, 'How did your day go, then? Any nasty shocks?'

Adam nodded. 'Could we talk in your office? I need advice.'

'Oh. That bad, is it?'

Bram said more than 'Oh' when he heard the news in full, cursing fluently and damning all people who set out to harm others for no reason. 'My father and yours! They'd make a grand pair!'

'I thought you'd understand, if anyone would. It's Ismay I'm concerned about, you see. How can I marry her – expose her to gossip and possible insult?'

'You could wait a little.'

'Yes.' It was the right thing to do, but it made him feel so bereft. He wanted to marry her soon, be with her, love her. Make a home for her and his aunt.

Was that so much to ask?

19

Rory was feeling impatient. Seeing Ismay had stirred up all his old feelings and he wanted her, as he had done ever since she grew to be a woman. It was more than wanting. She'd always been his. And now he'd put his mark on her, even more so. She was carrying his child. Even Father Patrick had said they should marry, so he was doing the right thing.

He hung around the Bazaar after work, seeing a final customer leaving, a dark silhouette against the lights gleaming up at the shop. Shop! It was an enormous place. How had a scrawny little runt like Bram Deagan got rich enough to own that? He must have stolen the money or committed some other crime, and whatever the damned priests said, it'd be worth putting your immortal soul in danger to be so rich you never had to think twice about where your next meal was coming from.

On that thought, Rory took a step forward, hesitated, then walked up the hill to the shop. He couldn't bear to wait any longer to confront her brother. Now that Bram realised the condition his sister was in, he must surely want her married off.

What would people say if her belly swelled and she gave birth to a bastard? That'd not be good for his reputation in the town.

An older man was standing near the door. 'I'm afraid we're closed, sir.'

'I'm wanting to speak to Bram, not buy anything.'

The man gave him a scornful look. 'Well, he's busy with someone else. You'll have to come back another time.'

Rory didn't hesitate. He shoved the old fellow hard and, as he stumbled backwards and fell, Rory pushed inside the shop.

A bell started to ring behind him and he swung round, wondering what the hell that was.

In the office, Bram broke off at the sound of the bell. 'There's trouble,' he called, already running out of the door.

Adam followed.

Bram stopped dead when he saw who was standing in the middle of his shop, looking like an outraged bull. He hadn't seen Rory since Ismay arrived and, after finding out what he'd done to her, he had a strong desire to smash the fellow's teeth in. He'd never succeed. But oh, he wanted to try!

'We'll fight him with words,' he muttered to Adam. 'I don't want my stock damaging.'

'He'll not listen.'

'Oh, he will. He's still thinking he can marry Ismay. We're three to one, but it'd create havoc

and cost me money. If I choose my words carefully, he'll save his fighting for another day.'

Adam made an angry sound but didn't argue.

Bram strolled forward, praying he'd find the
right thing to say. 'Is it yourself, Rory Flynn?'

'You can see it is. I want to speak to you.'

'Aren't you doing just that?'

Adam stayed in the darkened rear of the shop,
picking up a wooden walking stick with a knobbly
head in case it came to a fight. He kept outside
the circle of light near the entrance and Flynn
didn't seem to have noticed him.

'Privately,' Rory said.

'Oh, my old friend Sim won't tell your secrets.'
Bram could see that Sim was angry at being taken
by surprise. A former pensioner guard on a convict
ship, Sim was now his night watchman and prided
himself on keeping the Bazaar safe.

'It isn't just my secret. It's your sister's, too. You
won't want everyone to know about her.'

'Ismay has no secrets from me.'

'Then she'll have told you she's expecting my
child. We had a quarrel and she ran away to
Australia, but I came after her. I'm still prepared
to marry her, and the sooner the better.'

Bram forced a laugh. 'My sister isn't expecting
a child and I don't know why you want to pretend
she is. She's a decent young woman, and I'll thank
you not to blacken her name.'

Rory froze. 'I don't believe you. I *know* she's
expecting a child.'

Adam couldn't bear to stay out of it and moved forward. 'Indeed she isn't. Miss Deagan has been sharing a cabin with my aunt, since she's betrothed to me. I think we'd know if she was carrying a child.'

Bram had never seen such naked hatred on any man's face as on Adam's, and he left it to him to continue. He now had two furiously angry men to manage – along with his own anger as well.

For all Rory was much bigger, he took an involuntary step backwards when Adam moved towards him, hefting the walking stick in his hand.

'If I ever heard you blackening her name, Flynn, I'd make you very sorry indeed,' Adam said, his voice so loud it rang round the huge room.

'I don't have to blacken her name. She did it when she lay with me.'

'Willingly?' The one word seemed to echo, then there was a heavy silence as Adam waited for a reply.

Rory opened his mouth, then shut it again. He stood for a moment, then said thickly, 'It was with her father's permission, and that was as willing as I needed. I'm warning you to stay away from her. She's mine. Always has been.'

'She's always avoided you,' Bram said. 'She doesn't want you, Rory.'

Flynn turned his head to glare at Bram. 'That's just a woman's teasing way. They say one thing and mean another.'

Could the fellow really believe that? From the look on his face, he did. 'She meant it.'

Adam spoke again. 'And if she wanted you, why is she now betrothed to me?'

Rory gaped at him as this sank in. 'She isn't. She can't be.'

'Oh, but she is.'

'Well, she won't be staying betrothed to you for long.' Rory bunched his fists, seeming about to lunge forward. But something held him back, the sense of faint shame he'd felt occasionally ever since he'd forced her. He did no more than shuffle his feet and growl under his breath.

The silence seemed filled with anger.

Suddenly Adam thwacked his stick against one hand and Sim took a step forward, hefting a lead-weighted belaying pin.

'Three to one, Rory,' Bram said quickly, desperate to protect his stock. 'You'll not win.' He held up one hand to stop his companions moving any closer.

They waited, expecting at any minute to be attacked.

Rory watched them. Should he, shouldn't he? No, he shouldn't hurt her brother or they'd never make it up. He drew in a deep breath, then another. He'd wait till another time, plan it out more carefully. Perhaps he could catch her on her own and tell her it was all right. He still wanted to marry her.

Swinging round, he strode out, slamming the

door back against its hinges as he went. As he lumbered off down the hill, he kept his anger chained. It wouldn't do any good to hit out blindly, never did. Old Mr Largan had taught him that the hard way, by having him whipped several times when he was a lad.

Her engaged to marry that scrawny sailor fellow? Never. He wouldn't allow it. She'd only done it to give the baby a name. But it was Rory's baby.

As he strode down the street, he gradually slowed down, frowning. Bram and his friend seemed very certain she wasn't carrying a child. She had been. He knew that for certain. Had she lost it, then?

He stopped walking to think about this. She must have done. If she had, it'd be a pity, because it meant he'd lost his bargaining power.

For the moment.

He smiled. They couldn't watch her every minute of the day. He'd find a way to take her from them.

He'd come all the way to Australia for her, hadn't he? If he'd managed to do that, he'd find a way to get her back again.

The watchman looked from Bram to Adam. 'You'll want to be private. And don't think I'll go blabbing about what I've heard.' Sim walked outside and they heard the sound of his feet crunching on the crushed limestone path, growing fainter as he started a circuit of the building.

'Well, we got out of that without a fight, at least,' Bram said. 'But Ismay will need protecting carefully. Rory Flynn never gives up when he wants something. The only one who could ever stop him was the old master. Even before Rory had grown to his man's strength, everyone in the village was afraid of him.'

Bram paused to think. 'Rory never came after me and mine before, though he thumped me a few times as a boy – me and most of the lads in the village. He's a devil of a bully, that one. Even if Ismay was carrying his child, I'd not want her to marry him. She'd have a miserable life.'

Bram waited, looking at Adam. 'Maybe you should marry Ismay as soon as we can arrange it?'

'I've just been telling you what's happened to me, Bram. How can I marry her till I've sorted this mess out? Me owning that brothel would blacken her name, too.'

'You worry too much about gossip.'

'With reason. That house is a *brothel*, Bram. It makes me sick to think of it.'

'Then close it down.'

'I intend to. But however quickly I do that, the mud will cling, not only to me but to my wife. I have to talk to her about it, explain, give her a chance to . . . wait.'

Another long silence, then Bram said, 'Do you want to marry her or not?'

'Of course I damned well do! There's nothing I want more. But I want to do it properly. If you'd seen how my mother suffered from gossip, if you knew how cruel people can be . . . I want better than that for Ismay.'

'Doesn't what she wants matter?'

Adam nodded. 'Of course it does.'

'Then ask her. Let her choose whether to wait or not.'

'You think . . . it'd be all right to do that?'

'Of course I do.'

He watched Adam's expression lighten a little and clapped him on the shoulder. 'She's not your mother. And you're not your father. Let her do the choosing about when to get married.'

'Very well, I will. There's nothing I want more than to marry her, Bram. I've been torn in two, trying to do the right thing.'

'Come on then. Let's see what she says. Tea will be ready and I'm famished.' He raised his voice. 'I'm going now, Sim! Keep that cosh handy and ring the bell if you need help.'

Sim walked round the corner. 'Yes, sir.'

As they drew near the cottage, Bram stopped again to say, 'You should tell Ismay exactly what you found out in Perth. If I know my sister, she'll be ready to help you kick the people out.'

'She's a wonderful woman! So brave, so lively. There's no one like her.'

Bram hid a smile. As far as he was concerned, his own wife was the most marvellous woman in the world, but you didn't contradict a man in the first throes of love.

It was no smiling matter, though, and he was really worried for his sister and her husband-to-be. Rory Flynn would make a very formidable enemy, physically strong and doggedly determined.

The only thing that might stop him was them marrying.

When the two men went inside the house, they looked so grim, Isabella asked at once, 'What's happened?'

Bram sighed. 'We've just had a visit from Rory Flynn.'

'Oh, no!' His sister clapped one hand to her mouth.

'He still thinks he's going to marry you, even though he knows there's no reason to.'

'I'd never marry him. I'd die before I said the words, whatever he threatened me with.' Ismay looked at Adam.

He stepped forward. 'You and I need to talk. Let's go across to the stables.'

'I'll watch you across in case he's still hanging around,' Bram said. 'Better safe than sorry. And tell Les to be on his guard before you start talking. Maybe I should hire another night watchman.'

'I don't like to cost you money,' Ismay said.

'I'd spend every penny I have to protect my family,' he said. 'But don't worry. I'm not short of money.'

'I know. You're a clever man. I'm so proud of what you've done here.'

He flushed and Isabella stepped forward to take his arm. 'He is wonderful.'

Adam hurried Ismay across to the stables, where he had a word with Les. Together the two men locked the big outer doors earlier than usual while Ismay waited in the bedroom area at the rear.

When Adam joined her, they sat together on the narrow bed.

'What did you find out in Perth?' she asked. 'I saw you going up to the Bazaar after you got back and knew it must be bad from the look on your face.'

'It isn't good news.' He went through what the lawyer had told him.

She waved one hand dismissively. 'Is that all? I don't care about that.'

'Then I must care for you. I love you and I do want to marry you, but not like this, a hurried ceremony without any announcements or guests. Even imaginary mud clings where gossip is concerned.'

'Your aunt made me promise not to let you hold back from getting married, whatever your father had done.'

Adam sighed. 'Neither of you is thinking straight, then. I worked it out on the way back that we'd wait a while to marry, but now there's Rory to complicate matters.'

She tugged his hand to pull him closer. 'It's you who's not thinking straight, Adam darling. I don't care that you're bastard born. I don't care what your father has left you. I only know I want to be your wife. And if Rory is going to cause trouble, please could we get married quickly, so that he can see it's hopeless? I can't face him catching me again.' Her voice broke on the final word as the bad memories of that day overwhelmed her.

Adam's final doubts vanished. Pulling her towards him, he kissed her tenderly, then simply held her close. It was a while before he moved away, then he said quietly, 'If you're absolutely certain, we'll get married as soon as the banns can be called.'

'Could we not get a special licence and do it straight away?' She shivered. 'I don't want to give Rory three weeks to try to capture me again. He will try, I know. He's the most stubborn, pig-headed creature in this world, or he'd not have followed me all the way to Australia.'

Adam stroked the hair back from her flushed forehead. He felt so right being with her, touching her, and best of all he had a sense of belonging that he hadn't felt so strongly for many years. 'Very well, my darling girl. A special licence it is. But even after we're married, we'll be careful till we can think of a way to get rid of Flynn. I want him out of this town, preferably out of this colony.'

They sat there a little longer, then went to join the rest of the family and announce their news.

Rory went to the alehouse he used sometimes. The owner called it a public house, but the customers mostly called it a grog shop, because it was small and shabby. He ordered some beer and sat down. The woman who ran it most of the time came over to join him and chat. She'd done that before, and it was obvious she liked him.

He sighed. Tessie was a comfortable armful, pleasant natured and hard working, but she wasn't Ismay.

When he'd finished the one drink he allowed himself, he went out for a walk, inevitably passing the livery stables where *she* was sleeping. He even knew which window was hers.

He couldn't resist creeping round the back and tapping on the window. 'I'm watching you, Ismay Deagan. I'm not letting you go.'

When he heard someone moving inside, he hurried off, smiling at the thought that he'd probably ruined her night's sleep. And that fellow's too. Good. Serve them right.

He found his own bed, a mattress in the hayloft of the byre where he worked. He hated to see the poor cows shut up like this to give milk to the townfolk. Poor creatures. They never even saw the sun or got to eat fresh grass. He felt sorry for them.

But that didn't stop him sleeping soundly.

The next morning Adam went to St John's Church to ask about getting married quickly. Ismay said she didn't care which church they got married in, because she'd had enough of Catholic priests telling her to marry Rory. He therefore went to the Church of England, to which his Aunt Harriet belonged, attending services when she could.

The curate, a youngish man called Howarth, frowned. 'Why do you need to marry in such haste, Mr Tregear? Is your young lady, um . . . ?' He delicately didn't put it into words.

'No, she isn't. I've not bedded her yet. She's a decent young woman.'

The curate blushed.

After a moment's hesitation, Adam told him about Rory.

'Are you sure this fellow will continue to pursue Miss Deagan?'

'I'm certain of it. He followed her here all the way from Ireland, after all.'

'Ireland? Is she a Catholic? If so—'

'She's been worshipping at the Church of England since she came to live with my aunt.' He hoped he'd be forgiven this small lie, but he had to make Ismay safe.

'Oh. Right.' The curate chewed one corner of his mouth, then said, 'Well, given what you've told me, I think it'd be in order for me to marry you tomorrow. I'll have to check with the minister first, though.'

He came back a quarter of an hour later, still looking unhappy. 'He says it's all right, given the circumstances. Two o'clock tomorrow afternoon would be a convenient time for me, and you'll have to pay extra for the special licence.'

'Thank you.'

'You'll need to bring two witnesses, remember.'

'I know.'

Glad to see the back of the scornful curate, Adam rushed home to tell Ismay, who was looking tired after the night's disturbance.

'I'm sorry it'll be such a simple, rushed affair.'

She smiled. 'I'm not. I want to be your wife so much that the ceremony isn't important. It's our lives together that matter most.'

'You're always so easy to deal with.' He resisted the urge to kiss her again and pulled out his pocket watch. 'I'd better get on with things. I'm going to inspect my properties now.'

'Can I come with you?'

'Not to the sort of places I'm going. It would definitely cause talk if you went into a brothel.'

She sighed. 'I know, but I'm starting to feel like a prisoner.'

'It won't be for long. We'll be married tomorrow and then surely he'll stop pursuing you? You'd better work out what to wear.' He looked up as his aunt came in. 'We're getting married tomorrow. You'll help Ismay with her clothes, won't you, Aunt Harriet?'

'It'll be my pleasure.' She put one arm round Ismay. 'I'll make sure you have a clean shirt, too, Adam.'

He set off to visit his properties, something he'd been dreading ever since he'd spoken to the lawyer.

*   *   *

Livia woke feeling happier now that she had a job of sorts, even if helping Dougal was only a temporary thing. She and her maid spent the morning going through the old lady's possessions.

'Mr Deagan could sell some of these in his bazaar,' Orla said. 'If Captain McBride doesn't want the money, it'd be a good bit more for you. Well, he could sell them if we cleaned and aired them. At least Mrs McBride kept herself clean. It's the only good thing I know about her. There's a room at the back of the Bazaar for secondhand clothes and it has a separate entrance. The front-door people ignore it, but I found a pretty shawl there the other week, that blue one.'

'I'll go and see Mr Deagan straight away, then.'

'You could buy a newspaper while you're out, Mrs Southerham,' Orla said. 'We need to look for a position for you, or a house to rent for running a school. We can't wait till the last minute to do something.'

'Oh, we don't need to do anything yet. Captain McBride said we could stay here as long as we liked. But I will buy a newspaper. I'll enjoy having something to read.'

When she'd gone, Orla looked at Rhoda. 'Impractical. That's what she is. A good mistress, kind-hearted, but hasn't got a practical bone in her body, however hard she tries. Has to make lists to remind herself to do things.'

'If ever a woman needed a husband to look after her, it's Mrs Southerham,' Rhoda said, nodding her head several times for emphasis. 'And one with the money for servants and such.'

'You and I could keep an eye on the adverts in the newspaper. Men of all sorts put them in sometimes about wanting a wife. They don't give their names, of course, just *Gentleman seeks lady, object marriage.*' Or, *Farmer seeks wife, skilled in dairy work.*

'What about Captain McBride? Wouldn't he make a good husband for her?'

'He doesn't show any signs of that sort of interest. Nor does she. And anyway, he'll probably marry someone with money, him being a captain and owning his own ship. He'll need someone practical because he's away a lot. No, we'll have to look elsewhere for Mrs Southerham.'

Unaware that her two maids were conspiring to help her, Livia spent a few minutes with Bram and Isabella discussing the secondhand clothes, then took Isabella back to the house to look at the items which she thought were too good to throw away.

By afternoon, a pile of the better clothes and personal possessions had been carried across to the Bazaar and Orla had taken a pile of less attractive items to a secondhand clothing merchant Isabella had told them about.

Livia spent a pleasant evening reading the newspaper, after which she passed it on to her maids.

'Nothing here this week,' Orla said after scanning the advertisements.

'Never mind. She says there's no hurry for us to leave here.'

'She'll be saying that as they throw us out in the street. I don't know why I stick with her.'

'Because she needs you.'

Orla grimaced. 'She does. And it's a good place, working for her, all things considered. She's a nice lady.'

Adam found the brothel easily enough. It was a ramshackle wooden house with extra rooms built on at the rear, in great need of repair, with the paintwork of the door peeling. The blinds were closed and there was no sign of activity. He supposed its occupants were still sleeping after their night's work.

Since he was determined to close it down straight away, he banged on the door till someone answered.

A blowsy woman with a torn dressing gown pulled carelessly round herself opened the door a little way.

'We don't open till afternoon, sir.'

'I need to speak to the person in charge now.'

She hesitated, then said, 'I suppose if your need is urgent, I can find you a girl, but I'll have to charge extra.'

'I'm the new owner of this place, not a customer. My name's Tregear. The name on the lease is Neville Charrock. Is he here?'

'No, sir.'

'Then I'll have to give this to you.' He handed her the letter the lawyer had prepared for him. 'It says you have twenty-four hours to vacate the premises.'

She stared at him in shock, making no attempt to open the letter. 'Leave the house, you mean?' Her eyes narrowed. 'Can you prove that you're the owner?'

'Oh, yes. I have all the papers.'

She stared down at the letter, twisting it round in her hands. 'Look, surely we can come to some arrangement? We could perhaps manage to pay you a bit more rent. Not too much, of course. We're not making a fortune here.'

'I don't want rent money from immoral activities. I'm closing this place down immediately and I want you all to leave.'

It took a moment or two for her to realise he meant it, then she threw the letter back at him. 'You can't do that! Why should you close us down, anyway? We pay our rent on time, always have done.'

'I'm not having you running a brothel on my premises.'

'You don't need to be involved. You don't even need to visit us. I keep everything clean and tidy. You'll get your rent and we'll not cause any trouble. Nev keeps order here so there are no fights, no trouble. He'll—'

'I meant what I said: I want it closing down. *Today*.'

'How will we make a living? Where will the girls and I go?'

'You could try honest work for a change. But as long as you don't open for business again, I'll give you a couple of days to find somewhere else to live. No longer than that, though.'

She laid her hand on his arm, speaking coaxingly about the higher rent he already got for the place, how much money he'd lose. But he shook her hand off, bent to pick up the letter and shoved it into her hands again.

'I'll be back later this afternoon to inspect the whole premises. Get the women out of bed and make sure you're ready for me in two hours' time. And remember: you are not to open tonight. I'll be walking past at regular intervals to check and I'll also inform the constables and ask them to keep an eye on the place.'

As he walked away, she started to curse him, but he didn't let himself react to the filth she was spewing out. The way she spoke only made him more determined to get rid of her.

Madge stopped cursing but watched Mr Bloody Tregear walk away before she went inside. What was she going to do?

She shivered as she closed the door. Nev would throw a fit when he heard they'd been told to leave, and when he was in a rage, he didn't mind who he took his anger out on.

He'd go after the new owner, she was sure of

it. And Mr Tregear didn't look like a fighter. She frowned. He didn't look a coward either. He seemed very determined to get rid of them, so was probably some sort of Holy Joe.

She went to the kitchen to get the stove hot again, shoving wood in till the fire was blazing nicely, then setting the smaller kettle on top of the hole.

As she sipped her first cup of tea, she tried to think what to do, how to make the best of this, but could see no way of placating Nev, let alone stopping this happening.

He'd not be back from Perth till later tonight. She and the girls had better start packing up their things. She'd didn't dare pack Nev's stuff. He didn't like anyone messing with the stuff in his room.

Surely he wouldn't blame her for this?

She'd send Chrissie out to look for rooms to rent temporarily, but the only houses vacant would probably be shabby places on the outskirts of the town. Not good for her sort of trade to be away from the centre. Sailors wouldn't want to go too far from their ships and would patronise the nearer houses. And the neighbours on the outskirts would probably get fussy, too.

There were too many stuffed shirts around Fremantle these days, people like the new owner, causing trouble for hard-working girls who needed to earn their daily bread as best they could, like everyone else.

Madge looked round with tears in her eyes. This house was nice and central, just off High Street. She'd been happy here. Why couldn't that stupid fool just take his rent money and leave them alone?

Oh dear, she was dreading Nev coming back.

She drained the cup. Time to get the girls up. They'd a lot to do today. Nev might be a good fighter, but that Mr Tregear had a determined chin. And anyway, he had the law on his side.

Adam went to look at his next property, the pub or 'grog shop', as the lawyer had scornfully called it. It was a wooden building, probably originally a house. The property looked sound enough, but was in need of some maintenance work. When he went inside, he found people drinking already.

The woman behind a small counter smiled at him. 'What can I get you, sir?'

'Are you in charge here?'

'No, sir. Tommy is.' She indicated a man taking a long drink of ale in the corner.

'I need to speak to him privately.'

Her expression immediately became wary and she went across to whisper in Tommy's ear.

He looked round with a scowl and heaved himself up, lingering to joke with the man next to him. He came slowly across to the counter. 'What can I do for you?' As an afterthought, he added, 'Sir,' in a way that was an insult. Clearly Adam wasn't welcome here.

'I'm the new owner. My name's Tregear. I'm

closing this place down immediately. You have two days to vacate the premises.' He held out the lawyer's letter. 'This is your official notification.'

The man's affable expression changed immediately. 'I don't think my customers will like that.'

'They don't own the house. I do.'

'I've paid my rent and I'm staying.'

'It's all explained in the letter. If there's rent paid in advance, you'll get a refund. As long as the premises are in decent order, that is.'

For a moment Adam thought the man was going to attack him, but the woman, who'd been listening to them, grasped Tommy's arm and gave it a shake.

Adam nodded at her in thanks but she only scowled at him.

'I'll be back the day after tomorrow to see you move out.'

As he walked out, he heard someone say, 'Wait till Nev hears about this. He'll throw a fit if he loses his favourite drinking place.'

That name again. Who was this Nev person?

A voice called, 'You'd better watch your step, stranger.'

Adam swung round. 'Are you threatening me?' He had no idea who had spoken, but the voice came from someone at Tommy's table. 'Any more talk like that and I'll bring in the police constables to throw everyone out this minute. From what I've heard, I'm sure they'll be glad to see you lot go.'

A sullen silence greeted his words. He met their gaze defiantly, waited a moment or two to emphasise that they hadn't intimidated him, then turned and left.

After that he went across the street to look for the house he was supposed to live in. He saw a shabby place and prayed that wasn't the one. But when he counted the numbers, it was. He stopped and let out a disgusted choke of sound.

Not only was it shabby, but it looked filthy. As if he'd bring Ismay and his aunt to live here! One of the steps up to the veranda was broken and a windowpane was cracked. There was only sandy soil in the garden, with a few weeds struggling here and there, wilting in the heat.

He went carefully up the two rickety steps on to the veranda. One of the planks in front of the door was loose, another creaked and sagged beneath his foot.

Using the key the lawyer had given him, he went inside, wrinkling his nose at the sour smell. The door opened on to a narrow passage. There was a bedroom on either side and, as he moved towards the rear, he passed another two rooms, smaller ones. All were empty, apart from dust and spiders' webs.

The passage opened into the kitchen, where he found two men sleeping. The place smelled foul, of unwashed bodies and something rotten. Clearly they'd been using it for a while. The rear door was hanging off its hinges and, as he moved across to study the back garden, a large hairy spider scuttled for cover. The back garden was as neglected as the front one, but it had a couple of trees at least and a few plants he didn't recognise which seemed to be coping with the poor soil and heat.

Amazingly, the men hadn't woken. Anger filled him and he took the poker and banged it on the rusty stove. 'Wake up!' he yelled at the top of his voice, continuing to clang it.

They jerked awake, blinking at him warily. One scratched himself, the other yawned.

'I'm the new owner and you two are trespassing. You'd better find somewhere else to sleep from now on because, if I find you here again, I'll have you arrested.'

'We've not done any damage,' one whined. 'The door was already broke.'

'It won't be by nightfall. Get out and do not come back.'

When they'd gathered their pitiful bundles of possessions together, he followed them out at the back and down the side to make sure they left. There was a gate, sagging on its hinges. He managed to drag it across the space between the house and the fence and shove the rusty bolt into a hole in the wooden gatepost. Anyone could kick it in if they really wanted to, but a closed gate said something, at least.

He sighed as he went inside to examine the six rooms again, with their bare, creaking boards and dust floating in the sunbeams slanting through the windows. Upset by the place, he went out and locked the front door carefully behind him.

Bram had told him how to get to the police

station, so Adam went there next and introduced himself, explaining what he'd done.

'Bit difficult for them women to find somewhere else to go in one day,' one of the constables said. 'They aren't bad sorts, sir, don't give us no trouble.'

The other scowled at his companion and said to Adam, 'They're an ungodly crowd, both the women and their customers. And so are them at the grog shop. I'll be glad to see both places closed down.'

Adam saw his chance to start spreading the word that he was respectable. 'So will I. When I inherited them, I was horrified to find one was a brothel.'

They both nodded and one said, 'I'd advise you to let the Justice of the Peace know as well, sir. Get a paper from him authorising us to help. Once we have that, I'll call in and let Nev know I'm watching to make sure he gets his girls out as you've told him to.'

'I keep hearing this man's name. Who is he?'

'He's a bad sort, Nev is. Not a convict, but ought to have been, if ever anyone ought. You want to watch out for him.'

'I will.'

The other one said, 'We'll both go to Tommy's boozer. Quite a few people will be upset about that closing.' He looked at Adam. 'You'd better take care, sir. Angry men can be violent.'

'Thanks.' Just what he needed. Irate people after his blood.

Adam spent the rest of the day hurrying to and fro, too busy to keep an eye out for Rory, too busy even to spend a few minutes with his bride-to-be.

By dusk, the back door of the house was closed with a new bolt and he'd checked on the brothel and grog shop twice, making sure the people at each place saw him doing it.

He could manage no more for now. Tomorrow he was getting married. The thought of that seemed unreal . . . and yet, wonderful.

Suddenly, fiercely, he couldn't wait for a wife and children, his aunt: a real family, people who belonged to him.

20

Ismay waited impatiently for Adam to come back, but he didn't do so until just before the evening meal at her brother's house.

She saw him coming down the street and ran to the door to greet him, stopping at the sight of his grim expression. 'Were the houses very bad?'

'Yes.' He caught hold of her hand, smiling at her. 'I'll tell you about them in a minute, so that I don't have to repeat it for the others. I just need to wash my hands. I won't be long.' He planted a kiss on her cheek then hurried across to the stables.

Over the meal, he told them what his inheritance was like.

'I can clean our house out,' Ismay said at once.

'I can help,' Aunt Harriet said.

'I'm not having you two going near it till it's been cleaned out. The place *stinks*!'

'I'm sure Rhoda will do the scrubbing for you,' Isabella said. 'She's always glad to earn a bit extra. She's got a friend who helps out too. You can nip up to their house after we've eaten and ask Livia if Rhoda's free.'

'Good. And after that, we'll need to buy furniture.'

'I've got some pieces to start you off,' Bram said. 'It'll be my wedding present.'

'I can afford to pay for them!'

'Ismay's my sister. I'd like to help out, so let me give her a present or two,' Bram said gently.

Adam realised he'd spoken sharply. 'Thank you, then. Sorry if I sounded ungrateful. I'm just . . . a bit upset by it all. Will it be all right if we stay on in your stable quarters for a few more days?'

Ismay's heart went out to her beloved. He looked upset. It mattered so much to him to stay respectable.

When they'd finished the meal, she said lightly, 'I'll walk up to Mrs Southerham's with you, Adam.'

It was the first time they'd been alone all day. When they'd passed the Bazaar and waved to the watchman, she pulled him into the shadows. 'About time you kissed me properly. We *are* getting married tomorrow, after all.' She put her arms round his neck. His kiss was still a butterfly touch but he held her close, rocking her slightly.

'I love you, Ismay.'

'Good. Because I love you too.' As she felt him relax a little she said quietly, 'Don't forget that my family lived in a two-room cottage in Ireland. It had earth floors and there were ten of us sharing it, some of us sleeping in the roof space. Do you think I'll look down on a five-room house after that?'

'It's like a pigsty.'

'Pigsties can be cleaned up.'

'I wanted everything to be perfect for you.'

She laughed. 'We'll make it perfect together, and your aunt will help. I'll enjoy doing that and so will she.'

'You're a wonderful woman. I don't deserve you.'

Hand in hand they went on their way.

Nev got back from Perth at dusk. He erupted into the house, yelling for the outside lanterns to be lit. 'What are the customers going to think?'

Madge came out to greet him. 'That we're not open. Nev, we've been closed down.'

He stared at her, the pulse at his temple throbbing, his fists clenching. 'Who says so?'

'The new owner.'

'I don't believe you.'

'He came today and left a letter for you.' She went to the mantelpiece and got the envelope, holding it out with a hand that trembled slightly.

Nev snatched it from her, ripping it open and scanning the words. Then he cursed and flung it on the ground. 'He can't do this to us.'

She didn't contradict him.

'Get those lanterns lit.'

'Nev . . . the constables came round. They said we weren't to open. They had a paper from the magistrate.'

He kicked a chair out of his way, then picked another up and hurled it across the room. 'Damn you, I go away for a day – one day! – and I come back to find my business closed.'

With a shriek, she dodged out of the way. 'It's not my fault, Nev. I begged the owner to let us carry on, offered him more rent money, but he didn't want it, not from a business like ours. He won't change his mind.'

'Old fellow, is he?'

'No, quite young, about your age. And Nev . . . I heard he went to the pub afterwards and closed them down too.'

Without a word, he slammed out of the house. Shuddering, she poured herself a glass of port and then another. She was dreading him coming back.

Nev went to his local pub and grew even more furious when he saw that it was closed down too. There were lights on inside, though, and he heard voices, so he banged on the door.

Tommy came to see who it was. 'Oh, it's you. Come in. I'll stand you a drink. I can't sell drinks but there's no law about giving them to my friends.'

'Why has he closed you down?' Nev asked.

'Didn't say. Just told me we had two days to vacate the premises and handed us a bit of paper from his lawyer. Then the police come round and said we had to do what he'd told us or the magistrate would lock us up. I don't want to deal with the magistrate.'

'The new owner is a sod and needs teaching a lesson. Do you know where he lives?'

'One of my customers says he's staying at that place behind the livery stables.'

'He can't be a toff, then.'

'He speaks like a toff. Looks down his nose at you like a toff, too.'

'He'll have trouble speaking at all by the time I've done with him.'

Tommy grasped his arm. 'Nev, it won't do any good.'

'It'll make me feel better, and it'll teach him not to mess with me in future.'

The sky was lightening by the time Nev staggered home, drunk, supported by two friends.

Madge let them in and showed them where to dump Nev, relieved that she didn't have to face his anger tonight.

Then quiet reigned for a time, but she knew it was the quiet before a storm.

Ismay slept badly that night, wondering if she'd pushed Adam too hard to marry her. Aunt Harriet heard her tossing and turning and came in to find out what was worrying her.

'He loves you, dear, and you're going to make him a wonderful wife. Now, let me tuck you in and go to sleep.'

It was lovely to be treated in this motherly way, something Ismay had never experienced before she met Aunt Harriet, because her own mother had always been too sick with the new baby, or too busy once it was born.

When she woke up, it was morning. Her wedding day! She bounced out of bed and twirled round, then went to look at herself in the mirror. Her hair was shiny because Isabella and Aunt Harriet had insisted she take a bath instead of washing with a cloth, as she usually did. She'd washed her hair too, and Isabella had produced a piece of silk to polish it with.

They suggested she rest, but she could never bear to sit still and do nothing, so she insisted on helping Isabella and the maid Sally around the house. For a time she played with little Louisa, who was such a shy child but who always came to her. There was a set of skittles, which Adam had already shown Louisa how to use, and the child always asked to play that. Ismay took her outside at the back and they enjoyed a few games together.

Isabella came to the door, smiling at them. 'Could you clear those away now, Louisa? We have to get ready. Bram's putting up a couple of trestle tables in the rear part of the shop and we're closing that area off. I want you to help me carry things up.'

Ismay looked at her in surprise. 'You didn't say anything about that.'

'We decided last night. Did you think we'd not

celebrate your wedding? We've invited some of our
friends, including Livia and Dougal, to join us
after the ceremony.'

Louisa pushed the wooden skittles into a corner
and helped carry the plates and glasses up to the
shop.

'You're doing her a world of good,' Isabella
whispered. 'I'm so busy that I don't give her as
much time as I should.'

'Do you mind me asking . . . Is she staying on
with you?'

'Yes. She's my cousin's child by her first
marriage, but Alice is too lazy to look after her.
Poor Louisa saw some dreadful things, including
her father being killed right in front of her, so it's
no wonder she's quiet. She seems to have taken
to you, though, and very quickly, too. And to those
skittles, heaven knows why. She carries one or two
with her everywhere.'

'I love children. I want to have several of my
own – though not as many as my mother.' She
shuddered at the thought of that: always expecting
one, then losing half the children to a variety of
illnesses or accidents. What sort of life was that
for a woman?

After a midday meal, Aunt Harriet insisted on
bringing Ismay's clothes across and the two women
helped her dress. Aunt Harriet lent her a pretty
silver necklace and Isabella gave her a silk scarf in
just the right colour to bring out the green in the
checked material of her dress.

Then they did her hair, arguing amicably over which style would suit her best. Isabella produced a hairnet to enclose the chignon. 'A little present for my new sister.'

Ismay looked at it in awe. It was made of black silk lace, with beads threaded through it. She'd never had such a beautiful thing.

Then Isabella produced a fashionably small bonnet as well. 'This will be perfect to finish off your outfit.'

'I can't accept so many presents,' Ismay protested.

'You have no choice. You're going to become my sister in another hour or so, and I'm older than you, so I can boss you about.'

By the time the two women had finished with her, Ismay was glowing with happiness and dared think she'd never looked as good in her whole life. She hoped she wasn't vain – well, she'd never had enough money to indulge in that sort of thing – but she did want to do credit to Adam.

'Just one more thing. Bram's arranged for a photographer to come to the Bazaar afterwards and take your photo. I hope you can stand still for a whole minute.'

Ismay was beyond words at this further generosity and had to wipe away a happy tear or two.

The men got ready across at the stables annexe, with Bram nominated to give away the bride and look after the ring Adam had produced, a slender gold circle that had belonged to his grandmother.

'I should have checked that it fits Ismay,' he worried. 'I meant to do that yesterday.'

'If it doesn't, she can crook her finger until we can find someone to alter it,' Bram said.

When they came across to the house, the other people stood back, leaving Ismay at the doorway to face Adam across the circular space in front of the stables.

No doubt about it, he was the most handsome man she'd ever seen. He was dressed in his best: a grey morning coat over a single-breasted waistcoat, with a watch chain looped into one buttonhole and the watch in his waistcoat pocket. His trousers were narrow, and on his feet he was wearing well-polished black boots. His dark hair was gleaming and his eyes were bright with love.

'You look beautiful,' he said quietly. 'I'm so lucky to have found you.'

Aunt Harriet sighed sentimentally and everyone else smiled.

'Let's be going,' Bram said. 'We don't want to be late.'

They all walked to the church together, with Ismay taking Adam's arm. She had only one worry now, which she hadn't dared voice, not wanting to spoil the day. But to her enormous relief, they didn't see a sign of Rory.

The curate looked surprised to see the happy group of well-dressed people accompanying them, as if he'd expected only the couple getting married.

He conducted the ceremony in a very loud voice – did he think they were deaf? – and then declared them man and wife with a flourish of the hands.

Ismay turned to Adam. 'Is it really true? Are we married now? I'm not dreaming all this?'

'If you are, so am I, and a wonderful dream it is, too. I love you, my darling wife.' He kissed her cheek, then offered her his arm. Once they'd signed the register, they led the way out of the church and started walking back to Bram's house.

It was too much to hope her luck would hold, Ismay thought, as she caught a glimpse of Rory in the distance. She tugged Adam's sleeve and hissed, 'It's him. Rory.'

No mistaking that burly figure with its big, mucky boots. He was leading a young cow round to the byre where they kept the poor creatures while they were in milk, but he stopped dead when he saw them. Tying the cow's halter to a post, he strode over to walk beside them, staring.

He didn't say a word, but he radiated menace, and she was suddenly sure they'd not heard the last from him.

'I won't let him hurt you,' Adam said in a low voice.

She realised she was digging her fingers into his arm and tried to hold him less tightly. 'I'm more frightened of him hurting you. He fights unfairly.'

'I think I can defend myself. Don't let him spoil our wedding day, my darling.'

She tried not to, but she couldn't help worrying because, though Rory fell back, he continued to follow them, silent and scowling, all the way home.

Here, Bram fell behind. 'I'll join you in a minute.'

Isabella hesitated, then led the way up to the Bazaar.

Bram stared at Rory. 'You're not welcome on my property, Rory, especially today.'

'She's gone and married him, hasn't she?'

'Of course she has. She loves him.' He was startled to see the anguish in Rory's eyes. 'You can't tell people who to love, you know. Find someone else, man. She can't be yours now.'

Rory stared at him, looked up at the Bazaar, then turned and strode away.

'And I hope that's the end of that,' Bram muttered. But he'd tell Adam to keep an eye on Ismay, nonetheless. You could never quite tell what a Flynn was going to do. The whole family were chancy tempered.

Inside Deagan's Bazaar, someone had finished setting up the table at the rear, which was now closed to visitors. They'd decorated it with fresh flowers and it was loaded with plates of sliced meat, cheese, pickles, loaves and scones. A real feast.

A couple of lady customers stopped what they were doing to watch her pass, and when Bram came hurrying up to join them, he called, 'I've just been marrying off my sister.'

They both wished the newly-weds well, finished making their purchases and walked out smiling.

At the rear, Sally and the two maids who worked for Mrs Southerham were standing in a row, beaming at her. Their aprons were white and gleaming with starch. Little Louisa was playing in a corner with a few of her skittles. She gave the bride a shy smile, then bent her head again.

Mrs Southerham was standing to one side, waiting for them. Ismay had only met her once, but she too was smiling and came across to wish them happy and offer a small wedding gift, a pretty pot with a plant in it.

In the centre of the table stood a large cake decorated with butter cream, with glacé cherries and angelica leaves round the edges.

'Rhoda made it,' Isabella whispered. 'She's surprised us all by how good her cakes are.'

Bram had hired a couple of fiddlers and, when he signalled, they started to play an Irish tune from the back corner.

'Sure, what's a wedding without music? Let me take a turn with you myself, little sister.' Laughing, he pulled her into a dance that was popular with the young folk from their village.

As it ended, he said gently, 'I hope you'll be happy, Ismay darlin'. He's a quiet fellow most of the time, but I don't doubt he loves you.'

'I'm sure Adam and I will be happy together.'

Even as she spoke, she thought she caught sight of a man outside the window. But before she could say something, he'd vanished again, so she didn't say anything. Rory couldn't do anything to them with so many protectors around, surely?

Then it was Adam's turn to dance with her.

'I'm not very good at dancing,' he whispered as they started off.

'I am. I'll pull you round.' She forgot her fears in the pleasure of counting out the steps until he got used to them, then dancing with him, forgetting for the moment that anyone else existed in the whole world.

Afternoon turned into evening. Sally and Rhoda went down to the cottage to bring up more food and the shop closed to customers early. People were sitting now, servants and mistresses, forgetting their differences and chatting with the ease of old friends who enjoyed one another's company.

When Ismay fanned herself, Adam pulled her to her feet. 'I'm taking my bride to get some fresh air at the front door.'

With his arm round her shoulders they walked to the door but, as they stepped outside, something slammed into Adam and Ismay was sent spinning sideways. She cried out as she fell, shouting for help.

All she could see was a big dark shape, raising one hand to pummel Adam, who had been taken by surprise.

Screaming, she hurled herself upon the fellow,

expecting it to be Rory. But it wasn't. It was a complete stranger.

Clearly an experienced fighter, he kicked her feet from under her and she called out again as she fell.

Before she could get up, there was a roar of anger and another man hurtled forward to join in the fight, yanking the one who'd attacked Adam away from him and punching the stranger hard.

By now people were at the door of the Bazaar, but Bram yelled to them to stay back.

Adam crawled round the two men, who were fighting so furiously they seemed unaware of him. He helped Ismay up and, as he did so, one of the struggling men cracked the other one over the head and he fell motionless.

That left Rory standing panting and glaring down at the one on the floor. Slowly he turned to look at Adam, such a menacing look that Ismay squeaked and tried to push herself in front of her husband. But he wouldn't let her.

'Stay back. This is between me and Flynn.'

But the man on the ground chose that moment to hurl a chunk of rock at Rory and, as he staggered, the stranger pulled a knife.

This time it was Adam's quick thinking that saved Rory, because he kicked the knife out of the man's hand before he could throw it, while Bram picked up the little stone statue from Singapore that stood by the door for luck and thumped it down on the stranger's head.

He dropped like a stone and this time didn't move again.

Warily, Adam watched Rory, who was panting and glaring at the newly-weds but didn't seem sure of what to do next.

'Sure, you can't be attacking a man who's just saved your life, Rory Flynn,' Bram said, his voice sounding more Irish than usual.

There was dead silence, then Rory looked at Ismay, a look so filled with longing that she realised suddenly how much he cared for her in his own way.

She spoke from the heart. 'Please leave me alone from now on, Rory. I've married the man I love and I'll not change my mind, whatever you do. I'm sorry, but I can't love you.'

He shook his head from side to side, his scowl returning.

'Who's this fellow?' Adam asked, following Bram's lead in trying to defuse the situation with words. 'And why the hell did he attack me? I've never seen him before in my life.'

It was Rhoda who answered. 'He's Nev Charrock. Ran the brothel you closed – and some say he did a bit of stealing on the side, though he's never been caught.'

Adam touched him disdainfully with his foot. 'What are we going to do with him?'

'*We* are not going to do anything.' Bram looked at Rhoda. 'Could you go and fetch the constables? I think he'll be charged with assault and attempted murder. Isabella darlin', will you find me some rope from the back of the bazaar? He's beginning to stir, and he's a strong brute.'

Rory was turning away, as if preparing to leave, but Bram called him back. 'I need your help in case this fellow tries to escape. You'll have to talk to the police about him trying to knife you, so you might as well get it over with now.' He smiled wryly as he added, 'You're a hero, Rory Flynn, did you not realise that?'

Rory gaped at him.

'Yes, a real hero. And so is Adam. He saved your life and you probably saved his.' He took the rope from his wife and bent to tie up their prisoner, then clapped a hand to Rory's shoulder.

'Come inside and have a drink of ale. It's thirsty work, fighting.'

For a moment all hung in the balance, then Rory grunted and accepted a glass of beer, hunching his shoulders, not attempting to join the others.

From time to time he glanced at Ismay, looking sad and puzzled now.

Adam put his arm round his wife, keeping a wary eye on Flynn. He had to admire his brother-in-law, who used words as cleverly as other men used their fists or weapons, but he wished Bram hadn't kept Flynn around.

He felt his wife shudder as they walked inside, so he found them seats as far away as possible from Rory, who had accepted another glass of beer, then a piece of cake from Rhoda.

'Trust my brother to stop a fight,' she said in a low voice. 'He often did it when we were children, and only he could control Da.' Then she really looked at her husband. 'Oh, dear.'

'What's the matter?'

'You're going to have such a black eye.'

Aunt Harriet put plates of cake in front of them and turned her nephew's face up to examine it. 'Let me get some water and bathe the dirt from your face. We've just boiled some in the spirit kettle.' As she moved behind the big trestle table, she stopped at Rory and said cheerfully, 'I'll tend to you too, afterwards, Mr Flynn. You'll have a black eye to equal Adam's.'

He nodded, seeming stunned into silence by the way things had turned out.

While Aunt Harriet bathed Adam's eye, Ismay cuddled Louisa, who had been standing trembling in the corner, clutching a skittle and rocking to and fro. She remembered Isabella telling her of the dreadful things the child had seen.

A stir by the door had her jerking round, grabbing the skittle, ready to protect the child, but it was only the constables. They came round asking questions and listening respectfully to Bram and the other men, who said nothing about Rory's plan to attack Adam, but painted him as the hero of the evening.

When Aunt Harriet had finished bathing the

grazes on Adam's face, she did as she'd promised, carrying another bowl of water across to Rory. 'Come here, young man. You don't want to leave a cut dirty. It might fester.'

He opened his mouth to refuse, met her eyes and shut it again, letting her minister to him.

By the time she'd finished, the constables were ready to question him.

During a lull, while Ismay was talking softly to Louisa, Dougal moved across to join Adam. 'This isn't a good time to approach you, I know, but the matter is rather urgent. I've just bought another schooner, smaller than mine, and I'm looking for someone to captain her. Are you interested? I have the feeling Joss will be on the Sydney run for a while and I doubt Ismay will want to move away from her brother.'

'I'm interested.' But his eyes were on Flynn.

'That's all right.' Dougal grinned. 'As long as I know I don't need to look elsewhere. You get back to your wife.' He too stared along the table, watching Aunt Harriet bathe Rory's face. 'Trust Bram to turn the tables on him. And your aunt Harriet's helping keep the peace. Look at Flynn. He doesn't know what to do or think.'

When the constables had finished questioning him, Rory drained his glass and stood up.

Bram was by his side in a minute, watchful. 'Are you all right now?'

'I'm past my anger, if that's what you mean,' Rory said. 'They're wed now, damn them.'

He walked out, turning once at the door to look back at Ismay, then striding off down the slope.

Bram let his breath out in a whistle. 'It was touch and go there for a minute or two.'

Adam had come up to stand beside him. 'It should have been me protecting her.'

Bram laughed. 'Didn't you just save a man's life? Leave some of the glory for me, brother-in-law.' He slapped Adam on the back. 'You'll make her happy, I know. She sparkles when she's happy, our Ismay does.'

Then he fell silent and stared out into the darkness. 'I just hope the rest of my family will agree to join me here. It's been my dream ever since the Bazaar was opened.'

Another silence, then, 'I don't suppose I could bring my parents now, though. I'd find it hard to forgive Da for treating Ismay so badly. But I've more brothers and sisters over there and I could do so much for them if they came to Australia.'

'Perhaps they will one day.'

'I have to hope.' He smiled. 'In the meantime, get back to your wife and I'll get back to mine. This is supposed to be a joyful occasion. We'll pull out our dreams and see if we can make them come true another day.'

The guests left soon afterwards, the three maids began clearing up and carrying the food back to the cottage, and Dougal escorted Livia home to the street behind the bazaar. Isabella had been hinting he might consider marrying her, but Livia felt more like a sister to him. He just . . . couldn't think of her that way. What was wrong with him that he couldn't find a woman to love?

Adam and Ismay parted company from the others and, to her relief, there were none of the usual crude wedding jokes, just a chorus of good wishes.

They went to the small room behind the stables, which they'd now be sharing, a room nearly filled by two single beds lashed together.

He stopped by the door, grimacing. 'Not a very fine place to spend our wedding night.'

'It seems very fine indeed to me. Ah, Adam darling.' She twined her arms round his neck and smiled up at him, all her love showing in her eyes. 'It's our time now.'

But as she started to pull the pins out of her hair, he saw the smile fade a little, though she tried to hide it. 'I wonder – are you nervous, Ismay?'

She swallowed hard. 'Not of you. Not exactly.'

'But all you know is the rough treatment that lout meted out to you.'

She nodded, relieved that he understood, that he was holding back, not grabbing her.

'We could wait till you feel more . . . ready.'

Her response was instant, a shake of the head that set her lovely hair tumbling from its remaining pins to curl softly on her shoulders. 'No. No, we'll not be waiting. This is our wedding night and I want it to be a proper one.'

He took her hand and raised it to his lips. 'Then we'll take it slowly, Mrs Tregear, and I'll show you how wonderful it can be when a man and woman want to give each other pleasure.'

Very gently, he helped her take her clothes off, kissing her and making her feel so well-and-truly loved that her fears gradually left her.

Safe in the shelter of his arms, she found that the way he touched her didn't frighten her now. The loving and kisses made her feel as if she was flying, soaring above everything in a cloud of happiness. She hadn't realised how happy the right man could make this joining together, and, from his reactions, Adam was enjoying it greatly too.

Ma had been so wrong. This wasn't something you put up with, not when your husband cared deeply about you. This was a way of celebrating your joy in one another.

As they lay entwined together afterwards, she sighed happily. 'I love you so much, Adam darling.'

His voice was slow and drowsy. 'Not as much as I love you, my Ismay. And as long . . . as there's breath in my body . . . I'll show you how I feel.'

She gave a sleepy chuckle. 'If that's how you show it, I'll be looking forward to it.'

She wasn't sure he'd heard her, though, because

his deep, steady breathing told her he'd fallen asleep suddenly.

Smiling, she dropped a kiss on his hand, which was still clutching hers. Then she let sleep wrap itself round her like a soft caress.

She had never been so happy in her whole life.

ABOUT THE AUTHOR

Anna Jacobs grew up in Lancashire and emigrated to Australia, but she returns each year to the UK to see her family and do research, something she loves. She is addicted to writing and she figures she'll have to live to be 120 at least to tell all the stories that keep popping up in her imagination and nagging her to write them down. She's also addicted to her own hero, to whom she's been happily married for many years.

CONTACT ANNA

Anna is always delighted to hear from readers and can be contacted via the Internet.

Anna has her own web page, with details of her books, some behind-the-scenes information that is available nowhere else and the first chapters of her books to try out, as well as a picture gallery.

Anna can be contacted by email at
anna@annajacobs.com

You can also find Anna on Facebook at
www.facebook.com/AnnaJacobsBooks

If you'd like to receive an email newsletter about Anna and her books every month or two, you are cordially invited to join her announcements list. Just email her and ask to be added to the list, or follow the link from her web page.

www.annajacobs.com

Discover the whole spellbinding Traders series

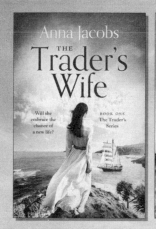

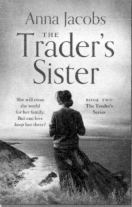

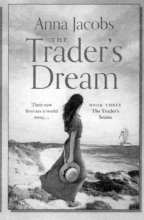

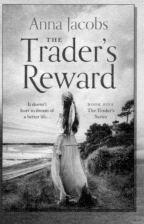